MISSISSIPPI SWAMP

Volume 1 of the New Africa Chronicles

John Hatch

Cover design by Chris Hall, CHd Graphic Studio

Text design and composition by Dickie Magidoff,
Archetype Typography

Printed in U.S.A. by McNaughton & Gunn

Published by 2ndsightbooks.com
2625 Alcatraz, Suite 368
Berkeley, CA 94705

ISBN #0-9706854-0-8
Library of Congress Catalogue #00-193471

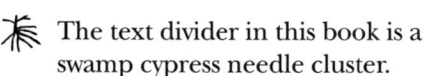 The text divider in this book is a
swamp cypress needle cluster.

To the spirit of life

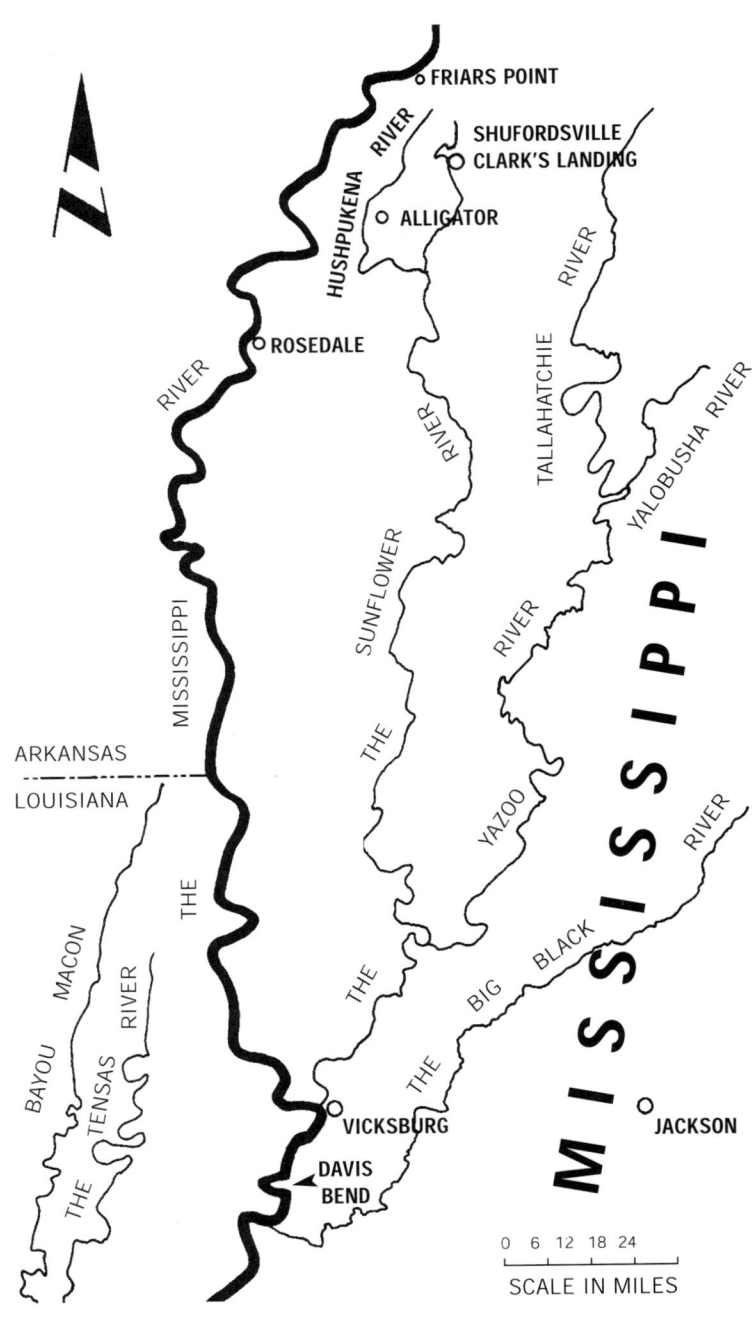

IN THE BEGINNING, a nurturing darkness embraced my land and water as one until they flowed apart and light is said to have emerged from the dark. Eons would pass before life appeared, a rambling rose shooting tendrils in every direction, each turning thorns against all but itself. Came the rule of tooth and claw, gone the nurturing darkness, the oneness of things. Came the mischief of mind, tribes forming to fight each other's gods, the most zealous always eager to kill in service of the light, darkness be damned.

Now Then

Inside The Swamp, Spring of 1879

> *Whatever happens in Florida, no matter how many different courts can't agree, we remain a government of laws.*
>
> Spokesperson for the challenged
> Republican candidate Rutherford B. Hayes

Taxpayers Pay For Hayes-Tilden

Yesterday afternoon, the Auditor General disclosed that the War Department had spent $20,461,045.02 it could not account for. The leadership of both parties reaffirmed their commitment to erasing the national debt.

After the 1877 election, a war of words attended President-elect Hayes' decision to pull troops policing the surrender out of the South and to kill potentially costly Reconstruction giveaways. With less controversy, the government began to repair Southern roads and levees. That expense exceeded the Interior Department's budget and was charged to the War Department.

Republican Rutherford B. Hayes, our readers will recall, recently won a much-disputed victory over NY Democratic Governor Samuel J. Tilden. Tilden received more popular votes, but Hayes won a majority of the states. The Electoral College was poised to elect Hayes until electors were challenged in 3 states including Florida.

An effort to resolve the stalemate in the House, Senate and Supreme Court failed when each voted along party lines. Constitutional paralysis was averted by the statesmanlike compromise between representatives of President Hayes and Governor Tilden on troops, public works and negro welfare programs.

There can be no return to the liberal spending of the Sixties. It is perhaps a comfort that the cost of big government could not avoid the scrutiny of the Auditor General, our democracy's shopkeeper.

Evening Star
(Washington, D.C.)

"**W**hat in the world are you reading, cherie?"

"My newspaper from Washington."

"Um hunh."

"Nothing worth talking about."

"You just read it over'n over."

Cicero wrinkled his mouth toward Rose.

"Actually, I was amused by a quote from an immigrant saying 'In America, they give everybody opportunity.'"

"Where he from?"

"Somewhere in Europe. More opportunity than Joe Woods, but assuredly less than Adelbert Ames."

"I don't follow you."

"Never mind."

"Oh, I do mind. You teaching me to read makes me want to follow how you think about the world out there."

"It's not just a black-white thing, Woods being one of us, Ames being white. It's about money and power hiding its face. Joe Woods has no notion how the people on top scheme to keep us all worshiping the right to grow rich. In time, most of the Radicals I knew went looking for a piece of the pie. Meanwhile, schools teach and newspapers preach that *the only issue* is having an equal opportunity to succeed."

"Big fish been around long enough to know how to hide."

Cicero folded the newspaper, pointed and passed it to Rose.

"Go on, read it carefully . . . This one article is the epitaph for my generation."

3

"Politics, you mean?"

"New Democrats, new Republicans, can't tell them apart
. . . This is the first newspaper to report the whole backroom
deal between President Hayes and New York Governor
Tilden."

"So they the bad guys, cherie?"

"Just two white boys with armies of lawyers fighting for what
they think is power. The richest people don't care who wins
because the candidates are pretty much alike, and poor people run around screaming and yelling about the issues. None
of which have anything to do who wields the real power.
Bankers are getting richer parceling out the national debt,
and you and I hide from all of it by living out here in the
swamp."

"Cherie, you and me sharin' this space is the most important thing in my life. Ain't want it no other way."

Rose settled into her chair and traced the whole article
with her finger. Then she sighed and read it a second time out
loud. Her finger stopped on one word.

"'Com-pro-mise'."

"Makes me want to goddamn scream."

Love In Grim Times

Vicksburg, Mississippi, Winter, 1846

Holding Negroes Accountable

A sage legislative wisdom requires free negroes to register with the police. Too many slaves are disappearing, and the blame falls squarely upon the free ones among us.

Millions of acres of swamp ceded by Choctaw and Chickasaw treaties have quadrupled the land of this state. Every acre cleared multiplies the value of negroes whose productivity Mr. Whitney's cotton gin has already doubled.

Protect our investments! No liberty for those who foment unrest!

Vicksburg Herald Editorial

Flecks of foam at the horse's mouth led Morgan to tug the buggy whip away from his five year-old son.

"Sit your little tail still."

"I like driving with the whip."

"Son, horsy is tired. We have to let him walk."

For hours, the wagon had been bouncing over a dirt road whose rutted clay was newly frozen. Hurricane Plantation a half day's ride south of Vicksburg was their destination. It was the largest of the plantations on a five-mile long peninsula that jutted like a thumb over into Louisiana and forced the Mississippi River to flow around it. Everyone called the place Davis Bend.

By the time Morgan turned off the mainland and headed into Davis Bend, a cold wind was blowing patches of vapor off the river and into forest at the center of the peninsula. Anticipation of being with his wife hurried Morgan through and into the flat fields of Hurricane Plantation where the distant mansion came into view.

Not quite a mile further, Morgan turned onto a service drive toward the cookhouse. The child jumped out of the wagon and ran up the stairs ahead of his father. As Morgan stepped inside, two women preparing supper nodded their heads politely.

"Excuse me, would one of you go tell Nancy her family has arrived?"

He stepped aside for the woman to leave and followed her out. Old George, the Davis family butler, was walking toward him and waving.

"Morgan you scamp! Take yourself on back inside that cookhouse."

"Are you sure that'll be alright?"

"Ole masta ain't around, so you go back inside. Got work myself, or I'd come sit with you."

The cookhouse like the other buildings on Davis Bend were built above flood level, and Morgan took his time climbing the long stairs a second time. By the time he stepped inside and opened his coat to the welcome warmth, a pan clattering to the floor made him grab the boy and order him to quit running. Before the child finished sulking, there was the sound of feet on the stairs. Nancy rushed in and wrapped Morgan in a moaning embrace. Cicero began yanking on his mother's skirt until she bent to pick him up.

"How's my sugar?"

"No, Momma Nancy. Don't kiss all over me."

"I'm still working, Morgan. Woman you sent gonna let me take her place here. Since masta knew you was drivin' in and he ain't give me time off, ain't wise for us to ask. Take the boy and go git warm."

The cookhouse had worktables in the middle, storage shelves on the walls and three huge stoves. Morgan relaxed when steaming coffee and a hot piece of skillet bread were placed in front of him. As he sat down, his son filled his mouth with bread, dashed to the door and outside where he charged around in circles. All of which led Morgan to recall his own childhood. A little food had been the beginning of all else, the comfort that set him apart from his always-hungry playmates.

Coming out of his reverie, he settled back to watch Nancy work. Grace equal to size a satiny cream of skin that Morgan imagined puddling into darkness at her nipples made him yearn to be alone with his wife. The second cooking woman whispered something that caused the women to share a laugh as Nancy finished packing salt meat and greens into a huge cook pot.

"You wash these taters'n wipe down, Nancy. Don't worry about the bread."

Daylight faded along with the sharpness of Morgan's initial passion. He became anxious for trusting so much, for ignoring all the caution now screaming inside as it did whenever he visited his old plantation.

"Go on over to the house, Morgan. I got to carry mistress a night meal."

Outside, Morgan looked up at the sky thinking, anything for a moment with his wife before the child reappeared. He hurried to the big house and through the back door. Once inside, he began chuckling. To whom, he wondered, should his prayer have been addressed? As if in answer, there was a blast of cold air, and Nancy rushed in.

"Surprise! I'm all yours."

The cold had blushed Nancy's cheeks like ripe peaches, and Morgan caressed a film of perspiration as he breathed in her warmth. When they moved into Nancy's little room, light from the hall lamp illuminated a rough dresser with keep-sakes on top.

"That picture, Nancy, of you as a girl and who else?"

"That's the mistress beside me, just after she married."

"You're the beautiful one."

Morgan lifted his wife and carried her over to the bed.

"Mistress used to tell me anybody could make theyself look beautiful."

"Hush up! *You* were born beautiful."

Morgan kissed Nancy's lower lip, moved his tongue to her eyes.

"That tickle me, Morgan . . . Guess I was right handsome."

"You could teach it you got so much of it."

"A woman could lose her mind over a man talk like you."

"Go on undress, before you know who."

Nancy raised her hips to pull off garments. Morgan ran to latch the door.

"You're whispering to yourself again," he said, snatching at his belt before dropping like a stone to remove his brogans.

"I was just thinking how lucky I am."

Morgan crawled to his wife.

"I'm a hummingbird feeding from a big ripe peach."

"Morgan! . . . You give me chills."

"What is this I feel between your legs?"

"Waiting for you to come visit."

Embracing, arms and legs intertwined, shirt and dress were still in place as Morgan slipped inside the woman he loved. Just as suddenly, the wind started whipping around the house as if to conceal from the world all the razor-sharp desire and precious memory living apart forced them to cram into their moments together. Soon, Morgan relaxed, still in the grasp of Nancy's thighs.

"If Ben only knew why I worship my Queen Lady."

"You the one started that?"

"He didn't call Mary, 'Queen Lady' until he heard me call you that."

"Well, I b'damn. What else you know I don't?"

"Nothing I'm unwilling to give up."

"Well, sail my ship into shallow water, you got me wantin' to sink."

"You don't mind if I climb aboard again?"

Morgan hesitated, reached down and began stroking Nancy's hip. Then he rolled onto his side.

"We need to have a talk before the boy walks in."

"Hold me, Morgan. We talk about trouble later."

"How do you know it's about trouble?"

"Cause it's a grim time to be in love. I'm a slave woman an' you here on account a evil old white man tryin' to out-smart you."

Someone rattled the door.

"Let me in, it's me!"

"Keep your voice down, baby."

Nancy bounded out of bed. On her way to the door, Nancy retrieved Morgan's trousers and threw them into his chest.

"Ouch!"

"What you doing in there, ma?"

"Just me teasin' your pa."

When Nancy opened the door, light from the back-hall lamps flooded the room.

"See, he went to bed, but I got work to do."

The boy ran over and leapt into bed beside his father causing him to grimace from the cold in the child's clothing as Morgan refocussed on Nancy.

"I'm curious about your momma."

Nancy joined her family in bed.

"Why is pa talking about your momma?"

"This is grown folks business," Nancy told her son.

"You may," Morgan said, "have to raise a daughter of ours."

"Oh, Morgan."

"I don't want to be around all this kissing. Can I go back outside?"

"Stay here with your pa and me. We tryin' not to raise too much ruckus over his visit. Look over there on my dressing table."

"Over here?"

"Yep."

"Fried apple pies!"

"Happy birthday, sugar. Eat what you want. There's other food, but you can eat a dinner of pie if you want to."

Nancy threw her leg on top of Morgan's.

"A man is a sweet thing, you know."

The sliver of hall light coming in the door left ajar barely made shadows of them all. Nancy left the bed, swept up her underthings and moved to light a lamp.

"I have to go bed down the horse," Morgan announced. "Doesn't anybody want supper?"

"Not me, pa."

"Me neither," Nancy added.

"Guess I got to go out in the cold alone."

"Not yet, sugar . . . Baby boy?"

"Yes, momma?"

"Lift up that tray your pies on . . . That's right."

"OOoooo, momma. It's ham sandwiches."

"Go eat, Morgan. It does me a world of good to do for my own when you here."

"Bring it over here, Cicero."

Cicero obeyed, then went back to his pie. As Morgan ate, Nancy sat cross-legged on the bed and began to unplait her hair.

Some time later, Morgan unhitched his horse and led it over to the barn. Nancy's only chore was to re-stock the fireplace in her mistress' room. One trip to the woodpile and back was not so time consuming as to take her away for very long.

I N THE MORNING, Nancy bundled her son up in a blanket and carried him out for his trip home.

"Kiss your ma goodbye."

Instead of a peck on the lips, the child stuck his nose into the shawl covering his mother's bosom.

"Boy like my lilac powder. And you love your momma. You are the sweetest thing on earth."

"You smell good, momma."

"I suppose," Morgan said, climbing aboard the wagon, "we should not feel guilty in accepting the benefit from working around rich white folks."

"Y'all drive careful."

"I always carry my freedom paper."

Nancy settled her son on the seat, then walked around the wagon to offer Morgan a kiss. He slid to the ground, and they held each other.

"Don't have to tell you the price masta askin' for me gone way up."

"Maybe I should go offer Davis another down payment."

"Nothing to worry about or Ben would have told me."

"How is my friend?"

"Still masta's favorite."

"Boy, get back in the wagon!"

"Can I go over to the sawmill?"

"No!"

"God bless you, Morgan. I know you doin' everything you can."

Morgan touched Nancy's cheek, hesitated, and then pulled himself aboard the wagon. He waited for Nancy to re-wrap Cicero inside his blanket before strapping his horse into motion. When Morgan reached the main drive, he stared angrily at the two-story mansion. It was twice as big as the nearby marble building with twelve foot pillars supporting overhanging porticoes where he had once worked. Both buildings were white and sparkling clean, surrounded by crushed rock, grass and clusters of massive oak trees. All the property of Joseph Davis, as was Nancy. Morgan felt the boy's hand.

"The man said that's a temple."

"Yes, built to look like a Greek temple—the master's library. Now . . . what do you remember me saying about this place?"

The boy sighed, rested his finger alongside his cheek in imitation of his father and looked all around. His eyes came to rest on a group of black men wielding shovels along the riverbank.

"You said that lots of folks want to be rich, but that don't make what they do to other people right."

A flick of the reins started the horse moving. Soon, the white rock of the carriage drive turned to common gravel and some time later, dirt, as the wagon entered the forest. There was another plantation to cross near the mainland.

"Damnsuh!"

"What's the matter?"

As the boy opened his eyes, two riders rode toward the wagon. White men, they slowed and circled at a distance. One pulled a pistol from under his coat. Morgan raised his hands.

"I have my freedom paper. I work for Mr. Joseph Davis."

One man rode forward and took the papers. After a brief inspection, he threw them into Morgan's face. The wind took them. Morgan dismounted to chase them down.

THE OUTLINE OF Vicksburg on its bluffs rose slowly into view. The wind was pushing a cloud of vapor off the river up against the great rock beneath the city. On the heights sat regal homes and below them, the business community growing with the new steamboat commerce fueled by cotton shipments. All was surrounded by more modest homes and even more numerous shacks.

Where the heights of the city descended toward the water, just above the boat docks, lay the market district. Home for Morgan and Cicero was a converted produce shed. Morgan drove on past it.

An hour later, in a small home six blocks from his own, Morgan was staring through the window thinking of Nancy. The gusting wind was rattling shutters in the neighborhood. Marcellette Coleman glanced up from her knitting.

"No one is coming out in this weather."

"Fewer and fewer the past two months," Morgan said, turning back inside. "This is the first time nobody showed up."

"You and the boy welcome to have supper with us."

"Thank you, ma'am, but no. I'm nervous about teaching so openly. Seems Mr. Davis warned my Nancy I'd come to harm."

"Forgit that old devil. He just want you back workin' for him."

"We ought to hold school somewhere else."

"Morgan got the same feelin' as me." Jacob Coleman's voice boomed out from the back room. When he walked in, Cicero ran over to grab his huge arm and swing on it. "This new law give police the excuse to barge in anywhere, anytime."

As Morgan turned to look through the window, the wind screamed even louder.

"Jacob, my life is a trouble wind. I may need your help."

"Whatever for?"

"I can't leave Nancy on that plantation much longer."

"If you serious, go 'cross town tomorrow and talk to our choir leader. Use the wagon 'cause I ain't goin' nowhere."

The wind quieted as Morgan led Cicero outside and lifted him aboard. The usually busy market was deserted. Against the quiet, the occasional slapping of loose shutters continued their eerie counterpoint.

THE FOLLOWING MORNING, Cicero awakened to footsteps in the front of his small two-room home. When he stuck his head out, Morgan was gone. Because it was still cold, the child ran back and jumped into bed. Light filling the small room reminded him of reading, and he ran into the main room for Morgan's translation of Marcus Tullius Cicero.

As Cicero returned to his room, he was trying to remember exactly what else Morgan had told him. Something about the Roman Cicero being sufficient reason for ignorant people to learn how to read, to learn of something beyond greed, how standing up for what's right made a human being heroic.

The ever-present wind gusted again.

"Trouble wind," he mumbled.

By the time the wind receded, the child realized that he had begun napping, and someone was banging on the front door. Icy air rushed through the chinks in the wall of his room, which meant the front door was open. Cicero's heart started pounding. Voices filtered into the back.

"Gotcha dead to rights, nigger! Don't give us no trouble."

Up like a rabbit, Cicero bounded toward the front. In the doorway, Morgan stood with his hands in manacles being yanked forward by a burly white man.

"Pa!"

"Go to Jacob, son. Send word to Mr. Davis—"

"Shut up, nigger, it's off with you."

"But my boy has no—"

Morgan pitched forward. He caught himself on his hands so as not to sprawl. As he struggled up, a big fist grabbed his collar and shoved him against the iron bars of the lock wagon. Two men standing in the wagon seized him by the shirt and hauled him aboard.

Marcellette broke down crying when she heard the news. Jacob lay his huge hand on Cicero's shoulder.

"We lost the house this morning. Man come wit a court paper. Cain't go to no court—wouldn't help your pa, neither."

"What about me? Momma Nancy?"

"Just hush precious baby," Marcellette said. "You stay with me."

"I'm takin' Morgan's message to Davis Bend. When I get back, I'm gonna go visit your pa in jail."

"Mr. Jacob, are you gonna run away?"

"First, gonna make sure your pa got his own movin' plans."

House Rules

Davis Bend, Winter, 1847

> *"Until lions produce their own historian, the story of the hunt will glorify the hunter."*
>
> African proverb

"**N**ancy, we have arrangements on the Underground Railroad."

"Oh no!"

"For all of us."

"But once they find us gone, the road be blocked."

"We can do it, ma. Listen to pa."

"How we git up to Vicksburg?"

"In two months, on the last day, halfway between midnight and sunrise, a wagon will drive by the road into Davis Bend."

"Who be driving?"

"Just a friendly white man doing business in Vicksburg. He is an abolitionist."

"So, this white man drive us where?"

"Toward Jackson. Joseph Davis will be searching the river and the road to Vicksburg. We'll hide in Jackson for a week before we move toward Vicksburg."

"And we hook up with somebody in Vicksburg."

"Yes, she's a—"

"She?"

"Shhhhhh! . . . Yes."

"Some woman willin' to risk everything to lead you—"

"Not me—us, my dear."

"Don't you 'my dear' me."

"She is a woman of grit and purpose. Being a woman helps her to escape detection where a man might not.

"Where you meet her?"

"Her husband came to my school. Jacob Coleman would visit me in jail and bring her along as his wife."

"Ain't this Jacob married?"

"His wife knows everything. Please, just listen."

"I do that."

"I stayed in jail to complete our plans before I let myself be brought here. A stranger coming to the plantation would have raised too much suspicion."

Benjamin Montgomery was Joseph Davis' most trusted slave, a man Davis relied on for all crop decisions. After Morgan's arrest, Jacob Coleman had bundled Cicero up like a package and delivered him to Montgomery who accepted the child and took him to his mother.

A few months later, Benjamin Montgomery again brought Nancy news about her husband.

"Morgan lost his appeal."

"Are they gonna punish him, Ben?"

"No, no, Nancy. Be happy, the fightin's over."

"When can we see him?"

"Well that's still to be decided. Masta want Morgan to come back to the plantation and work off the money advanced toward his fine. Morgan hasn't yet agreed to that."

The sound of wheels on gravel brought everyone outside the cookhouse. Nancy was the first down to the carriage. Mr. Ben followed in silence. Morgan was sitting across from the master. He was skin and bones, dressed in filthy trousers and shirt.

"I shall provide you and Morgan a cabin, Nancy," Davis said as he climbed down. "Tonight, though, you may take him into your room."

"Yessuh, masta."

"None other like you, masta." Mary Montgomery added.

"Enlightened husbandry, Mary. Your boys, Morgan's son, will each pay dividends for my support of you. Slavery is the way of our world. Hurricane is your home."

Benjamin Montgomery bowed, then turned back to helping Morgan down from the carriage. Nancy and Ben helped Morgan toward the rear of the mansion.

"You gonna have your old job," Ben whispered. "We seen to that."

Morgan made a teeth-sucking sound.

"And I," Nancy said, "got a surprise."

She left them at the back door and ran inside to fetch a cloth bundle.

"Your fried pies, sugar. Made them last night to feed you in bed. Only way I could think to welcome you home."

Benjamin Montgomery smiled and pulled a protesting Cicero away with him. Mr. Ben, his wife and toddling son lived in one of five small cabins along the river. In another cabin, three older Montgomery boys slept together.

"Jes go on in there and make yourself comfortable, Cicero."

"I want to be with my pa."

"What you want don't count. A plantation got rules. Now go on where you goin'."

The following morning, Cicero waited outside the cabin that he had slept in. The other children had rushed off mumbling about special chores. Soon after, Nancy appeared.

"We got big white folk's doings."

"What's that?"

"Church today. Carriages out front from Masta Jefferson's plantation. A real preacher drivin' in."

"Hello, son."

Morgan stood in the doorway.

"Paaa!"

Cicero pulled away from his mother and ran to hug his father around the knees.

"It's awful here, pa. The white people—"

"Stop that!"

"Leave him talk, Nancy."

"No! Cain't say what you want if you ain't livin' free . . . Son, that's the way it is. Now git yourself down to the pump'n wash. I got clean clothes for you back in my room."

That night, Nancy was in a very good mood. The mistress, upon whose good opinion Nancy's position in the household depended, had told her how very friendly to the guests she'd been. Left-over food made their first supper special. Morgan ate very little, but Cicero ate his own food and reached for his father's.

"Your father sick. Don't eat his food."

"Let the boy have his fill."

"You need your strength more than him," Nancy said.

"For more reasons than you know."

"Go on tell her, pa."

"Hush . . . Nancy, we need to go talk. Somewhere comfortable and not so close up under people in the cabin next door."

"We talk right here. I been on my feet all day."

"Nancy, we have arrangements on the underground rail-road."

Morgan decided to postpone their escape because he still wasn't at full strength. The problem was how to pass word to his contact in Vicksburg.

Spring was a time of sharing of opinion about weather, and often seed. Each plantation set aside more of its good seed than needed, which made it possible for other plantations to have some of the best. Usually that was seed from Benjamin Montgomery's cotton crop on Hurricane.

"Say, Ben?"

"Yeah?"

Morgan took him by the arm.

"If the master sent me along, you could handle all this spring's trading on one trip. I could help load stuff, drive, and the master would see me volunteering. I could keep accounts, too, and that leave you free for other business."

"I was gonna trade seed tomorrow."

"Do all your trading on one big trip around The Bend."

"Masta ain't dumb. He'd know we got something up."

"Consider, where had you planned to sleep tonight?"

"I was going to the Woods place and coming on back home."

"If we do it my way, you bunk down at the Woods place, then by saving travel time you cover the final two plantations the next day."

"Oooo . . . "

"Tell the master I volunteered."

"My pal, Morgan! Don't you tell nobody where we stayin'."

That evening at the Woods Plantation, the day's hog butchering was winding up. Huge cauldrons were suspended over no longer roaring bonfires. Into them all of the scrap from the animals slaughtered was being rendered of its fat. Benjamin Montgomery emerged from the seed shed a short distance away.

"We got to stay here overnight," Ben said conspiratorially. "Too late to start for the next plantation."

"You the boss, Ben. I'll take the wagon to the barn."

"Well, thank you, Morgan. They made me a bed in the kitchen behind the big house."

"You gonna eat good."

Benjamin Montgomery winked.

"When you finish with the wagon, come meet the cook."

Some hours later, the sounds of frogs and crickets were loud in Morgan's ears as he eased up from his blanket. Dust from the pile of straw he'd slept in was making him sneeze, and he was frantic to smother the noise.

He had left the mules in harness, and now he walked them away from the barn until a stand of trees closed around. Momentarily, there was a whinnying horse, and Morgan froze. He waited until he could be sure it was moving away. Then he eased aboard the wagon and started driving.

Morgan heard the other wagon before he saw it. In the light from its lantern, a shadowy figure pulled to a stop. Morgan ran out of the sheltering grove in which he'd been hiding mindless of the chance he was approaching the wrong person. A woman's voice called out.

"You'd be the teacher?"

As Morgan pulled up, the woman jumped down, picked up Morgan's lantern and hurried over to him.

"Where is your family?"

"I came alone. We have to wait another month."

The woman shoved her lantern into Morgan's face, smiled, then turned back to her wagon.

"Don't assume you haven't been seen. Next time, go down about a mile below The Bend. That's where I'll pick you up."

"But. . ."

"Steal a boat, but don't push out into the channel. Just let yourself drift while you count to a hundred twice. Then come ashore. Walk as fast as you can up off the riverbank toward this road. Just close enough to look out for my wagon. I'll be hauling a casket."

"A what!?"

"You'll drink a potion that'll put you out heavy for hours. Your wife and I will be a grieving wife and your sister. You will have died of a horrible contagion. If anyone insists on opening your casket they'll be hit by stench from a dead varmint, and they'll see your face all marked up with dried porridge."

Two days later, Morgan had a real pain in his chest and could hardly move. Mr. Ben agreed that it was inflammation from sleeping in a drafty barn and told him to stay in bed, that he'd inform the master. As Nancy worked the big house that day, she ran back and forth. Cicero remained at his father's side.

As the days passed, Mr. Ben warned Morgan that he could not afford to linger abed. So, with Ben's help, Morgan walked over to the library where both of them began their usual work, until Ben left to handle an emergency. A man working the saw at the mill had allowed a log to kick up and strike him in the head. When Ben returned, Morgan had collapsed on the marble floor. A handkerchief in his fist was stained with blood.

That evening, a frail Morgan called his son over to the bed.

"I have something for you . . . Open your hand."

He dropped a folded paper into the boy's hand.

"I have written down the names of books I could remember that you should read. You won't have that paper for very long. It will pass away, like me."

"Pa, you're scaring me."

"What's in your hand will last if you commit it to memory. My books will be your friends, hide you from your problems, teach you what you do not know, and occasionally they will utterly delight you."

"Can I find them in the library?"

"Just grow up and find a way to freedom for you and your mother. Here's a name . . . Lean close so I can whisper . . . She's the conductor up in . . . "

Morgan began coughing.

"Does it hurt?"

". . . No pain. Probably means I'm going to die."

Cicero was up and out of the door in an instant. He didn't stop until he had found his mother in the big house.

"Come quick, it's pa!"

The master paused with his fork in mid air. Nancy grabbed her face and ran to the door. She outran Cicero. By the time he arrived, she was already kneeling.

"Do you want the preacher man, Morgan?"

"I won't feel better in this world, even if Jesus wills it."

"What that mean, pa—Jesus will it?"

The adults looked at Cicero.

"So tell me, son. When things go bad, what do you believe in?"

A knock at the door distracted them.

"Just me, Nancy," Mr. Ben said. "Word travel fast."

"He real sick," Cicero said, "and he . . . he talkin' about Jesus and stuff."

Benjamin Montgomery became rigid.

"Young'un, you got to keep your mouth closed. We cain't keep you away from the white folks all the time."

"He mean Mr. Davis, sugar. We cain't keep makin' excuses for how you talk."

That night, with no note except the tears of his wife lying alongside, Morgan gave up the struggle.

漾

MR. BEN HAD Morgan's body laid out under one of the oak trees near the cabins. Those who served the house gathered to mourn. Joseph Davis walked over. Cicero was standing silently beside his father's body.

"How's your reading, young one?"

When Davis touched the child's head, Cicero jerked away.

"Lord God," Nancy said. "Don't pay no attention to this boy. He sick from grief."

"No, I'm not!"

"Then what is your problem?" the master demanded.

"I hate you!"

Nancy ran her son down.

"Show you sorry, boy! Show you sorry!" she kept saying, as she struck him.

One morning an overseer from the field dragged Cicero outside and began paddling him because the overseer had heard two slaves laughing about Cicero saying that he had put a curse on the master. Joseph Davis appeared, riding crop in hand.

"You have been privileged . . ." He struck the child across the face. ". . . because of your blood line . . . Your damn sire left Nancy with child . . . She will bear it without chasing you around."

The master spoke to the overseer who dragged Cicero a half-mile to the edge of where the slave barracks were lined up, to a large gray shed surrounded by hard-packed dirt.

"Git back 'way from the door!" the overseer yelled, putting his shoulder to it.

There was giggling and scrambling as a host of little bodies moved. The dim interior reeked. When the door slammed shut, there was only darkness.

Once Cicero's eyes focussed, he saw boys in front of him, each wearing a burlap sack shirt or a piece of burlap sewn on like a badge.

"Who're you?" A girl's voice.

"Cicero Morgan."

She and some other girls giggled.

"He cute."

"Shut up, Lutie!" one of the big boys said. "Latrine out back. Me'n these others got to keep you little niggas in line."

"Who's your momma?" another boy asked.

"Her name's Nancy."

The murmur became snickering.

"I know somebody stickin' it to your momma."

"You take that back."

The blow struck home before Cicero knew it was coming. A knee in the stomach knocked the wind out of him. His head struck the ground and filled with stars. A big friendly youngster was squatting at his side when his head cleared.

"You all right?"

"Uh-huh."

"My name's Little Man."

"Mine, Cicero."

"You leave the big boys alone."

"They cain't make me do nothing!"

"Didn't say what you *got* to do. Just that things works a certain way."

"I kill anybody mess with me."

"With what?"

"I don't know."

"You better know. You sound smart, Cicero, but fightin' ain't your thing."

"Who's that?"

"Gimpfoot! He a cripple white man. Hear the way his walk sound on them planks outside."

The door whined open, and two men stepped in. The crippled man had thin red hair. Behind him was a taller, more stern man, the one Cicero had tangled with at the big house.

"What's goin' on?" Gimpfoot said.

"Nothin', suh!" a boy with a burlap badge said. "We showin' the new boy how things work."

"You little coons is nasty as buzzards."

"Yessuh!"

"Ain't no buzzard!" Cicero said.

The white men rushed Cicero and dragged him out of the mass of little bodies.

"Don't touch me, you old gimpy foot!"

"I'll wring your mangy neck," Gimpfoot said.

He snatched the whip from the taller man and would have lit into the child had not the other grabbed his arm.

"Gonna beat sense into the little nigger," Gimpfoot said.

"No, you ain't, not with my whip, but wait."

The man walked outside and returned stripping twigs from a bunch of willow branches.

"Use these. He be near valuable as his pa when he grow up and learn to obey."

One man put his foot on the boy's back and held him in place. The other snatched off Cicero's trousers and beat him until fine cuts welted all over and began oozing blood. A vicious stroke took the skin off one ear, and Cicero screamed.

When their anger was exhausted, the men walked away. Vows of revenge began to crust over Cicero's wounds.

"Ice water in your veins," Little Man whispered. "Hit's the rule. It ain't bein' no coward to keep the white man from knowin' how you feel."

Cicero was put to work carrying messages and hand-pulling weeds out of growing cotton. Then came carrying water buckets, serving it to grown folks in the field after his young arms toughened to the task, and finally came days of chopping with a hoe, the picking of soft white fiber out of brown prickly cotton bolls. He would become expert about hoes and cotton sacks, bleeding fingers, cold winter mornings and hot summer noons.

A Young Rose

Land's End, Louisiana Gulf Coast, 1845

"How God so great when he the one thought up the negro race?"
"Naw, fool! A white man did that, on a slave ship."
From a South Side of Chicago tavern

Below New Orleans, eons of shifting plates in the continental shelf had thrust a spine of rock to the surface. Over time, it anchored a ragged curving sieve of sand and mud between the Gulf of Mexico on one side, the Mississippi River on the other. This was Land's End.

The sky was mottled with color above the blackening water, and Rose stared off into the distance drawing out her enjoyment of the moment. The water seemed an extension of her young self. Tall and sleek her face held soft wide-set eyes that sparkled like black bottle glass. When she smiled, her blade of a nose gave a full curling top lip an air of haughtiness.

Then she saw the ship. It was dropping sails and drifting in toward the open doors of what looked like a prison of stone built up on a rocky outcrop a hundred yards down the beach.

She hadn't noticed a mast on the horizon. No work bell had rung and even the guard tower was still unmanned—a most peculiar circumstance—but not her problem.

Rose walked out to savor the tickle of water on her feet. As it slapped her legs, she giggled and chanted:

> *Black water*
> *sister water,*
> *all your water*
> *mine.*

Some time back, the girlish beauty that had made her feel so playful and good about herself had become a curse. Her own mistreatment had opened her eyes in a more radical way to suffering in the big world around her. Now, she held herself apart, at least in her own mind. She was not free, she was not white, she would not grow up to be a man, she was not willing to give others pain to savor the crumbs of Lige Coulter's praise, him being the white trader who ruled the thick-walled holding pen now coming to life. Only the black water, huge and all-powerful, seemed to Rose, friend.

Her job was dumping buckets of it on those who survived the ocean passage. She carried them gruel each morning. She flushed out the waste each evening. At thirteen, but after years of such toil, the one thing she kept telling herself was that everything she did was to help the people passing through.

The massive cook was the woman Rose called mother. Her name was Songhai. She had named Rose and taught her what she knew, though Rose had rejected much of that wisdom because all it seemed to promise was a life of endless toil for Lige Coulter. Songhai, it was, who'd explained how Rose had been delivered by the sea after a fever-wracked woman was tossed from an approaching ship.

Rose turned away from the depot back toward the open sea. She distanced herself from the world around her by opening to the sunset only to hear a din and clamor from the ship, and then the clinging tide made her stumble. A dizziness seized her. Into her, came a sense of lying in a floating room of black men tending a roaring fire that flamed into shadow. Someone bursting with a friendliness beyond what she had ever known was nearby, hidden in a darkness laden with the smell of spring flowers.

The vision faded, and Rose dipped water to refresh her face. Now, from the pens, came Lige Coulter's outraged voice. He was yelling at Jamaica Rex, his black major domo, for being drunk and for not announcing the late-docking ship. Screams and clanking chains almost covered the sound of Coulter's hollering as the first human cargo was whipped onto deck before being unloaded.

Rose splashed out of the water, off the sand and up onto a rise in the land strewn with gravel. Lige Coulter's house was ahead on the rise behind the pens. Rose ran to tell Songhai about the dizziness, and it was the time of month to eat the bitter berries that would keep her barren of new life. To kill the taste, that meant a crust stained with honey. Little explosions of noise drew her toward the open kitchen door.

"Ah be . . . hic . . . too much for your ass to bear, one day, um hunh!" a man's voice said.

"Too much," Songhai's voice said, "for a drunk-ass island man, now, or do you doubt me?"

Rose arrived at the door in time to see the woman's fist close around an iron spoon that resembled an axe.

"Next time," the man said, "you tell massa I stealin' his rum, is your t'roat I be grabbin'."

As Jamaica Rex backed out, Rose jumped aside.

"Get outta my way, black t'ing!" he said, storming past her.

"Come in, cherie. He ain't much to worry about," Songhai said. "We got woman business. Do what you got to."

"I been in the water watchin' sunset."

"You spend too much time in that water."

"What else I'm gonna do?"

"If I didn't love you, I'd call you touched in the head like all these other fools."

Rose ran outside to make sure Jamaica Rex was gone. When she returned, she walked up close to Songhai.

"Why people got to act like him?"

"How I know? Reckon he been cursed. Musta made the gods mad about somethin'."

"Musta done somethin' *awful*."

"For sure, if it could be done—it been done. That's the way o' things in this man's world. You see how things is."

"Hey, Rose!" Jamaica Rex called from a distance. "You hear the work bell?"

Rose dropped her eyes from Songhai and meekly trudged out and across to the holding pens.

The smell told her that there had been much death aboard ship. A bucket line up from the water's edge had already been formed. Jamaica Rex ordered Rose to the end near the holding pen. She'd have to walk her buckets inside and dump the water below.

Rose quit thinking and began working without looking, offering her water—rude as it might seem—as her welcome to those screaming below. Without intending to, she dumped a bucket too near Coulter as he and the ship captain walked inside.

"Damn you!" Coulter yelled up. "Leave off and bring me my accounts book."

Jamaica Rex pushed by and yelled out, "I got it sah!" He picked up the huge book of accounts on the work table near Rose, raised the trap door near the wall and hurried below grinning. When Rose looked after him, a tall young man chained at the end of the last coffle unloaded was shielding his eyes from the ship captain's torch and staring straight into her eyes.

"Now ain't he a healthy lookin' jasper," the captain said. "No plague atall."

"No pay," Coulter said, "'till I see 'em in day light."

The next morning Rose awakened before Songhai. She dressed, hurried to the kitchen and kindled the big wood stove. Working into the night, she had missed her allotment of honey bread, and she had put off her dose of the bitter berries. Guilty for that, she decided to make amends by helping Songhai before her own chores began. All evening the young man's eyes had stayed in her head. Then she heard the bag of shrimp dropped outside.

A slave named Zeke made a kissing sound as she bent over to grasp the wet sack. She glared back, and the man waggled his tongue. Only after he walked away did she drop her eyes and turn back inside.

Shucking the shrimp was quick work, snatching off legs, head, shell all in few motions. She washed and seasoned them with flakes of red pepper, then sought out the crusty sliced ham that Songhai had left on the counterboard. It would flavor the bland shrimp, which would give moisture to the ham. Fried on a smoking griddle and finished with lightly scrambled egg, the dish was a favorite of Lige Coulter.

After her chores were completed, Rose sat in front of the stove for warmth and tucked her legs underneath. Her vision in the bay the night before was again on her mind: the sense of springtime and of a fireplace on a boat. Then someone snatched open the door—Zeke again, grinning down at her.

She tried to jump up, but she tripped on her skirt. He was on her, reaching under her dress. She grabbed his wrists and held on with all her strength. He thrust his knee between her legs but overbalanced himself, and she managed to tip them over. Tall as the man, strength renewing with outrage, she wrestled him to a draw. Then she relaxed, and he rolled on top. When his hands again began exploring, she heard the door scrape open, then footsteps. Zeke gasped and rolled off, clutching his back. Songhai was standing over them holding a kitchen knife dripping blood.

Jamaica Rex ran in.

"Go git masta!" Zeke said. "They *cut* me!"

"Don't be a fool, Rex," Songhai said, "You know this ain't my fault."

"Oooo Lord! Massa no blame this island man! You done this t'ing before I come here this mornin'. You're bot crazy."

"Crazy or not, you know what happened here."

"I know you're t'ru givin' me problem. I going to be your masta from now on. I show you."

A FISHING BOAT put in at Land's End. Rose and three arrivals new to America were taken aboard and chained together. One was the young man whom Rose had heard called a healthy looking jasper.

In New Orleans, they were transferred into waterfront holding pens. Some days later, they were put aboard a steamboat. They were no longer chained together, and a white man led them down into a hot and fume-filled boiler room where he invited Rose to become his friend. It was a comfort to find herself inside a room on a ship with a fireplace.

On the morning of the third day, boiler fumes made one of the new men throw up. Their new owner, who had told Rose that his name was Laplace, insisted that his cargo be moved. So Rose and the others were marched up on deck, given blankets and chained to a cargo winch.

The wintry air had them huddling together, Rose closest to the tall young man who'd been called a jasper. From time to

time, he would point to her and say a word she didn't understand. Thinking the word in some way meant her, she touched
her breast only to have the man touch her likewise. Her anger
ended that, but the young man touched one of the others and
opened his arms as if to embrace them all.

"We the same," Rose said.

"Saame," the young man said.

As time passed, Rose lost count of the days. She heard
them call out Natchez. Since leaving Baton Rouge, one side of
the river had become Mississippi. Late one morning, they
were ushered off the steamboat and aboard a ferry that took
them across to the Louisiana shore. Laplace obtained a livery
wagon and motioned Rose aboard to drive.

Just a little ways inland, ditch-sized stagnant sloughs closed
around the trail. They had a rest stop, raw corn for food, and
then they continued for several more hours before resting
the horses.

As dusk came on, Hubert Laplace dismounted and walked
ahead leading his horse. The trail had narrowed and forced
the men to cluster in the center of the wagon to avoid tree
limbs. Rose was surprised when she looked up and saw a building in a clearing ahead. It was a big rough-hewn steep-roofed
cabin whose sides and back had been built out to more than
quadruple the original space. All rough planks chinked with
mud, it had been white-washed sometime in the past, and
there were new wood shingles on the roof. Out back, three
rickety slave cabins leaned against one another.

A dark-haired white woman with thin, sharp features
dashed outside and down off the tiny porch. She was wearing
a gown that seemed made for a ballroom. Below it, work
shoes. She stood all smiles and confidence waiting for Laplace
to approach.

"Welcome cherie," the woman said as Laplace hurried toward her, but when he leaned in to embrace her, she pushed

him off. "Dammit! You have dirt on you, and this is my Christmas dress."

A wizened old woman popped out of the house wearing a bright red headrag and a faded red dress with yellow dots. Laplace and his wife waited as she struggled down off the porch and scrunched up her eyes to take a look at the new slaves.

"Good lookin mens, y'all. Beaucoup good!"

"Mammy Lucy, you see after Rose!" Laplace yelled into the old woman's ear. "Take her to our kitchen and walk her 'round it."

Old Lucy moved stiffly, took Rose's hand and led her around toward the rear of the house.

"Tired o' that man yellin' at me. Been cook here since Hubert's papa quit the French army an' hid out. Was a thief to git started and build this place. Then he cleared the land and had a baby by some gal ain't been seen since. That was young masta, and I raised him. Now, he married what he call quality, but he ain't the man his father was, an' he don't know quality from gator meat."

"What you mean 'quality'?"

"'Tween me'n you, cherie, I ain't sure. Something the white folks talks about when they got ten, fifteen us doin' all they work."

"Who that out back?"

"Wheah at, young'un?"

"That girl out there, lookin' inside?"

"Oh! That's Lucy's Lucy. She my daughter. You may as well meet her."

"Don't you like her?"

"She my daughter. I don't have to like her . . . C'meah, cherie—this is Rose."

The daughter was a curly-headed woman who seemed angry about something. Even so, young Lucy leaned in to touch Rose's cheek with her own.

"Pleased to meet you, Lucy."

"Bitch! You ain't take my mamma's kitchen from me."

DURING THAT FIRST week, the cabin that had been the old cook's became Rose's. On Sunday of her third week, Rose was summoned to the field. When she reached it, Jasper was hunkered down in front of the overseer talking to himself.

"Goddamn nigger challenges every order I give."

"What he do wrong?" Rose asked.

"I'm tryin' to show him he got to move down a row o' cane like so, all the way to the end. Then, next row."

"What he do wrong?"

"He go chop, chop—cutting all around in a circle. Girly, you are his last chance before I bust his head open."

Rose marched over, snatched the machete from Jasper's hand, and beckoned him to follow. Down the whole row of cane she moved, bending as if to chop. When Rose paused, Jasper paused. When Rose started back up the next row, Jasper took the machete from her hand. His grunt seemed to indicate acquiescence.

That evening, Rose was washing dishes when Mammy Lucy's daughter walked in.

"Bon soir, cherie," Mammy Lucy said.

"Bon soir, ma ma . . . How you Rose?"

Rose nodded.

"Well," the daughter said, "I just come to visit my ma ma."

"You heah now," Mammy Lucy said. "What else you want?"

"Why you that way to me, ma ma? Ain't I your only daughter? You know I love you."

"Humph!"

"Weather was nice today, wasn't it?" Rose said.

"For you, up in this kitchen. Not for your friend."

Rose snatched her hands out of the dishpan, reached for a towel.

"Ahhhh," Lucy giggled. "You worried about the boy. That's so funny."

"It ain't funny to me. What happened?"

"Well, the poor man, he talk so fast. I was there, I see exactly what happen. Master Hubert lose all control, draw his pistol and hold it in midair . . . "

"Oh, no!"

". . . like he gonna shoot. Then he realize he killin' one thousand dollar wortha nigga, and he stop—poof—just like that. He order Jasper tied up and he whip that boy with his own hand."

Tears filled Rose's eyes. She lowered her face to hide them.

"They got him salved and wrapped up," Lucy's Lucy said. "I'm takin' care of that boy."

A tremor of Rose's lips was her only answer before she dashed out of the kitchen and on to the barracks.

Jasper was sleeping. Oil made his welts glisten in the moonlight. Rose dropped to her knees and stroked his forehead. One of the other Africans walked over and spoke to Jasper who startled awake.

Rose helped Jasper outside and settled him on the ground. An hour passed before seeking common words for things ended in awkward silence. When men approached from the barracks, Rose abandoned her efforts and ran.

As she trotted toward the kitchen, a leather band holding a charm to her waist began to chafe. For months now, she had ignored her vow to eat the bitter berries..

The next morning, sunlight coming through chinks in Rose's wall sprayed the room with warmth. A perfect day. Despite her encounter with the master the night before, her mind was filled with Jasper. Only good feelings. No confusion. Outside, she knelt to taste the dew. It was like having a piece of an old god inside as she began whispering Songhai's prayer.

> *Dew of morning*
> *Light of life*
> *Day forever from night.*

That morning, the mistress decided to show Rose how to roll out thick biscuits.

"The world is more civilized now, Rose. When my poppa was a boy, they strip a woman like you naked an' push her in a snake pit. Don't think you can take over my house."

"Yes'm."

The holiday season—Christmas, Three King's Day the next month—passed. With spring ahead, the master spent all day in the fields, the mistress at his side, which left Rose relatively idle except for mealtimes. Mammy Lucy was always around. It was old Lucy who told Rose about chapel time. Whenever the priest visited, the white people drank the blood of a god.

In wonderment about what she had heard, Rose rushed home and got into bed eager to enter her dream world. Lying there in the moonstruck darkness, inviting whatever might come, she began to giggle and to roll back and forth in an outflow of energy. She tried to imagine what it might be like to go ahead and move of her own choice into the realm of being a woman with a man. As she lay with one arm caressing the other, the shimmering silver moonlight gave her skin the look of a black flower's petal.

All of a sudden, her cabin door creaked open. A young virile body stepped inside.

"Same, same," he whispered.

"Same."

Moonlight flashed into Rose's eyes when he moved, and she couldn't see for a moment. His hand touched her as his face came into focus, so serious and almost sad. Something more a sigh than a word escaped his lips, and Rose remembered that he had been whipped. She reached up around his back to finger the welts until he winced, and she eased her hands away.

She swung her legs to the floor and darted outside. The young man tried to snatch her up but she squirmed free and turned. The sky behind Jasper looked like a starlit windowed house, the giant moon a door he had just walked down out of. She threw her arms around him for an instant and then took off running.

A quarter-mile farther on, the bayou that flowed behind her cabin opened into a pond fringed on the higher ground with pecan and sycamore trees. Troll-footed cypress crossed the water like giants frozen in mid-stride. A single willow fluttered in the wind. Wildflowers dotted the shore.

As Jasper dashed toward the water, the wind abruptly died. Rose hesitated in caution at the sound of a hooting owl, always an omen, but then she entered the water and swam toward a clearing. She was right behind Jasper when he crawled out. His touch caused her to shiver as she collapsed at his side. The water was tickling her feet so she eased further ahead into a glen of moss and sprouting grass.

No kisses, no caresses of face and lips, they struggled together, eager thighs pressing so that wet sounds rode the air displaced between them. Despite her effort to wrestle him around and to trap him with her legs, he had his own rhythm, more and more deliberate, steadier and steadier. He paused only to open the faded clinging chemise.

Then she quit resisting, conformed her body to his. The less she struggled, the more a dream-feeling seemed to build and to give her body a life it had never had. She moved her hips, and his answering voice smiled. She kissed his lips, taught him to linger there and to play. A sweet tension began to knot up her stomach. Tears pooled in her eyes, and a cry crept out of her throat. Water was now tickling her feet, whispering, sister, I have brought you this.

Later, with her arms around herself, she watched him walk into the water and go under to ease his healing back. Lying on her carpet of moss, she remembered Songhai's way of offering praise to the God of the Sky and sent her own praise skyward as Jasper frolicked in the water. When he returned, his finger toyed with her eyes, traced the outline of her nose. He growled and gently took her lips with his teeth, pulling her inside the calm eye of intimacy, free of beginning's uncertainty, the hot rush, the need to engulf and to exhaust, they became infants without language, giggling and cooing, touching soft against soft and marveling that each breath had become ecstasy.

When it became her turn to bathe, even the swirl of water brought pleasure. She crawled ashore and whispered, "Same, same." He opened his eyes and smiled, so she pressed herself into the warm hollows of his nakedness and closed her eyes.

A mischief of sunlight and breeze through chinks in the wall awakened Rose. She remembered returning to the cabin, pushing Jasper away and deciding to stay awake until morning. In a panic, she ran to the big house where the mistress was waiting.

"Dammit, Rose! I'll not be pulled out of bed to cook so you can carry on."

The mistress departed in huff leaving the housemaid hugging a bowl of eggs against her stomach, ham frying in a big iron skillet. When Rose reached for the eggs, she heard footsteps.

"You take this!" the maid whispered, backing away. "Heah come Masta Hubert."

Laplace stepped out from the narrow pantry built between the house itself and the kitchen annex. His face was trembling. He grabbed Rose's jaw, held it toward his face.

"Damn your soul," he said.

"What you want, masta?"

"I'll teach you to trifle with me. That nigger you was with—I'm sellin' him. Maybe then you act right."

Rose wrenched her face away, and Laplace slapped it. The skillet crashed to the floor. Rose took one step toward Laplace, then stopped.

"I got feelin's. I got . . . feelin'."

"You're black and ugly as sin. We give you a home—do you want Lucy to have your kitchen?"

"I kill Lucy! I will kill her!"

"Oh, no you will not."

Laplace swung at Rose, but she ducked and moved behind the chopping block.

"Jasper my only friend."

"That does not excuse your shamelessness."

"What that mean?"

"It means that you cannot consort with a man while you work my kitchen, you hear!"

"I hear."

That night, one of the Africans Rose had arrived with knocked softly at her door. She had difficulty understanding. Something about a bird. Then the man pointed between them.

"Get outta here, man!"

He began to flap his arms and run around in a circle.

"Same people go—go!"

"Do you mean run away?"

"We come."

Each day, a little cornmeal or flour disappeared from the huge crocks in the pantry. The salted meat was kept under the mistress's key and there was never fresh fruit until summer. Rose stuffed her apron pockets with sticky dried plums. In a sack under the dirt floor of her cabin, she buried it.

"What's wrong?" Mistress Laplace asked one day.

"Nothin'."

"Sure, there is. You got a pain?"

Rose nodded.

"Where is it?"

Rose cupped her palm around her forehead.

"Knew there was somethin' wrong with your head. Nigger girl like you cain't have better'n what I could give you." She stopped inside the pantry and turned. "If you tried to be nice, Rose, you could be so happy here."

"I 'spect so, mistress. This swamp . . ." Rose said, snatching at something she had heard the housemaid say to excuse an outburst of crying, ". . . it puts me in a fright. Folks out there cut your heart out."

"You just hush up!" Mistress Laplace wagged her finger in Rose's face. "I know you want that boy in the quarters. You best leave him alone and let me help you . . . None of them black heathens living in that swamp can touch you."

"Who they, mistress?"

"Never mind, you black silly. My daddy say civilized folk oughten even speak of such trash. Just living out there like animals, them niggers. Now, if you was to straighten up and learn to work my kitchen like a real chef cook, I could change things for you."

The rains came. In the middle of May on a night after an all-day rain, Rose's door creaked open and three men came inside—Jasper and the two Africans.

Rose motioned them down on the floor and giggled when the three men obeyed. She pulled on trousers under her nightgown, over which she pulled on all the clothes she possessed. She dug up her cache of food and drew a finger to her lips when the men began to speak excitedly.

They ran from the cabin in equal parts fear and exhilaration. North they moved, but after sloshing through mud and water for hours, they could only guess at direction. Rain hurtling down on the leaves overhead was deafening. Lakes appeared between usually narrow and clogged bayous. They finally rested near two giant oak trees, atop a tramped-down mound of vines and brush.

They slept until the skies began to lighten. The rain continued, and so did they, in a direction Rose hoped was still north. By mid-afternoon, they could hear water rumbling in the distance. Two of the men tried to talk, but they were drowned out by the noise. One of them took her hand and pulled her ahead. Jasper followed. Every few steps, someone would trip on a vine hidden beneath the shallow water they had to wade through. Then the ground began to rise, imperceptibly at first, and a line of giant trees loomed ahead beyond the highest ridge they had yet encountered.

A roaring noise filled their ears as they climbed to the top. Perched on a ribbon of mud, they gaped at a rain-swollen river. A hundred-foot-wide brown torrent was slamming broken trees into those still rooted.

They moved downstream, but no crossing was to be found. As darkness fell Jasper stopped them. The last thing Rose remembered after collapsing was the sight of Jasper on all fours gasping for breath.

Rose awakened to an argument. Jasper was pointing toward the river. The others pointed away from the raging torrent. They prevailed. Jasper and Rose followed in the dark.

Blindly they pushed on through the night, until the sky lightened and they all wanted to rest. Jasper refused. He began to yell, standing over one man, pulling on his arm. They pushed on through the day and into the night. Rose and Jasper walked together, bodies aching and worn out. At some point the sound of water began again, and Rose feared they had ended up back where they started. But they had left the interior. The sound was that of the Mississippi River. Because they all recognized it as the river they had been transported on, everyone took heart.

It was dark. They had to rest. There was no crossing such a great river at night. Back a ways from the shore, they squeezed together for warmth from the heat-stealing rain. The next morning, they awakened to gray sky and heard the dogs barking.

THE WHIPPING WAS terrible. Mammy Lucy prodded and dragged Rose over to the women's quarters where Rose begged sleep to take her forever away from her pain.

As Rose recovered, she neither challenged nor tried to please, and she was with child. Never with Songhai had Rose discussed child-bearing other than to avoid it. What she knew of birth at Land's End was bloody and pain-filled, and she was afraid without even the words to express her panic.

Lucy's Lucy was given Rose's place in the kitchen. She proved to be both less and more than the master and mistress bargained for. On the less side, young Lucy was barely competent, and she squabbled constantly with Luke and the housemaid. On the more side, she was energetic and determined to hold onto her long-coveted job. Laplace complimented her for wearing a flower in her hair, and Lucy began wearing one every day.

She was a sharp-featured and not very good-looking woman, but working indoors instead of in the sun began to fade the reddish-brown in her complexion. As time passed, Lucy became nearly as pale as her mistress, who took note of both Lucy's skin and her flowers. Her first guess was that Lucy had a man. The problem was, who—color being everything to the white woman, and all the men of the canefields black and seeming ugly. Unable to figure out who the man was, the mistress approached her husband.

"Do you intend to put Lucy to breeding?"

"Leave running the plantation to me."

"With a mate, Lucy would never finish my work."

"I'd never put her to a common nigger."

"Why? Is she special?"

"Leave running this place to me."

"Then you must train Lucy to handle my kitchen. Isn't that running the plantation?"

The mistress withdrew in a huff, and it took her only a moment of stewing to seize upon her response. She sent Luke to the quarters to summon Rose—whom Laplace never had stopped raging against since her run—to help prepare for a soiree. Rose was walking heavily toward the kitchen when she heard loud voices inside.

"You got to say again, mistress. I cain't do it."

"Dammit, Lucy! You spread butter over the pie crust . . . Then fold it over and roll it out again."

"Ain't no cook like that."

"Oh, sweet Jesus!"

Rose heard heavy footsteps, then a man's voice, Laplace.

"Excuse me, pet—Lucy, come see me in the library room when you finish."

Rose felt better hearing the master walk away. Easing closer to make sure he was gone, Rose saw the mistress muttering and Lucy grooming her face with water, smiling as she toweled dry.

"I be fine tomorrow, mistress. Don't worry. I do good."

"You mean you understand how to make dough flaky?"

"Yes'm—just like that," Lucy said, snapping her fingers as if the mistress were her friend. "Masta want me now."

Rose was about to reach for the door when she felt dizzy, and she stumbled backward. This was not the time to encounter an angry white woman whose attitude was unclear from the scene Rose had witnessed. Then, in a realization like a daydream, she saw herself spying on the master and mistress, and they were fighting.

She hurried around the house to crouch under the library window. Low voices could be heard.

"Wasn't ever nothing against you, Lucy. Just thought it best you and me didn't live under the same roof."

"I know."

"I let you have the kitchen, but now . . . it's the way you're dressing."

"You don't like it!?"

"My wife knows nothing about us, and here you are sporting yourself like a tart. Quit doin' all that in her kitchen."

"Just want to be pretty for you, masta. You like it, non? What's wrong with—"

What might have been a gunshot rang out, but it was only the heavy door slamming into the wall as the mistress stormed into the room. Rose had to move back from the window to see her slapping and scratching at Lucy.

"Control yourself, pet," the master said. "What's gotten into you?"

"You shut up!" Then, to Lucy, "You, get out of here!"

Lucy pulled free and ran.

"What is troubling you, pet?"

"Don't you say a damn word! I want Lucy locked up— tonight! Tomorrow, you whip her, and I'll watch."

"Slaves can't help—"

"I am not a fool, Hubert, and if you say another word on her behalf, I'll go stay with my momma and daddy."

"But what of your soiree?"

"Rose can cook! You tell Luke to bring her here tonight. Right now, you hear?"

Rose walked away from the window holding her mouth to keep from being overheard laughing, back around to the kitchen and inside. What she knew, the mistress apparently did not. Mammy Lucy had explained that Young Lucy was Laplace's half-sister.

IN THE FIRST DAYS of December, eight months after her recapture, Rose delivered a baby boy whom the master named Joseph. As soon as she could get away alone, Rose took the infant with her into the swamp and held him in her arms on the edge of the water. She named him Jasper.

For January, the Laplaces planned a big meal to celebrate Three Kings bringing gifts to their child-god. The master's favorite cousin, a Doctor Pierre Laplace, had arrived before Christmas and was staying through the Three Kings celebration. Mistress Laplace spent a lot of time describing to him what she called Rose's affliction.

The beady-eyed little man began to haunt Rose's path and to talk in words Rose could not at first understand. He would become most animated when she uncovered a breast for her infant. One day, he cornered Rose alone in the pantry. His hand reached to explore Rose's burgeoning breasts. She lifted her head and stared without a word. When his lips dropped down seeking what belonged by rights only to her infant, she pulled away.

"I will tell mistress."

"Be nice. I can make you feel better."

"Non."

"A healthy girl like you needs a man."

"Had all I need. Got it right here in my arms."

Each passing day left Rose increasingly anguished for having brought a child into the very world to which she had always avoided connection. Fear for her child's future and her own helplessness to do anything about it spawned little headaches that linked up and became constant.

She was stirring milk into sweetened butter and flour for a king cake. As usual, her month-old infant lay in a basket on the floor at her feet.

"Rose!"

"Yes, mistress?"

"Master Hubert and Dr. Pierre want you in the library room."

"Yes'm."

She scraped the batter off her spoon, reached for a piece of cloth to cover her mixing bowl.

"I'm sorry I ever let Hubert think of replacing you, Rose. It won't happen again."

"Yes ma'am," Rose said, eyes focused on the mistress picking at a pile of citrons meant for the cake batter.

"I will not say precisely what caused me to send Lucy back to the fields, but she cannot control herself around men." She walked forward and laid a hand on Rose's arm, "You know your place, and for that I shall be . . . well, your protector."

"Thank you, mistress."

"Go on, now. Dr. Pierre will make you feel better. Do you at least understand that?"

Rose sighed and nodded wearily. She had been talking with Doctor Pierre for weeks now, sessions that usually turned into groping. If this one took very long, her cake batter would go flat, and there'd be more time on her feet starting over again. The mistress seemed to want more of an answer, so Rose smiled.

"Yes'm, I understand."

Rose scooped her infant into her flour-covered arms and walked away. As she approached the library, she was thinking that white people had so much power that their words might possess some kind of enchantment. She would not allow it to touch her.

Rose knocked once and walked in. To her left was the tiny fireplace. The master and his cousin were on a cane settee across from it. Both ignored her and went on with their conversation. Rose's arm holding little Jasper was tiring, her legs too. Across the room, Dr. Pierre was folding and unfolding his fingers into a tent. He was a possum-faced man, blotchy and puffy, with gray around the edges of his black hair.

The library door slammed into Rose, as her mistress entered. Startled—the pain in Rose's back an omen if not punishment for daring to think of opposing white folk—she watched the mistress nod to Dr. Pierre and sit. Doctor Pierre crossed to the fireplace, reached a taper from the overhanging shelf and lit his pipe.

"Rose Laplace," he said, puffing smoke everywhere, "your problem is your mind."

Rose nodded her head, but she was alert against being enchanted by the words.

"At the Pennsylvania Hospital, Rose, I studied slaves who were a thorn in the side of the good people who provided them a living . . ."

Could white folks believe her so stupid as to blame herself for being a slave?

". . . Their minds were flawed. An African is heathen and demonstrably inferior." The doctor turned to Hubert. "Are you listenin' to me, cousin?"

Suddenly, Rose felt dizzy, and it was different from her occasional visions of the future. Everything looked tiny, as if she were back at Land's End peering at the world through the large end of Lige Coulter's telescope. In a panic because she seemed on the verge of some enchantment, she pressed her fingers against her eyes, but the tiny little world remained tiny.

Her wariness began to slide toward contempt for the bearded little man gesturing in front of her. He would never charm her into letting him play with her breasts. She rubbed at flour caking on her hands, and flakes of batter fluttered toward the floor. That the cake was to have been in honor of a god made her wonder if his power were making her dizzy and might raise up the flakes of his cake in such a manifestation of power as to command her respect. But the white dust settled, her heartbeat slowed, and again, she began to listen.

". . . her mind is not constructed for her to act like a good slave . . ."

The man is beginning to make sense.

". . . You suffer from a malady identified by Dr. Ahmonson, who interviewed runaways returned to their masters, to reality . . ."

What are you saying?

". . . a primitive mind too weak to tolerate even the simple demands placed on a slave who has no mortgage or crop failure to worry about. They disobey, lose weight, even run off. We call it drifting—"

Smoke and sparks belched from Dr. Pierre's pipe and he fanned at it but was forced to step away. Rose covered a smile.

"—Rose Laplace! You are afflicted with running, with driftomania!"

The master applauded his cousin who thrust his pipe back between his teeth and bowed grandly, into another large trail of smoke in the small room. Rose fought to control herself.

"Are you telling me that slaves got minds like us," Hubert asked?

"Course not!" Dr. Pierre said. "It's not so much having a mind, their feet run—they can't control them. *Draepedomania* in the Latin, but I say driftomania to keep from explaining—"

A delayed cough from choking on the smoke interrupted Dr. Pierre. When his little eyes bulged, Rose erupted in laughter. No possum could enchant her. She clapped her free hand over her mouth, but her laughter kept pouring out. As she sank to her knees, the expression on three white faces shifted from astonishment to anger.

"Git up, damn you!" Hubert Laplace said.

A spasmodic sobbing was Rose's reply. She drew herself up like a newborn and clutched Jasper to her breast to shelter him.

"Do leave her be for the moment," Dr. Pierre said.

"Silly, silly fool!"

It was the mistress following her husband away. Finally, Rose saw suede boots she had cleaned a few days earlier walk up to her and stop. A pen was scratching on paper. When it ceased, the suede boots went away.

No one came for her right away. The thought that she had only herself to rely on filled her up. Still, she had no idea what to do next. Suddenly feeling exhausted, sleep seemed that day's only escape from the hard floor she found herself on. Mammy Lucy stood over her.

"C'mon, cherie. Ain't got to git whipped. Mistress scared my Lucy have to be cook."

As Rose followed the old woman to the kitchen, the child made tiny smacking noises. Rose whispered into his ear before she fed him.

"Drink and be strong, baby, like your daddy."

She had never had anything worth saying to her child, but now all that had changed. Words that made sense for black people needed to be said about the world they shared, and she began to sing:

> *Sleepy by, cherie amour*
> *'till you grow up a flame*
> *to keep us free and warm at night*
> *these mastas all afright.*

ONE MORNING, Rose remained in her cabin. Days earlier she had brought home cooked beans and tomatoes that had developed a powerful stench. Now, she tossed them just outside her door, dribbling a few across the sill to suggest a sick person befouling it. Lucy's Lucy took over the kitchen that afternoon and soon enough aggravated the mistress, who ordered Lucy to go clean up for Rose.

That night, taking comfort in the noise of her master and his cousin drinking, Rose wrapped her son warmly and dashed into the thickest part of the swamp behind her cabin. She ran until she tripped and sprawled. After calming her screaming son, she walked more deliberately. Full of inexhaustible energy for the first hours, she had to force herself to rest and to drink some water.

Much later, as the sky lightened, she reached the same river she had reached during her first run. As before, it seemed uncrossable. Carrying her infant, she was even less eager to march into the unknown flow. So, she commenced to search along the shore until she found a fallen tree.

Without hesitation, she stepped into the water and sloshed ahead with the tree at her side. The water never reached above her chest, and by the time she reached the end of the log, the water level was dropping.

Then, suddenly, she was tired. Hours of walking, the weight of carrying her baby and provisions had worn her out. All she could do was head for a nook between the giant roots of a nearby tree and curl up with Jasper.

It was mid-afternoon when she awakened. Jasper was gone. She let out a wail and struggled to get up. A hand grasped her arm and pushed her back down.

"Easy, pretty girl, we take care o' you," a man's voice said.
"Non!"

A sack was thrust over her head, and more arms helped pin her down. All she could do was to yell and to kick, but at least four strong arms held her on the ground. Though she could hardly breathe through the foul sack, she kept screaming and struggling until she was too winded to fight or to shout. So close, freedom, she thought as she lost consciousness.

Some time later, light filtered into her eyes. The sack over her head was gone. The evening sun was below the tree line, and she had been moved.

On either side of her stood black men, one dressed in skins, the other in the ragtag attire of a slave. One was holding food toward her. On the ground a few yards away, Jasper was gurgling and smiling.

Out of Bondage

Davis Bend, August of 1852

> *"How might one describe a Roman lacking arms?"*
> *"Speech impaired."*
>
> From *Visigoth Humor*

Six years after the death of Cicero's father, Little Man weighed over two hundred pounds. In one day, the fifteen year-old could pick his weight in cotton. They were still housed together, now in the men's barracks.

"Are you sorry you followed me here?"

Twelve year-old Cicero eased his back away from the wall and began picking at his big toe. Little Man kept after him.

"You couldda worked another year with the children."

"Not under Gimpfoot. Come holding up some work paper like he can read off my name."

"Aw, you little string-neck nigga, don't let him git you down."

"Cold as ice water, that's me."

"Since when?"

"Since your momma give it up, you mule-dick bastard."

Cicero's baby fat was gone. He was all legs and arms, and his skin gleamed black from constant sun. He and Little Man were hiding inside the single men's barracks not far from where they'd finished snatching the tassels from a stand of corn.

"You messin' with Gimpfoot or you wouldn't be doin' this."

"He said, 'Don't do nothin' *I* don't tell you—I'm the boss!' . . . We waiting for him like he said."

In September, Cicero was ordered to cut and stack firewood. After working all afternoon, he looked up to see Mr. Ben approaching with his son Isaiah, followed by a girl near Cicero's age and Cicero's sister, Abyssinia.

"This here is Annye Mae, Cicero. I know you've seen her around. She been put in charge of these children and any others who want to come and improve their minds. She can't read, but she can write her name."

"Hey, Cicero."

"Hey, girl."

"This ain't play time, Cicero. You are going to teach these children. Twice a week, I'll make sure you come in from the field. Isaiah, you pay attention. Masta Jefferson needs a personal assistant."

As Mr. Ben walked away, Annye Mae unfolded a blanket on the ground and motioned the younger ones to sit. Isaiah was quiet, strangely so until Cicero noticed his eyes fixed on Abyssinia.

"Mr. Ben's older boys be comin' to learn," Annye Mae said. "They ain't got time today, but Mr. Ben said you oughtta know so you could figure out what you want them to work on aside from these young ones."

"Quit pointing at me," Abyssinia said. "I don't belong out here with you all."

"Don't be a fool," Cicero said. "I'm your brother."

"Un unhhh! You all just common niggers."

Cicero's eyes met Annye Mae's. She smiled and slowly walked up the long cookhouse stairs. She was already sporting breasts but wearing the short dress of a little girl. Before she disappeared, Cicero was struggling to keep his pants from reflecting his excitement.

LATE THAT SUMMER, Cicero learned that he was to be allowed to live with the house group, and he took off running. Mr. Ben was waiting along the way to the cookhouse. He grabbed Cicero's arm, but the young man pulled away.

"You got responsibility now, boy! I need to talk to you!"

As the old man faded in the distance, Cicero felt self-conscious. He was bare-chested wearing burlap field pants. His nose told him to go wash. So he headed toward the river bank.

"Come on race me again, race me again!"

Cicero could see Annye Mae hanging off the dock, long legs bare, wet shift bunched up around her waist as she climbed. Cicero walked out onto the dock grinning. Annye Mae squealed, opened her arms wide and threw herself back into the river.

"I'm coming to live here."

"What you say?'

"Said I'm coming to live in the house!"

"What?!"

"I'll swim out to you."

Abby paddled in to shore as her brother ran out to the end of the dock and jumped. When he surfaced, Annye Mae swam to him.

"You better not let him rub his nasty thing on you," Abby yelled to Annye Mae.

Annye Mae giggled and tread water. Cicero moved off and began to dive. When he came up for air, he looked ashore. Abby—he noticed for the first time—had been swimming fully clothed.

"Cicero!" she yelled. "I don't want nothing to do with you running off from work."

"Grow up, girl," Annye Mae said. "He's your brother."

"I'm gonna tell mistress he sneaked out of the Quarters."

Annye Mae swam over and wrapped her arms around Cicero. He blurted out that he was to join them serving the House.

"Oh, we gonna have fuuun!"

"You all better get dressed," Abby said, "else Momma Nancy be blamin' me for what you ready to do."

Cicero shrugged off Annye Mae's arms and charged through the water yelling at his little sister, and she ran away. Cicero and Annye Mae moved back out into the water and kissed. When it became serious, they splashed over to stand underneath the far edge of the dock. Her well-fleshed thighs slid wetly along his slim flank. Eager as well as noisy, they ground against each other, bumped apart. Cicero dropped his hand to fumble toward consummating the wet joining. He was almost there when footsteps rang out overhead.

"Who that down under?"

"Who is it?" Annye Mae asked sweetly.

"You know who this is Annye Mae. C'mon out."

The young people pulled their clothes into place and climbed onto the dock to face a stern Mr. Ben.

"You know you did wrong. There's white men who would turn you into a play thing, Annye Mae. And you Cicero—did you ask yourself if somethin' like this would make the masta happy?"

"I don't know."

"That's my point. *You* don't know. Didn't even give it a thought—now that ain't politic."

"Politic?"

"It ain't wise. You know that word?"

"Yes sir."

"Then both of you straighten up. If it's romance, it can wait. Cicero, you go to my cabin. Mary got you some clean clothes waitin'. Annye, you got work. Go to it."

Annye Mae pulled her dress over her wet shift and dashed toward the back of the main house. In his wet trousers, Cicero walked down to Mr. Ben's cabin. He didn't expect to see his mother there.

"Momma! Did you hear about me?"

"Oh yes, sweetheart. Praise the Lord. Now, follow me."

"Where?"

"Masta give us same cabin me'n your pa had so I could live with my son. Remind me so much of your pa, you do."

"What about Abby?"

"Oh, *that* one. She's taking over some of my chores for the mistress. I do not understand how two people so different and one so much older can stay up in each other's face."

Well past midnight, Cicero and Annye Mae lay alongside each other underneath the cookhouse.

"You like me don't you, Cicero?"

"Yeah."

"Well, you better not let Mr. Ben hear you talk them dozens. He say, 'Vulgar ain't tough. Tough is when you can stand up to anything.'"

"He said that to you?"

"I got a salty tongue when I git riled up. So the way you talk don't prove nothin' to me."

Cicero lay his head on Annye Mae's stomach.

"Cicero, is Mr. Ben your father?"

"My pa got arrested. He wanted to run away with me and momma, but he died."

"Oh, Cicero, I'm sorry . . . You really do like me."

"Yes."

"Do you want to get married?"

"I never thought about it."

"People jump the broom all the time."

"I sneak and watch what happen later."

Annye Mae was silent. Cicero touched her face. There was not enough moonlight to reflect the tears wetting his fingers.

"Why are you crying?"

" 'Cause."

"Come on Annye Mae . . . You wanted to do it."

"Yes."

"Good."

"You won't tell on me, will you?"

"Why you ashamed? Everybody do this."

"But a lady ain't supposed to. That's what the mistress and them say. Your momma and Miz Montgomery, too. If I had a momma she be sayin' the same thing."

When Cicero tried to roll atop Annye Mae again, she closed her legs and turned onto her side.

"I think you like to use a woman and leave her."

"I can't leave you, I'm a slave."

"Don't you know nothing."

"I know plenty."

"I feel like slapping you."

"Why?!"

"Talk like a baby instead of a grown man."

"Then why you like me so much?"

"If you and me fall in love, when you buy your freedom maybe you remember me."

CICERO THREW himself into teaching Isaiah and the others. Abyssinia's determination to out perform Isaiah, Annye Mae's dogged resolve not to be found wanting in comparison to one of Mr. Ben's older sons, Cicero's growing pride at being able to accomplish a task on his own—all blended together in a way most serendipitous.

One morning shortly after Cicero began working in the library, Joseph Davis led Nancy in.

"Nancy, be proud of your boy. Still excellent manners even after years in the field. I am amazed your influence has not worn off."

"Thank you, masta. Kin I go back to work, now?"

"In a moment, Nancy. Boy, I was telling your mother how pleased Benjamin is that you have done so well tutoring the young ones. You read all the newspapers my political brother arranges to be delivered . . . Have you yet made acquaintance with our business accounts?"

"No sir."

"Not so? What shall we make of this, Nancy? Not a business man? So he lacks the constitution of his father—what do you say?"

"Me, master?"

"I don't wish to overtax your son. Do you think he has his father's talent?"

"Of course, sir."

"Good. Well, then, Cicero. I shall offer you a small responsibility. Will you rise to the task?"

"Yessir!"

"Benjamin will give you information every week-end. Each Monday, I make it a practice to examine all business transactions conducted on the plantation's behalf. That is how important your chore is. What you will do is to enter each and every business transaction into a single big book I call a ledger."

"I can do it, sir."

The white man clapped his hands together, and walked away.

In the weeks that followed, Cicero was enthusiastic about mastering every part of any job he was given. He was challenged, and his mother and Mr. Ben encouraged him to show how talented he was. One day, he returned to brag about his work to Little Man. Unfortunately, only those too old or ill to work were sitting around the barracks.

"He been lent out to work across river," said an old man they called Stacks. "Why you come back out here anyhow?"

"To see my friend."

"You young mother huncher, your momma's titties your only friend."

"Go on tell it now!" another old man said.

"Damn that," Cicero said, warming to the ritual challenge. "You just started something you can't finish."

"Plantation pussy made you bad, is that it—like your daddy? Your momma need a good old nigga like me."

"Your momma sell coochy rides, got my stick stuck inside. She buck up and down, and out popped your hide."

Everybody laughed then. Stacks, too.

"I'll tell the big fool you was here," Stacks said. "What they got you workin' at?"

"I'm keeping records. Sometimes, Mr. Ben let me work the plantation store. It's real easy."

"Think so, huh?"

"Yes, I do, Mr. Flapjack Stacks, and I ain't stealin' no bacon for nobody."

"See? No fool like a young fool." He winked at an old woman nearby. "He barely know how to work his tool, move up when a woman want him down. White man trick him, he fall in an' drown."

"You talking like a fool," Cicero said.

"You the fool, youngster. Don't you know I'd kill that white man if he was to do me like he done your people. And you actin' proud to work for his raggedy-ass."

"Shut up, Stacks!" the old woman said. "Nigga lyin', son. Full o' lies like the devil."

"What did masta do?"

Stacks smiled at the woman, who walked away.

"Come here and listen, youngblood . . . The white man was hunchin' your momma on the sly, like they does. Then your pa come along and git a baby outta her—he buys you right off, too. So the white man think 'My, my! This nigga some smart, good breeder, too.' And he commence to schemin'—ain't you never heard this?"

"None of your business."

"Well, when the price of all of us went double, triple—back nine, ten years ago—your momma was prime breedin' stock. Hadn't been for that old Benjamin nigga, you would of had lots more brothers'n sisters. Instead, Mr. Ben give masta the idea it be better to leave your momma be. Idea was to let your poppa work hisself silly tryin' to buy you all's freedom, then force Morgan back into the plantation and let him make more babies like you."

Cicero was silent.

"Well?"

"I don't believe you."

"Didn't you think it strange your pa got arrested in his own house when nobody'd bothered him up to then? Everybody knew him. Hell, I say your pa got chunked in jail when masta give the word. So he could buy Morgan out. That way he got a smart nigga owed everything to him. He hung onto Nancy and got you back, too."

Cicero returned to the cookhouse trembling. The sudden awful reality of his father's enslavement had him hating everyone, hating himself for having his parents' blood, hating Mr. Ben and all the people around him for being weak.

"Mr. Ben!"

There was motion inside the library window. Benjamin Montgomery walked outside with his finger raised to his lips.

"It's about my pa!"

"What are you upset about?"

"About my pa, what you and masta agreed on."

"Come on away from that Library a little further . . . Son, cain't no man our complexion survive being a goddamn hero, not never like you doin' here with me, going straight ahead at things like you think a man supposed to. See, it's about power, and we ain't got none. What you been hearin' about was a bad time. Your momma was going to be put to breeding—you wanted the truth! So to stop that, I meddled in, though I talked to Nancy first."

"About my pa coming to the plantation?"

"Yessir, I did. Not that I was part of havin' him put in jail. God as my witness, I don't know if masta was behind that or no. All I know is, when your momma and me talked, we couldn't figure out how Morgan was gonna be able to buy her. So I began whispering in the masta's ear easy-like, when he wasn't full of worries, and I commenced to tell him he ought to hire your pa. That would of helped everybody."

"So it *was* you brought pa here?"

"Hell, son, I didn't make the world. Didn't call no police on your poppa, neither . . . Me'n Nancy couldn't help the way things turned out, and cryin' don't help nothing."

BY THE TIME Cicero turned twenty, he did what he was told and no more. He never stepped out of place with the master, but he never again sought the man's praise. Benjamin Montgomery gave Cicero a wider berth, but the two still worked together.

Social events required all of them to serve, and usually the library would be transformed into overnight lodgings. As it was the night Joseph and his brother—now Senator Jefferson Davis—hosted a gathering of all of the planters in the area, along with their wives. It was not unusual for the planters on

Davis Bend to consult but seldom five at one time, and their families had never gathered, being kept apart and appropriately safe and ensconced within the sensibility one patriarch owning land on Davis Bend figured the others lacked.

Senator James Alcorn took a steamboat to Vicksburg and was driven down from the city. Jefferson Davis had returned from Washington and personally invited Alcorn. Something about communicating the latest from Washington to wilderness planters.

By the time the sun was poised to disappear below the tree line across the Mississippi, a bevy of carriages were parked between the cookhouse and the barn. Abyssinia had been running out of the big house every time the rattle of a carriage was heard. When the Woods plantation carriage arrived driven by a sturdy young slave with dark curly hair and smiles for everyone, Abyssinia burst through the front door and stood waving to him.

Abyssinia was followed by the dark and handsome visitor named Alcorn. He started bowing and carrying on with Abby in a manner that Cicero—even as far away as the library—recognized as a kind of mock courting. Alcorn even circled the young coachman with sword arm outstretched as if offering a duel. Both men seemed cut from the same physical stock: tallish thick bodies with an admixture of Indian hair and swarthy complexions.

By the time Cicero reached the big house, Alcorn had moved to stand beside the Woods Plantation carriage and was offering a hand down to Eulalia Woods, a woman whose heft had run way past ample. Her tittering and give-away high color encouraged Alcorn in more profound bows and clever speech, until Mr. Woods snatched her away.

"Keep your hands to yourself, you hustler."

"What is it that troubles you?"

"Got a levee district taxin' white trash to build levees that benefit you."

"Surely sir," Alcorn said, "this is a conversation for after supper."

"Not with a man who'll stick his face up in my wife's like she ain't married."

"Again, my apologies . . . As for my business, being a lawyer in a steamboat town I accepted deeds to swamp land as fees. Others hadn't the foresight. I have no shame for it."

"I came to eat. Your business does not interest me."

"Ah yes. I shall not steal your time from supper."

"You stole slaves."

"Perhaps your excesses made them run."

"You are a thief!"

"Libel can be expensive, even for a sober man."

"Oh, I can prove it."

"Reasonable men may differ."

Alcorn downed his whiskey. He made a little hop and winked in Abyssinia's direction.

"Don't ignore me, James Alcorn. I've lost many a sable property I daresay turned up on your dear—is it the Mound Place farm."

"Plantation."

By now, Abyssinia was speaking intimately with the young carriage driver, and he was helping her aboard. Joseph Davis appeared with a couple other guests. Mr. Woods drew himself up and spit his words into Alcorn's face.

"You look like my coachman, a bastard by common knowledge."

The bloodrush darkened Alcorn's face.

"In my county of Coahoma, dueling is for women. Shooting a varmint satisfies."

"Gentlemen," came the voice of another guest, "misunderstandings are unfortunate. We are gathered to plan for continued commerce in these uncertain times."

"I apologize for any offense to your fine lady," Alcorn said. "I grew by the use of Irish labor as well as slaves. Contractors

bring them in to build my levees. As for your runaway negroes
. . . Let us take a lesson from our host. He is an enlightened
businessman. I daresay he has not suffered the defections of
property that some of you may."

"Thank you, James," Joseph Davis said. "Gentlemen, refreshment awaits."

In the dining room, small lamps along the wall reflected in
the crystal and silver for twenty adorning the mammoth table.
Extending into the parlor, a second table covered with matching linen and an overlay of lace provided space for another
twenty guests.

Serving that many was intricate. Food was run over from
the cookhouse by Mr. Ben's sons. Food cooked ahead of time
that needn't be served piping hot was stored in a room the
width of the house off the back door. George the Butler was
an imposingly dressed figurehead. Mr. Ben roamed everywhere barking out orders.

Jefferson Davis, the Senator, did not put in his appearance
until the soup had been served and removed. He never apolo-
gized for being tardy and commenced complaining about a
farm chore his brother had overlooked. To a tolerant stare
from Joseph Davis, he continued.

"Of late, Varina accuses me of being away too much."

"I'd travel for the cause, too," one guest said to Jefferson,
"if my brother was willing to manage my affairs."

"There is a government outside of government in forma-
tion, gentleman," Jefferson Davis said. "We are focussed upon
protecting the textile trade that is our lifeline, finding mills in
Birmingham, England, to replace those of Cincinnati and further east should Northern politics lead to rupture. Having access as a Senator, I am charged with keeping several nations
aware that there are two states of America, one commercial,
one agrarian. Northerners have a diverging view of the future.
God forbid, they should bring us to violence."

"Some of us," Alcorn said, "wonder at all the effort to prepare for this rupture no sane man admits to wanting."

"Gentlemen," Joseph Davis said, "my brother did not mean to provoke a debate. He is merely sharing what burdens him every day."

"How can you oppose arming ourselves?" a now even more drunken Woods said to Alcorn.

"You would be the expert," Alcorn muttered under his breath.

As the tittering spread, Cicero moved away from the front door where he was posted to call grooms in charge of horses or carriages of guests who might depart early.

"An' we cain't let ourself git out-voted!" Woods thundered, dropping back drunkenly into his seat.

"We are already outvoted!" Alcorn said. "This conversation has run by me so often that I cannot bear it. If another state is allowed into the Union, Northerners would control the congress. Sure, they have money invested in the slave economy, but freedom has always been the worshipful pose of Yankee greed."

As the occasion wound down, guests prepared to drive home. The crisis mood that serving so many people had fostered among the house slaves eased. The Montgomery boys began to sample left-overs, and Mary Montgomery became frazzled trying to shoo her sons away from prematurely doing what everyone would in due time. Old George was catnapping open-mouthed leaning in a corner of the back room. Cicero drank as much whiskey as he could lay his hands on without being seen.

His final chore was to light the fireplace in the library. The grates had already been cleaned, wood stacked nearby. He raked a pile of kindling together and lit it. As it burst into flame, the door opened, and the wind swept inside and across the grate on its way up the chimney. Cicero's small fire died.

Inside the door, stood James Alcorn, a flagon in his hand. He raised it to his lips before focussing upon Cicero.

"An evening of snakes and bears."

"If you say so, sir."

"Bears who pronounce themselves champions of the white race. Snakes who would steal the gold from your teeth . . . No comment?"

"No sir."

"Your master has trained you well."

Cicero nodded.

"Your master is among the few who understand the business we are in for what it is. There will be movement toward a more liberal condition for those of your race."

Cicero remained silent.

"Understand, please . . . I am not seeking an out-of-place conversation. I am drunk and talking to myself. Once, upon visiting London, I was taken into their St. Paul's Church. Now there is a confused church . . . What I recall amidst all of their history of conquest on the church walls is the one word, 'empire' . . . Do you have any idea what it really means?"

"No sir."

"The lower class Englishman can't pronounce his 'h's'. He says 'E for He. I had drunk a decent quantity of claret, and inside my head, I heard such a one—a cockney they call them—pronounce the word 'empire' backward."

"Backward?"

"Yesss . . . in my imagination."

"If you say so."

"'E rip me! is what I heard. That is the word 'empire', backward." Alcorn paused to drink from his flagon. "The Queen of England sails her bloody ships over and rips some little brown bugger from stem to stern in the name of her god and country."

Cicero bowed and lowered his face.

"Go ahead and laugh. It is the truth of history, and you're a bright young man who happens to be a slave. Years from now, it may be that educated men of your hue will be holding conversations about some small empire of their own. It is the few of enterprise and vision who will always prevail. But now, it is scamps like me doing the talking, men who got here when the getting was good. We've been consecrated by our money."

DURING SUMMER and fall, the newspapers filled up with reports of bitter presidential campaigning. Cicero and Annye Mae had wrapped their feet in rags and were waxing floors in the library when the master's telegraph began clicking.

Cicero ran into the master's study and grabbed a handful of tape. The word "war" leaped out at him.

"Annye Mae! War been declared!"

"Where they fightin'?"

"Go tell Mr. Ben I'm bringing the master here."

The telegraph key was still going when Davis walked into his office. He bent over it and studied the words being punched out.

"Holy Jesus!"

It was so unlike him, Cicero jumped.

"Fort Sumter's been attacked. Go get me my overseers, Cicero, and if they don't come right away, I'm whipping you."

At the sawmill, Cicero found Davis' chief overseer. He ordered Cicero to go round up certain others. Afterwards, Cicero ran to the cookhouse to make sure Mr. Ben had been informed of events.

"I'm waiting for Nancy and Mary to put together a tray," Ben said. "I need me a better reason than curiosity to go barge in."

A short time later, Mr. Ben walked up onto the stone esplanade in front of the library, whistling. Isaiah and Cicero ran around back to listen under the window of the master's study.

"Come right in, Ben. Thank you for your good work."

"Thought you might be in here a spell," Mr. Ben said. "Rough times ahead."

"I have business with these gentlemen, Ben. Leave us."

Moments later, Mr. Ben was around the back with Cicero and Isaiah. Inside, voices were rising, the clearest that of the master.

"Quit screaming about your feelings! Hurricane is business. I do not want you running off . . . All right, two of you—cast lots. I want the rest of you to promise me six months before you do anything. What would I do with all these niggers running wild?"

Mr. Ben walked back around front and inside. The master was bending over the telegraph again, writing out the message coming over it.

"Give me a minute, Ben . . . I know you heard what I just said—no, don't deny it. You listen in. I depend on you for that."

"What's wrong, masta?"

"Jefferson is right in the middle of it all. He's resigned his commission. He'll be impeached in the Senate . . . We're in for it."

Davis sighed, dropped his eyes to the message in his hand again and read from it.

". . . 'General mobilization in Vicksburg. Consult the commander of the principal defensive battery for the city, Colonel . . .' So on and so forth. You see, Benjamin, the main force Southern army must remain in Vicksburg. With its guns over the river, the army would protect those guns. Another army inland at Jackson is only logical. However, there is all of the river between Vicksburg and Natchez a day's river travel to the south of us . . . We are the hole in our defense."

In March, Cicero awakened to find a small army of unknown white men assembling slaves from the Quarters on the lawn of the big house. Joseph Davis emerged accompanied by the mistress on his arm. The crowd began murmuring. The master raised his hands for silence.

"I am moving your home inland. We cannot remain here with the Union Navy taking over the river."

The murmurs became a din of consternation and surprise punctuated by outbursts of anger.

"Look sharp! Anyone attempting to sneak away or to cause trouble will be dealt with harshly."

As suddenly as he had appeared, the master held his hand out to his wife, and together they walked into the library to the applause of some of the armed white men. One of them led Benjamin Montgomery inside.

When it sank in that people Cicero had known almost all of his life were being taken off, he didn't know what to do. He separated himself from the house group and walked the line of guards until he found the group of men from his old barracks. Little Man was there, but the guards would not allow them to talk.

Mr. Ben appeared behind Cicero, grabbed him roughly by the arm and led him back to the house group.

"Stop abusing your privilege. This ain't no day to make a white man mad."

"Where is Annye Mae? She's not with our group."

"I got business inside with the master. Ice water, now—you know what that mean. Just wait until I come back."

When Mr. Ben ran back toward the library, Cicero began searching for Annye Mae. He stepped into the milling crowd when the guards separated to allow a water wagon to leave, but they ran him out.

AFTER THE PLANTATION was shut down, the small group of families abandoned their cabins and moved into the mansion. No one saw the gunboat steam up from the south. It steered in close to shore and eased ahead until it reached the plantation dock. Two dories were lowered. Ten men paddled ashore.

Quickly, they fanned out to the sawmill, up from the river to the utility buildings, to the cookhouse. More men came ashore when the landing party signaled that there was no opposition. Isaiah noticed the landing as he was driving a wagon back from Brierfield. He whipped his horse ahead and ran inside Hurricane.

"Daddy! Daddy! They got men outside with guns."

Everyone poured outside and stood in wonder. One of the dories was returning with an officer aboard. Holding his fancy hat under his arm, the man marched through the ranks of his men and made directly for Benjamin Montgomery.

"My name is Farragut. We are an expeditionary force out of New Orleans."

"Yessir. You . . . ah, would be with the Union?"

"We have to secure this area immediately."

"Oh, you ain't got nothin' to worry about. The white folks all moved away some time back. They figured this was comin'."

"Would you kindly show us the house of Senator Davis."

"This Davis Bend. All you kin see is Davis land."

Cicero appeared at Mr. Ben's side.

"Davis broke his oath to preserve the Union," Farragut said. "His treason will not go unpunished this day."

"Sir, my name is Cicero Morgan. I want a gun to fight."

"Is that so? And why, young man, do you wish to fight?"

"Because white folks owe me for making me a slave. That

man, Davis, forced my father into slavery after he'd purchased our freedom."

"How tragic." The commander turned again to Ben Montgomery. "Is that the Davis house there?"

"Yessir," Cicero blurted out. "That's his house right over there, the big one beside the little library building."

"Thank you, young man. Just so you all may know, I am Commander David Farragut. Be sure and tell the Senator who visited his home today."

"Sir?"

"Yes, young man?"

"Leave me a gun if you can't take me with you."

"I like your diction. You certainly stand out."

"Don't you need another fighter?"

"Mainly, we have need of a cabin boy."

"But . . ."

"Cabin boy or nothing."

"I want a gun, not a spoon."

"Excuse me then. I must confer with my non-com."

As the commander walked away, Ben Montgomery grabbed Cicero's arm.

"Fool! He was looking for the Jeff Davis house."

"So, send them over to Brierfield."

Commander Farragut and the men he was huddled with headed toward the house. In the doorway, stood Abyssinia wearing one of her mistress' cast-off dresses. Farragut bowed to Abyssinia and motioned one of his men forward. A moment later, when the sailor put out his hand to prevent Abby re-entering the house, she tried to slap him. Abyssinia planted her hands on her hips as Farragut walked over.

"You can't be the Senator's wife—much too young, though of dark hair and eye. You are a beautiful young lady."

"I am a distant relative. I was simply attempting to enter my home."

"I intend to burn this house. It is a symbol of broken faith."

Abyssinia's mouth gaped open before she spoke.

"I have trunks in the maid's room. There is a closet full of my things upstairs."

A bemused Farragut looked up to the sky.

"Be quick."

"Can I get some help?"

A sailor snatched his cap off and stepped forward. Isaiah joined him.

Two trunks and several armsful of various articles of clothing were carted out. Meanwhile, other navy men stripped the cookhouse of foodstuffs. From the main house, many took souvenirs. A small team of more ominous purpose poured kerosene and tar into corners, and they broke up and piled furniture underneath the stairs.

"Quartermaster, report!"

"Provisions obtained, sir."

Farragut tossed the first blazing faggot into a waiting pile of saturated kindling. The flame ran inside the front door, along both sides of the stairs and begun to climb. Minutes later, a cheer went up when the fireball exploded into the second floor. As Commander Farragut stepped aboard his gunboat to head back downriver, the flames broke through the roof.

Hurricane burned into the evening lending unreal color to the watching faces. As night fell, Mr. Ben roused everyone to carry necessaries into the library. After the house fell into embers, they claimed sleeping space on the library floor.

Not quite a year later, Joseph Davis appeared with ten men in uniform. They rode straight for the barn to feed and water their horses while Davis himself helped dig a hole behind the main house. Not even Mr. Ben knew what they were looking for until they pulled out a cache of gold coin in pillow cases.

In April, a Confederate officer who said that he was down from Vicksburg showed up and told everyone that he had been asked to have a look at the Davis plantations. Curiously to those who lived there, he asked questions about the locations of plantation houses all over Davis Bend and wrote down the information.

Those left on the plantation became increasingly anxious. There was the prospect of planting food the Union Navy would seize as it pleased come harvest time. Even worse, the Confederate officer from Vicksburg began galloping into the Bend at the head of a band of rag-tag volunteers to take whatever they could find.

Mr. Cicero's Book

Davis Bend, 1863

Union boats soon established completed control of the Mississippi River. As they put in at Davis Bend for supplies, the sailors shared information about the stalemated war along the River. To the south, New Orleans had fallen. North of the Bend, Confederates had continued to build gun emplacements on bluffs facing north and west over the Yazoo and Mississippi rivers that flowed together below Vicksburg.

The Great Mississippi Swamp blocked the way north and east, leaving attack from the south the only way Vicksburg could be taken. The problem was how to ship the whole Northern Army past the city's guns. Several failed efforts had cost one general his job and tied up the Northern Army for almost a year. Ulysses S. Grant was now in charge.

For her own reasons having little to do with the war, Abyssinia moved across the Bend to sleep in the vacant Brierfield house. One day, Mary Montgomery complained about Abby reporting back to Hurricane late for chores, and an argument broke out. Old George walked over and put his arm around Abby.

"This girl got too much spirit for her own good. Some dancin' git it outta her."

"Anytime Old George want a party," his young wife said, "I'm all for it. Let's all go to Brierfield."

Inside Jefferson Davis' house, they poured through the food hidden from seizure and selected what could easily be prepared. Then they started on the whiskey. Mr. Ben was over-ruled. Abby took George's wife up into the big master bed-room and dressed them in gowns of their Mistress Eliza. Abby brushed out and curled their hair with an iron warmed over a lamp. When the two returned to the group Abby had become a wan and elegant Eliza Davis attended by George's wife.

"Oh, we are certainly free," she said, downing a glass of whiskey punch. "We must have music and dancing. Would you please, George?"

Old George clapped his hands and sang. Isaiah pulled Abyssinia into something between a waltz and a square dance. The fun became contagious, and George's wife chose Cicero for her partner. There was a muffled rumble, and Abyssinia clutched Isaiah.

"My lord! Is that thunder?"

"Come on, Abby, quit worrying. We dancin'."

Soon there were other explosions, no longer solitary rum-bles. The sounds washed over them all, deep rumbling sounds counterpointed by staccato bursts.

"They're running Vicksburg!" Cicero yelled.

Nancy started humming, and Cicero leapt in the air. Isaiah and his brothers started cheering, and the older generation joined Mary and Ben Montgomery singing. Cicero ran outside with Isaiah behind him. The trees of the Bend were between them and a view north on the river toward Vicksburg. Cicero raced Isaiah for the dock more than a mile away at Hurricane.

There was no view north to Vicksburg other than at the neck of the Bend, but they ran anyway. All while the sky was

flashing orange and yellow, lightning before the thunder.
Gunpowder rode the wind. When they reached the pier, all of
the young men, including Isaiah's brothers, gathered and
cheered and shook each other's hand. More than an hour
would pass before the first Union ironclad rounded the bend
in the river and came into view.

"My lord!" Isaiah said. "Look like a big black turtle with his
red-eyed self."

In a spectral line lit by the faraway occasional cannon fire,
a flotilla of warships was puffing its way toward the little dock
behind where the Hurricane mansion had stood. From inside
the turret of the lead vessel, night lanterns leaked pools of
shimmering red out onto the river's blackness. It resembled
a cigar-shaped black stove belching dense smoke in the
moonlight.

Lashed to it was a boxy wooden vessel that had been inade-
quately shielded from the guns of Vicksburg. It had burned
but was still afloat. Another ironclad ran free, engine coughing and humming like a demon.

Cicero started running again to burn off the frustration of
sitting around so long. A rich hearty singing from sailors filled
his ears, and he veered back toward the riverbank and ran
along listening as the sound passed downriver. By the time he
found himself nearing the Brierfield dock, one of the first
ironclads was already tied up.

Suddenly keen to rejoin his family and talk about what it all
meant, he started running across the fields to return home by
the shortest route. As he slowed to rest, Hurricane's utility
buildings came into view. They were surrounded by uni-
formed men.

Caution led Cicero to circle. He found more men milling
around fires built on the esplanade in front of the library.
There was a hostility that Cicero did not connect with them
being Union forces in hostile territory as he sneaked behind

the ruins of the plantation house. An ironclad and two other vessels were tying off of the Hurricane dock.

He made his way back around toward what had been the front of the mansion and crept from tree to tree as close to the cookhouse as he could. As soon as he marched out into the open, an armed marine blocked his way.

"My master left us in charge," Cicero said, only to feel a bayonet prodding him away from the cookhouse.

"You sit down," the marine said. "The other fella come in before you. He say he was in charge."

A fire in the yard reflected off their faces. When Cicero tried to move toward the cookhouse, a gun barrel poked into his back.

"Be still," came a new voice from behind. "Do you folks in there know this man?"

"Yessuh," Mr. Ben said. "He with us."

That night, the cookhouse floor seemed as hard and splintery as the new freedom world outside. Mary Montgomery worried about having to cook for the whole navy. Old George and his wife feared they would lose cabins to the military because the library and Brierfield big house had been commandeered. Mr. Ben worried about planting food crops before the spring was lost. Everyone feared the unknown, and no one knew how long their liberty would be restricted.

Well after midnight, Isaiah—who had been led off by a guard before Cicero's arrival—rejoined the group.

"Daddy, the commander told me that Admiral Porter is comin'. He would of been here already, but his boat run under Vicksburg last."

"Where is Abby?" Cicero asked.

"Miss Abyssinia Morgan is entertainin' the commander of one of them ironclads with lady-like conversation."

"Doing what?"

"Why, actin' just as fine as she can be," Isaiah said in parody of Abby's grand manner. "First Union men was no-counts, like that boy outside. They thought she was the lady of Brierfield 'cause of the way she was dressed."

"So, where is she?"

"Look, Cicero, these Yankee boys seen some pretty sunburnt white women, but that commander got to know Abby ain't white. But she acting' like she is—I mean, talkin' about her balls and parties like they was her own, stead of Miz Eliza's, and ole navy goin' along with it."

"She's safe?"

"Excuse me," Mr. Ben said. "What we have to worry about is feedin' ourselves. Soon be more niggas around here than these Yankees know what to do with."

"How do you figure?" Cicero asked.

"There's food here, and there ain't a lot anywhere else. Why you think the navy come here so often?"

That first evening of freedom, flight entered Cicero's mind, as if he were standing over the river up on the bluffs of Vicksburg with the wind whispering jump. Back in the real world of the cookhouse Nancy stirred on a pallet she had been keeping to whenever her eyes were ailing. Cicero had no idea what he would do with her or with Abby. In a painful reprise of what his father must have felt, he knew that he couldn't leap without first arranging for his family to get away.

COMMANDER GREY was the Union officer that Abyssinia had charmed, and he told her that fifty thousand slaves were drifting south along the river shadowing both the Navy and Grant's army to remain free of enslavement. On her return to the cookhouse the first morning after occupation, she was full of herself.

"Commander Grey says we can move North if we want, and he wants to take me to Boston."

"Don't be a fool," Nancy said. "Man sweet talking you or just plain lying."

"No, no. Isaiah heard him."

They all turned to Isaiah who got up and walked away.

"What's wrong with him?" Cicero asked.

"Hush," Nancy said, then to Abyssinia. "Daughter you ain't got no sense."

Abyssinia turned away in a huff and hurried past Isaiah. Outside, a guard provided by the commander awaited her. Nancy whispered to Cicero.

"Isaiah been sweet on your sister for the longest."

With daylight of the next day, Cicero put a piece of bread in his pocket and began to walk around Davis Bend. Naval barges were coming in from the Louisiana side of the river to unload soldiers and black people. After unloading, the barges would return across river for more.

"Where you folks from?" Cicero asked a man camped near the Hurricane slave quarters.

"Upriver from the Quitman place here. Call it Riverhome."

"Why are you here?"

"Ain't you know there's a war on?"

"Of course, but why didn't you stay home?"

"'Cause here it's safe with the navy around us. No Confederates. Anywhere else, you liable to get horsemen whoopin' and hollerin' through every night. Ain't no food, neither."

"I only have one piece of bread, but I'll bring you more."

Curious to know how many others were around and now beginning to wonder if the fifty thousand people Abyssinia had reported as shadowing Grant's army might not be close to the truth, Cicero walked to the Woods Plantation at the neck of the peninsula. Hundreds were lined up there, all clamoring to be let onto Davis Bend. Guards had been posted, and wire had been strung to close off the entrance. The Army was still bringing in boatloads of ex-slaves while keeping others out. Cicero sought out an officer.

"We have orders," he said, "to admit only those of your people who are trustworthy. Letting everybody in creates security problems."

"How many do you think will fight you? Look at the lines. Some of these people are sick."

The officer shrugged.

"Been the same up and down the Mississippi for almost a year. They followed the General and lay around all day. But those are the ones we feel we can trust because we are bringing them here."

The people listening seemed to give up for the afternoon. Recent runaways, they had braved the lines for hours and now fell out to lounge on the dune grass along the sandy expanse that connected the Bend to the mainland.

Back at Hurricane, Cicero scraped together a small store of provisions. Isaiah refused him more without his father's approval, which Cicero decided to forego. He'd heard Mr. Ben promise Isaiah a whipping if he mentioned the hidden food cache to anyone.

When Cicero returned to his new acquaintances, people were swimming out into the river from the riverbank north of the Bend and coming ashore where no guards were posted. As the night came on, Cicero found himself huddled around one of hundreds of bonfires blazing on Davis Bend that night under threatening skies.

"I'm eighty years old," the old woman who'd challenged Cicero earlier in the day said. "Just weaned 'em and wished 'em well as they was taken off."

"They sold me twice," a man said, "once 'cause a master needed the money, second time 'cause my master wanted women to breed. Said I wasn't the right type of buck . . . I talked to ten folks today. They all promised to carry my name to any woman name of Bertie they meets up with."

Cicero thought of Annye Mae, of Little Man, shared his own story.

"If we run into them, we tells 'em you lookin'," the old woman said. "Lots of our people got a whole list of names in they head. Me—look here!"

With a palsied hand, she pulled off a faded turban and unwound it. Inside was a piece of paper.

"I cain't write," she said, "but a man writ down all my chil'ren's names. Young man?"

"Yes ma'am."

"Can you read'n write?"

"Sure I can."

"Well, damn it all!" the man who'd spoken earlier said. "Sure would feel kindly if you would bring us some paper."

"I could write up one list for all, maybe give you here a copy. I won't have enough paper to copy lists for everybody."

"We use our heads," the man said. "Got to carry 'em on our shoulders like always."

A DRIVING RAIN BEGAN before Cicero made it back to the cookhouse. By morning, the grounds were a quagmire, and it rained all day. Cicero postponed visiting Commander Grey and attempting to advise him of the problems people were facing. Despite the rain, a sentry appeared at the cookhouse seeking Isaiah who departed with him.

Hours passed before Isaiah returned bedraggled and dripping to pull his father aside. Mr. Ben motioned Cicero over and whispered, "My son is gonna meet the Admiral tonight."

"That's what they told me," Isaiah said.

"I would send one of my other sons over," Mr. Ben said to Cicero, "but you know a lot more about things."

"Let's go," Cicero said to Isaiah. "There's a lot we need to tell the Admiral."

"Don't forget," Mr. Ben said. "The man know what he want from us. Pushing ain't the way you deals with white folks."

They set out immediately. Cicero was shivering and soaked like Isaiah by the time they arrived, and they had to wait outside for what seemed more hours. Finally, they were ushered before a bearded, tallish man with sagging skin and brown hair who barely looked up at them from behind his desk.

"I am Admiral Porter," the man said.

"We all ready to work," Isaiah said. "This my cousin. My family the one been runnin' both these plantations, and we can build levees or whatever you pay us for."

"Can't guarantee all of you work, but some, yes."

"We save the money to see us through our trip North."

"We can't guarantee that either."

"Beg your pardon, admiral sir," Cicero said, "but I want to fight. I'm able-bodied, and I can read and write. You won't have to worry about me."

The admiral took a deep breath.

"That is a fine ambition, young man, but the services do not encourage the enlistment of your race."

"But you have black soldiers at Millikens Bend. I've met people from there."

The Admiral put down his pen. His face grew tense. Cicero could see Isaiah's eyes flashing.

"Milliken's Bend is a military resettlement area, which this will soon become. We armed freedmen there for self protection because our army was moving away to march around Vicksburg." The admiral walked out from behind his desk and pulled aside the lacy floor-to-ceiling white curtains with which the undistinguished windows at Brierfield were masked. "I'm sorry, young men. I have no doubt of your bravery."

"But admiral—"

The admiral clapped his hands together.

"No more about that, now. The general will be here any day. For security reasons I can't tell you exactly when. I need people familiar with the river south of here and especially with sources of provisions. You there, young Isaiah?"

"Yes sir!"

"Do you know where the gunboat, Indianola, went down close to here, some time back?"

"You bet, sir!"

"Good! Good! She's got valuable hardware on the bottom."

Cicero tried to catch the white man's eyes, but he couldn't.

"If young Isaiah will agree, I'll make him my cabin boy and, to be fair about it, I'll send him and the rest of you to Cincinnati on naval transport when the time comes."

"Yessir!" Isaiah let out a whoop. "Anything you need, we do."

TENS OF THOUSANDS of freed women and men had been assembled inside the Bend. Thousands more were said to be yet accompanying elements of the Union army remaining across river in Louisiana. Admiral Porter placed Hurricane and Brierfield under Mr. Ben's direction to grow food and to shelter the ex-slaves. All would be kept at the Bend for the duration of the war.

"I need you to do me a favor," Cicero told his sister

"Empty-headed me? Surely you jest."

"I need something from your Commander Grey."

"Whatta you want?"

"He seems a decent enough sort compared to folks we've called master."

"And . . ."

"I want a quantity of paper, quills, ink."

"I don't have time for foolishness."

"Have you been looking around? The one thing I see over and over is people promised medicine or food being relocated. What happens after that is, nothing. Navy can't locate the people, or nobody cares enough to try. If I volunteer the time to keep records of every soul brought into Davis Bend, I can offer it to the military. If they don't use my journal, I'll offer it to the people looking for family."

"You can do all that?"

"Get me some paper—I really want a ledger book like I kept for the plantation."

"I could do that for you, Cicero."

Rumor had General Grant putting in a brief appearance on Davis Bend, though none of those who had served the Davis household ever saw him. His army had been bivouacked just south of the Bend to rest up from its march through the Louisiana swamp.

Within days, General Grant marched the Army of The Mississippi toward Jackson, the capitol. It was a strategic move. During an attack on Vicksburg, a Confederate army guarding the capitol might attack Grant's flank. To counter that possibility, Grant set out to dispatch the smaller army before laying siege to Vicksburg.

The campaign against Jackson was brief. Large numbers of Confederates surrendered when faced with a superior Northern force. Within days, Grant reorganized his army and marched back toward the Mississippi River. It was imperative to seal off the City of Vicksburg before elements of Confederate forces that had not surrendered at Jackson could rush over and reinforce the garrison. Though Grant's troops had scant rest, the long battle of entrenched forces on both sides of the line around Vicksburg would allow for ample rest.

The siege commenced from the southeast, the city's least defensible side. There were no Confederate guns on superior elevation there, no rivers Union troops had to cross. Grant's mortars bombarded the city for days before foot soldiers moved forward and dug in. With Admiral Porter controlling the rivers north and west of the city, it was cut off on all sides. Northern and Confederate forces were soon living in trenches. Confederates dug caves into the hills, and Union battalions dug holes in the ground. Nobody attacked the other for weeks at a time.

At Davis Bend, Cicero began his work. He wrote down the names of men, women and children, their origins, relatives they knew. Lines developed at his work space on the esplanade outside the library, and he came to expect a crowd whenever he arrived. Someone started calling his work *Mr. Cicero's Book.*

Late one morning, military police brought Cicero a prisoner to be questioned.

"Why is he in chains?"

"They brought him from Louisiana in shackles so he must be dangerous. Wouldn't talk to us. Figured he might talk to you so you could put him in your book."

"Is he charged with a crime?"

"Not by us."

"How long has he been in custody?"

"'Least a month. They moved him around while the army was crossing the river. Ones who captured him ain't around no more. So here he is."

Cicero grabbed a military transit sheet from the guard and began to read.

"Says he was armed and uncooperative—What does this mean?"

"All I know is we got to question everybody in the stockade, and he won't talk to us."

The boy was over six feet tall, lean muscled, and so broad in the shoulders Cicero understood why he was treated gingerly by the guards. He wore homespun, skins on his feet despite the season. His smoky-eyed, black velvet look had a couple of young women smiling brazenly.

"My name is Jasper."

Surprised that the young man had spoken, Cicero motioned him closer.

"What is your last name?"

"It's Jasper."

Just then, Cicero looked up to see Abyssinia approaching. The skirts of her dress were rustling as she held both them and her chin a little too high. She was followed by none other than Commander Grey. She hopped up onto a nearby desk and offered her hand to the commander.

"Thank you for accompanying me."

Cicero sprang out from behind his desk.

"You have work, Abby. Sit in your chair. Good morning, commander."

"I'll move when I am good and ready . . . My brother has poor manners, commander. He does not understand that gentle conversation graces civilized people."

"Do you mean," Cicero asked, "the ones who owned us?"

The young prisoner giggled.

"Who are you?" Abby asked him.

"Tell me your name first."

"Don't play with me."

"You want my name, give me yours."

Commander Grey cleared his throat.

"I brought Miss Abyssinia over to work, Cicero, as you suggested."

"Thank you, sir, for the job."

Sensing that the commander was tiring of Abby, Cicero had tried to fashion a way to keep her away from the man and benefit Abby at the same time. That previous Monday night, Abby had visited her mother and gossiped about how little time the commander had for her. Now, sitting on top of her desk, Abby leaned forward and hissed at her brother.

"I am a colored girl with only one thing, it seems, I am to be valued for, and I must do with it what I can."

Abyssinia snatched off her sunbonnet and shook her hair out as the commander bowed and withdrew. The guards watching Abyssinia's little drama left the refugees unrestrained, and the room began filling up.

"Get those people back in line," Cicero said, "and turn the prisoner loose."

After a moment's hesitation, one guard unshackled the young man. The other left the prisoner's side to help Cicero direct people back outside and into a line. Cicero watched the good-looking boy trying to get Abyssinia's attention, until a guard's voice intruded.

"Move away from the door . . . Let her in!"

The people moved aside for a black woman as tall as Cicero. She bowed to one, gave a howdy-do to another as they stood aside, but she remained polite. Her eyes sparkled when they settled on the prisoner, and the two embraced.

"I'm free, momma. This man gonna let me out."

"You free long as you live, cherie. Just let me hold you."

No one disturbed them until the woman kissed her son's face, and they moved apart.

"You look like his sister," Cicero said. "The young fellow has some size."

"So do I."

"Oh, yes. Beautiful enough to . . ."

"Make a rooster crow?"

"Well, I'll be damned!" Abyssinia mumbled.

"This the man makin' me free, momma. He kin read and write, too."

"Where," Cicero asked, "are you from—I mean, the boy and you?"

"Everywhere and nowhere, mister. We maroon from across the river. My name is Rose. What's yours, please?"

"Cicero Morgan. Forgive me for loosing sight of my manners. Over there is my sister, Abyssinia."

"Pleased to meet you," Rose said to Abby, who looked away.

"Miss Rose, I have business now. It's what I do, keep records of all the people brought into Davis Bend."

"Don't say?"

"You seem surprised?"

"No, not surprised. You could probably do anything need doin'. It's just that I don't look to another for much, and I kinda feel what you feel for these people. You a good man, but you probably ain't had the choices I had."

"Civilized people owe each other a certain debt, and working to help these people is so much better than working for somebody who owns you, know what I mean?"

"Cain't disagree. I'm just a woman from the swamp, but I ain't never met no civilized people nowhere."

"Stay in line! And leave me be."

Abyssinia was yelling at a woman who'd become impatient watching Cicero and Rose talk.

"Momma," Jasper lowered his voice, "don't you think she pretty?"

"Don't matter what I think," Rose said, then to Cicero. "When you have time, we could talk some more."

"I'd be delighted."

Jasper sat against Abyssinia's desk, but she picked up her bonnet and walked away.

"Come see me down by the riverbank," Rose said, pulling Jasper behind her, "past the big plantation house that burnt down."

"I'll look forward to it."

"Tell you a little about my life."

The Swamp

Eastern Louisiana, Winter of 1861

"You old people treat me like a slave."
                    Young Jasper's lament.

The sky was devil red and glowing as if storm lanterns were burning behind the curtain of cloud, and to those who had learned to bow to the inevitability of nature, that meant snow. Already a drizzle was beading on the fur of Rose's bearskin coat. Killing it had been part of a ritual, her learning to shoot, to kill before being killed.

Rose pulled the pelt around her body and secured it with two wooden pegs. All afternoon a chilling mist had been gathering along the ribbon of dirt road. A store surrounded by a handful of cabins was a mile ahead, and the only travelers since morning were just moving past where Rose was hidden. Clothes of rough and common cut, horses with a gaunt and mongrel look had persuaded Rose not to waylay them. As the riders disappeared, Rose noticed Mack easing out of the trees.

"Ain't no purpose in sittin' there, Big Rose. Give it up."

"Give what up? I ain't frosted my tail half a day to give nothin' up. Besides, you a married man, cherie."

Mack grinned but before he could reply, his brother appeared accompanied by adolescent Jasper.

"Y'all quitin'?" Jasper asked.

Mack nodded.

"Aw, we been here all day, and that store in town got soldier guns y'all been wantin'."

"Chance for another gun ain't worth bein' shot at. We goin' home and sleep."

"Y'all damned scared!"

"Say again, young critter?"

"Nothin'."

Mack motioned Brother off into the trees. Jasper collapsed on the ground and drew his legs up under him.

"Come on, cherie."

"Don't take his side, momma. You ain't his wife."

"Well now, Mr. Jasper, I ain't married to nobody. You bring your tail on back to camp."

They were all a family, maroons they sometimes called themselves, from a French word for people who ran away from the colonizers to live in the wilderness. The name referred to natives of the land before Europeans, to deserters from French and Spanish armies, and to those stolen from Africa who refused to live in slavery. They were the ones Mistress Laplace had called swamp trash, damned as heartless animals, and it was this one small group who had stumbled upon Rose and Jasper fourteen years before. Macklin was the leader's given name. He and his "Brother" had taught Rose how to survive in the wilderness.

"Don't mind the boy," Rose said, coming abreast of the men. "He's feelin' his manhood."

Mack cleared his throat and spat. Brother answered.

"We know, Miz Rose, but it's hard to find patience for chil'ren when there's folks paid to kill you on sight."

Rose nodded, remembering her run from slavery. A teen-ager herself not much older than Jasper, she had been terri-fied to see her infant smiling up at gruff-looking Mack. She'd crawled over, snatched her infant away and begun singing. Brother starting to sing along with her had broken the ice, him making up verses about living free, making like a flame in the night to scare patrollers away.

Yellow Woman was Mack's wife, together from the time Mack ran away and hid out with her people. Ten others had joined the family since Rose, but none remained. One man died of old age. The rest had returned to the outside—gone North—but for a couple of young men who had moved away to start their own camp.

Back along the road, Jasper was hunkered down. Fear was weakness. Brother had caned Jasper's hands when he hesi-tated as a child to reach a snapping turtle out of a trap. Later, after Jasper pleaded to keep it for a pet, Brother had tossed it into the soup pot and pointed out that the strong always ate the weak. Now, every time Jasper heard one of the men urge caution around white people, he would remember his own caning and hear weakness in his elders.

Barely thirteen, with a long coal-black face dominated by his mother's slightly hooked West-African nose, he stood a head taller than Rose. Just the year before, coltish sleekness had begun giving way to the broad-shouldered body of a man.

After the others moved away, he headed toward the town. It was only a handful of cabins surrounding one clapboard building. Not even a stray dog stirred as Jasper crept along to avoid being seen, right up to the general store's porch. A fine white powder replaced the drizzle on his raccoon skin cloak, and the wind gusted as he used a window for footing and gained the roof. Tiny cypress shingles that he pried off blew away in the wind as he dropped to the floor.

Next morning, Jasper walked into camp with an armful of guns and stopped in front of Mack.

"Looky here," Jasper said. "Spencer rifles. They repeaters with breach loading."

"I b'damn! They took these guns from Northern soldiers."

Brother was struggling to hang a wild pig under a tree. He came running as Mack began rolling around like a squat bear, aiming one of the new guns.

"Let me see," Brother said.

"Got one for everybody," Jasper said.

"Ain't they grand!" Brother said.

Mack quit rolling around. Came to his feet and approached Jasper.

"You know, them Confederates say a Yankee can shoot all day without reloading one o' these."

"Got them cloth cartridges with shot and powder inside," Brother said. "Oh, they grand."

"Then you like 'em?"

"Don't be a child, Jasper. Guns is guns. Git your ass on home 'fore I git mad 'cause you stayed out all night."

West of the Mississippi River was where they made home. Only a few miles west of it at some points lay the Black River. It ran half the length of Louisiana. All along this inland river and its extension called Bayou Macon was maroon country—fugitive slaves, Indians and not a few white outlaws.

Everyone heard the twig snap, and Mack leapt up. Brother let go of his precious hog and scrambled for his new gun. It was Rose who said, "Runaways, Brother! Go easy."

Jasper had just fallen asleep. He awakened in time to watch two men and a woman walk into camp casting wary glances toward Mack and Brother. Mack put his rifle aside and approached one of the newcomers.

"Always happy to see another get away, but don't take it unkindly if I say you got to move on quick. This here our territory, and it's just a little winter camp. Too many live here, the white folks get wind of it. Send a posse after us."

"We headed North," the woman said. "Be pleased you help us."

"Get you good'n fed before you leave, for sure," Brother said. "'Fact, one of y'all can come help me dress down this hog."

"Howdy do," Rose said, joining the group.

"How're you ma'am," the woman said. "I be happy to help do any work you got."

"This here is Yellow Woman. You come on over with us. Woman don't talk much, and I can't get enough of company."

"Why that is?"

"If you'd spent my years in this swamp, you be full of time alone, too. Me'n Woman workin' together right now, but most often we off workin' alone."

"Sound like a life I be grateful for."

Yellow Woman began showing the visitor woman how to season a stew. She and one of the men were Mack's age. Mack and the man sat on the grass and struck up a conversation while watching the younger man help Brother clean the wild pig. By this time, with the new woman settled grinding corn, Yellow Woman moved away.

"Got work on a skin," she said.

"Yes'm . . . You work it with yo' teeth?"

"Way my momma taught me."

"Are you married?" the visitor asked Yellow Woman.

"No."

"That your man over there, ain't it?"

Yellow Woman nodded, walked back out of her shelter and knelt between the woman and Rose.

"He was runnin' away from the white folks. Me, too. I left a treaty farm across the river 'cause they wanted us to dig up the ground and grow corn, just grow corn and sell it to them, like your whole life was nothin' but corn—no explorin' or huntin' or movin' with the seasons. Me'n Mack took up with each other after a winter together."

"Sound like there's more to tell," Rose said.

"He was used to workin' hard." Yellow Woman smiled. "Bein' a squaw was too much work until Mack come along."

"Be pleased you come with us, Miz Rose. We gonna follow the North Star to freedom."

"No place for people like you amongst the white folks," Yellow Woman said. "You be slave again."

"No ma'am, beg pardon for disagreeing, but we goin' North. Ain't no slavery up there."

"Didn't make no Injuns into slaves neither," Yellow Woman said. "But they got shot up'n run out for thinkin' they could live with them devils."

"If you go west," Rose said, "at least you have space around you. Stay in the wilderness, don't trust nobody."

Mack wandered over.

"Hell, Rose, That Injun Ter'tory like a prison. I was out there with Woman, here. Army treat you like dirt, and 'cept for Seminoles, some o' the tribes don't like free negroes mixin' amongst they own slaves."

"Injun agents," Brother said, "come from slave country. That's who them fools tryin' to live like."

"I ain't," Rose said, "tellin' these folks to leave the swamp, but if they got to go, I'd still go west. There's a lotta other places out there, mountains and woods."

"Yeah?" Brother said. "We like it right heah." He reached for his Spencer rifle. "Y'all ain't never seen a nigga with somethin' like this."

"That was me, mister!" Jasper yelled from across the clearing. "I stole them guns."

He had on his best hide shirt with bead work. Rabbit-skin wrappings had replaced his boots. But instead of leggings he still wore his wool pants, pants on which Rose knew he secretly doted. He was preening for the newcomers as he walked. Mack, who had gone back to reclining, jumped to his feet.

"Boy, take off them pants! You tear 'em up'n then you won't have nothin' blend in amongst the slaves if you git chased."

"Aw, leave him be, Mack," Brother said.

"Naw! He do what I say. Come creepin' in here after being out all night—and I almost forgot that goddamn bigfoot gal he been hangin' 'round."

"But he a cute young fella," the woman said.

"Is that a reason," Mack said, "to bring some child to where I make my whiskey? Just because he discovered a man's thang between his legs?"

THE END OF RAIN followed by warming weather found the family at its ease, especially Mack, who loved to spend idle days flat on his back.

"Woman! Bring me some more of that rabbit!"

"Ain't no more, Mack!"

"Git your gun, Jasper. Go shoot us some varmints. I'm dyin' for some roast squirrel, rabbit—don't much care which."

"Why you treat me like a slave?"

"Go on, Jasper," Yellow Woman said. "You claim to be the big hunter."

"He ain't my boss."

In a rage, Mack scrambled to his feet and ran at Jasper, who tried to stand. Mack's big hand slapped him coming up and dropped him to his knees again.

"That's for not moving quick."

"Damn your rabbits!"

Tears streaming down, Jasper grabbed Mack around the legs and tried to wrestle him to the ground, but Mack kneed Jasper and slipped out of his grasp. A knife appeared.

"Back off, young critter. I'll cut you."

"Quit it, Mack!" Brother said. "Come away, boy. You ain't man enough."

"Yes I am, and I'm leavin'."

"Oh," Mack said, "is that so?"

Rose hurried over from where she had been sitting with Yellow Woman.

"Put that knife down, Mack!" Then she turned to her son. "Always knew you was a drifter like your momma. Didn't know you'd be leavin' this quick."

Disbelief showed in Jasper's eyes. His mother was supposed to beg him to stay. Mack turned away smiling.

"Yeah, I be goin'—right now, momma." Tears glistened in Jasper's eyes. "You git ready."

"No, son. Ain't time for me yet. This something you want to do. You the one cain't live here."

Yellow Woman stopped scouring her cooking pot and joined the group. She put her arm through Rose's. Neither spoke, and Jasper turned away in bravado. From inside her lean-to Rose ran to pull out the giant bear pelt she often wore.

"This critter kept me safe'n warm. Do the same for you. But be smarter than he was, non? Learn when not to growl."

Jasper reached the Bayou Macon around midday and turned northerly, every stroke of his pole taking him further out of the swamp he was familiar with. It was spring and every bush and vine was claiming as much space as light and water would allow. The clogged channel slowed Jasper, and it focussed the current against him. A family of turtles scrambling ahead atop the muck nearer shore seemed to mock him as he inched along. When a crane stood its ground on a submerged stump, frustration led Jasper—against all good sense—to shoot it.

Afterward, the echoing explosion made him feel caution, on account of the big outlaw gangs a few days ahead near the well-traveled Vicksburg-to-Monroe, Louisiana, highway. Even so, Jasper fancied himself superior to any man he'd ever known, a solitary road agent, a scourge of white people, the nightflame his mother sang about.

As the afternoon turned amber and slowly shadowed, shelter came to mind. Wispy new cane growing down into the water caught Jasper's eye as he looked for a landing. He poled mightily, intent on ramming his boat into the cane brake so he could pull himself ashore. Unfortunately, the leaves were sharp, and the boat heavy. Jasper cursed as one hand slipped and dripped blood from a cut at the very moment that a snake slithered up over the side of his canoe.

It wasn't the deadly moccasin, but Jasper gave up moving into the stand of cane and pushed himself backward into the channel again. A fallen tree lay half in the water half on the opposite shore. He was content to have found another landing that would not wet his feet or pants that night.

Finally ashore, caught up in stretching, he realized too late that the current had coaxed his boat away. Now he had to hop in and splash after it. Back up on his log, his rage was too huge for anything but cursing, certainly not hiding himself or his boat. It was getting dark when he stepped onto land, into a rustle of crawfish and frogs scrambling away.

To dry out, he scorned Mack's rule against disturbing the darkness with fire. Only later did a nagging uneasiness prod him to shield the glowing fire with a blanket over a frame of sticks rammed into the earth.

He lay there enjoying the heat, casually touching himself. He wondered who might be trying to take his place with Maidy. His first time with her had convinced him that she was all he needed in life, and he began to consider turning back to see her. She had been cutting cane when he sneaked out of the rough and offered whiskey. He ended up fighting a red-boned young man who claimed Maidy was his girlfriend.

All of a sudden, the campfire seemed to leap into his eyes, and he crumpled to the ground. He was aware of being handled and dragged along, and before his senses returned, he was bound and blindfolded. He struggled once, which brought unconsciousness.

Some time later he came to, no longer blindfolded but surrounded by a crew of white men. He greeted them meekly enough, fascinated by the largest camp he'd ever seen.

"Likely 'nough nigger," an old man said. "What you think?"

"Thought he was a fighter, but maybe no. He make a good camp slave if he ain't."

"You reckon?"

"Ain't nobody buyin' slaves with the Union so close. But we got use for him."

Shame at having been captured and his mother's remembered warning made Jasper lower his head rather than growl. The outlaws were led by the old man, a Tennessee farmer who'd lost his land after war made farming impossible. He beat Jasper without mercy for a whole week, every time he forgot to say "master" or "mister" to one of them. They lived in plank shelters in groups of two or three, playing cards and drinking when not out stalking loot, which they did in the same small groupings. During the day they hobbled Jasper with a leg chain and kept his hands manacled unless he were working. When the last of them left camp, Jasper was always chained to a tree behind the farmer's shanty near where the loot was buried.

Jasper was chained and in misery. Misting rain had soaked his clothes, and he hadn't eaten since morning. It was a rare day when no one had returned to camp. Toward evening, the gang leader from Tennessee straggled in drunk supported by two of the young men.

"Git the nigger some food," the farmer said, "or I'll have your worthless hides."

"My ma ain't teached me to nursemaid no nigger," one of the young men said.

"Well, your ma ain't here, boy. You do it."

It was dark when the young man, who'd delayed to have a drink of the common whiskey plentiful in camp, brought food to Jasper. What Jasper was handed smelled like fish, and he wolfed it down, looked up for more. That was when he saw the young man peering through a chink in the shanty wall and heard him curse the old man lying there sleeping off his belly-ful of whiskey. Never before had there been so few in camp to deal with.

He waited a minute listening for any who might be return-ing, but there was only the patter of rain. The young white man was waiting to chain him up for the night. Quickly, Jasper took stock. That man would have to die, and there were leg chains to be rid of.

"Need to use the toilet, mister. I been holdin' on all day."

The man turned and grunted. Light from a fire in front of the shelter outlined his back. He fished in his pocket for the key to the chain locked around Jasper's waist. It took awhile, but he found it. Before he succeeded in opening the lock, however, footsteps approached in the wet leaves.

"Use this," the third outlaw said. He offered a lantern, then turned away. "I'm goin' to sleep."

In the flickering light, Jasper calmed himself and held out his manacled hands.

"I got to go bad, mister. Cain't do my business if you don't loosen these."

"Take yer shit away from here, unnerstand?"

The man searched another key from his vest, knelt and inserted it. The manacle lock stuck.

"Be still, goddammit!"

"Well, sir, if you stand up and I be on my knees, it go better, non?"

Don't rattle a chain, don't startle the man, Jasper kept thinking as he eased to his knees. Then the key began to turn. One manacle slipped loose. Jasper seized it in his free hand and leapt like a panther. The outlaw gasped only once before the chain circled his neck.

Jasper wrenched him to the ground and pulled the struggling man atop of himself. He could feel the knotted links of chain clicking as they straightened and, in the process, tore into the man's flesh. A warm wetness spread over Jasper's hands. The only noise in his ears were feet thrashing in wet leaves, and it all blended with the sound of the falling rain.

When the man quit struggling, Jasper lay gasping for a moment to catch his breath before he tossed away the loose end of chain. As he tried to push the man off, it seemed as if the body convulsed. He jumped on top and seized the man's neck in his hands, squeezing for all he was worth. Then the man's hands fell loose, and Jasper let go.

The key for his manacle was on a ring near the dead man's hand. When Jasper reached for it, a loud exhalation of air rushed out of the body. Panicked, Jasper leapt up and stomped all over the unmoving chest, wet feet skidding off.

Then he freed his remaining hand. When he knelt to free his legs, the key again stuck until he quit forcing it. When the leg chain fell away, Jasper started running. Like a rank newcomer to the swamp, he ran into the darkness without regard for noise or direction. Fear of recapture mated with a kind of self-loathing for the corpse he'd left behind. It spawned a hundred terrors out of common noises. The boy part of him wanted to run all the way home until a root in the spongy wet floor of the swamp became the neck he had just trampled. He tripped leaping off.

He lay there gasping for breath and slowly coming out of his panic. Then a sack went over his head and two figures leapt on him. He felt too sick to scream, too terrified. It did not occur to him that outlaws would have no reason to stifle his screams, not until he heard the voice of a woman.

"Just hold still, child. Had a vision o' sorts. Knew you was in trouble, but it took us some time to make sure you hadn't left the river back up closer to home. We followed them outlaws. They led us here."

Jasper tried to speak but he couldn't for sobbing.

"Where they keep the gear?" Brother asked. "Your new rifle, son? You want to go back and tell Mack we run off from two drunk white men and didn't help ourselves?"

"It's gonna be cold this winter," Rose said. "Be good to git that bearskin back, too. You could keep it. I'll hunt another."

Brother circled and led them in from the west, just in case the old farmer and the other man had discovered what had happened and headed in pursuit of Jasper. Relying on the rain to mask their sound, they came out behind a shanty across from the one where Jasper had been chained. As the others waited, Jasper moved toward the fire.

Two figures were lying nearby, a jug on the chest of one. Jasper's hand signal brought Rose and Brother at a trot. They got the drop on both men, made one tie up the other before roping the second. Rose looked at Brother, and he winked in the firelight.

"Ain't no need kill 'em, Rose. Don't care how mad they be 'cause we ain't got to come back this way no time soon."

They settled for nondescript rifles after failing to locate Jasper's Spencer. He stuffed a sack with his pistol, a knife and provisions and pulled on his bearskin. Brother dug up a half barrel of jewelry and coins Jasper pointed out, and they stuffed pockets with as much as they could. As an after-thought, Jasper grabbed a handful of paper money. Because the white men kept it, he would not believe it was as worthless as his mother told him.

THAT FALL, Jasper returned with a young woman on his arm. Yellow Woman looked up from her sewing, and Jasper's girl-friend pointed.

"Who that heifer?"

"Her name is Yellow Woman," Jasper said. "She nice."

"Who she married to?"

"To the headman. That's Mack."

Yellow Woman walked over. She said nothing, but she began to push on the young woman, toward the sewing blanket.

"Keep your hands offa me!"

"Don't git mad," Jasper said. "She want to show you how to sew."

"I know how to work. Ain't gonna be her slave."

Jasper pulled Maidy away toward his sleeping hut. Mack and Brother were away hunting. Rose walked over and bowed to the big-eyed young woman before addressing her son.

"Are you gonna fight Mack, cherie?"

"This Maidy, momma. She run away 'cause they found out she been leavin' the plantation."

"He saved me, Miz Rose. A ole jealous boy turn me in for quittin' him."

"That so?"

"Yes'm, Jasper my hero."

"Just be sure you two want a family of your own. If you do, it's time we head off."

Jasper leapt to his feet.

"I know the place to go. 'Cross the Mis'sippi an' down from a town called Friar's Point. So much swamp up there, it's big enough for us never to have no problems with people again."

"Where is that, Jasper?" Maidy said.

"Thatta way," he said, pointing nonchalantly. "Won't even be no runaways bustin' in."

"How you know?" Maidy said.

"Some outlaws I robbed was talkin' about it. Ain't hardly no plantations up there."

"Then," Maidy said, "how my people be able to find me?"

Jasper knelt and encircled her with his arms.

"You with us. People outside the swamp ain't our kind."

When Mack returned, his response to Maidy and to hearing of the move surprised Rose. His nostrils flared, the only sign of emotion she could see, and he walked off to sleep. Brother remained at Jasper's hut. He dropped onto his bottom and smiled toward the young woman.

"Howdy do."

"Howdy to you," Maidy said.

"Listen, Jasper. If you really going away, you need to hear some things Mack ain't never said. There's other camps around here maybe you ain't know about."

"I know more than you about this swamp."

"Jasper. You Big Rose's little boy. I carried you half the places you been."

"I been places on my own, too. Places you ain't seen."

"That, too . . . But listen to a old customer for a minute. Bein' a maroon ain't like what you seen here amongst us. Most maroons ain't so easy goin'. There's them just ahead o' the dogs. Scrappin' for every little bit o' time left—they can git downright hard on folks they don't know. Dangerous, you know? Then there's folks like us who settled down. Trouble is most folk live in this swamp ain't like neither one. Most is newcomers stayin' here 'cause they ain't got nowhere else to go."

"Ain't that why you here?" Maidy said.

"No, little miss, it ain't. I'm here cause I rather be. That's different. I likes the life. Rise when I want, work hard, drink a little. I knows the varmints, snakes, big critters. World outside ain't so friendly in my way o' lookin', so I stay put."

"Still sound the same," Maidy said.

"Talk to this gal, Jasper. Got to be clear why she here. Cain't be fightin' like mos' men and women does. Right now, I doubt either o' y'all got a notion about bein' a maroon 'cause you ain't never thought about makin' no choice. Jasper was raised here. You, little miss, was brought in. You got to make a choice."

After others were settling in for the night, Brother walked over and sat in front of Rose.

"I admire you, Miz Rose—you know that. Figured we be man and wife one day. I ain't big'n bad like Mack, but I truly do admire you."

"Sit down, Brother. Let's eat a meal together."

Awkward as a teenager, the big man reached for Rose's arm.

"I be real sad you was to leave on account of me or Mack being unkind to you or your boy."

"Now listen," Rose said, patting the back of his hand, "I been here a good spell. It's time for me to be in the wind. Y'all showed me true kindness, something I never seen except from my momma. Don't know how ornery and lonely I might be today if it hadn't been for you all . . . But if you want a woman, then the answer's no. Go on and eat, now. My boy and that gal of his be over this way in the morning."

Jasper was up before anyone. He walked over and waited until Yellow Woman emerged, and he asked her if he could speak with Mack. When Mack stuck his sleepy face out, Jasper sat in front of him.

"I got two trees already picked out for boats."

"Why you tellin' me this, youngster?"

"I be real obliged you was to help me git 'em down and hauled in close where I can work on 'em."

"Could use some help, that right?"

"I could."

"That's all you need say."

"Thank you."

Two trees were cut and lined up along the edge of the camp. Yellow Woman gave Jasper his directions. He chipped away at the insides with a small axe. Then came heated stones, red-hot from a fire kept going all day and banked at night, to leave the shell light enough for a man to pull. The hot stones were tucked into bow and stern to burn away the last inches of wood without risk of an errant axe stroke puncturing the hull.

"You ain't no expert," Yellow Woman told Jasper, "but green wood keep your mess-ups from turnin' into a cook fire."

When work on the boats was finished, Maidy began ducking her chores and disappearing into the swamp with Jasper.

"We got to talk, Maidy," Rose said one morning in March. "Leave us alone, son. We got women business."

"What you want?"

"Tell me what you and my son got in mind."

"Hunh?"

"Non, non, cherie! Don't flash them big eyes at me. What I want to know is how you plan on feedin' the family you be havin' soon."

Maidy kept silent.

"Yellow Woman say you went off and left her to cook for everybody."

"Jasper said to go with him."

"Then where is it you be goin' all the time?"

"Nowhere."

"Come on, now, if you got somewhere more important than chores I want to know. Ain't about to cook'n fix for everybody when we leave here."

Maidy shrugged.

"I'm waitin', daughter."

"For what?"

Rose snatched the young woman to her feet.

"You ain't going nowhere with me until you quit bein' a child. That manchild you married, I refuse to carry him in my pocket—you neither. You got to live your own life. You understand me?"

"Whatever you say go, don't it?"

"Yes, it do! Don't you nor him come near my food again."

In time, the last of the good feelings evaporated, and each group kept to itself. Mack mumbled about ingratitude and snapped at everybody to the point of embarrassing Brother. Jasper and Maidy were eating at their own fire, avoiding everyone else.

On the day of parting, regrets were brief, and no words disturbed the tears Rose and Yellow Woman silently shared. Even so, the young people were so impatient to be away that Rose had to run to catch up.

They set out on the Bayou Macon and continued north past the Monroe-Vicksburg highway that Jasper had failed to reach earlier. Just beyond it, they pulled their canoes into the trees and hid them. Then they trekked into the swamp and used the highway to guide them over to the Mississippi River.

Snow runoff from far to the north had the big river at flood stage. Neither Rose nor Jasper considered the Vicksburg ferry, and even if they had, they would have found it shut down because Vicksburg was in a state of siege from the Union Navy to draw attention away from Grant's march around the city on the Louisiana side.

There were a couple hundred people camped in the open near the end of the Vicksburg-Monroe Highway. Rose and Jasper remained apart. They camped inside the edge of the swamp on a modest rise in the ground where Jasper could climb a tree and follow the condition of the river.

Jasper was building a lean-to when a three-man advance for the main force of Grant's army came upon him. His hammering had drawn them and kept him from hearing their approach. Deep in Confederate territory, they eased into the open, guns at the ready.

"Stand easy there, fella," a burly man ordered Jasper.

Jasper knew that slaves like the hoard on the riverbank had been waiting for the Union Army to free them for more than a year, but that meant little to him. He was already free. Even more, memory of captivity made him frantic about any white man holding a gun on him.

"Where you come from, young man?" a sergeant asked.

Jasper pointed into the swamp.

"Can't you talk? I asked you a question."

The man's obvious annoyance unsettled Jasper. He leapt into the underbrush, toward where a rifle was lying. A bullet from one of the soldiers kicked dirt into his face and he froze knowing that he'd made things worse.

A quarter-mile away on the riverbank, Rose heard the gunshot. She wasn't alarmed at first, only later, when three men in blue marched Jasper out of the trees with his hands on top of his head.

"What's wrong, mister?" she called, running toward them.

"Young man took a gun against us," one of the men said. He showed her the rifle he'd taken off Jasper.

"Why, son?"

"He your boy?"

"Yessir, and this is his wife, Maidy—where you at, Maidy?"

The young woman was crouching among a group of onlookers. She continued to ignore Rose.

"Bring your tail over here, Maidy!"

"No ma'am!" Maidy said. Then, to the sergeant, "I ain't

with them people, mister. We ain't really married. This man here . . ." She pointed out a young man with coarse, reddish hair, ". . . He my friend."

"Maidy! Why you goin' back to him?"

Jasper moved toward the other boy. Maidy folded her arms and stepped between the two.

"I ain't agreed to gittin' locked up, Mr. Jasper."

Like the bear whose pelt Jasper wore in winter, he came growling after Maidy.

"Stop, son!"

A soldier leveled his rifle, but the sergeant pushed it aside.

"Break 'em apart, soldier! Don't kill the boy."

Two ran forward and clubbed Jasper away from the young woman. Maidy fluttered away like a frightened sparrow.

"Nigga tried to strangle me. Y'all saw him. Hit him in the head. Ain't nothin' but a thievin' road agent!"

Rose watched it all, shaking her head.

"Is this girl telling the truth?" the sergeant asked.

"No truth in what a woman say to cause her man trouble." Rose turned toward Maidy. "You ain't his wife. That much for real, little girl."

"Got a boy his age at home," the sergeant said. "Have to keep him in irons, though. He's too hot-headed for his own good."

The Unbearable Joy
Of Being One

Davis Bend, Autumn of 1863

"A newborn baby feels one with its mother, the organic first stage of love." Common Clinical Observation

After staying up all night talking, Rose and Cicero were sleeping when Jasper, who had taken himself off after supper, returned looking for breakfast. As much to get him out of the way as anything, Rose volunteered Jasper to go tell Mr. Ben that Cicero would not report for work. When he departed, they snuggled up close in their blankets and competed to see who could pretend to be awake smiling at the other longest.

Now, Jasper had his own sense of time. Things were done when done, nothing before eating or other calls of nature, including a visit to the Brierfield house for another look at Abyssinia. He located her on her way to the cookhouse at Hurricane.

"Why are you bothering me?"

"I kin walk where I want to."

"Well, it was embarrassing to see you in my yard last night."

"It ain't your house. The white man own it."

"How stupid you are. Commander Grey is my friend."

"What you doing friends with a white man?"

"What is your mother doing with my brother?"

Abyssinia walked off. Jasper was so flabbergasted, he followed at a distance. When they reached the cookhouse, Abby went inside. Moments later, Nancy appeared at the door.

"Is it your momma sleepin' with my son?"

"Yes'm. He sent me to find a man named Mr. Ben and tell him he cain't work today."

"And she is your natural mother—the one my boy is with?"

"Course she a natural mother."

"You go on. I'll tell Benjamin. He's too busy these days to have just anyone barge in."

Their second morning together, after another night of talking, but not nearly so late, there was very little small talk as Rose and Cicero roused themselves. It was as if each of them felt embarrassed to have spent so much time hanging on each other's words. Neither had been raised to a life of leisure, and some sense of needing to get back to ordinary life was compelling. Cicero went off to Mr. Cicero's Book. When Jasper showed up, Rose handed him a handful of twisted fibers.

"What's this?"

"I need me something to trade with. Just how good are you setting snares?"

Food on the Bend was scarce, and in the days that followed Jasper proved himself very good indeed. The varmints were skinned, cut into pieces for trading. By the end of the second day, Rose had swapped most of her trade goods for two dresses.

Cicero had never been busier. There were fewer newcomers being brought onto the Bend, but many of those already interned had yet to be interviewed. On their behalf, often the neediest, Cicero was on a crusade.

One morning, before they had pushed off their blankets, Cicero rolled close and smiled into Rose's face.

"You and I are going for a boat ride."

"Ain't you supposed to be at work?"

"Today is about me'n you. I want to celebrate."

It had already been arranged to take a small boat from the Hurricane dock. The guard winked at Rose. Within the hour, Cicero had negotiated Palmyra Island in the bend of the Mississippi where it turned north toward Vicksburg.

"We just aim the boat at Warrenton, and at the last minute we turn in toward shore. Our momentum will carry us, but so will the current. It'll pull us away from so close in to town."

"What's the matter with that town?"

"Confederate irregulars make Warrenton their base from time to time."

"I don't like this much, Cicero."

They struck a sandbar. The jolt threw Rose forward and left her hanging over the bow. Cicero scrambled to drop sail. Rose pulled herself back aboard.

"Move slowly," Cicero said.

"You shake a body up some, Mr. Cicero."

Cicero pushed off with a paddle, raised sail again to gather headway, then cut toward the riverbank. They came ashore at a sandy point. Both of them were laughing as the skiff grated on the shallow bottom.

"Help me drag this boat behind a dune."

They stepped into the shallow water and pulled the little boat ashore. Rose leaned on Cicero's shoulder.

"What now, mister sailor?"

"I take the mast out of the bottom and lay it alongside. So it can't be seen from the river."

Tufts of coarse wild grass sprouted here and there, but mostly there was just sand and debris in the hollows where refugees had been camping during the summer. Cicero flopped down atop a dune and turned his face up to the sun. He reached for Rose, but she was not there. When he opened his eyes, he saw her searching the river. He crawled over and ran his hand along the soft cotton of her pants, up toward her hip. She pointed toward a raft of some sort laden with folks waving at them.

"Follow me."

Rose led Cicero down onto a sand hollow. As they settled down, Cicero again turned his face up to the sun. Rose began whistling, and when Cicero opened his eyes, she was smoothing back her hair.

"Sure like the way naked sunlight makes you look."

"Thank you, sir."

"The river is so beautiful. Too bad we can't watch it from down here."

"It cain't see us, neither."

"All I need is you."

Cicero took Rose into his arms, but she avoided his lips.

"I don't," she said, "do this every day."

"How about every night?"

"Why you got to make a joke? . . . Just hold me awhile."

"Am I doing something wrong?"

"No, cherie, I was tryin' to tell you something." She draped her arms around his neck. "It's the peaceful part of us being together that give me so much pleasure. Dreamin' on a sparkling day, sittin' here with the man I'm gonna find a home for."

"Would you really?"

"I don't even want to let you out of my sight." She grasped the sides of his face with her hands. "Oh, Cicero, there's a place somewhere just for us. You and me could be free to love and to live our lives like any other two people."

"Just stay here on Davis Bend and help me."

"No, no, not here. Not permanent."

"This is my home. You don't have to find a new one."

"But it isn't mine. Cicero, living out here means giving up freedom, and I couldn't do that so easy."

"But, Rose . . . Give us a chance. Ever since I was little, I have wanted to do something for people. That's why I want to stay here instead of moving to Cincinnati. What I do, the people need, at least until the war ends. Then, there'll be the whole question of finding these people a new life."

"For every one you help, Cicero, there's a thousand more out here what need the same. I spent my girlhood in a slave depot. If you wasn't bein' sold through, you come to near hate yourself for bein' part o' all that. Me, they called crazy 'cause all I wanted was to be alone. I was lucky when I finally made my escape . . . You'n me two drops o' water. We make a little splash, but it don't change the river. It take you wherever it's goin'."

Rose leaned in to be kissed, then laced her fingers together behind her head and lay back.

"Look at your Mr. Ben. He know he ain't gonna change the world. Be the same when the war over. That's why he going North."

Cicero sighed and began caressing Rose, running his hand all over her hip as he lay alongside. Somewhat awkwardly, he picked at opening her dress.

There was the barest whisper as they embraced and pulled at clothes. When they kissed in earnest, sand that had been blowing since they came ashore rasped inside their mouths and left them spitting.

"Let's jump in the water."

"Oh, cherie. You are stirring up a warm feelin' I do not want to lose."

"We'll get rid of this sand."

Cicero shucked off the rest of his clothes, and raced to the water. When he plunged in, the cold water chastened him. He followed a current into a pool of sun-warmed river trapped inside a circular sandbar. Careful not to disturb the sand holding the pool in place, he sank to his neck in contentment.

Rose scanned the river before removing her pants, but she left her dress in place. As she waded in, the wetness shadowed her womanhood through the clinging fabric. Cicero held his arms out to draw her into his warm circle, and the river slapped deliciously against their skins as they began to make love.

No leverage, up against each other at the whim of currents, they touched and squeezed in expectation of pleasure that was returned even as given, until Cicero tried to pull Rose's dress over her head, and they bumped heads. Which provoked the laughter that upset their balance, sending them grabbing and falling.

Frisky and silly business after that, the motions meaning more than fulfillment, kissing Rose wasn't enough, Cicero tried to capture her lips with his teeth as if to consume them. He was gnawing on her giggling face and trying to whirl her around in the water when the sand shifted. Cold water rushed in and engulfed them.

Rose was still giggling when they surfaced. Cicero cursed, splashed water into her face and gave chase, but she swam as well as he did. When he abandoned the chase, she retrieved her dress. After pulling it on, they floated out into the channel.

"Ain't," she said, "grown old all of a sudden, have you?"

"Old enough," he said, closing the distance and struggling for an impossible embrace as they treaded water. They went ashore holding each other, down into their sheltered space. With a blanket from the boat, they stayed there into the night.

"Woman, you taste like ripe paw paw."

"Taste as much as you want. I could spend the whole day feeding you in bed."

"It's almost dawn."

"I don't care. Bein' here with you is like part of my dream-time."

"What is your dreamtime?"

"Ask me later. Ain't much time before the sun rise, and folks be up and about."

"So?"

"I met your Mr. Ben. I got a good idea how you was raised."

"Not really. I started out free, remember?"

"Yes, but your people worked the house."

"I spent ten years in the field. I know both sides."

"So don't waste time. Separate parts here, introduce 'em again."

THE DEMAND FOR Cicero's time continued to grow. He departed early and returned to camp later. As Rose was left alone, she had what seemed like too much time. Because neither wild animals nor wild white folks were likely to come after her, she was more secure than ever before. She tended her and Jasper's snares, traded some, did a little cooking.

Isaiah returned to the Bend for a rest leave after his first tour as Admiral Porter's cabin boy. Following the admiral's meeting with Mr. Ben, Isaiah remained ashore to help with planning the family move. He was not much older than Jasper and quick to note Cicero's new sleeping arrangement. Cicero brought Rose to a supper welcoming Isaiah home. Toward the end of supper, Isaiah took Cicero aside.

"Full moon woman. She got you by parts you don't understand."

As Cicero laughed, Mr. Ben joined the conversation.

"You wastin' precious time while these Northerners here. They be gone one day, and then it'll be too late for you to find a livelihood. Git married, if you want to. Just make sure this is the marryin' kind you took up with."

The following day, Isaiah came looking for Cicero who had already left with Rose for his interview station. Isaiah found Jasper sleeping. Being a stranger, Isaiah received blank looks instead of answers to his questions, until Isaiah mentioned a message from Abby.

"Miz Abyssinia?"

"Yeah, you know her?"

"Un-hunh. Met her my first day here. I go see her almost every night."

"She wouldn't see you."

"Course she do. All the girls like me."

"Why would she? Me'n my daddy run these plantations."

"Me'n my family sell whiskey 'cross the river."

"Wouldn't brag about something like that. My family movin' North, and I works for the Admiral, on his ship."

"We ain't ordinary niggas like that. Me'n my momma is maroons. You know what that means?"

"Well, yeah."

"We don't live like y'all who was slaves."

"The Montgomerys ain't no common slaves. We been runnin' the plantation by ourself ever since Masta Davis left."

"Y'all didn't run away?"

"Where was we gonna run to?"

"The swamp. Like anybody got good sense."

"Naw, like I say, we wasn't common niggas. Even white folks knew that. We didn't have to run nowhere."

Such encounters aside, young Jasper, too, had began to chafe under the restrictions of internment. He could carry no weapon. He had no way off of Davis Bend beyond swimming or sneaking at night through the Northern lines. Repression of his youthful sense of adventure as well as a growing jealousy toward Cicero began to take hold.

Rose and Cicero were meeting with the group that swapped information about refugee camps when Jasper found them.

"Momma, kin I talk to you?"

Rose led Jasper out of the meeting.

"Now what?"

"Are you plannin' to stay here?"

"Why you askin'?"

"You ain't gonna be a regular nigga, is you?"

"A reg'lar nigga? What's that, cherie?"

"Time for us to drift on, momma."

"Well, I ain't sure what gonna happen, but I got a feelin' we'll see a lot of Mr. Cicero. I hope you don't mind."

"Non, non, ain't that I mind, but you gonna stay here with him?"

"Didn't you bring Maidy home with you?"

Jasper nodded.

"So, I figure you give me the same rights I give you to pick who you wants to spend time with."

"Cicero all right, but we got to go."

"If you feel that way, where would we live?"

"I got a idea where to go scout around."

"Then go do what you need to and come on back for me."

"Noooo, you gonna stay with him."

"Did I complain about your Maidy? Chest so big her feet ain't seen the sun since she was twelve."

"Aw momma!"

"You go do your scout-around. I be ready when the time come."

"Then I'm goin'."

"May I ask where?"

"Miss'ippi River bottoms up north of here."

"What do you really know about the land up there?"

"Lots, momma, from when I was with them road agents."

"Think you'll be safe this time?"

"Yes'm."

"So be careful."

"I growed up in the swamp. I know things you don't know 'cause I growed up in it."

"Just don't die in it, cherie."

A couple of times after Jasper departed, Rose hinted that it might be time for her to return to the swamp. Cicero's response was a shrug. They were curled up in front of a fire whose light glinted off Rose's well-oiled calves under a blue dress she had traded a lot more varmints for than she thought the dress was worth. Matters other than Rose's legs had Cicero preoccupied.

"Grant's naval support," Isaiah had said, "is finally pulling out.

"Who will guard the plantations?"

"One gunboat and a company of marines."

"A single company?"

"Somethin' called a Freedman's Department from Washington is supposed to take charge of us."

Rose's voice called Cicero out of his recollection.

"You paid no attention to my new dress."

"Are you tempting me?"

"I don't know."

"I think that when you can't make me stop working any other way, you buy a blue dress."

"Don't . . . Let's enjoy tonight, we may not have many more."

"What's wrong?"

Awkwardly, Rose attempted a smile.

"You and I can share," Cicero said. "Like Mr. Ben helping out poor little farmers who don't understand the land. Helping means giving up a little of your own life."

"I never asked a man this before, but what about me?"

"What about you? You'd be my wife."

"Man and woman make a home. One of them ain't sup-posed to be gone all the time."

"Who said I would be? I'll be with you like this always, right here."

Seeking a Home

Into the Great Mississippi Swamp, Autumn of 1863

As Jasper walked toward Vicksburg, he was angry. He could not understand why Cicero resisted living in the swamp with his mother. Nor was he happy that his mother had remained behind. The sound of a wagon in the distance made him wary as it rolled closer. When near enough for him to see two rows of blue uniforms seated alongside each other, he jumped into some bushes along the road. After the wagon passed, he felt guilty for acting like a child, and as he gained the road again, he fought to control his anxiety. The old maroon named Mack would have been laughing at him for calling attention to himself by running off-road like a witless child.

The main thing was he didn't want to be searched and to lose the pistol he was carrying, so he left the road as he closed on the city. It took him hours to circle around the deserted fortifications. The people looked like skeletons. There was not a dog, not an uneaten cat abroad. Men in blue uniforms kept their guns handy.

Evening found Jasper nearing the other side of town, moving toward the sun and eager to find a place to turn in for the night. Before dark, he reached the top of the great bluffs north of the city. A short distance away stood the biggest gun emplacement he had ever seen. Union soldiers were dismantling it.

Upriver, a ribbon of cultivated fields hugged the Mississippi River on both sides. All else was swamp. Directly below Jasper, the Mississippi was joined by a smaller river, and toward its source the bluff he was standing on descended toward water level.

He retreated from the crest of the bluffs toward a wooded area far enough from the activity around the gun emplacements for him to be more at ease. In the rough he spread his blanket and daydreamed about Maidy and her perfectly remembered brown form. Lacking home and permanent shelter, neither of them had been reluctant to frolic outdoors. His breathing quickened as he recalled the accommodations he'd explored, the whiskey he'd stolen from his family to drink with her, and always she had been eager, mischief in her eyes, brown loins thrust against his own to bursting—his only word for the wet completion. She would continue long past his finish to whisper and to move and touch, leaking invitation from her eyes, until his hands remembered to move and to touch, the two perspiring bodies again rubbing skin to skin. After the initial rush, her long lean limbs would wrap and cling as he lay counting her heart beats in the twin berries that refused to soften against his chest. And always the awkward groping to embrace all of her giving way to another explosion of sweet loss.

The next morning, a shrill whistling awakened Jasper. He hurried out of the trees over to the edge of the heights. Down below him, the little river from inland was clogged with cargo boats. A paddleboat on the Mississippi continued to blow its whistle, and it finally had to alter course to avoid a barge floating toward it out of the smaller river's mouth. After watching the near collision, Jasper pulled two corn cakes out of his pouch and walked along the buff eating.

By late afternoon, he had reached the edge of the small river, and he could see in the distance a third river branch in from the north through a network of out-of-repair docks. He re-settled his bedroll securely around his waist cheerful in the belief that he had reached the southern edge of the Great Mississippi Swamp.

As he approached the docks, he saw a wiry old black fellow helping a white man load baled cotton onto a barge. Walking nearer, Jasper heard the white man laugh. The two were trading insults, and a second white man who was directing the work joined in. The novelty of joking white men made Jasper linger, but he hung back until the white men turned away.

"S'cuse me, mister," he said to the old black man.

One of the white men heard him and asked what he wanted. Jasper swallowed. Aside from Union soldiers and outlaws, he had never talked with a white man.

"I need to know the name of that little river?"

"It's called the Sunflower, son."

"The river?"

"It's a fact, young fella, but I'm from New Jersey, and I run barges up a piece and back down here to the Yazoo River. If you want to know more, ask the old coot there. He'll tell you about his mother if you let him."

Jasper turned to the old man.

"S'cuse—"

"S'cuse your black mammy! S'cuse you for what?"

"Can you tell me where I'm at?"

The two white men walked off and sat down to rest leaving Jasper in conversation with the old man.

"The Yazoo Docks, is where you be. Want to hear how the Union tried to burn 'em before they took Vicksburg?"

"Non."

"Then whatcha want to know?"

"Why you with them outlaw men?"

"Who—them?"

"Yeah."

"They white men, son, but they ain't outlaws jest 'cause they heah in the edge o' the wild. You sound like a swamp boy."

Jasper shrugged, and the old fellow started away. Just then, three barges whistled nearly in unison. The old man grabbed his ears.

"Damn that noise! Traders flockin' in now. Them Confed'rates ain't studyin' no em-bah-go. With Vicksburg took, the North buyin' all the cotton they want, and the farmers makin' money they need. Comes down that Sunflower River into the Yazoo here, then on past Vicksburg to N'awleans. Then they send the boats back up here, and they goes back up the Sunflower to search out more cotton. They does convoys—know what that mean?"

"Non."

"Non? See, I was right. You ain't from no plantation."

"I was raised in the swamp, me'n my momma."

"Where she at?"

"She—why you want to know?"

"Quit bein' persnickety! Answer my question if you please."

"Me'n my momma got took over here by the Union Army. They put us into this place called Davis Bend. She there now."

"Why you ain't with her?"

"'Cause."

"Well, I ain't used to talkin' to myself."

"She with somebody ain't no swamp man, and I'm looking for a place for us, so she can leave him."

"Sound like her business, not yours, young'n . . . Say, I ast you about convoys, does you know what that is?"

Jasper shook his head, no.

"Means the boats go up'n down together. You welcome to sign up, they lookin' for able bodies . . ." He glanced at his white boss and leaned in close so as not to be overheard. ". . . Most of these is Northern boats. They ain't gonna turn you down 'cause you been a slave—or whatevuh. Nawsuh."

"I ain't lookin' for work," Jasper said.

"Well, damn your no-workin' mammy, too. I'm tryin' to show you how to git a ride on that river. Thought you wanted to see the Great Swamp?"

"Yessir."

"Well, you listen to me . . ."

Make money while good white folks were still around was the message, peppered with asides about the Sunflower and the Choctaw people who once lived all along it. The old man had run away from slavery many years before and lived among them until the treaty officially expelled them.

". . . Lived in the swamp, boy—like you, I 'spect. Come out here to make some o' this Northern money." The old man stood up. "You got a place to sleep?"

Jasper smiled but said nothing.

"Sleep there, gawdamm you!" The old man spat on the ground. "I'm takin' my black ass home."

Jasper hadn't eaten all day. He let the old fellow go and moved away from the docks and back downstream into the scrub on the edge of shore. He baited several hooks, secured them to a stump and tossed them into the current. All around was cane, big pithy and dry as well as small bore green shoots, perfect for a raft. After roasting a fish and eating, he withdrew to sleep.

All night he dreamed of what the old man had told him of the Choctaw who had lived all around and called the river sunflower because of the giant blossoms along its bank. It flowed down through more than a hundred miles of swampy bottoms country.

The next morning, Jasper traded a knife for a length of rope to bind dry and pithy giant cane into a square frame. For the surface, he unraveled the rest of his rope and bound fishing-pole-sized cane on top. Then he sought out the old man.

"Appreciate your help," Jasper said. "What else you know?"

"Watch them docks you pass, the next day or so. Many a rough type be hangin' round up there to keep clear of the white man's army. You ain't even got slave value to 'em now, so keep your eyeballs cocked."

"I got what it takes," Jasper said, pulling aside his shirt to show his pistol. "I done killed outlaws before."

"Go on with you, boy, I'd of never . . . But don't let that gun take your scaredness away or you be dead right soon."

The river meandered, never straight for long. Jasper put aside his concern over where he was headed because he was still ashamed of his fear. In fact, his discomfort around white men had led him to reject the old man's suggestion he hire on as a barge poleman to get to where he wanted to go and end up with a handful of money on top of it. Instead, here he was on a tiny raft, unable to take more than one step in any direction without upsetting it.

Away from bluff country, the Great Swamp closed in along the river. Jasper poled diligently and rested only once to eat the remainder of his corn cakes. When the sun dipped below the tree line, he knew that he had less than an hour before darkness. Already it was too dim to pick out every log submerged in the channel, so he quit for the day and nosed into an inlet. He pulled his raft ashore, then walked back to sleep near the main river, to allow him to hear any who might float along following.

He had barely dozed off when the splash of a paddle brought him alert, and he watched a pirogue nose across the inlet in the moonlight. He could make out shadows of men sitting with their paddles raised, ears cocked for noise. A draped lantern in the bow bounced light off a tiny patch of water ahead of them. The boat paused and drifted backward, then moved into Jasper's inlet searching the edge of the water. Sure enough, Jasper's raft drew the men ashore. They moved slowly and carefully until they spied his sleeping blankets.

Two men dashed forward and pounded the blankets with rifle stocks. In the light from their lantern, Jasper watched them recoil as they sensed his trap. The bigger man dropped the lantern and whirled, rifle at his hip. The shorter man raised his hands.

"Come on out, nigger!" the big one said. "Where you gonna hide?"

Jasper fired a single shot into the man's chest. His companion started pleading even before the echo faded. Confident now, Jasper climbed down. He ordered the survivor to sit, and he roped him to a tree.

"Amazin' Grace . . . How still the—Help me! I'm a white man!"

The cries startled Jasper awake near dawn. Angry at what he heard, he cocked his pistol and pretended to take aim.

"Sweet Jesus, please don't kill me!"

"Then hush up."

From a rat skin bag Jasper selected a piece of lead, then cord and a bone fishhook, and he threaded it into a length of rope he uncoiled from around his waist. He stooped down and crawled along, shuffling his hands under the carpet of leaves and muddy debris. A beetle crawled onto his hand, and he seized it. Then he eased his hook beneath the insect's collar to leave it wriggling. He heaved the little critter out onto the surface of the water.

While awaiting a bite, he assembled kindling and drew out his flintstone only to realize that his tinder was damp. Now he had to walk inland and run his hands along the sides of trees for dry moss. Happily, the spark caught almost at once. He was still blowing it into flame when a splash announced his breakfast.

He pulled an eel-like gar ashore and hacked off the long snout with its needle-sharp teeth. Next he ripped a knife lengthwise through the armored hide and groped inside to peel away the thick rope of flesh. When the fire began to roar, he lay his fish on top to cook. He rolled the fish back and forth to sear evenly and then smothered the flame with damp marsh grass.

Only then did he inspect the dead man, nudging the corpse with his foot. No squeamishness like the first time, and he still felt like crowing, until it occurred to him that another killing decision had to be made. Avoiding the white man's eyes, Jasper returned to his fire to think things over.

Turning his prisoner loose to trail behind and take revenge made no sense. He grabbed up a piece of fish, threw it into the weeping man's lap and walked over to loosen his hands. Allowing him to eat postponed doing what had to be done. As fate would have it, pulling at the rope to free the white man broke a blister on the inside of Jasper's hand, and he began curse. Poling the river would be agony, and then—like a fish leaping in a pond—the solution to everything surfaced.

Jasper ate quickly. He tied the pirogue to his raft. The two rifles he hid under canvas in the boat. From a piece of green cane, he stripped tough, sharp fiber and fashioned them into a noose. Then he snatched off the white man's pants.

"Quit wigglin', goddamn you!"

The white man was named Ralph, and he whimpered as he saw what was happening. He screamed when the noose tightened around his male parts.

"Don't do that there—please Jesus, not that! Kill me first. I bleed to death anyhow."

Ignoring the plea, Jasper secured fibers from the frayed end of his rope to the threatening noose and passed the other end of the rope down and through the pants bunched around Ralph's ankles.

"Putcha pants on, white man, if you want to live."

Still weeping, the little man obeyed. Even a gentle tug of the rope pulled a scream out of him. He stood up as ordered, sat just as obediently. Jasper circled his own waist with the free end of the rope, making it look as if Ralph were a slave master with a rope around Jasper's waist.

It all seemed fitting, and poling upriver took them past many curious travelers.

"Beat that lazy nigger!" yelled an old man struggling to keep a raft overloaded with cotton afloat. "You a disgrace to all the South is fightin' for."

"Nigga," a black man yelled, "you be free!"

Full of glee at that, Jasper yanked on his rope, and Ralph came obediently to his feet. When Jasper sat down and Ralph started polling, the passing man's mouth dropped open. Jasper laughed until he cried. With Ralph presented as his master, not once did Jasper have to draw his gun, and after poling all day, Ralph slept as if dead.

Toward noon of the fourth day, hours after intersecting with what looked like a major river flowing in through cavernous banks, Jasper noticed that the cypress trees and burl that grew down into the water like wooden knees had been cut back from shore. Ahead of him, appeared a flat-topped mound marking the edge of farmed and already timbered land on both sides of the river. Over a sturdy platform set with winches was a sign that Ralph translated to be Clark's Landing. On the opposite bank, a broken-down river steamer listed badly against a second dock. A distance back from it stood a majestic home, bigger even than Jefferson Davis' Brierfield mansion on Davis Bend. All was surrounded by piles of newly harvested timber and stumps.

Two local boys began cursing and throwing stones at Jasper. So he barked at Ralph to sit down, then stood up and began poling in the opposite direction back downriver. The current did all of the work, and by dusk they had again reached the intersection of the river flowing in between steep and mounded banks—what would later be called the Hush-puckena River. There, Jasper and Ralph made camp for their fifth night together.

At first light, Jasper located a sturdy log and hog-tied his companion to it. Without a farewell, heedless of cries about drowning, Jasper launched the little man downriver. Let the swamp take him. It was enough of a compromise with outright killing.

He explored for the rest of the day. The land was uniformly rich, in some parts clay, elsewhere sandy, all covered with the debris of untold cycles of flood and renewal. He was ravenous after his river diet of fish but ate few of the wild plums still in season knowing that they could throw an empty stomach into turmoil. Toward evening, he returned to the Sunflower itself and spread his sleeping blankets.

In the morning, Jasper was surprised to see perch and cat-fish lazing in the shallows of a bayou that intersected the Sun-flower. Trapped in the bayou by flooding, the fish had grown ponderous on a rich swamp diet. He eased his hands beneath the green scum of spores and scooped out one that could have filled a dish pan. He ate as much as he could and re-turned the left-overs and the charred remnants of his small fire to the bayou to leave as little sign as possible.

He followed the intersecting bayou along one of the ridges that confined it, away from the Sunflower. All morning, he moved through seeming virgin swamp to a fork in the waters. He chose the southerly course, into a shallow meandering lake. Stripping off only his foot wrappings, he swam leisurely. Since leaving the Sunflower, he had seen no sign of others. Floating in the quiet, gazing up at a friendly sky, he felt safe, euphorically alone.

After a midday nap in a sunny glen, clothes spread to dry, he continued in the direction of the sun, seeking where he figured the Mississippi River should be. As the sun approached the tree line, he reached another river, narrow but set inside steep banks—clearly not the Mississippi. He took a guess that it must have an elbow bend downstream, that it was the same river he had seen flowing into the Sunflower. Thinking that he had confirmed his bearings made him glad. Now, he pressed on with no concern for hiding his trail and, when light ran out, he curled up under a balmy sky.

The next morning, he walked for an hour before eating. The new land seemed such an extravagance that his hunger was satisfied in the knowing that food was all around him. There were clusters of wild fruit trees, young ones sprung from fruit dropped by the old. In every direction, pecans and black walnuts crunched underfoot from the previous fall. And there were signs of wild boar, fowl, squirrel and rabbit for the taking. Then the land turned sandy and he came at last to a ridge from which he could see what he had aimed for. In the distance was the Mississippi River.

Now, he had clear and certain bearing. If he wanted, he could follow the Mississippi a hundred-odd miles back to Davis Bend. On the other hand, a couple three days walk due east would place him back on the Sunflower.

That night he watched the stars. How could living in the outside world be better? He did not like the talking and eating together around a big table he had witnessed down at Davis Bend. Nor the rude people who dressed-up and sat in a room singing a magic that they called church.

"Hey, white folks!" he yelled up at the pin pricks of light in the sky. "This swamp mine! Come in here, I kill you!"

He danced in a circle, clapping his hands to a music in his head, clapping as he had seen the people do in their church meeting on Davis Bend.

Stuff Happens

Davis Bend, Winter 1863

Commander Grey's replacement was a no-nonsense man whose air was as pestilential as his breath. He spent a portion of every day aboard his guardboat that was moored in the Mississippi River near where Davis Bend connected with the mainland. Sometimes, though, like the previous commander, he would steam downriver to the opposite side of the Bend to the big house at Brierfield.

A former non-commissioned officer, he had risen as far as he would go, and he knew it. No pretense to special military skill or to gentlemanly manner. As soon as he took command, he noticed Abyssinia. He winked at her during their first meal together, but, with exaggerated politeness, she leaned forward in her chair and shook her head.

Notes began to appear in Abyssinia's bedroom, one suggesting a river trip to New Orleans as soon as the new commander could arrange leave. Abby offered no reply. Those who'd served Brierfield before the new man's arrival joked that his campaign with Abyssinia was like his fighting record.

No small matter, this disregard in which the new commander was held. Two junior officers from Grey's command made a pact to quit saluting their new boss. Neither of them could expect promotion now that Vicksburg had been taken and they had been left behind guarding a backwater camp for negroes.

Their lording a presumed superiority of class over the new man—who was just as intent on bullying them into saluting him—saw no downside. Neither feared being charged outright with insubordination because, with two witnesses against the new commander, they figured he would not provoke a fight he might not win. Even so, when the gibe about Abby reached the commander, he retaliated. The offending officers were moved to the Wood's plantation, given personal charge of marching the earthen wall security perimeter.

JASPER REAPPEARED on one of the days Rose had relented and agreed to help Cicero. Jasper watched for awhile before walking over and allowing his mother to hug him. Then, he went away. No word to Cicero, nothing to either about his trip.

That evening, he took supper with his mother and Cicero. It wasn't until Cicero began to go over some papers that Jasper told Rose a few of the details about his trek. Within the hour, as if he were simply respecting his mother and Cicero's privacy, he disappeared again.

Over at Brierfield, Abyssinia was undressing at her leisure as she often did near the second-floor window. She happened to look out and noticed a man wearing skins, and she knew it was Jasper.

The very next day, Abyssinia glimpsed the skin-clad young man again. With nothing better to do, she kept her eyes open for Jasper that night when she went for a walk over to the flower garden at Hurricane. A short distance from Brierfield, Jasper appeared at the edge of her view. She waved. He vanished.

The new commander also noticed Jasper and concluded that he was the reason for Abyssinia's nightly walks. More aggravating to the commander was a report from another guard-boat captain that the two banished officers were telling everyone that their commander had lost Abyssinia to a wild nigger from the swamp.

"My dear, I know you go walking with a young man."

"What do you mean?"

"I've watched the two of you. He comes, you go. You go, he follows. I was once a young buck."

"I have no idea who you mean."

"Don't make me the fool! I could be just as grateful as your former commander."

"Grateful?"

"Yes, perhaps some further assistance in your family's move to Cincinnati."

Abyssinia leapt up from the dinner table.

"Sir, Admiral Porter is in charge of that. Perhaps you would care to inquire."

"Just who do you think you are?"

"Why, I am Miss Abyssinia Morgan of Hurricane Plantation."

The commander's chair scraped noisily as he pushed back from the table and marched away.

When Abyssinia entered her bedroom, she walked straight for the window to gaze out at the river. From below materialized a shadow that became an arm and finally, Jasper. He had scaled the outside of the house and was hanging there.

"I come to visit."

Abyssinia reached an oil lamp from a table and hesitated only a moment before she tossed the burning lamp through the window. Just in time, Jasper leapt to the ground and fled.

The blaze of flame brought men running. Up in her room, Abyssinia stood laughing as the men below looked up. The commander knocked on Abby's door.

"Seems you do have admirers."

"Do you think I would allow a man to climb through my window?"

"No, I thought—"

"That I would trifle with a swamp person?"

"I apologize, Miss Abyssinia. Earlier, I spoke unjustly, but in the heat of admiration, I assure you. Might I have the privilege of walking with you tomorrow evening?"

Abyssinia had eaten supper alone and was gazing through the charred window frame that had yet to be repaired. She had resigned herself to Cincinnati with the Montgomerys and was lamenting the fact that her prospects did not exceed the hard work that her mother and Mary Montgomery seemed to think life was given for. She was thinking that if the new commander really were the fool he seemed, she might be able to cajole a helpful favor or two, but he hadn't shown up.

She walked downstairs and stepped outside for her walk over to Hurricane.

"Evening, Miss Abyssinia."

The commander had come by river and walked from the dock. His brilliantined hair glistened in the moonlight.

"Oh, sir. I had thought you changed your mind."

"Such a beautiful gown . . . How did you come by it?"

"What are you asking?"

"It is not the gown of a slave woman."

"Oh, commander, you flatter me."

Abyssinia took a deep breath and the commander's arm. She smiled and led him away from the house.

"I want you to know that it was my job to cultivate most of what you will see just ahead. I had boys to do the labor, but I selected flowers to grow. I decorated the old mansion with them."

"The house that Mr. Farragut burned?"

"Only a ruffian would have destroyed such a mansion."

"David Farragut is a fine officer."

Communication seemed to have broken down, and silence prevailed. When the aroma of gardenias came upon them, Abby raised her nose into the sweetness and sighed. The Commander halted her stroll.

"I am sorry, Miss Abyssinia. Farragut is a true Southern gentleman. He remained loyal to the Union. I do apologize for my abruptness. I would not wish it to lie between us this evening."

"Why commander, whatever do you mean?"

"You have such beauty, woman . . . Need I say more?"

He pulled her arm against his body as the gazebo came into view, but she pulled free and ran ahead.

"This was my absolute favorite place as a child."

"Shall we be at our leisure?"

Jasper was hiding in the edge of some shrubs. He had followed the couple with his eyes. Their initial skirmish had his heart beating fast. He had no weapon beyond a knife, and the commander's pistol seemed huge. Abyssinia's hooped and bustled skirt convinced Jasper that she had dressed up for the white man. He hated whatever it was that could make an old man more desirable than himself.

Moonlight outlined Abyssinia as she moved toward the gazebo. The commander ran ahead of Abyssinia and held the wood-slatted swing motionless while Abby seated herself. When Abyssinia ducked away from the commander's lips, the man stood pensive for a moment before sitting beside Abby and commencing to push the swing back and forth with his feet.

"Never knew a yellow wench."

"Why commander that is a rough way of putting matters."

"Girl, I am so tired of your evasions."

"Well, this conversation is not benefiting your cause."

"You've wasted enough of my time. Now what is it to be?"

"What in heaven's name do you mean?"

As soon as the man's hand touched Abyssinia's bosom, she grabbed his wrist.

"You should be ashamed of yourself!"

Abyssinia tried to rise, but the man grabbed her skirt and yanked her back down.

"There's no doubt you know how to take care of a man."

"No, no! This won't do atall."

Jasper was hiding nearby. So near they should have seen him, he watched Abyssinia stand up only to be dragged back into the swing.

"Let me go!"

"Gal, I can do things for you."

She screamed only once before his hand covered her mouth. The swing bucked and finally tilted, spilling them in a mound of bunched-up petticoats and thrashing legs. When the commander crawled on top, there was a blur of motion and a growl.

Jasper leapt on the man's back and grabbed his neck. The commander's fists flailed the air as the two bodies lurched about atop the planks of the gazebo, then out onto the ground as Jasper's arms locked around the commander's neck. There was an audible snap, and both men seemed to relax.

ROSE WAS MENDING clothes, Cicero reading by candlelight when Abby's sobs preceded her. Cicero saw her staggering toward him out of the night, and he ran to her. Abby collapsed in front of her brother and grabbed him around his knees.

"Ain't hurt her," Jasper said. "She cryin' 'cause the white man tried to force hisself on her, one called commander."

As Cicero lifted Abby to her feet and led her over to where Rose was waiting, Jasper explained what had happened, how he'd heard it being planned.

"Jasper, it's not so simple. Military men don't usually accuse higher-ups of misconduct."

"No, you make 'em listen!"

"I'm trying to decide who might become a witness for us."

"Them two in charge of your guard. I know they didn't like that white man."

"But to accuse their commander would embarrass the service. Just to make the charge would put those two in a quarrel they might not want."

"It ain't my fault."

"No, but you killed the man. I have to deal with that."

From comforting Abyssinia, Rose turned on Cicero.

"What's botherin' you? What could you have done?"

"Look, Abby off doing what she will, Jasper killing the man—they could put either one on trial, accomplice if not perpetrator. If it happens, all of my work would be in peril."

"It ain't all about *you.* Stuff happen." Then to Jasper. "We got to get away from here."

"We maroon again!"

"Are you really going back into the swamp?"

"Ain't got no choice, Cicero."

"There must be a better way. I'm not ready to break up this family."

"Fam'ly—since when you ask me? All your time go to your work . . . That's how you been, and I don't believe in tryin' to change people. So, for my boy's sake—your sister, too, I 'spect—I'm goin' home."

"But where to?"

"This new place Jasper found. You ever ask him about it? No, didn't think so."

Cicero took a deep breath, opened his mouth and closed it. A sob from Abyssinia drew everyone's attention.

"What do I do with Abby?"

"We take her with us. It be her word against these navy men. Do you want to chance they'll admit what was tried?"

Abyssinia pointed to Jasper.

"He, he hit me!"

"Ain't so, Mr. Cicero." Jasper paused from rolling two rifles inside a bearskin. "She was actin' crazy, wouldn't move."

"You did hit me!"

"You two shut up!"

"Would you rather," Rose said to Abby, "we left you to fate, hunh? Don't act a fool all your life."

Abyssinia quieted down, and Rose offered water from a canteen.

"I can't," Cicero said, "just up and vanish. I've got my work, my mother. In her condition, she'd never make it in some swamp."

Jasper poked his finger at Cicero.

"The white man dead! Momma say you cain't stay."

"I can't leave. Mr. Ben has a favorite old saying . . . There are people who depend on me."

"I got to live, too, cherie."

"Jasper, would you run over to the cook house?"

"What for?"

"My mother, Nancy—bring her here."

"Do you think," Rose asked, "we got time for that?"

"No one's going to learn about what happened until day break. I want Momma Nancy here. She ought to hear what happened."

"Maybe," Rose said, "she go along with us?"

"No, I want her to help calm Abby down."

When Jasper arrived at the cookhouse, Mr. Ben refused to hear of Nancy going off into the night. Then Jasper explained what had happened. While the old man walked around talking to himself about what a calamity it was, Nancy took Jasper's arm and walked out.

It took them a half-hour to reach the camp where Abby

launched into a long winded complaint about how unfair the world was.

"I been listenin' to you, baby," Nancy said. "You keep sayin' the same thing."

"Then why I got to go away?"

"Because you don't know what these white men'll do."

"They'll listen to me."

"What if, like when the master tell his overseers he don't want no trouble and a slave be around when some trouble happen. Who you think git blamed—slave man or the overseer?"

"That's the way it could happen," Cicero said.

"I want to go home!"

"Shouldda brought your tail on back from Brierfield," Nancy said. "Had to do things your way. Well, now, look like your way come to the end."

Another round of weeping was Abby's response. Nancy turned to Cicero.

"You right about this, Cicero. Tell the young man—"

"My name, Jasper."

"Jasper, thank you. You can take me back home now. My head hurtin' somethin' fierce. I got to go lay down."

"Momma, don't leave me!"

"I ain't leavin' you, girl. Miz Rose help you along 'till you on your feet and we make contact again."

"But, momma, you goin' to Cincinnati."

"You can join me there when the time right . . . Miz Rose, I'm sorry to say we ain't got to know one 'nother. I'm deeply sorry."

"Your daughter can abide in the swamp just long as she wants to. She can leave when she got somewhere to go."

Abby rushed into her mother's arms.

"Let this woman care for you," Nancy said.

"Momma, how I'm gonna take Miz Nancy all the way back over to the plantation and pack up at the same time?"

"Jasper, one more problem outta your mouth and I will take the nearest stick to you. Just go!"

Two hours later, the four of them were sneaking up on the guardboat dock where several skiffs were moored. The plan was for Cicero to steal one and sail them all up as close to Vicksburg as possible. Jasper and Cicero left the women on shore and waded into the shallows, cut loose a boat and eased it away from the dozing guard.

They put ashore to pick the women up.

"I won't get in the boat!"

"Get in," Rose said, "or, I'll have Jasper tie you up."

"Rose!?"

"Cicero, I'm too tired to put up with more o' this girl."

"Get in the boat, Abby!"

Cicero had to balance the weight. Rose ended up sitting between his legs back near the tiller, Abby and Jasper on either side forward.

A westerly breeze, cool on the face, pulled them into the river and on toward Vicksburg.

"How this thing work?" Jasper asked.

"You never sailed?"

"Ain't likely inside a swamp," Rose said.

"Well, Jasper, the wind pulls on the sail or pushes it."

"Like now," Jasper said, "wind comin' from behind us."

"It's pushing."

"Kin I sail it?"

The question was so incongruous with what the older couple were feeling, they broke out laughing. Rose turned to Cicero, and their faces touched. Abyssinia cried again, and Jasper began to sing around her sobbing, a song about sailing in a river of tears.

"Didn't know he could sing," Cicero whispered to Rose.

"Me neither."

"Must be love."

"It ain't very good singin' either."

Miles later, the night almost spent, they glimpsed lights along the southern edge of the city. After the hours of being motionless aboard the tiny boat, all were stiff stepping ashore. Jasper slung the largest of the packs on his back and was ready to move out at once. Abby flopped down on a patch of dune grass.

"Ain't going into no swamp!"

"She'll be safe with us."

"We find her housework if she want it," Jasper said. "You come along too, Mr. Cicero."

"No," was all he could say as tears welled up to mingle with Rose's.

"I'm sorry," she said, "we got to part like this."

"Abby, if you want to go North, you still can."

"We help her with a little money," Rose said.

"It's so unfair," Abyssinia said, as Jasper pulled her to her feet. "It wasn't my fault!"

Rose grabbed Abyssinia's arm and pulled her around to listen.

"Be glad that we here. You ain't never had it hard, but I throw you to the varmints if you cross me, understand?"

With the same angry energy, Rose threw herself into Cicero's arms.

"I will see you again," Cicero said.

"I know, I know. I'm cryin' 'cause I 'spect it be a while."

"Mr. Cicero?" Jasper was holding out a scrap of paper with four lines on it. "Up where we goin', it's a place got rivers top, bottom and all around—this one is the Sunflower River . . . this the Mississippi. Other two is big bayous up top and bottom of where I'm gonna take momma'n Miz Abyssinia. That 'X' mark a town on the Sunflower. You cain't miss it, but I couldn't read the name."

Cicero was busy wiping at Rose's tears. He reached for her a final time, but she turned and walked away. Jasper grabbed Abby and hurried to catch up.

Who warrants the pedigree of words that serve memory? It is neither his story nor hers, not white nor black, nor time's own, nor memory time's master. Splinters preserved are always subject to the mind that arranges them, and eons of planetary time loom too large to sort. What you know are the human turns around the world. Emancipated from the servitude of being thought about as if now were unique, the human circus wheels back upon itself. This is the wisdom of dirt, that what comes around goes around and around to come again. Beyond the earth's curve, the spin of the moment that leaves you staring into an empty sky you call the future, the past remains underfoot ahead.

The Mississippi
Theater of War

Coahoma County, Mississippi, 1866

Killing Of Negro Sparks Lynch Mob

An angry mob of negroes attempted to hang a former Confederate general accused of killing a laborer. Sheriff Wirt Shaw reports that when his deputy reached Greengrove, General N. B. Forrest was barricaded inside his home.

The following morning, the deputy secreted the general onto a riverboat to Friar's Point. Upon finding the boat teeming with Union soldiers, the general retired to the barbershop. When the soldiers discovered the war hero, the esteem in which he was held led one soldier to buy him a bottle of champagne.

The Coahomian

With the end of the War, there was an exodus from plantations all over the state of Mississippi. The population of freed men and women in Memphis, Tennessee, on the Mississippi border surged from 3,000 to 15,000 by mid 1866.

Unlike Hurricane Plantation in the old part of the state, few of the swamp plantations like James Alcorn's in northern

Mississippi had been confiscated as spoils of war. As their owners sought ways to move back toward cotton production, competition developed for workers. Plantations offered wages to ex-slaves who had not moved on.

For a hundred thirty-odd miles north of Davis Bend all the way up to the hills of Tennessee, the swamp remained much as Jasper found it a few years before. A below-water-level basin into which the Mississippi surged almost every spring, overflowing inland streams like the Sunflower or the Coldwater or Tallahatchie or Yalobusha—names given by the previous inhabitants of the land. To the south lay the Yazoo River into which all the others drained, ultimately to return to the Mississippi at Vicksburg. East beyond all the rivers, the land turned red and mounded into hills that stepped down from Tennessee.

A plume of spring run-off from the Mississippi might spill though Yazoo Pass near James Alcorn's plantation north of Friar's Point—where General Grant had been unsuccessful in dynamiting the River over into the Coldwater—or it might surge into the Hushpuckena or even the Sunflower, both of whose headwaters arose in sandbars and marshes along the big river. Not in Cicero or Rose's lifetime would the Mississippi ever completely change course again.

General:

I am here for the purpos of making application to the Pres for a pardon. I find it necessary to first take the amnesty oath and took the oath to the application . . . and strove to have governors approval.

I have Setled for the present at my plantation in Coahoma Co Miss have gone to hard work have a fine crop of corn if the Seasons hit wil make a fine crop.

Mrs F is making Buter and Rasing chickens so come to
See us and Bring Mrs Lee. if you go to planting the Miss
River is the place to do. So Give my kindeste Regardes
to Mrs Lee and allow me to Remain as Ever

> You friend
> N. B. Forrest

Nathan Bedford Forrest spent his formative youth as a slave
trader. He retired to a thousand-acre plantation in southwest
Coahoma County before the Civil War broke out. By the end
of the war, he had become a cavalry general. Forrest told a
Congressional Inquiry that the rules of war did not apply to
black soldiers. When he captured them, he hanged them.

Not his bankers, though. A debt secured by Forrest's plantation had not been paid during the war, which was why he
was in Memphis and why he had just sold half of his acreage. A
liberal campaign of corn liquor held his demons at bay. His
dark hair was thinning, his shoulders slumped and he was pi-
geon breasted. Though he lacked size, he was a firecracker
when his powder was dry.

Of late, it had remained decidedly wet. Impulsively that afternoon, he had invested some of his land proceeds with a
commodity merchant who bought and sold farm products.
The lure had been how high the price of food had soared in
the time after the war. Now, as Forrest stumbled aboard a
steamboat for the return trip down into Mississippi, he fin-
gered the remaining money in his belt and considered what to
do with it.

A previous short-term loan to plant crops and repair the
sawmill would be paid, followed by a set of new wooden teeth
for King Philip, Forrest's faithful horse. A few weeks back, the
warhorse had charged and tried to bite a group of occupation
troopers. They knocked his teeth out.

Greengrove Plantation was less than a mile in from the
Mississippi River. During flood time, timber could be coaxed

into the flood and on into the big river for floating down to Vicksburg. Other times, the timber and finished lumber products could be shipped by wagon a few miles north to Friars Point.

When the Forrest reached home that evening, to control a breakout of personal demons, he reached for another bottle and retired to his study. His wife—who had been surprised by the timing of his return and eager to hear of the business—withdrew. From experience, she knew that a frontal assault through the general's alcohol was unwise.

She heard it first. Someone outside accused of being lazy. The voice was that of Major Diffenbacher, a partner her Nathan had taken in the face of financial distress. Which was only the first of many reasons Nathan's wife did not like Diffenbacher. Too cozy with the nigger women she had told Nathan. What she said to friends was that the major had no soul. Fight for the Union one month, come begging to be Nathan's business partner the next. Her exact words were, "Grinnin' up at Nathan like a nigger at Christmas 'cause he want some o' what Nathan sold his soul for."

One of those yelling was Thomas Edwards, a man Diffenbacher had accused of beating a mule to death some time back. In the way of small men, little Tom Edwards overcompensated. Greengrove had been one of the early plantations to offer wages to freedmen, and Edwards had negotiated wages for the entire group.

"Lie to me again, and I'll whip you!" Diffenbacher said.

"Git me a stick and whup you back, like I would a mule," Tom Edwards replied.

"Alright, you black bastard—come on!"

A knife used to trim cypress shingles passed from one black hand over to Edwards. Diffenbacher, a huge man possessing some subtlety, halted. He pointed to a black man in the crowd.

"You there, Milam Woods. Fetch me my whip."

"No sir, I ain't doin' that."

It was Milam Woods' face in which the white man shook his fist.

"If I was to tell you to whup Tom Edwards, you better do it! Or you can pick up'n move on."

"Well, ain't leavin'. Ain't whippin' Tom Edwards neither. He represent all of us."

Johnson Steers Middle Course

New President Andrew Johnson has granted amnesty and pardon to all Southerners except those in certain categories, including high Confederate officials and officers of the military. The President has also appointed William L. Sharkey as Mississippi's new governor. Johnson has shown other signs of accommodation, perhaps in order to influence southern votes in the next presidential election.

Johnson, a former slaveholder himself, has promised that he will not add to the war debt to promote the interests of former slaves.

The Coahomian

JOSEPH WOODS had just finished building a new house. It was north of John Clark's farm on the banks of the Sunflower and across from a small white community around a general store. An uncle, sister, and brother had moved with Joseph from the Jones Plantation along Moore's Bayou inland where they had been kept as slaves.

Joseph and his brother, Eugene, were master carpenters. They were moving closer to the new Northern white people they presumed had the money to hire them to build things. Also to help build the new black community that Joseph was convinced would blossom just above John Clark's farm.

One Sunday afternoon, Joseph and Eugene crossed the

Sunflower and drove west to reach the logging trail to Green-grove. When they arrived, Joseph leapt from his wagon.

"Cousin Milam, the doctor of muleology!"

"Hey, Joe! God damn, I'm glad to see you."

As the men hugged, Eugene Woods stepped to the ground and stretched. Milam took his cousin Joe's arm, pulled him away from the nearby workers toward Milam's cabin. Eugene followed leading the wagon.

"The white man here told me to whup a man."

"Are you lyin'?'

"Naw! Old evil Nathan stay drunk 'cause he got money problems, and his new partner act like we still slaves."

"That is a bad situation."

"I got to come stay with you 'till we git our business goin'. Then I kin afford to have you build me a house."

"Wouldn't look right, you movin' now."

"Nigga, what do you mean?"

"We want to haul Greengrove timber."

"Listen to Joe," Eugene said.

"Naw, I got to move."

"Cain't be like that, Milam."

"You tellin' a free colored man he cain't move?"

"Old man Jones," Eugene said, "got mad when Joe and me left the land."

"Don't care. I ain't stayin'."

"No, no," Joseph Woods said. "You gotta invest some of your self in this business. We cain't have Gen'ral Forrest think I'm pullin' you off the land, certainly not just yet."

"I don't care."

"You will, if we don't git a freight contract from that bastard."

A MONTH LATER, Forrest stormed out of his commodity part-ners' Memphis office. No commissions, he'd just been told.

Not yet a full crop season since the end of war. The brokerage had had to invest its funds in Northern war debt bonds.

Once again, Greengrove needed cash, desperately. The only fall-back plan was to sharecrop 1500 acres Forrest had already sold months back. He would have to give up one-half of the crop to the current owner of the land. The other half would go to his commodity partners against which they had just agreed to loan him enough money to run Greengrove for 3 more months.

After making the deal, Forrest had an awful taste in his mouth. For a white man to sharecrop was an embarrassment, especially to crop what had once been his own land. As he reached the street, a pane of glass reflected his face. His eyes had become yellow. His complexion was off, too. As he raised his hand to slick back his hair, he heard crowd noise.

Not half a block away, a white policeman was arresting a black man. Walking closer, Forrest learned that the man had refused to step off the narrow planked sidewalk and allow a white man to pass. A crowd of black soldiers was pouring out of a nearby saloon.

Suddenly, the soldiers and the surrounding white crowd began to push and to shove each other. A wrestling match broke out. The policeman drew his revolver, and two shots were fired in quick succession. The policeman and a soldier fell.

Forrest ran for cover. He drew his own weapon as sniping from nearby drove the soldiers back into the tavern. Some time passed as the crowd took cover, and the street cleared save for a second policeman attending to the wounded man. Then a buggy drove up, and a man declaring himself the sheriff helped drag the wounded man to safety.

The general continued on his way from doorway to doorway. By the time Forest had made it all the way to the end of the block, a sporadic sniping turned into a volley. Forest took shelter, and looked behind him. The soldiers were now retreating from the saloon and falling back doorway to doorway as the general himself had, but in the opposite direction, toward south Memphis and the growing black community there.

Abolitionists demonstrated in Northern cities to protest what newspapers called the Memphis Riot. Senators who had opposed President Johnson's emerging policy of looking away from violence in the former Confederate states now filibustered. The work of Congress came to a halt until a consensus appeared to emerge against a slide back toward the abuses of slavery. With Lincoln dead and Johnson from Tennessee in the White House, the problem was that no one could agree what should be done to help settle the newly freed black people, and there were not enough votes to pass any legislation over a certain veto by Johnson.

NATHAN FORREST went back to Memphis seeking longer term financing, but he failed. On his return, the general was, as usual, hungover and dispeptic.

Milam Woods and his cousins, Gene and Joe, were loading the last of Milam's furniture when the newly arrived general was informed of the move and came storming back to the former slave quarters.

"What are you damn rascals doing?"

"I am taking my leave, sir," Milam Woods said.

The general pulled his pistol.

"Go git Mr. D! You niggers just hold on 'till we sort this out."

Tense moments passed without a word. Then, in the distance a figure appeared running. As it came closer, everyone recognized Tom Edwards.

"You can't make folks a slave," Edwards yelled as he approached. "This man can go where he want to."

"General," Joseph Woods said. "My apologies. I had no idea you had a claim on my cousin."

"I don't give a rat's fart if he is your cousin."

"No sir, you wouldn't, but if he owes you money, I'm here to pay up."

Congested laughter erupted from the old man's chest. His eyes were cloudy, his shirttail out, suspenders draping down over his knees.

"Where the hell is Mr. D.?"

"He wasn't at the sawmill," Tom Edwards said. "That's why I'm here."

In the distance at that moment, an open-shirted Diffenbacher stepped out of the buffer of trees between the main house and the workers' cabins. The general shaded his eyes when he glimpsed Diffenbacher, and he addressed the three black men.

"Is that Mr. D.?"

Tom Edwards turned around and stared motionless as if not comprehending what he was seeing. Then his whole body jerked as an infuriating awareness overwhelmed him.

"Where that fool comin' from?"

"Tom," Milam Woods said. "I 'spect you ought to go on back to the saw mill. I don't need no more help."

"This ain't about you no more."

Edwards bolted toward Diffenbacher a hundred yards away.

"Come back here nigger!"

Forrest fired as he yelled, but he missed. The gunshot made Diffenbacher—who could see what was going on—duck his head. Edwards hesitated only momentarily before shouting toward Diffenbacher.

"You just stand there 'till I git my gun," Tom Edwards said, beginning to circle back in the direction of his cabin.

The general fired and missed again, and Edwards made it to his cabin at approximately the same time Diffenbacher arrived beside General Forrest and the Woods cousins.

"What's the problem, General?"

"These rascals are runnin' off." Then he looked down at his pistol and shook his head. "I cain't hit nary a nigger today."

"Now, General, you let me handle this," Diffenbacher said. "First off, you boys . . . Milam, if you got to move, go 'head. Gimmie your gun General. That crazy Tom nigger comin' after me."

"Why'n hell old Tom after you?"

"He beats on his wife, and I won't allow—"

"Put your clothes on!"

It was Tom Edwards' voice from inside the cabin, followed by a woman's scream.

"Stop brutalizing that woman!" Diffenbacher yelled.

"General," Milam Woods said. "the only reason Mr. D. cain't git along with Tom Edwards is Miz Edwards."

"What you say?"

"Him and Tom fightin' about Miz Edwards."

Original Settler Charged In Killing

Friars Point residents were surprised to see General J.L. Alcorn sitting with a client on the porch of the Friar's Point Hotel. The client was Moore Bayou's Wm. D. Jones. He is accused of killing a colored tenant in a dispute. Alcorn has agreed to represent Mr. Jones in his up and coming trial for murder.

"The past is past," said Alcorn of the rumored spate of killings by high profile citizens. "Violence will not return us to a normal commerce. Bill Jones' peers will understand that he committed no cold-blooded act."

The Coahomian

WIRT SHAW WAS no champion of the white race. He was just Wirt, chewing on a cigar inside his Friar's Point office when the wagon arrived, and he looked up to see two black men.

"What name you boy's go by."

"I'm Joe Woods. This my brother, Gene."

"Ah, Joseph Woods. Notable opinion say you got a level head."

"That Greengrove killing scared my cousin away. A lot of folks is scared. We represent all the skilled workers and a lot of people Tom Edwards used to talk for . . . We just want the law to take its course."

"Law take its course . . . Where you get that from?"

"Mr. Alcorn said it."

"What's wrong—Eugene ain't it?"

"Here come Mr. Alcorn. Gittin' off his horse right now."

The front door scraped open. In the distance behind Alcorn stretched the Mississippi River.

"Greetings, Wirt."

"General, are you representing the individual in question?"

"Why no. Nathan Forrest has committed an act that goes against the logic of our surrender."

"Pardon me if I take a dip o snuff 'cause I'm a simple man. A few months back, Nathan was leading his cavalry. Then git challenged by a boy on his own land."

"What I want to explain," Alcorn said, "to the two men here is that I stand for a law that protects us all."

"That's what we been trying to say," Joe Woods said.

"Ain't for me to decide," the sheriff replied.

"Go talk to the circuit court clerk, members of the board of supervisors. You will find almost unanimous sentiment that Nathan must stand trial."

"Stand trial?"

"Leave that to the court."

"You done talked to the people?"

"Some of us talk all the time. The vote is being prematurely thrust upon the newly emancipated, and that is provoking the real struggle. Mr. Woods?"

"Yes sir?"

"There will be a few episodes like this, but the races must never become warring camps. I have been persuaded to offer my name in candidacy for the coming constitutional convention."

"What convention that, suh?" Joe Woods asked.

"No white man of sound mind favors your people getting the vote, but we accept it. The problem is that you will be voting before your race has gained the experience to keep it free of the depredations of scalawag Northerners who will use your people for their own purposes."

"Tell us how you mean, sir?"

"They will convince you to support them in their cause of holding onto seized Southern land. That will be the beginning. Then they will turn on men of prospect like yourselves."

"You mean us?"

"Joseph, you and your brother underestimate your futures. You are talented, hardworking. You have needed trades. You know how to build connections with people."

The black men nodded in agreement. The sheriff was silent.

"Mr. sheriff, I would not represent Nathan Forrest because I cannot be publicly associated with his defense while I offer my own program of progress."

"You gonna run, then?" the sheriff asked. "You got old John Clark's money behind you?"

"My brother-in-law has always urged me to run."

"That for real, Mr. Alcorn?" Joe Woods asked. "You gonna run for this convention?"

"Yes."

"Well, I—we—been tryin' to git Mr. Clark to hire us. I'm a master builder, and I sure would be grateful you was to put in a word for me'n Eugene."

"Yes sir, we be most grateful."

"If I help you, would you attend the Loyal League meetings? I know you have little interest in politics."

"Whatever you want, sir. We be happy to help you."

"Lack of education while enslaved is the only reason I fear your people getting the right to vote. I cannot re-write history. I can make sure that schooling becomes available."

"Bravo, Mr. Alcorn."

"Schools for black and white youth alike."

The sheriff snatched the cigar from his mouth.

"Ain't that seem a trifle extreme?"

"It may sound that way, sheriff, but it isn't."

"God bless, you Mr. Alcorn," Joe Woods said. "We . . . I never knew you stood for something like this."

Alcorn Tenant Housing Burns

Sheriff Wirt Shaw described as cowardly the ruffians who advanced under cover of darkness and torched a group of farm tenant buildings recently constructed on the Mound Place plantation of J. L. Alcorn. A colored tenant described them as an army of men wearing sheets. Investigation of the crime so far has failed to identify the perpetrators.

A spokesman for Alcorn said that Mr. Alcorn was most concerned that someone might have been injured. Temporary housing is being provided the local colored.

The Coahomian

Mississippi Grass Roots

Davis Bend, Fall of 1867

All of the Montgomerys did move to Cincinnati, but they turned right around and returned to Davis Bend the following year. Mr. Ben didn't like to talk about it, but Isaiah explained to Cicero that they found themselves just another anonymous group of negroes without prospect. Demagogues had stirred up Ohio white people with dire warnings about black refugees seizing all the good jobs. The Montgomerys sold out and departed Ohio on the eve of a referendum to prohibit freedmen from voting.

Down in the Mississippi Theater of War, General Ord was commander. Appointed before Lincoln's assassination, he had already dismantled a short-lived militia that Southern whites attempted to form. Unfortunately, state law enforcement holding over from Confederate days was just as hostile to people of color, and it did nothing to protect black people from violence.

In Warren County—from Vicksburg south and including Davis Bend—local landowners understood that General Ord couldn't see everything. Freedmen leaving their land were harassed and arrested, charged with vagrancy, and ordered to serve out their detention working for certain well-connected landowners. Former slaves who escaped took the riverboat up into the swamp counties like Coahoma where cash wages were the magnet.

Cicero had received a letter from Abyssinia. She was working as housekeeper for some landowner on the Sunflower River, and she had given directions to have her clothes freighted to a place called Friar's Point.

Cicero's mother had returned with the Montgomerys. She was now cooking for Cicero and several of his helpers. The huge marble library building was home for them all. There were others from the days of Mr. Ben's management of the plantations for the military who had returned to help work the farms, both Brierfield and Hurricane. Then, Mr. Ben was appointed Justice of the Peace by General Ord, and he and his family put in a bid to the Army's Freedman's Department and were awarded a lease of the plantations to run as a private venture.

Mr. Cicero's Book was now too valuable to be handled by the public. Paid assistants looked up information for people. Cicero kept current records on behalf of the Freedman's Bureau, a department of the Treasury that was in process of taking over management of freedmen's affairs from the military.

Isaiah couldn't contain his excitement about the success of the Montgomery business.

"Back in '65, took about 200 people to farm these plantations. Admiral Porter showed us papers say they pretty much broke even, and they was payin' wages near $25 dollars a month."

"Mr. Ben got paid that for you and your brothers," Cicero said.

"Well, since the Freedman's Bureau took over from the Army, ain't nobody down here below Vicksburg payin' over

$10 a month. They ain't got near the kinda workers we got, and daddy say we gonna make $10,000 profit this year. That's after food, seed, fertilizer, housing—everything! . . .' Course we gotta split it up amongst the group."

Cicero's mother didn't like the new arrangements. Working for someone else was one thing. Working for herself kept her nerves on edge even though she had no hand in the big decisions. She had the caution of a woman who'd spent her life as a humble servant. The cookhouse was the only world in which she felt comfortable. She was as disinterested in the Montgomerys' talk of getting rich as she was frightened by her own son's ambitions.

"Watch your face," Nancy said when Cicero complained about people in Washington. "White folks on Davis Bend look at you close when you ain't even notice. I see 'em."

Rebel States Readmittance Delayed

Late last evening, a majority of the Senate joined the Radical-led majority in the House of Representatives to force President Johnson to hold off readmitting former Rebel states."

Radicals in the House refused to release appropriations for the War Department until Johnson's policy was clarified. Precipitating the stand-off was the call for a Mississippi convention in which no former slaves were allowed to elect delegates.

The compromise requires forces upon rebel soil to recognize only new governments organized in convention in which former slaves are accorded the vote. No details could be agreed upon. Executive and Legislative powers agreed to monitor details worked out by army commanders in the field.

Evening Star,
(Washington, D.C.)

IN THE FALL OF '67, when Nancy might have been coming into her own for the first time in her life, she had a full-blown stroke. Mr. Ben sent Isaiah to fetch Cicero to the cookhouse.

"Momma?"

The muscles in her face moved, but she couldn't speak.

"Just leave her rest," Mary Montgomery said. "You know she worried 'bout the way you argue with the new white folks."

"Is that all?"

"She been listening to you talk about what you gonna make people do when you git into politics. She don't know how you got that in your head, and she scared for you."

"Don't you worry. With a little luck, we'll show those fools in Washington how bad things really are."

General Ord issued orders for a constitutional convention to be held and required that there be two lists of voter registrar candidates: one white, one black. At least one freedman in each county would be selected by the general's office to over-see the election of convention delegates.

The current naval commander at the Bend had personally interrogated Cicero about Jasper and Abyssinia. He cut the whole investigation short in order to concentrate on becoming acquainted with the area. After the war, he bought a parcel of land downriver. As commander of the Bend, his duties were now minimal. His time was spent overseeing the building of a new house, to which he invited Cicero to meet several associates.

"You are a most remarkable young freedman. You deserve to be the first colored man elected from this area."

"Yes . . . I've been listening to you ever since we met."

"You have?"

"Yes sir. You always seemed to talk about big issues, so I listened."

"Ah, yes."

"I understand the administration of the plantation system, managing displaced people, crop husbandry, even what's going on in Washington."

"Cicero, that is not everything."

"Of course not. There is a public man's responsibility to serve the public good."

In walked two men, one stocky with a genial farmer look about him, the other lean and stooped in the shoulders but well tailored with immaculate fingernails that reminded Cicero of his old master.

"Please greet ex-sergeant Francis O'Grady and Mr. Elsworth Doolittle. Gentlemen—Cicero Morgan."

Cicero rose from his chair and held out his hand. O'Grady seized it, Doolittle bowed.

"This is the young man who kept *Mr. Cicero's Book*," the commander said. "He is known by every voter of sable hue in this district . . . You know, I keep forgetting the damned county name."

"Warren," Doolittle said, "estimated three-fourths slave—freedman, that is—one-fourth white. This Cicero may have some reputation, but how will the voters see him?"

"I can be elected."

"The interests that I represent," Doolittle said, "will neither purchase nor loan money against local holdings until the political situation is stable." He turned to the commander. "What convinces you of his appeal?"

"Personal experience. I have been stationed around the locals since—"

"The man," O'Grady said, "wants to know who's payin' who to vote." He turned to his companion. "Worked a New York ward myself, Dooly."

"It's *Mister* Doolittle, thank you. Your little 160 acres are nothing compared to thousands of acres of railroad land. And now that our simple-minded regional general has decreed that at least one registrar of the three in every county be a freedman, politics down here is worse than Irish ward shenanigans."

"I'll not stand for bein' put down," O'Grady said.

"What are your interests?" Cicero asked.

"You have some sense of politics," the commander said. "You answer the question—whose side are you on?"

"You may not wish to think this way but we're all in the same boat, white and black. I hold to the view that politics is ruled by the common good, to help the needful people of the moment."

"Come on, boy," Doolittle said, "I've no time for darky wisdom."

"Have you ever read Marcus Tullius Cicero?"

"Don't be impertinent. Have you?"

"Yes."

"The man's got a tongue on him," O'Grady said. "No ruffian, this one. You're a credit to your race, lad."

"A fine speech for a fish fry," Doolittle said, "but do you understand our economy?"

"What do you mean?" Cicero said.

"The economy, man—land, roads, levees, money changing hands smoothly—all that."

"My family ran Hurricane Plantation for many years."

"Is that correct?"

"Yes, it is!"

Doolittle bowed in conciliation.

"No offense intended. I have certain personal investments like O'Grady here . . . I could offer a farm management job."

"Saints alive!" O'Grady said. "Leave the poor man where his heart and soul are, Doolittle. 'Tis politics we're about."

"He's right," the commander said. "Mr. Morgan is a rare specimen. I'm sure you agree that compared to others of his people, a man like him could well represent his *and* our interests."

"Why don't you," Cicero said, "describe your interests."

O'Grady held his hand up to silence Doolittle who seemed disposed to reply.

"We're here to carry on the work of abolition, lad. Don't you have a doubt about it. Never again will your lovely people have to answer to them bastards who was your masters. Nor the damned shanty Democrats, either. Good Republicans all, is how you have to vote. That's why we're here, to build a grand old party, room for all and all for one."

That November, a black churchman named T.W. Stringer and Cicero Morgan were elected delegates to the first authorized post-war convention in Mississippi. Even the usually reserved Mr. Ben celebrated. Old George played his harmonica off and on all that day. George had a daughter born a few years prior to his May-December marriage. Her name was Suzy. Years before, she would bring Cicero food while he worked. She had—as Isaiah had whispered more than once—a willowy frame fleshing out spectacularly.

The party wound down. Cicero asked why she was so happy.

"You the Honorable Mr. Cicero. We waitin' for you to help our people."

In January, Cicero boarded a train in Vicksburg bound for Jackson and his swearing-in. He marveled at the sound, the steam, the feel of power riding in a machine, and he hogged a window as the countryside passed. He wore new gray boots and a matching suit of broadcloth over a hard-starched white shirt. His high-top hat sat on the seat across from him. He watched it jiggle close to falling off.

Close to the capital, the train slowed for Clinton, which was the first settlement of any size on the line. Ten passengers came aboard, including a burly black man in tight-fitting trousers who startled when he saw Cicero, then smiled broadly. Cicero stood to greet the newcomer.

"Nice of the white folks," the man said, "to leave us these good seats."

Cicero's hat fell off. The man grabbed it before it rolled into a nasty gob of tobacco beside the spittoon.

"And the most excellent of company, too," Cicero said.

The man flipped up the tail of his coat and sat down.

"My name is—"

"Niggers out of place!" The speaker was a white passenger across the isle, a dandy wearing a blue swallow-tailed coat and matching silk hat.

"Gracious me," Cicero's companion said, staring across at the white man before turning back to Cicero. "You bound for Jackson?"

"Yes, sir. To build a government."

"You be a delegate?"

"I am."

"Me too. Name's Caldwell, Charlie Caldwell."

"I am Cicero Morgan. Pleased to meet you, Mr. Caldwell."

"Likewise. Folks call me the Blacksmith."

Leaning across the space between, the two men erupted in a parody of the handshaking and back-slapping.

"Was a time when a buck knew his place," said the dandyish white man across the isle.

Caldwell planted his foot on the armrest beside Cicero and rolled up his pants leg. Strapped to his ankle was a pistol.

"My second time on a train, Mr. Morgan. What about you?"

"My first."

"Shake a nigga up, don't it?"

Caldwell then offered Cicero a drink. As Cicero accepted, the man across the aisle moved three rows away.

That night, in Cicero's room on Yazoo Street near the Capital, he had just finished toasting Mr. Caldwell.

"Why politics, Charles?"

"Call me Blacksmith, dammit!"

"We don't know much," Cicero said, "at least I don't. Our people don't even know as much as us. There's the old masters, the poor whites, a growing number of Northern whites— some as poor off as us. There's this one-legged ex-sergeant back on Davis Bend. He drinks all day. You should hear the stories he tells about poor white folks in the North. The sheriff is always kicking him around."

Blacksmith sighed, then rolled his head around as if to ease a kink in his big neck.

"I know you ain't askin' if I'm scared, so . . . hmmm, ain't easy to tell. Things got to be done, and I'm a ornery old blacksmith ain't backin' down from nobody that can die like me."

"Some poor white people suffered like us."

"Oh, is that so?"

"Yes. A Mr. O'Grady swears his father worked like a slave in a coal mine. Came over on a boat, too."

"Shit! White folks come over, but most come by choice or what pass for that. Old Dutch man owned me—ever meet any of them Dutch rascals?"

Cicero shook his head, no.

"Well, he had this little beady-eyed wife used to talk like you. Claimed they'd been whupped around worse'n clabber in milk. Next breath she'd be sayin' how blessed they was to be in this fine country and to own me'n my brother. What's I supposed say? . . . I just grin."

"I feel so uneducated sometimes. It's like there must be answers I don't have. Like what you said about your owners—I never thought of that . . . There's this colored man named Ira Aldridge. He's a big success on stage in London, England."

"Damn, Cicero, I ain't even sure what being on stage mean."

"That's what I mean. So many things we don't know about."

"So what about this Ira fella?"

"I read about Mr. Aldridge in a magazine. White people in London pay to see him perform . . . You got any more liquor?"

"Naw, and I can tell you had enough. Get a good night's sleep."

AN OVER-LONG breakfast was interrupted by one guest after another begging to shake Cicero and Blacksmith's hands. They had to pull themselves away from their landlady's family and head for the capital. Horses had been provided by Republican Party functionaries.

They rode past clusters of freed men and women cheering and clusters of white ones pointedly ignoring them. A lifetime of dreams came to mind as Cicero entered the capitol grounds, trees waving bare in the winter like a sad shadowy multitude lining the path.

At the gray stone rotunda of the statehouse, Union soldiers took their horses, bowed. T. W. Stringer stood in the lobby.

"Greetings, Mr. Morgan. I've invited our colored delegates to caucus."

"This is Charles Caldwell," Cicero said. "From Clinton."

"I've heard of you, sir," Stringer said. "Your reputation for organizing our people in their own defense has preceded you."

"Ain't so much, Mr. Stringer. Same as any man would do. You all go ahead."

"You have private business already?" Stringer asked.

"I'll be along soon as I go count and see how many rednecks versus niggas we got."

"Excellent idea, Mr. Caldwell."

Stringer led Cicero toward a side room. Inside, seated around a table were nine black men, four of whom rose.

"Hello, gentlemen," Cicero said.

"The white delegates claim it ain't right for us to be here."

"If we keep separate," another said, "others do the same. That's dangerous for us colored."

"Don't white folks meet," Stringer said, "hold their caucuses?"

"All politicians have meetings," Cicero said. "Our color and our history sets us apart."

"Bein' a slave ain't nothing' to be proud of."

"Fighting will get us nowhere." Stringer said. "And for those of you who haven't heard, General Ord—our military governor—has been reassigned to San Francisco. I'm told he has already been shipped out."

An ominous silence followed.

"What does that mean?" Cicero asked.

"Southerners have been wanting what they call a more even-tempered army boss, one who won't appoint black men as registrars next time. A general named Gillem, from Tennessee like our President—you all heard me right—has taken Ord's place."

"There's shit in high and low places," came a voice from the door—Blacksmith's. "Man name Alcorn—"

"Did you say Alcorn?"

"Sure is, Cicero. You know him?"

"Not on a personal basis."

Everyone chuckled at the obvious.

"He was a guest of my master. Seemed to hold progressive views for a slaveholder."

"Well, he the boss out there. They sayin' that it was the niggas up in his county that elected him."

Not quite a hundred delegates assembled. Cicero walked the rows of lecterns lining the hall and found himself captured by this white delegate or the next in discussions of progress. Toward noon, Cicero went looking for Stringer only to run into Blacksmith.

"I counts seventeen of us folk," he said.

"Is that all?"

"Twenty-nine is old mastas turned Republican. The rest split between local Democrats and Northern Republicans."

"That makes . . . about forty-three of us and Northerners combined—no majority."

Boots resounded on the marble floor as a military entourage marched in. A gavel struck for quiet. A voice boomed out.

"Honorable gentlemen! The General Officer of the Mississippi Theater of War—our brand new commander—General Alvin C. Gillem."

"Stand easy, gentlemen," said a short, gruff man, declining the lectern. "I bring you all greetings and godspeed. My Commander-in-chief, the President, wishes you to begin your deliberations with a single virtue in mind—prudence."

There was weak applause. Into it a voice yelled, "He won't be President long," followed by murmuring and side conversations punctured by a single cry to impeach the president. Gillem walked away, boots quick-stepping across the stone floor and out of the hall. Before the echo had died, another voice filled the hall.

"My name is Eggleston, General Eggleston. I am an elected delegate originally from New York state. I have been pressed by a goodly number of you—on the north and south of the isle—to offer my name in humble consideration for president of the convention."

Electing a president took hours. Other names had to be submitted, seconded. Position speeches had to be made. Members of the convention spoke in support of various candidates. It was well after the noon meal that Eggleston spoke in favor of his own candidacy.

"I am proud to be a Republican, a guardian of Union and of human rights. But I am no Radical, not one who would tear down our ways of doing things and plunge us into chaos."

There was light applause. Blacksmith caught Cicero's eye and grimaced.

"Nor should we or any other fair-minded Americans, add our emotion to the boiling pot. There is heat enough between our President Johnson and our Congress. You and I should not ask, who is right, who wrong. Impeachment is no issue at this convention. The issues are tradition and respect for property, principles many Republicans find too much in disregard as our national government assumes unprecedented powers in binding up the wounds of war and, incidentally, trying to resolve the negro question.

"But let no colored delegate think that his race is at issue. You will not be returned to Africa, nor be shipped off to Mexico. Trust us, us fair-minded, enterprising men of business and agriculture dedicated to your uplift."

By the end of the day, Eggleston was convention president. Four standing committees had been formed. Stringer and Cicero were members of the Appropriations Committee.

The following morning, a group of them were standing in the rear while someone was speaking from the podium.

"Well, if it isn't our star delegate."

"Good morning, Mr. White," Cicero said. "A pleasure to speak with you again."

"Can you gentlemen imagine what talent this young man possesses—a former slave who learned to write and to read the classics? I am forced again to apologize for the evil of slavery."

"You gentlemen," Cicero said, "should probably introduce yourselves."

Cicero's new admirer spoke first.

"The Honorable Gambrel Allington White, here."

"I am T. W. Stringer."

"Some of you know me," said a man who had joined the group unseen. "I am James Lusk Alcorn of Coahoma County."

"You!?" Cicero said, belatedly taking the hand offered. "I have never shaken the hand of a slaveowner before."

"Even before the war had ended," Alcorn said, "I counseled moderation."

"Cicero Morgan, from Warren County."

"Felicitations, Mr. Morgan."

"Actually," Cicero said, "we have met before."

"Oh."

"I helped serve a supper at Hurricane Plantation before I became free."

Alcorn hesitated, pursed his lips.

"But, Mr. Morgan, I assume we would not be holding this charming conversation if I had done you wrong and you had a pistol in your pocket."

All of the tension that had been building with the arrival of a former slave owner exploded in laughter.

"You are correct. In fact, I found you remarkably forward thinking even though I was deemed capable only to light your fireplace and hear you tell the story of empire."

"Yes! By god, I do recall. You have an extraordinary sister whose name is Abyssinia."

"Yes."

"Dear Abyssinia."

"She is employed somewhere near your home."

Alcorn placed his hand on Cicero's shoulder.

"Mr. Morgan, I bring you good tidings. Your sister is employed by my brother-in-law."

"Are you certain?"

"Very much. She is well. We must not tarry in this personal exchange."

When they turned to the group, a pensive Stringer was stroking his mustache. The other men were chatting amiably but without purpose. Every eye had been on Alcorn and Morgan.

"Mr. Alcorn?" Cicero asked. "I hear that you were elected by black voters."

"That is true. Before the war, I urged the emancipation of your people within twenty years. I am no redneck."

Alcorn made a face and then laughed at himself. He had a hearty laugh and a manner that made the men around him comfortable. Another round of handshaking and backslapping left a smile on Cicero's face.

"My position on public schools," Alcorn continued, "delivered a lot of freedman votes up in Coahoma County. It also led local thugs to torch my tenement houses."

Alcorn threw his arms around Stringer and Cicero.

"The Appropriations Committee has business to conduct. I think of only one person who is not present, and I have his proxy."

"So we meet right here, then?"

"Yes, Mr. Morgan . . . As for the matter of salaries, I should propose twenty dollars a day."

"Second."

"Thank you, Mr. Morgan."

The vote was unanimous.

"Now, Mr. Morgan," Alcorn said, "would you undertake an errand to the governor?"

"Why . . . yes."

"Good. Just follow me."

"Right now?"

"Protocol. We make a courtesy call on Governor Humphries and leave details of money for stationery and such to our clerks."

It was a bright and sunny morning as Cicero followed Alcorn outside, a perfect day for Cicero's first foray into the statehouse controlled by Confederates. While waiting for the governor, they sat in his anteroom. Cicero was about to inquire further of Abyssinia, when Alcorn spoke.

"We might give up this errand right now, for I do not believe the good governor will entertain us."

"What?"

"I want you to hear me out before you leave. What I would request is that you try to grasp the delicate task before us. We have to frame a government that black and white can agree on, but it must have as little to do with free food and land as possible."

"Those are the greatest needs of my people—and some of yours as well. I've seen ex-overseers begging handouts."

"We must bind up our economy, Mr. Morgan. It is in the flow of money and commerce that the bread of the poor is baked. Work, not give-aways, lead to productivity. I hope that you will accept the role of a moderating presence among your race at this convention . . . Did you know I moved into The Great Mississippi Swamp—what we are now calling The Bottoms—on a flat-bottomed boat? We weren't penniless, my sister and me, but I suppose you might have called us opportunely impoverished."

"I think I know what you mean."

"My sister married John Clark, one of the first white men to settle inland in my county—your sister's employer, by the way."

"Can it be? Abby is your sister's maid?"

"Housekeeper, I believe."

"Well I'll be damned."

"Ah, Mr. Morgan, it is not for us politicians to ponder the mysteries of damnation or salvation. I became a lawyer but soon saw that my fortune was in the land. I took land as fees, bought what I could. I organized a levee district to protect our wild new land—all near a town called Friar's Point."

"Ah, you did use public money."

"Public improvements. The price of land began to climb for everyone. Aside from marrying quite a wealthy woman some time after the death of my first wife, I built a modest but respectable fortune. And then came the blasted War. It killed opportunity . . . Let me share something . . . During the war whenever I could, I sneaked home and paid men willing to take risks to ferry me and cotton from my land over to Arkansas where I would hide the cotton. Selling it was illegal, so I had to sneak into Helena looking for someone willing to buy."

"Had people like me not raised that cotton without pay, I would be weeping on your shoulder."

Alcorn chuckled.

"Well put, Mr. Morgan. My point is that the economic growth I and others enjoyed back then cannot be resurrected if you and I turn all our energy to hominy and cornbread."

"Your opportunity came from enslaving others."

"No, the opportunity was in the land. Paying wages or livelihood for slaves—all the same. It was in that miraculous land the Indians did nothing with."

"You took it from them, made us work it for free. Now, what?"

"So many hysterical words, Mr. Morgan—forget the past which neither you nor I can do anything about. Your historic challenge right now is to help us dispel the silly expectations the Northern Army left behind."

"We people have been slaves of your economy. The same amount of cotton will grow no matter who grows it—thousands of ex-slaves on their own land, or a handful of old masters."

"Would you throw over the institution of property? It was not government that built this great state, it was men like me."

"And like me. I toiled in cotton fields for 10 years."

"You were a field hand?"

"The only hands we need discuss are yours and mine. We have *power* in them. The only issue is what to do. How do we use it? We don't have to be pigs protecting our troughs."

Alcorn laughed again, briefly, as if disavowing mockery.

"Ah, that is the Governor's secretary coming out, probably to tell us to leave. I want to speak with Humphries about a private matter, and he would not condone a person of your race in his private office. Would you excuse me?"

By the time Cicero arrived back on the convention floor, the holdover governor had sent word that no state money to support the Convention would be provided. The news had the place in an uproar. A motion to vacate state offices had been made. Cicero talked himself hoarse for the first time in his life. The motion was defeated.

Alcorn, who had opposed the motion, now stood up to the applause of well-dressed men seated around him.

"Mr. President!"

"Recognize the honorable gentleman from Coahoma County."

"What has been attempted here is fruitless. You yourself promised prudence and moderation. There is no cause for disrespect to our state. There can be no radical remedies."

"Sit down!" Blacksmith yelled.

A mixture of cheers and boos greeted this outburst. Alcorn held the floor, but before he could speak again a man from among the group known to be Democrats jumped up.

"Mr. President! You allow votin' like this here again and you'll answer to me, you carpetbag swine!"

"Order! Order!"

Eggleston banged his gavel, but a fight broke out between a black delegate who'd sat up with the white folks and the Democrat on the floor. After the peace was restored, the convention adjourned for supper.

Stringer collared most of the freedmen and pulled together a second caucus, but they could find no common ground. Several remained convinced that a black caucus was unwise. Back on the convention floor in emergency session that night, the only motion to enthusiastically carry was to go seek financial support from General Gillem.

A FEW DAYS LATER, as the designated black delegate, Cicero found himself in Gillem's office.

"I am from Tennessee like the President," Gillem said, unable to keep from laughing, "but that does not mean I hate radicals, niggers or scalawags."

"I most strenuously object," General Eggleston said, "to your use of those scurrilous terms."

"Which term, General?"

Eggleston turned red.

"Don't bait me, Gillem. Business aside, I will have your ass if you trifle with me."

"Hell, Eggy, I am not triflin' with you. I just want you all to understand who is the boss. I like my President, and he likes me. You come in here with your hats in your hands like children. So, I want you to understand who the poppa is."

"That is more than enough!" Eggleston thundered. "If this were a personal matter, I'd call you out, sir."

"But it isn't personal. Now, let's get down to business."

"What we desire," Eggleston said, only to have Gillem raise his hand.

"Didn't you hear me? I don't give a damn what you desire. Talk to me about what you think you can get. You tell me why *I* should want to do something for you."

"To begin with, you have to enforce the will of the Congress."

"What's that?"

"That a convention be held. That it write a new constitution. To do that we can't have the state people refuse us money. You have to order them out of office. Or give us Federal money and leave it to the courts—your choice."

"Well, look. I won't dismiss state officials, but I am willing to give you some money. You come to me with your hands out, so you have to do things my way."

"And what would that be?"

"Well now, Eggy, let's get down to horse trading. I got some ideas. You got some, too."

A sense of impotence pervaded the convention after the committee reported back. First the stalemate with Governor Humphries. Then Gillem's back of the hand. Cicero—who had found himself restive during negotiation with Gillem because he'd been warned to keep his mouth shut—discovered that his Appropriations Committee had nothing further to do. All of the action was in the Drafting Committee. Alcorn was on it, also Eggleston. But not Cicero Morgan, nor any other freedman.

In the weeks that followed, drafts of language were circulated for comment. The stated purpose was to build a consensus by distributing language addressing critical issues as discussion progressed. No full convention vote on anything was planned until the drafting committee finished a draft of the whole constitution.

"We cannot," Cicero said during a speech urging adoption of a Bill of Rights prohibiting arrest for failure to pay a debt, "continue to ignore the real problems of the people. Brutality at the hands of unreconstructed whites holding debts, torture of so-called vagrants in jail by hold-over sheriffs—this is the face of the new slavery. My people languish, shackled to old plantations, afraid to move."

"Point of order!" It was one of Alcorn's cronies. "We have an agenda. We do not have the time for digression. I ask that the delegate from Warren County be ruled out of order."

"Sorry, Mr. Morgan," Eggleston said. "This matter is just not on the agenda, only the report of the Drafting Committee. Your recommendations should have been addressed to them."

Weeks became months. Dissension was managed, though as the delegates became more familiar they sometimes behaved like a pack of adolescence boys. Argument would be throttled, then allowed about the most curious matters. The Drafting Committee allowed a Democrat to propose constitutionally prohibiting black men from cohabiting with white women. Blacksmith proposed an amendment to prohibit white men cohabiting with black women. The other side offered amendments to safeguard men in "longstanding" relationships. Blacksmith sprang to his feet.

"Nigga dicks git just as hard as white ones."

About the only thing delegates of color accomplished by the end of March was to convince the carpetbag delegates to join in passing a resolution requiring the return to former slaves of property taken from them by masters during the last years of slavery. No one considered this proposal very radical, and some of the Northern whites applauded black delegates for standing up for property rights.

Within hours, though, General Gillem sent word that he would authorize no further money because the property-return resolution had exceeded the convention's mandate. A hastily arranged negotiation freed up the money. As part of the delegation calling on the General, Cicero had to acknowledge a great political lesson: power may corrupt, but money controls.

Cicero walked to his room to hibernate for a few days, only to find his landlady waiting in her front yard.

"Lord, lord, son. There's been a shootin', and white folks got Mr. Caldwell dead to rights."

"What happened?"

"Him and some others—white mens, they was—went walkin' downtown, and some other young white mens commenced to meddle. They got to shovin' and pushin', and I hear this one young man pulled a pistol. Mr. Caldwell had to kill him."

⍟

CICERO LOCATED Blacksmith sitting on a lectern in the legislative hall.

"Glad you're safe."

"Don't be a pure fool. These folks are hiding me."

"Not hiding—sanctuary," Gambrel Allington White said. "A goodly majority has agreed that the shooting was in self-defense. We have witnesses among us here. Of course it's another story if you ask these townspeople, all kinds of rumors are circulating."

"What are we to do now?" James Alcorn asked. "Some of us are fair, but there are positions we cannot take."

"No sense," White said, "embarrassing local folks like yourself, James. As a body, we'll demand that the military governor take the action."

"He'll keep local police away," said a delegate known to be a lawyer. "This is a body constituted under Federal law. State police have no authority, just like they can't arrest a member of the Congress. So everyone agrees Mr. Caldwell belongs in our custody. Or in General Gillem's."

"Why," Cicero asked, "should Gillem arrest him?"

"State judges have no business meddling in," the lawyer said. "No member of a convention decreed by the Congress of these United States should be accused under state law . . . But there are political considerations. Mr. Alcorn has persuaded a number of his Southern colleagues to go along with our plan if we generally respect this state's legal process and do not block prosecution altogether."

Prosecution testimony about the shooting took all morning of the first day of trial. The prosecutor called witnesses whose testimony the judge allowed despite objections that not all of them could have seen the act in question. Blacksmith's lawyer, a Mr. Stubblefield, was a cigar-chomping local white chosen because he was in business with one of the Northern delegates.

"I go by instinct," Stubblefield said. "Don't get his honor's dander up. He already got enough heat on him over this nigger."

Defense testimony then proceeded, and when the last of Blacksmith's witnesses left the stand, trial was adjourned. Several hundred people were being restrained by soldiers behind a barricade across the street. The delegates exited together under a barrage of rocks and horseshit.

The following morning, the judge never showed up. Hundreds of screaming protesters ringed the courthouse. All morning, the accused and a few of his fellow convention members waited. Blue-coated men marched around the building with rifles at the ready. An army messenger galloped up before noon and ran a dispatch pouch in to the prosecutor. It announced that the judge had taken ill. His ruling was, not guilty.

Cicero danced outside and got hit on the head. He was barely conscious when Gambrel Allington White pulled him out of the mob.

"Things will change," White said, running alongside. "We'll put these Confederates down yet."

"Just get me out of this mob."

"You must have been hit pretty hard."

"Where are we?"

"Inside my carriage. Here. . ."

"What's this?"

"A telegram. Your mother is gravely ill."

CICERO SPENT THE evening of his arrival at his mother's side. No pain, no labored breathing, she sat with her mouth open, propped with cushions into the corner she had lived in since the first stroke. Her ailing eyes had been just one symptom of the high blood pressure that brought on the strokes. On toward morning, what had been soft snoring abruptly ceased. Isaiah, who had sat up with Cicero most of the night, touched his shoulder and led him away from the corner. The first burning tears fell as Mr. Ben entered the cookhouse.

"Nary a deed left to be done. Come on outta there, Cicero. Me'n these others got to make her ready."

"Mr. Ben—"

"Hush! . . . Be a man."

"I appreciate everything."

"We family, son, ever since your pa left this world. Don't you grieve no more now. She in the bosom of Abraham."

Cicero started for the door, then turned back. He wanted desperately to put arms around his mother a last time, to cry or to scream, to do something—anything—to mark her passing. Ice water, he thought, remembering how he'd lived, but the thought was not very satisfying. Even worse, he felt embarrassed showing how he really felt. Old George was already at the top of the stairs carrying the cooling boards so he and the women could lay-out Momma Nancy for all to come pay their respects. It was then, suddenly knowing that all his life his feelings had been on a cooling board, that Cicero lost control.

The household had gathered below the stairs. Cicero waded into a sea of tears. Old George's wife and daughter were the first to drape arms around him. He could think of nothing to say as hands pressed upon him from every direction. He was a little boy again, and again comforted by arms powerless to heal his hurting. Mary Montgomery started humming, and others took it up. When the humming softened and comforting hands left him, the light of day and sounds of life brought him outside of himself. He sniffed the frost in the air, opened his eyes. Two women were climbing the stairs with cloth to prepare the body for burial.

A World Apart

Inside the Great Swamp

Civilization Called Slavery

Special to your Coahomian. (Reprinted from California's Altadena Eagle)

"There is rich living on garbage," says Orrin Swift, negro recluse. Altadena authorities investigating the disappearance of sheep discovered a cave littered with refuse in which the recluse has lived for twenty years. "Civilization is evidence of how slavery can be lifted up and made more refined outward. The man on a plantation, the man in a factory is nothing more or less than a slave. Lamb chops are my downfall. I am guilty of thieving."

The recluse was reported rational, though strange. He showed no interest in details of the recent Union victory. With a sum of coin, he paid for the missing sheep. The officers left him to his lonely life.

The Coahomian

In their first spring in the Bottoms, Jasper guided Rose to watch broad brown flood waters surging below Friar's Point into headwaters of the Hushpuckena and Sunflower rivers. He had already shown his mother how the Hushpuckena ran parallel to the Mississippi for almost thirty miles before bending east and dumping into the Sunflower.

It was between the Hushpuckena and the Sunflower, some distance below John Clark's farm, where Rose and Jasper claimed the land. Jasper built a cabin of rough logs sealed with mud, and Rose made it home while he explored like a cat marking off territory. She soon began exploring herself, learning where to trade, one place being John Clark's Landing. That was where Abyssinia had moved after a single winter in the swamp. To the southwest of the landing, there was a tiny settlement on a wide, shallow lake full of alligators.

Rose and her son encountered a number of individuals passing through like silent harbingers of another time. Rose had a few Choctaw words that Yellow Woman had taught, and most of the wanderers knew a smattering of English. They told Rose of being hunted like runaway slaves after a treaty ordered them beyond Arkansas, into what was called Indian Lands. As they came to trust one another, they guided Rose to where others lived inside the Great Swamp.

ROSE WAS TRIMMING the hearts from a pile of rose hips when a twig snapped outside. She ran to her window port and looked but saw nothing. She pulled aside the quilts that blocked drafts between timbers in the walls and peered through, first to the south, then west.

Rifle in hand she eased the door open and dashed outside. Nobody could catch her once she reached the trees. She would then circle back and surprise whoever in her own time. But that morning, running for the trees, she ran right into a short, wiry, skin-clad man hidden just beyond the clearing. She wriggled out of his arms and darted away, only to trip.

"Won't hurt you," the little man said, ambling over like a lean bear cub. "I see you here many a time."

"How—without me seein' you?"

"My blood," he said, soot brown hands draped over the barrel of a rifle planted on the ground.

"What kinda blood you got?"

"Ain't only a nigga, my ma is Choctaw."

"You bleed like me, mister, only I ain't a liar."

"Why I got to lie? I got a gun, you already layin' on the ground."

"Go on with yourself," Rose said, coming to her feet. "What's your name?"

"Name's Bill."

"Hello, Bill." She offered her hand. "Don't never sneak up on me like that again, 'less you want to be a shot-up Injun."

"Ain't likely."

When Rose turned back toward the cabin, Bill followed, sniffing the odor of her stew.

Bill counted fifty springs he'd kept track of. Said he was called Musty Bill because he only bathed when forced to swim a bayou, and even then he never removed his buckskin. Other folks called him Pussy Bill, from the time he'd been named Pusillanimous Bill by a white man with whom his mother had traded. Like Rose he had no last name, though he called himself Bill Williams whenever he wanted to avoid explaining that his mother was Choctaw.

"How you come lookin' for me?"

"You sell roots'n stuff."

"That what you want?"

"No, I bring you something."

"Ain't nothin' I need."

"You need a man."

"I got me a man. You too little to whip him, too. So be on your way."

"Why? You know you like Bill, or you wouldn't feed him . . . Chew tobacco?"

"My stars! Where you buy this?"

"It ain't the stuff they sell in the store."

"I can see that, so soft and fresh."

"Taste good like your food . . . So, why you feed me?"

"Any man deserve a meal before he die."

"That mean I kin stay 'till I die?"

"If you ain't scared of dying."

WHILE COURTING ROSE, Bill became as much of a father to Jasper as Mack had been, and they never argued. Jasper soaked up Bill's tales of the flatbottomed steamboat that made so much big river travel possible, of the wood supply towns that grew up and cleared the land along the big river to feed the boats, of the land worth less than a gallon of whiskey an acre, of the slaves brought in to farm, of the levees built to keep out the river, of gunfighters hired to keep Arkansas landowners from blasting Mississippi levees that threw floodwater into Arkansas. All in all a rough and ready place that just fit young Jasper's disposition and cunning.

Bill showing the way, Jasper ranged farther than ever, following Indian trails. He learned to track as never before and to use skunk scent to block the man smell while hunting, which was no small part of why some folks called his teacher Musty Bill. After the two became whiskey partners, neither Bill nor Jasper said a word about Rose leaving the window and door open. When it turned cold, she made them both go bathe.

In early winter, Bill lay a beaded deerskin tunic and trousers at Rose's feet.

"Why all this, Mr. Bill?"

"My gift. I ain't got whatcha call a reg'lar woman."

"A reg'lar woman?"

"Ain't got a squaw."

"I look like a squaw to you?"

Bill cradled his rifle and scratched his forehead along the barrel.

"You a fine woman, beautiful on the outside and inside. Make a good wife."

"Go somewhere, Jasper. You see this my business, non?"

"But I didn't say nothin'."

"Did I sit watching you and Maidy?"

As Jasper left, Rose turned to Bill.

"Got to tell you, I been with two men of my own choice. One, he'n me gonna be together again. Non, non! Don't say nothin', I *know* it's gonna be that way."

"I got a bigger house an' other things make a good life for you'n young Jasper."

"Bill, let's go visit your house'n talk this over some more. I think you see my point after I explain more about me."

Remnants of the giant flowers that sprouted and died in a season on the banks of the Sunflower were withered and tangled as Rose sat on a raft being carried along by the current. Bill stooped beside Rose with his pole balanced on his knees.

"Lots of the sunflower places got trampled when they started shipping cotton down to Vicksburg. Convoys camped in the clearings where the flowers grew."

"Oh, they are grand."

"Got a short little life, a flower."

"Why you lookin' at me like that, Bill?"

"You a woman in bloom. My old stalk is witherin'."

"Don't say that, Bill. You show me around. It's a real honor for a woman to be cherished like that. Don't nobody have to know I ain't your squaw. I sleep where you sleep. Go where you go. Just don't make me lock up my feelin's 'cause you taking 'em the wrong way."

Bill nodded, then settled cross-legged beside Rose.

"You see, this is what so special about you. Ain't never met nobody got words so powerful."

"Why, Bill."

"You mix 'em like medicine. All I got is a old man's feelin's, some stories to tell. Late at night after I sweat, I need medicine words, and I need to feel you near me. If you give me that, I won't do nothin to upset you."

"Why you standin' up?"

"First stop is here. We visit your neighbors."

"I ain't got no neighbors this close."

"They told me about you."

It was getting dark as they pulled their raft ashore. When Rose shivered noticeably, Bill picked up his flask and shoved it toward her. They hid the raft behind some bushes.

"Don't bother erasing sign," Bill said. "Tomorrow I come back."

"Why, thank you, sir."

"Just 'cause you got such friendly parts."

"Quit lookin' at me!"

"You got medicine words and parts friendly to the eyes."

Rose started climbing the steep embankment. The water was a good fifteen feet below. The earth was brittle and crumbled underfoot.

"Keep your hands off my bottom, please."

"I'm just pushin' so you don't have to carry all that weight by yourself."

They moved inland. Thorns and prickly bush had them moving carefully. Bill led the way. He paused at a clump of vines blocking progress, stooped and swung them aside. He crawled through a hole to emerge inside a grove of trees, trees so tall and canopy so dense they shut out all light. He set off along a trail of soft ground. Rose followed by extending her hand to Bill. He sang a little every time she touched him.

It was full dark when they glimpsed the camp. Nothing more than a cabin set upon a base of logs against flooding. Light flickered from a truncheon of fire notched inside a box on the cabin wall.

"Who that out theah!"

"Listen here, Luther," Bill said. "If I wasn't your friend, you'd been dead years ago."

"And if I ain't figured it was you, you be dead too."

"I got a woman want you to meet."

The door of the cabin creaked open. A woman stepped out.

"Bill, you a real surprise. Ain't remember when you brought nobody here."

"How are you, ma'am?" Rose said.

"Name is Merlene. What's yours?"

"Call me, Rose"

"Rose! You the woman sell medicine? Hell, you finally met up with this old nigger."

Bill and Rose broke out laughing.

"Guess you all really is good friends. This here my husband. His name is Luther. Humph . . ." She walked over and put her arm around Luther's waist. ". . . he a right friendly man too."

"Well," Bill said, "this my woman friend."

"Mmmm mmm!"

"Shut up, Merlene. Go on tell us about it, Bill."

"I'm takin' Rose to see parts of my life I can still find."

"Your life, nigger? What that mean?" Merlene asked.

"It means," Rose said. "I thank you all for sendin' me this little man. A place inside of us both is real happy."

"Oh Lord!"

"Shut up, Merlene!" her husband said.

"Make me feel like doin' the swamp trot," Merlene said.

What is that?" Bill asked.

"It's what people do when we git happy. Tonight, we gonna build a fire'n drink an' dance till the sun rise."

"Miz Merlene," Rose said, "I packed some bear meat, corn cakes."

"Oh no, you keep your travel food. Luther!"

"Yes'm."

"Build us a fire. Me'n Miz Rose goin' down to the river and empty the crawfish trap. You ain't never seen critters this size, Rose."

"Bet I have."

"Naw, see—once we ketch 'em, we got this cage stuck down in the mud under the water. Every week or so, we go down and scatter old corn meal, left-over fish. Them little suckers eat like it's judgment day. Also bring lots of other fish around for us to catch. We gonna eat crawfish'n . . ." She leaned in to whisper. ". . . I got a good man, an' it's his birthday. I cooked a pot o' plum stew this mornin' while he was gone."

"You know how to treat a man."

"Rose, I treat that man so good he ain't studyin' 'bout leavin'. He got me comin' back for more. I'm makin' sho he do the same."

"Well, if you don't mind, be much obliged you was to teach me about plum stew."

"Why, sure I will . . . Honey, Bill's parts in workin' order, but he ain't got the teeth for sweets . . . Ain't got no more to say neither. There's a man somewhere prob'ly don't know what all you been doin'."

Sometime the next morning, Rose awakened. First thing she thought of was crazy Merlene tryin to strip her husband the night before. As Rose mustered the energy to turn over, something unfamiliar poked dangerously near. Rose turned and shook Bill.

"Shhhh . . . You was pokin' into my backside. I thought we was gonna just be friends."

"Hey Rose?"

"Yes?"

"Little things like this wouldn't hardly matter if you was to think of me as your sister."

"Your what!?"

"Like the sister you ain't never had. C'mon lay back and let me git close to my sister with the friendly parts."

FLAKES OF EARLY snow were melting on his face as Jasper and Mule drifted south on the Sunflower past the cavernous mouth of the Hushpuckena. The snowflakes reminded him of childhood in Louisiana when snow had meant a trail for strangers to follow and he'd been whipped for playing in it.

He and Bill made whiskey three times a year. They were starting late because Bill had been away with Rose. The past summer's corn crop had been expensive, though it mattered little because farmers would always accept a gallon in trade for three or four bushels of corn. And because Bill had lived in the Bottoms all his life, he knew which farmers traded and asked no questions.

Mule snorted as the raft approached the mouth of Black Bayou. Jasper poled upstream into it. He had less than a mile to go inland before putting ashore. When the bayou widened, he poled toward a narrow rill draped with debris to hide it. Two gunny sacks packed with glass jugs were clattering on Mule's back, and Jasper rubbed the mule's flank to calm him. While his attention was diverted from poling, the raft paused and slid backward in the current. He had to dig in his pole and launch forward, again unsettling the animal.

"Whoa now!"

Then the raft bumped the obstruction disguising the opening. Quickly, Jasper lowered the clanking bottles from the animal, hopped into the water and yanked on the halter rope to pull Mule into the water and lighten the raft's load. He was so intent on controlling the thrashing mule and holding the raft in the current that he didn't see Bill sneak up, until the little man's hand grabbed Mule's rope.

Jasper waited while Bill led Mule ashore, until Bill could return to help lift the raft over the brush blocking the mouth of the inlet.

"Take ol' Mule into camp, goddamn him," Jasper said. "I'll hide the raft a piece away."

He leapt aboard and strained at his pole to warm himself, but already the wetness was stealing his heat, making him irritable. He put ashore a distance in from the main bayou, hid the raft. He was so cold he hadn't thought once about why Bill had summoned him. He trotted to keep warm, blundering through the brush until he glimpsed the flame.

A line of stones marked a cistern where hot alcohol vapor was already condensing. Bill was hunkered down inside a lean-to stirring the fire. The smell of roasting meat soothed Jasper's feelings as he pulled off his pants to dry at the fire.

"Quit sneakin' up on me," Jasper said. "Else, you be dead."

"Rose would not like that."

"So what about you'n my momma? You mad at her?"

"Why be mad? Her'n me just not to be. She already wife to somebody inside herself." Bill tapped Jasper's shoulder. "But you'n me got business."

"Oh, the white folks?"

"They will bring us trouble."

"But they over east of the Sunflower. We live on the west. They won't bother me'n momma."

"White man never stop movin'. More white men and camps will come. We have to put fear into these men. First, we go to their camp and do a lot of shooting just for fun. But later, the first time we see one west of the Sunflower, we got to kill him."

Jasper said nothing.

"Only that will keep them away."

"You mad 'cause of Momma."

"No, young man! This has to be. They won't cut trees πwhere they get shot at. If we act smart, they will remain east of the river."

Bill tossed away a stick with which he'd been stirring the fire and began separating glass jugs according to size.

"I help you scare them white men for you and Rose. What happen to me ain't important no more. May as well kill me, 'cause I'm old . . . You know this land? Won't be the same as you and me know when they cut down the trees to build the railroad."

"Railroad?"

"I hear talk of one." Bill paused and touched his chest with both hands, then opened them toward Jasper. "I treat you like my son, and I tell you that one day you must show your son the way of railroads and the changes they bring long after the railroad come through. I be too old to help." He chuckled. "I be dead. All this change comin' on the land make a old man like me nothin' but a boy. Old memories cain't teach in a new world. They somethin' to play with, I reckon. I seen enough change . . . Just wish your momma was cookin' for me."

Toward Statehood

Jackson, Mississippi, Summer 1868

> *"The promise of America is not about doing right. Ours is a money-changing-hands kind of place. Everyone desires to become rich, no matter how poor, how abused."*
>
> Address to Mississippi Constitutional Convention,
> by the Honorable Gambrel Allington White

A tame convention was going through its final motions. Alcorn's Planter Republicans together with senior Northern army men arranged a working majority. Sections of the proposed constitution materialized as if from out of nowhere.

Delegate Stringer negotiated the only successful challenge of the controlling coalition by putting a majority together to disenfranchise all who had borne arms against the Union and not subsequently sworn an oath of loyalty. Cicero, Blacksmith, Stringer and a handful of other delegates were now officially branded as Radicals by Alcorn, who spoke against the measure. And suddenly, the convention was over.

Cicero invited Blacksmith, Stringer and White to a supper in his and Blacksmith's lodgings. The roominghouse was now frequented by so-called Radical delegates. It was a time to rest up, plan. The battle had just begun. After all, the former Confederate state didn't even have a constitution yet.

"We have to break through the voting impasse we experienced as delegates," Cicero began.

"Nothing is being done," Gambrel Allington White said, "about anything we hold dear. Nothing for the people."

"Right you are, Gamble."

"Blacksmith—it's Gam-brel!"

"He he, I know. Fact is, Gamble, I'mma make you a honorary nigga."

"Oh please don't use that detestable word."

"I got the right. Just don't you take it outsidda this room. Niggas be all over you."

Gambrel Allington White hailed from Massachusetts. Months before, Blacksmith's initial greeting to Gambrel White had been "Man, you look like a goddamn long-haired hound dog." It was an accurate image of a thirty year-old man with the florid pink of dissipation streaking his fleshy cheeks and prominent nose. White wore his dirt red hair bunched around his ears and full in back. Since taking a prominent role in Blacksmith's murder defense, he had sat with Cicero's group during the convention.

"Our strategy up to now," Cicero said, "was to foster good will and seek out allies like Gamble here. Trouble is, whether the delegates hail from the North or the South, all of them want to get business in the state up and running because they've bought land. And that is all they want to talk about. That's Alcorn's objective. One thing, we have to forget about people liking us. We have to set goals and plan. No one else will."

"So what do you want to do?" Blacksmith asked.

"We have to increase our power, not merely our associations."

"What that mean?" Blacksmith asked.

"The most basic power there is," Gambrel White said, "getting out the vote. Once you have some power, you can again reach out."

"Take the rest of the week off," Stringer said. "Rest. Let's reconvene next Monday."

A few days later, Cicero's landlady gave him a message from a black delegates disappointed not to have been invited to supper.

"Name is Brinson," the man said. "I been votin' close to Radical right along. Some of us come from places ain't got so many of our folks like over in your Warren County. I know who live where 'cause I worked for General Ord a spell . . . Here's a map I brung with me. If you look—see, there's thirteen counties we black delegates represent."

"That's true."

"Look here . . . In addition to counties we already represent, you got Bolivar, Coahoma and Tunica straight up the river from Washington which we already control. Them is the counties on either side o' Jim Alcorn's Coahoma. Black folks control the vote in all of 'em. Then that leave only two river counties we maybe cain't control. If we move smart we run a Northern Radical like old Gamble White in the Alabama state-line counties."

"You call him that, too.?"

"Gamble sho do look like a hound dog. Him and his playin' cards and drinkin' . . . See, if we was to ask him to go to them state line counties and appeal to his carpetbagger brothers settlin' over there, I think we could put a certain category of Northern votes and black votes together."

"And if we concentrate on building leadership in the counties where we have majorities, we'd elect more black representatives."

"Damn right, suh!"

"Just so you'll know, a group of us delegates are inviting the black registrars that General Ord appointed to become our local contacts. Some have refused. We'll need more help."

"Lots of black soldiers been mustered out and gone back home."

"Do you know many?"

"I know one man up in Coahoma County name of Bill Pease. He got a organization o' soldiers he formed last Christmas when that Confederate governor started taking guns from black folks. My cousin was in the army with Pease."

That Monday, at the next meeting of the group, new members including Mr. Brinson were introduced. Cicero took the floor.

"Our primary goal is to build black leadership. That's what it is, leadership for black people. But, I'm going to suggest that we call what we are setting up Councils of Elders. It sounds the least political, and we don't want Northerners complaining just yet that they're being shut out of an all-black thing. Gamble—Mr. Gambrel Allington White—will be our token white member and assist us in this regard."

"Gentlemen, I understand my place."

In the months that followed, controversy continued to center around the proposed constitution. Some white delegates damned it as the spawn of evil Northern money come to take over. Others warned that it was the Trojan horse of a coming black take over. Meanwhile, Cicero's group seldom discussed the constitution. Uncast black votes were their focus.

Come election time, the new constitution was voted down. The provision disenfranchising Confederate soldiers who had not sworn loyalty was said to be what killed it. Most delegates understood that white folks preferred the friendly military government of General Gillem from Tennessee. They voted against the specter of more black people being elected under the new constitution.

There was good news, too. As a result of the holdover

Confederate Governor Humphries using some of the state militia to bar black voters near the capitol, the War Department—after another skirmish with Republicans in the House of Representatives—was forced to order General Gillem to remove Humphries by military decree. Convention delegate, General Adelbert Ames from Maine, was appointed interim governor.

All of a sudden, movement toward new government began to pick up momentum. New Governor Ames now consulted several Councils of Elders and began appointing black men to vacant county offices previously held by Confederates. A running battle of orders broke out between Ames and a hostile General Gillem.

That fall of 1868 was also a presidential election year, and Ulysses S. Grant won. In April of the new year, Congress authorized Grant to resubmit the rejected constitution to Mississippi voters. Grant eliminated the clause disenfranchising former combatants, and a quickly convened state Republican convention announced that a new vote on the constitution would be held in November. James Alcorn declared his full support of the constitution. Cicero Morgan announced his support of Alcorn for governor in the election to follow.

Meanwhile, Democrats changed their name to National Union Republicans in what most opposed to them saw as an effort to confuse black voters. The centerpiece of the strategy was the nomination of Lewis Dent for governor. Another Northerner seeking his fortune in Mississippi, Dent was also the son-in-law of President Grant.

A CELEBRATION SEEMED in order. In addition to the good political news, the Montgomery clan had just come to terms on purchasing Hurricane Plantation from Joseph Davis after he obtained his pardon. And there was need to mark the passing of a generation. Mr. Ben was retiring.

The family was pleased to host The Reverend Doctor Stringer and the Honorable Cicero Morgan in the plantation library that had become their home.

"Since your return to Mississippi from Cincinnati," Stringer said, "I have followed the fortunes of the Montgomery family. You are outstanding businessmen—you Mr. Ben, your sons and daughters—a beacon to upstanding colored men and women everywhere."

"Thank you, Reverend Doctor," Mr. Ben said. "We have a small amount of capital, and it is growing. All is in God's hands."

"Daddy's being humble," Isaiah said. "They call us black entrepreneurs. They wrote us up in that newspaper, Cicero—the one used to be abolitionist, out of Boston."

"I saw it," Cicero said. "The writer of the article is a fellow delegate."

"I didn't know that," Isaiah said.

"I suggested he do the article. Too many former abolitionists seem to think being negro means to be poor, and while I am neither a businessman by profession, nor by dint of believing that commerce is the salvation of the world, still it seems right that images of our people in all walks of life be known."

"Ain't that right," Mr. Ben said.

"Well," Isaiah said beaming, "you can still congratulate us about that article."

"Yes, congratulations. Maybe now, Isaiah, you'll donate more time to our political work."

"Awww c'mon, big-head boy—that's what I used to call the old Honorable here, Dr. Stringer—tell me somethin' I want to hear."

Cicero swallowed his immediate reply. Instead, he raised his whiskey glass to his lips. The flush of success around him was heady as he poured more whiskey. The table quieted as he stood up.

"Isaiah, let me tell you my own goals. I don't remember too clearly what at first I thought I could accomplish in politics. Now, I'm more clear. First thing, we have to secure the vote, which we already have but are not yet using as we should. Second, we need a redistribution of the old plantations or of as much land as is possible to our people. Finally, security is becoming a problem as the Northern army is pulled away." Cicero took another drink of whiskey. "I've not accomplished two of my goals, so I don't feel so merry."

"We've actually done quite a lot," Stringer said.

"Perhaps, but not about land . . . Isaiah, having a black businessman stand up against all those white men and say we should never forget the needs of the people would be powerful."

"Don't be a wet blanket," Mr. Ben said. "There's opportunity everywhere for enterprising colored men."

"Mr. Montgomery is quite correct," Stringer said. "Opportunities have begun appearing. Our new national administration is making itself felt, praise God."

"Here's to opportunity." Mr. Ben raised his glass.

"Say somethin', Cicero!" Isaiah said.

"Dr. Stringer taught me not to be so trusting. President Grant or no, the mass of our people stand to be cut off from any kind of decent life, just like that river that now cuts Davis Bend off from the mainland in spring. We've got to fight against our people becoming an island of poverty."

"We can't help every scamp don't cotton to work," Isaiah said.

"They can earn," Stringer said, "twenty-five dollars a month in some of those swamp plantations."

"And they're being arrested," Cicero said, "for trying to better themselves."

"Damn if that's so," Isaiah said. "How you run a business if you can't hold a man to his word?"

"So you want the government to arrest them," Cicero asked, "to help keep your wages down?"

"What in hell you mean?" Isaiah said. "You want us black businessman to follow rules the white man don't?"

"If you paid a decent wage, they'd have no reason to move."

Mr. Ben cleared his throat.

"Hold on, Isaiah . . . You're right, Cicero—in part. Nonetheless, the world is not as simple as you see it."

George Woods' daughter Suzy had her leg against Cicero's under the table, and it wasn't long before he dropped his hand to it, tentatively at first, just a pat. Until she dropped her hand on top of his and pulled it over into her lap.

"Mr. Morgan!" Mr. Ben said. "Are you with us?"

"Yes, of course."

Cicero grinned when Suzy squeezed his hand between her knees. When he looked at her, Mr. Ben smiled.

"Oh I see. Got a sixteen-year-old gal on the mind."

"We proud of our Cicero, Dr. Stringer," Isaiah said. "He is our future as much as this land is."

"Cheer up, Cicero," Mr. Ben said. "Ain't no more redneck sheriffs runnin' wild through here. And you know we'll help folks willing to work."

"It's time," Isaiah said, "for you to think about your own career."

"Gentlemen, please," Cicero said, "a call of nature."

As he stood up, Stringer lifted a final toast.

"You are a fine young man," he said. "When you reach my age you'll know how valuable all of life is, even the time you do nothing with. Take some for yourself, including the advice you're getting tonight."

Take some for yourself. The idea echoed back and forth in Cicero's brain as he relieved myself out back in the rough.

Reeling back toward the library, as he was about to emerge from a stand of oaks that had formerly framed the Hurricane mansion, Suzy stepped into his path, smiling.

As her arms opened, his went around her and she whispered "I want you, Mr. Cicero. Man like you need a woman crazy 'bout him." She was two arms full, wielding lips and a wicked wiggle as she embraced him. And all because he had become the Honorable Mr. Cicero, enough of a catch to transform a well-raised young woman into a vixen.

"When dinner's over, come to the swing house"

"Man, why I ought to do that?"

"Because you want the same thing I do."

"And what's that?"

"All that wiggle in your walk, your eyes on fire. Surely you know what you got."

"Umph, sure do talk fast. So what I'm supposed to get out of this?"

"I don't want to be the first to explain."

"I could stay here to help Isaiah's sister clean up."

Suzy kissed Cicero again, hard on the lips. He didn't see Isaiah's mother Mary watching, smiling from the darkened back door of the library.

Cicero kept a bottle near as he waited for the evening to end. Sitting there, he thought about two planters who had come to the door earlier and offered a contribution toward Stringer's and his campaigns. It reminded him that he hadn't had a salary since the defeat of the constitution. He had to quit living out of contributed money, for if he followed his instinct, he would soon be fighting the people who had money to give.

Isaiah tried to pull him back outside to continue drinking, but Cicero begged off. Before Isaiah could return, Cicero shook hands with Stringer, said his goodnights and ran for the old gazebo.

The latticework had fallen away since the war, and no one had worried to repair it. Screened by untended hedges and shrubs, the sweet scent of some flower that Cicero couldn't identify led him to Suzy waiting in the shadows.

To Our Readers

We proudly announce the sale of the COAHOMIAN newspaper from Harrison Reid, Esquire, to J. L. Alcorn. With this edition, the name of the newspaper becomes the WEEKLY DELTA.

Former Senator Alcorn wishes the readership to know that he intends no change in operation of the county's only weekly newspaper. "My purchase is to finance expanded coverage of business news for my neighbors and supporters."

Weekly Delta

SUZY WAS A hard-working young woman eager to snare what everybody told her was a good catch. She was voluptuous enough to push aside both Cicero's loneliness and worry about the future—theirs and the world's. He spent many evenings with Suzy in the months that followed, but he would always believe that it was the first time that made him a father.

In that time of organizing to get out the vote, Gambrel Allington White worked diligently to pull in white support for black candidates, but he made a personal decision not to run again that he politely but stubbornly refused to explain. He made preparations to return to Boston after the election.

That November, Mississippi voters ratified the resubmitted constitution. What was even more momentous, forty black people were elected out of one hundred fifteen seats in the new legislature. There had been only seventeen black delegates to the convention, and the increase had come from organizing, turning out a huge vote for black candidates. James Alcorn profited from the same black vote. He became governor-elect.

Cicero was elected to the Assembly, and he began making a two-day trip each way to and from Jackson at least twice a month on Republican caucus business, though none of those elected would have offices to fill until the U. S. Congress officially approved Mississippi's new constitution.

Into the new year, Cicero continued his active travel and correspondence. He had so little time for Suzy that she was in continual uproar. As her pregnancy progressed, she pushed for a formal marriage. What Cicero might have considered before their living together turned into a battle, he now refused. When he did, Suzy followed him from Hurricane to Brierfield screaming that he should act like a man. Her mother and Mary Montgomery took her side. Cicero learned that all of the women had encouraged Suzy to "go courting" that first night.

In April, a child was born, and Cicero hurried home from Jackson. Suzy was installed in the Hurricane library in her father's room. When Cicero arrived, the men were sitting on the esplanade toasting Old George and his new grandchild. The women—Mary Montgomery, Suzy's mother and several of their friends—were packed into Suzy's bedroom doing their own form of celebrating.

"Here come my stepson," Old George said, rising rheumy-eyed and unsteady.

The former butler was so old now he had no chores. Isaiah had taken off work to come greet Cicero, and as Cicero climbed off his horse, Isaiah rushed over.

"Hey, Cicero. Before you go in, we got some business."

"Leave the boy alone," Mr. Ben said. "He a daddy now. Let him go on inside and congratulate the new momma. Cain't be a bachelor scamp all his days."

"How're you Mr. Ben, Old George? How's Suzy?"

"I'm a gram'pa," Old George said. "Pretty li'l boy, he is. His name is Buck."

"Congratulations," Mr. Ben said. "You got a fine boy, pretty skin like his momma and some of Momma Nancy in him, too."

Cicero was more than a little nervous as he walked inside to see his son and Suzy.

"Oh you! I already give him his name."

"Couldn't we change that to Morgan, after my father?"

"What rights you got? Just cause you got the Montgomerys givin' me a little money, that don't give you no rights."

"Didn't you think I'd have some interest in my son's name?"

"I get confused. I *thought* you was gonna marry me."

"I never said so."

"And I never said you could name my baby."

Shaken, Cicero took comfort in making one decision. He would postpone supporting himself no longer. In the days that followed, he visited families at the Bend and announced that he was available for tutoring children. For the rest of that year, he became first and foremost a schoolteacher.

The U. S. Congress did not approve the new Mississippi constitution until March of 1871, the following year. To fill the time, along with teaching, Cicero began catching up on his reading of Latin.

Then, an emergency message arrived at the Bend. A man who had been a voter registrar back in '67—and was serving on one of the Council of Elders—demanded that all of the Radical group return to Jackson.

What the man reported was that fifty-four assassinations of political workers, office-holders or schoolteachers had occurred in 1869. The number had climbed to eighty-three in 1870. In just the first three months of '71, the number had reached seventy one. He did not count homicides, rapes, whippings and arson against ordinary people.

Pomp and Circumstance

Jackson, Mississippi, Early Spring of 1871

> *"Methinks a confiscation of all wealth upon death, 'twould endorse a better use of life."*
>
> Anonymous Pre-Revolutionary War Broadside

A young man on horseback rode down Capital Street past a jostling throng waiting for the important people to arrive. Ahead of him, the gray stone rotunda of the legislative hall rose above monumental columns atop a supporting base of arches that were rustic but reminiscent of L'Enfant's gray stone in Washington.

The rider dismounted and accepted a dipper of water. Someone pushed forward a full cup of whiskey. He downed it quickly, before some officer might see him and object. It was now less than an hour before dark when festivities were to begin. After the summoning bugle, he would march up and salute General Adelbert Ames. To him would be given the guilt-encrusted envelope containing the personal good wishes of President Ulysses S. Grant. Ames would pass the envelope on to Governor-elect Alcorn.

Someone grabbed his arm. None other than General—formerly from Maine—Adelbert Ames.

"You should be inside. Go there now."

"Yessir!"

He gave the eager salute of an enlisted man to a general and ran faster than need be just to show that he was good at following orders. Following orders had, in fact, got him chosen for the detail, his being willing to carry documents in an army pouch that he knew had nothing to do with army business. That and being discrete. There was a lot of land being quietly purchased by army men.

An explosion of laughter behind him made the messenger turn around. In front of him was an old man dressed in what looked like a hand-me-down suit, ill fitting as suited a clown. Shuffling his feet and playing a harmonica at the same time, he was the funniest sight the young man had ever seen.

"Here come them goddamn Radicals," someone whispered.

Two black men dressed for the celebration were approaching. The one, slim but of more than average height, marched right up and broke the circle around the old man.

"Will you celebrate a free government with this kind of display?"

"It's perfectly good fun."

The Radical pointed to the old man.

"His bows and ribbons are an affront to us who suffered worse at some of your hands."

"Who you, suh?" the old man demanded.

"I am Representative Cicero Morgan from Warren County. I was a slave just like you."

"I needs this job jes much as y'all needs one."

Cicero stiffened, at a loss for words. Some of the onlookers began to applaud again, and the old man began cutting an even livelier caper. From out of the audience, stepped another well-dressed black person.

"Be still, brother man. We the party o' Lincoln. Don't make

no monkeyshines here. That old man got to eat like us. An' he funny."

"He is an affront!"

"Why, Cicero, 'cause he po'?"

"No. Because someone finds being black and poor something to poke fun at."

"Ain't high-fallutin' enough for you? He okay by me."

Former delegate, now Senator-elect Stringer walked up.

"What we do, Cicero, is to keep our eyes on the prize. We have turned this state around."

"Listen to Senator Stringer, Mr. Morgan," a member of the crowd said. "Back in Ohio we appreciate a little local color."

By now, the old fellow was on his hands and knees picking up coins. A hulk of a man the messenger heard called Blacksmith whispered to Cicero. Stringer addressed the crowd around them.

"My young associate wasn't wrong. He was too simplistic. We are here tonight because of common interest—not agreement about everything."

The festive mood triumphed, and the messenger followed the crowd as they made their way inside and on underneath the capital dome. The sight took his breath away. Chandeliers suspended overhead, each a festive tree of glass lit with what seemed hundreds of tiny gaslights. A sparkling marble floor so slippery with wax his hard-soled boots barely allowed him to stand.

Along the back wall, men held serving trays. Stationed between them, at attention but armed only with holstered small arms, stood dress-uniformed soldiers, their white gloves motionless against dark blue. Serving people sprang into motion, all moving so fast under the shimmering lamplight, white gloved hands passing tiny frosted cakes toward extended white cuffs. Momentarily, it all turned into a blur, and the messenger, young man that he was, allowed as how he might be a wee bit tipsy.

Applause drew his attention back to the doors. James Alcorn stepped inside dressed modishly and extravagantly in blue silk and wool, accented by white. His wife was attended by two women of color.

"Greetings, Chauncy," Alcorn said, offering his hand to another. "Good you could attend . . . Ladies and Gentlemen, secession ends tonight. The negro, Hiram Revels—he's the tall charming black minister who entered with me for those of you who do not already know the gentleman—he will serve out the pre-war term of our beloved Jefferson Davis. May he be granted pardon soon."

Stubborn but thin applause for the Confederate President eventually died. Alcorn pulled his hand free of his wife's and walked forward.

"The good General Ames will take our other Senate seat. In dear Adelbert I have appointed a fine man to represent a fine state . . . And I—poor me—I shall be stuck here in Jackson minding the plantation, just a simple governor."

There was wholesale laughter. A black legislator others were calling John Lynch walked forward and began introducing his wife to the Alcorns. Cicero Morgan was nearby. Lynch spotted Cicero and moved in his direction. His wife excused herself to Mrs. Alcorn and followed her husband.

"Well Mr. Morgan," Lynch said, "you can congratulate yourself."

"If you say so."

"No, no! I mean it. I am to become Speaker of the House. It was pressure from men like you brought it about."

"And our organization."

"You must be proud—forty-odd black legislators elected, me chosen as Speaker of the House, a Secretary of State of sable hue—bravo, Mr. Morgan. You and Dr. Stringer had the right idea—organize!"

From Africanamericans in the vicinity, there erupted a hearty applause, and they surrounded Morgan and Lynch.

When Hiram Revels moved out of a conversation near the entryway, all eyes turned toward him. He bowed to the assembled room but marched to join the group around Cicero and Lynch.

The Senator and the House Speaker embraced. The orchestra's drum saluted them to general applause. As it died down, Alcorn spoke.

"Right over there . . . That is Senator Revels, and of course I call him a friend."

"You are a friend of the colored, too," Revels replied.

Cicero moved out of the black group and stood near Alcorn. As if his silence were the art of anger, Cicero bowed, barely civil.

"I hear," Alcorn said, "you've been your usual busy self tonight."

"Nothing that would concern you, I suspect—or dare I hope so?"

"Why, of course not. Things are going splendidly. How are you again, Mr. Lynch—forgive me—Mr. Speaker!"

"Fine, thank you, Governor Alcorn."

Cicero grabbed the governor's sleeve.

"Our report on violence to the U. S. Attorney finally got General Gillem removed."

"Not at all. I suggested removing Gillem. Governor Ames was appointed military commander until tonight because he was acceptable to all of us."

"Were you also consulted before they mustered out every single black soldier left in Mississippi? Governor, we are neither pawns nor fools like that old man out front."

Alcorn pulled Cicero away from everyone. Words continued to be exchanged, though not loud enough to be heard at a distance. Eager not to miss whatever might be going on, the messenger eased closer as Alcorn began hissing.

"That old colored man works for Chauncy, over there. Chauncy supports him and a very large family who wander about but always come on back to the plantation when things get rough. If you Radicals had your way, great plantations like ours would be broken up. Our labor would be marching off in search of scandalous wages, or demanding free land . . . Tonight, let us put difference aside and enjoy ourselves."

"Yes!" John Lynch said from a distance. "We have fought the good fight. Slavery is dead, Mississippi is reconstructing its ways. As the official host of this noble eve, I ask you all to raise a glass, to a future never before imagined."

A tidal wave of confirmation poured out of the crowd. Lynch raised his hand and snapped his fingers twice. Doors at the perimeter of the hall noisily opened. Liveried servants walked in carrying more trays. Lynch seized a glass and raised it.

"A glass for every hand!"

Cicero stood unmoved as the drinking and toasting commenced. "Much as any o' them," the large man called Blacksmith was heard to whisper, "me'n you deserve a drink for puttin' up with shit like this."

After the ceremonial drink had been consumed, groups of acquaintances began to coalesce around ubiquitous flasks of corn whiskey, and the noise increased. Until a rich baritone voice sliced through.

"I-in, that great gittin' up mornin', fare thee well . . ."

Senator Hiram Revels was singing. Staring him in the face, John Lynch didn't wait. His voice pounced on the end of Revels' and twisted the phrase a different way. Then, some worthy person unknown to the messenger threw his arms around Lynch and Revels and did his own vocal turn. A free-for-all, it became, each challenging the other. Encouragement from all sides kept them at it. Louder and louder, they sang, and before the improvising flagged, a wicked soprano egged the male voices into one more verse.

The young messenger found himself singing along with everyone. As the singing became a humming, the messenger pulled at his uniform and prepared to march up and present the President's best wishes. Before the summoning bugle, though, he heard a muffled thump behind him.

Near the door already, he walked outside. In time to see the troublemaker Morgan again slam his fist against the wall. Blacksmith was angrily trying to pull him back inside.

"Excuse me. I saw you out front. What makes you so angry?"

"Ah, a young man in blue. You probably think this is a wonderful evening."

"That it is. What's troubling you?"

"Something I don't believe you would understand."

"Weren't you a slave before?"

Cicero nodded.

"Come on, colored man, tonight is what we fought for. All these colored been elected. You wearin' fancy clothes. . ."

"It's everything you fought your war for."

"I fought for the Union! My brother died at Shiloh. This war was paid in blood and won for all of us.

"No disrespect to the dead, but you don't understand what's really going on tonight."

"Hell, I got the President's letter congratulating us right here. This gonna be a real state again. Why don't you act right?"

"You want me to . . . act right."

A bugle sounded inside the ballroom.

"Come on—quick, mister. Tell me what's bothering you 'cause I got to go."

"The plantation owners who will run this government say that little people owning land is not very important because we have the great gift of freedom."

"I know. That's why we celebrating."

THE NEXT MORNING, the newly leafed trees around the Capital were sparkling under full sun as Blacksmith and Cicero entered the legislative hall. For ceremonial purposes, a joint session of the legislature had been arranged.

James Alcorn entered with the rest of the new legislators en masse. Alongside John Lynch and the rest of the leadership, he was chatty and humorous judging from how Lynch was laughing as Cicero caught Alcorn's eye.

"Ah, Mr. Morgan. Our disagreement last night did not dispose me to thank you properly for your support in my election."

"Perhaps, governor, you will support some small part of our program."

Alcorn halted, and so did the party around him. He put his hand on Cicero's arm and stepped aside to whisper.

"Let me share this . . . I planned to move to Canada when the war ended. I could not see how my small commerce in land and cotton could recover. But it has. That accomplishment—and the new enterprises that others from the North have begun—I cannot jeopardize with a program of free land."

"Even if it wouldn't take an acre away from you?"

"Who would work for us if they had their own land? . . . You should consider moving to Canada. A move can be restorative. Some of us might assist you in becoming more of a man of affairs than grubbing down here in Mississippi for outdated liberal ideals has left you."

As the morning progressed, lists of political appointees were passed from the Governor up to John Lynch for reading to the Joint Session. Alcorn had insisted on having his appointees confirmed, though there was no law requiring him to do so.

A Black Caucus was scheduled for that afternoon. Aside from the foreboding matter of security, there was the general question of strategy, how best to let Alcorn know with the least confrontation that he would have to accommodate a sizable voting block bent on addressing the land issue. Gambrel Allington White's final suggestion before departing had been to put aside all thought of confiscating existing plantations and focus exclusively on swamp land.

Cicero left his seat and walked outside. He opened an unread letter.

> Dear Cicero,
> Congratulations on success—or dare I hope so. We did pursue the correct way. It will remain to be seen if chance and circumstance favor our cause.
> Many happy days for you and for your family.
>
> Gamble White
>
> ps: I am reborn! In the bosom of my family. The only cloud on my horizon is a strike against a family paper mill, but we shall prevail.

Loud applause drew Cicero back inside the Joint Session. Stringer was frowning as Cicero took his seat. Blacksmith had his flask open. An explosion of applause focussed Cicero's attention on Alcorn at the podium shaking hands with John Lynch.

"What's going on?"

"Just listen!" Stringer hissed.

". . . I will not bore you," Alcorn continued, "with dry detail—those of you yet recovering from last evening. Let me repeat the good news you heard from Mr. Speaker Lynch. I signed papers this morning to purchase a college for the colored.

"If you gentlemen do me the honor and grant it the money for full staffing, that school will become the first college in this nation for the education of men like Hiram Revels, John Lynch. To my honorable associate from Warren County, the

Honorable Cicero Morgan, I urge your continued support. You see, I am on your side."

A foot stomping ovation accompanied James Lusk Alcorn's exit. Cicero found himself applauding. He knew of the former white private college. It sat on a couple hundred acres of land-scaped hill along the Mississippi less than a day's ride south of Davis Bend. Then Cicero's hands froze. He looked to Black-smith who offered whiskey. Stringer just shook his head.

"That man," Stringer said, "has just cut our throats."

"Niggas gonna love that white man 'till he die, or my name ain't Blacksmith."

An earthquake had reformed the political landscape. Al-corn could no longer become the enemy they had all hoped would pull black legislators more tightly together. The wild applause—even cheering—coming from black legislators meant that Alcorn could now pick and choose his support. Hiram Revels in Washington, John Lynch in Jackson would be—already were—forming new and separate constellations of allegiance. There was no way to forge a progressive voting block, not even by those whose skins had marked them as slaves. A logical absurdity, but fact.

In the weeks that followed, friendly newspapers trumpeted Alcorn's plan for the college. Democratic opinion damned him. The conflict was a siren call to black people who rushed to Alcorn's defense. All effort to brand Alcorn a rich man's governor failed. For most of the public, white and black, the public issue of the day was reduced to one, whether former slaves deserved a college.

Meanwhile, the legislative agenda remained controlled by the native white Republicans and their landed Northern allies. John Lynch, whom they had appointed, parroted their desires. The legislature would consider—in order of priority —levees along the Mississippi, new roads in the wilderness counties, the disposition of hundreds of thousands of acres of virgin swamp land to finance railroad expansion.

BUSINESS AS USUAL, not an inherently pejorative phrase, but it became the mantra, the holy cause in white and black mouths as they muttered in mutual congratulation of their accomplishment in those early days of what would be known as the Alcorn administration. Talking about doing business as usual sugar-coated ignoring the opportunity of Reconstruction for people, made it easy to become a booster for the plantations almost everyone in government now owned. Who could disagree with protecting land from the river, building roads to move the harvest, financing railroad building.

Cicero fled Jackson. Home to lick his wounds. He was sprawled in the Hurricane library looking at catalogs from the University of Mississippi he'd acquired some time before. Now that land for the people was no longer in the cards, he turned to his own life. He had always dreamt of college. Now, bitter though circumstances of its birth had been, the new college had lured him into imagining a course of study.

He had already read many of the classics including the works of Cicero, and he had taught himself Latin grammar. All that remained of First Term requirements was English composition. Even the Second Term courses were already familiar. He had not read Livy, but the rest was more Latin grammar and composition. Were he to enter the white university, he would probably begin as a sophomore, possibly a junior.

On the bed, beside his application letter to the new college, lay little Buck. The child seldom cried, but he was fretting. Cicero picked him up and lay back with the baby on his chest. The door opened.

"You tryin' to teach the boy somethin'?"

"No, Suzie. Just resting."

"I'm happy you come spend time with us. I don't know if you need this school, though."

"What did Isaiah say to you?"

"Oh, just that you won't stay and help us work the farm. You rather go mingle with snooty folks at the new college."

"Don't blame me for what you think of other people."

"Shit, I'm good as anybody. I'm tellin' you what Isaiah said."

"So that you understand, I can keep doing what I was doing last year. I make a little money. Or—and this is why I want to go to school—I can prepare to teach older students. Maybe teach in a college myself."

"You mean Isaiah don't know what he talkin' about?"

"What I just told you is what I'm doing."

"Well, gimmie my baby."

"Leave him here."

"I got work to do—less you want to keep him all night."

"I'll keep him."

"Naw, I just remembered he got a cold. Look at his nose. Giv'm here."

"Just a little dribble. I'll take care of it."

"You don't know nothin' about children. C'mon, L'il Buck. We gotta go."

As soon as Cicero arrived at the college, he was upgraded to third year courses on account of his grasp of Latin, the core of all beginning work. A handful of upper class students along with Cicero negotiated areas of reading to be guided by faculty. He also discovered that he couldn't simply be a student. He was a celebrity.

A young woman whose father was a faculty member began issuing supper invitations, but Cicero declined them. The first serious conversation they had led Cicero to tell her that he preferred friendship ahead of marriage. Though he would often see her on campus, he maintained his distance.

No one seemed to understand his single-minded interest in books either. He deflected equal scorn from men as from the handful of women in his orbit, all of whom were studying to move up in the world. None of the miscellany of social pretense they lobbed his way drew a response beyond a practiced political smile.

He read a translation of a French book, Candide. The wide-eyed character who was always willing to believe tomorrow would be better in a most perfect of worlds reminded Cicero of most of those who'd elected him, always hopeful and seldom aware of the real issues. Then he began to wonder if his own recent political quests had been equally silly, and then he laughed. At least he did not believe in a most perfect of worlds. His delusion, if that is what it had been, was that people could reshape their own future, to make it serve them. On his birthday that April, he was thirty-two.

Blacksmith summoned him back to Jackson. Cicero excused himself from classes, and rode a horse all the way straight to his old room near the capitol. The landlady was all smiles. Blacksmith had paid her and left word to have Cicero sent on whenever he arrived.

When Cicero stepped inside the rotunda, he heard the legislature involved in a dispute between two railroads over conflicting land grant proposals. When he wandered out he was puzzled as to why Blacksmith had summoned him. Then he caught sight of Hiram Revels emerging from a meeting room.

"Greetings, Senator!"

"Hello, Cicero," Revels said, seeming to lengthen his stride away.

"So good seeing you," Cicero said, matching the man's stride as a matter of courtesy. "You're back?"

"Yes, I am, but pressed for time."

"What brought you back here? I haven't heard you speak since you left for the nation's capital."

"No, but you know I've been busy. Doing what I could."

"And now?

"Business."

"Might I help?"

"No, no, I don't have time to talk about the state of the world. Good afternoon, sir."

The abrupt dismissal left Cicero irritated as he watched Revels climb into a waiting carriage. Cicero walked about the grounds distracted until he decided again to stick his head inside the legislative chamber. Before he reached the doors, though, he glimpsed Blacksmith, T. W. Stringer and a couple other black faces emerging from the same door as had Revels.

"A safe job," Dr. Stringer kept repeating, shaking his head.

"What are you men of the world up to?" Cicero asked.

Blacksmith strode forward and embraced Cicero, then turned to Stringer.

"Go on, tell him."

"Instruct me, my Doctor Pangloss."

"Dr. who?" Stringer asked.

"From a book I read at the college, a man who had explanations for everything."

"We had hoped you would reach here in time to meet with Hiram. He's resigning."

"What!?"

"Jim Alcorn," Blacksmith said, "has appointed Senator Hiram Revels to be president of your little college."

"My college!?"

"We had hoped," Stringer said, "that you could show him how insignificant it really is, how far from the corridors of power he would have had access to."

"Let me go after him. Where is he staying?"

Blacksmith waved Cicero off. Stringer stepped forward.

"Won't do no good."

"I can't imagine him giving up Washington. He's our voice."

"Hold on, Cicero!" Blacksmith said. "Hear T.W. out."

"All of us tried," Stringer said. "We could not change his mind because he is convinced that what he is doing is for the future of the race."

"And I thought I was naive. Who better than him to explain in Washington what's happening to the people?"

"Cicero, he walked out. He won't discuss the matter."

"Not that college ain't still the right thing for you, boy," Blacksmith said, "It just don't make no sense Revels giving in to white folks like he been doing. As far as that law against mob violence, word come back Revels did vote the right way, but he ain't leadin' no fight. He vote. He lose, he go home'n eat."

"He's the first Senator of color in this nation's history. Why would he be like that?"

"I'm just guessing," Stringer said. "Living in Washington, all the attention, always being made up to for being so cultivated or whatever—though he's really a simple man. Alcorn, I'm sure, has been massaging him with talk about all they've accomplished for the state's economy."

"Yes," Cicero said. "On occasion I, too, have fallen victim of Jim Alcorn's praise."

"Don't talk, Cicero. Just listen," Blacksmith said.

"We all," Stringer continued, "can start feeling uncomfortable telling the whole truth about them and us. As far as us Radicals, Hiram now thinks of our goals as unrealistic. Every soul who worships at the altar of business dismisses us to him. Not simply as wrong either, but crazy—crazy demented or crazy idealist, it doesn't matter."

"I'm gonna seek him out anyway."

"We had a pretty big fight," Blacksmith said. "Hiram up and cussed out T. W. here."

"His not understanding how important it is to stay in Washington is only a symptom of what we all suffer from. You see, I have purchased a small plantation."

"Oh?"

"We all have to do something apart from being a legislator."

"Tell him," Blacksmith said to Stringer, "what Hiram said to you."

"Hiram said that if I could become a farmer, he sure as hell could be a college president. He needed a permanent job, too."

IN THE MIDDLE of his second school year, Cicero was told that Senator Caldwell had arrived and was awaiting him at the president's residence.

"Our dear Master Alcorn," Blacksmith said, "has appointed himself to take Hiram's place?"

"Nooooo."

"He says he owes it to his sweet state to go represent the people."

"So, all information about this state, the violence, will now go through Nigga Jim."

"You got it."

"This is so depressing."

"Well, that's why I've come. I wish I could say we need you back in Jackson, but everything's already been arranged against us, and we have maybe half those we figured we could count on for votes."

"Only thing makes sense right now is a few glasses of whiskey . . . Tomorrow, you can ride home with me."

"And you'll feed me for free?"

Cicero nodded, and they fell into one another's arms laughing.

They set off early on borrowed horses to reach the Bend before dark. The good road running all the way, plus a mid-morning meal of cold bread pudding from the groundskeeper's wife, made the morning a lark. Until talk turned to politics.

"I also came visitin' to keep the Honorable Mr. Cicero from slipping away. We will need you back in Jackson."

"Who said I was quitting?"

"No you wouldn't, but what about reelection? . . . Things goin' downhill fast. You know all this killin' been goin on? People know it too, now that we been demanding Federal marshals. One out of three I talk with ain't votin' come November this year."

"You think I don't know that?"

"Why are you so touchy?"

"Nerves, I guess."

Blacksmith leaned over, patted Cicero's arm.

"Think," he said, "what it means in the House alone, that many folks not voting."

"I don't follow you."

"You can probably get reelected in Warren County—'least I hope so. How many others will? After this next election, we won't hardly have a presence."

"But, we now have forty people."

"Been some bad lynchin's this year—I mean like public hanging of a county official. They draggin' po' folk off in the night like always. It's us trying to stand up and make changes, we the ones marked."

They rode silently for a while. The sky was bright but overcast, the air was frosty but no longer numbing cold. A dull rumble to the north caused them both to look at the sky.

"This trip one crazy idea," Blacksmith said. "Hope that weather up ahead pass by before we catch up to it."

"If white folks don't kill you, a little rain won't."

"We got to keep a few of us in Jackson . . ." Blacksmith reached over and grabbed Cicero's reins. ". . . to push an' shove old Governor Ames."

"Did Alcorn replace himself with Ames?"

"Strange shit, ain't it? Ames could be our last friendly governor. And one more thing—Nigga Jim is boltin' the party."

"Whaaat?!"

"First appoint hisself, then Ames, then he tell folks he leavin' the national Republican party—all in a few months time."

"All this and I didn't hear a word?"

"Ain't so long ago happened, and the juicy stuff don't git in the newspaper. Him leavin' the party got to do with that Klan law. Alcorn didn't like the Republican platform that urges Washington to start prosecuting people for mob violence."

"So what is Alcorn's plan after leaving the party?"

"First, for all his faults, Alcorn was the only Republican who could pull in both sides of the white vote. Without him, who wins the next governor's race is a toss-up. Old Governor Adelbert Ames in a big marble game an' he ain't make the rules."

"You aren't saying that Alcorn—who just appointed himself to Washington—"

"That was to get Hiram outta there. After that, any white man do."

"You think Alcorn will come back to run for governor?"

"Who know? What I do know is there's deep unhappiness with Ames among all the planter Republicans. Couple years ago, Ames appointed too many of our people to county office. He's doing it again, especially up in them swamp counties where Alcorn is from. But you see, Alcorn had to appoint Ames governor as the price of Northerners voting for Alcorn to go to Washington. Now, the betting is that Alcorn will run against Ames. Meanwhile, Ames seem to be appointing folks he can count on come election time."

"Doesn't he know a lot of black folks won't vote against Alcorn?"

"Fact remain, a lotta his new appointees is our people."

"I don't understand Alcorn bolting the party. Especially if he plans on running for governor, as you say."

"Him and some Democrats got the idea to call theyself the 'Republican Party of Mississippi'."

"I see."

"Yep. He'll draw votes from all sides still, old planters, few more democrats and lots of black folks. Ain't that some shit?"

Blacksmith laughed, circled tightly on his mount while drawing a pistol. Not to be outdone, Cicero drew his pocket pistol. They spurred ahead like rambunctious boys.

"I got to say one more thing," Blacksmith said, slowing. "Here!"

"Here, what?"

"Take my grown-up gun. That little pocket pistol I gave you wont stop a flea in his tracks."

"Have you told me everything?"

Blacksmith shook his head.

"Go on talk, then."

"Political folks bein' ambushed all over. Forget the old arguments we had. Maybe you was right. Maybe there wasn't no actual conspiracy between the various white folks. But now, for the coming election, a group of thugs been brought in from outta state. Somebody paying them to disrupt our political meetings and then move on. This big increase in political killings is one of the things we 'spect they been part of. You, my dear friend, have been a thorn in the side—just like me. I got letters to prove they after me. Because you been away at the college don't mean your name ain't still on the Radical list."

WHEN THEY ARRIVED at the Davis Bend cookhouse, Cicero passed time in polite conversation with Mary Montgomery, Suzy, and Blacksmith, until Blacksmith drained his second glass of whiskey and started talking about Cicero being on an assassination list. Cicero hustled Blacksmith out and over to the library to get him settled in.

Late that night, after making love inside a cabin that had been provided for him and Suzy, Cicero was lying on his back counting his heartbeats.

"Thinking to build myself a house," Suzy said.

Cicero sighed and turned away before her words registered. "What did you say?"

"I'm tired of livin' back in the Quarters. Everybody around here is puttin' up a house of they own. I know you been fair with me and the boy, and Mr. Ben and Isaiah all help out, but I would truly like a house of my own."

"Whatever you want. Money can come from my teaching this summer."

"If you stay here all year, you could help run another sawmill before all that timber in the middle of the Bend git flooded for good. You seen how the river playin' games, like it want to run permanent through that guardboat canal and turn this place into a island."

"I'm standing for re-election. We're in the worst fix we've been in since before freedom. What with all this shooting and lynching going on, a lot of black people won't vote this time."

Suzy got out of bed then. Cicero pushed himself up on his elbows to watch her bending over a heavy cypress table lighting a kerosene lamp. Content to watch her naked bottom as she moved to locate her nightgown, he gave no thought to her having gotten out of bed so abruptly. In a peculiar observance of modesty when she turned toward him, she covered her breasts with her nightgown.

"Just got out of my bed. Why are you covering up like a girl?"

Suzy turned her back and commenced pulling the gown over her head. Her arm got caught up.

"Nigga," she said, struggling, "I didn't just git outta your bed. You're in mine!"

"What's the matter?"

"You can leave if you think I'm crazy enough to bind myself to a pure fool like you fixin' to be."

"Calm down."

"No, I won't!"

"Please."

"If you got to die, do it when the dandelions bloom 'cause I ain't saved up my little money for no flowers. I seen how much difference all your Honorable Mr. Cicero mess is makin'. White folks still treat y'all like fools."

She snatched her gown completely off, started again. She bunched it up and drew it over her free arm.

"Miz Mary say Mr. Ben didn't want to get married. He kept tryin' to run away when he was young. But you ain't even runnin' away. You askin' to get killed in this politics mess."

Suzy broke off and finished with the nightgown, smoothing it over her thighs. Cicero's eyes dropped to a tiny wet spot below the soft ridge of her stomach. From making love, he assumed, which encouraged him to turn the conversation in a more loving direction.

"Come here."

He lay back and opened his arms. Suzy rubbed at her eyes, and tears spotted her nightgown.

"Don't cry. Just talk to me."

"What is there to talk about?"

"About you and me."

"You and me what? Why you want to let these mad-dog white folks shoot at you—shoot at me and the baby, too?"

"You want to be my wife, you have to accept the risks."

"I ain't got to do nothin'. Isaiah and his people ain't so involved in politics as you. And they gittin' ready to quit what little they doin'."

Sensing Isaiah's hand in some of what he'd heard, Cicero scooted to the edge of the bed away from Suzy. Then he remembered Blacksmith's gift of the evening before—a new pipe lying on the table near the lamp—and he headed around the foot of the bed for it, brushing against Suzy as he passed.

"Left me with this baby to take care of, now you fixin' to git kilt."

"Just shut up and let me do my work."

Cicero sat back down on the bed and stuffed his pipe with tobacco. Silence hung between them, North versus South, no movement across the border without giving anger its freedom.

Then Suzy sat down, and they remained apart. Finally, Cicero lay his pipe aside and moved closer. When his arm encircled Suzy, she shrugged it off and flushed him with anger as she leapt out of bed and confronted him. Her hands had become fists.

"Oh hell, Suzy, grow up!"

Cicero tried to stand, but before his knees could unbend, Suzy slapped him, and the rage boiled up like mud during a flood. He grabbed her by one arm and pointed his finger to warn her off. She dug her nails into his face, and her muscled arms resisted polite disentanglement. He screamed in pain before slinging her away against the cabin wall. Suzy came up blinking, caught a foot in her gown. It ripped, and down she went to the floor again. She got to her feet more slowly this time, holding the ripped gown in front of her to blame him for it. Her brown muscled thighs came into focus through his pain, and passion flashed inside of rage. When she swung at him, he grabbed her wrists—they of the deadly nails—and wrestled her against the bed, which skidded away to the opposite wall. They fell to the floor snarling obscenities and clinging to one another in a parody of making love. But words kill only feelings, so they kept screaming, flailing about on the floor as if to continue for some hellish eternity. Then Benjamin and Mary Montgomery rushed in to pull them apart.

"How dare you fight a woman, Cicero! Go help the child, Mary."

"You poor, poor dear," Mary said.

Cicero dropped his eyes, and his mind sort of pulled away from those around him as he reached for his pants.

"I'm tired o' bein' used," Suzy said between sobs.

"Nobody blame you, child," Mary said. "You tried your best."

"Amen," Mr. Ben said. "Come here, Cicero, I got a word for you."

Cicero said nothing, hunting around for the shoes and shirt he'd been in such a hurry to shuck off before.

"Listen to me, young man. No matter how hard life is, there's never an excuse to hit a woman."

"I didn't."

"Did too!" Suzy said. "Look at this bruise on my head."

"You fell against the wall!"

"You knocked me 'gainst it!"

Mary took Suzy in her arms and murmured hush as Suzy cried on her shoulder. Mr. Ben's occasional "Lord a mercy" counterpointed the sound of sobbing, but as Cicero finally laid hold of his shoes he was thinking of matters from his own private perch. Suzy was purring in her ripped gown, like a well-fed cat.

THAT FALL, Suzy married a man who farmed forty acres with two older boys. Cicero saw his son sporadically when he visited the Bend campaigning for the November election and Suzy happened to relent.

A black paper-candidate entered the assembly race in Warren County. He was supported by the Democrats and split off some of the black vote, thus helping the white Mississippi Republican—the Alcorn man—to out-poll Cicero. With James Alcorn down personally campaigning for him, the Alcorn man captured a majority of the white votes and a good number of black votes. All Cicero could take comfort in was that Adelbert Ames remained governor and defeated Alcorn.

WITH THE NEW YEAR, Cicero decided to move. Nothing was holding him, not even his son, whom he knew to be in good hands. Increasingly, he felt like a pariah around Buck as their time together was parceled out by his often vindictive and always emotional mother. He booked passage to Friar's Point north on the Mississippi near where Abyssinia had written she was living. Other than it being home to Alcorn, Cicero knew nothing of the place. He'd figure out how to locate Abyssinia after he arrived.

On the day of his departure, the table for breakfast was set for a feast. Except that, of the Montgomery family, only Isaiah appeared. They ate in silence until one of the workmen who farmed land in loose federation with the Montgomerys showed up after the sun rose. After Isaiah finished with the workman, Isaiah walked behind Cicero's chair, put his hands on Cicero's shoulders.

"The man say he was proud to vote for you—any time."

"Thank him for me," Cicero said, "your mother and father for this food, too."

"You thank Suzy. She insisted on cooking, but she didn't want to hang around and have folks say she was still after you."

"I expect it's time we leave."

"Some men used to be daddy's deputies when he was justice of the peace is comin' over to ride us up to Vicksburg. Daddy say we ought not to be goin' alone."

"Isaiah, for once, be reckless. Let's go, you'n me, like old times. Take a bottle and we celebrate along the way."

"Well . . . Hell, why not?"

They reached the wartime canal and were heading onto the mainland when shots rang out. Wood splintered near Cicero's hand on the wagon seat. Isaiah turned the wagon while strapping his horses into a gallop. About the only comfort Cicero felt as they headed back into the Bend and relative safety was that the would-be assassin wasn't very smart. A second gunman bringing up the rear would have made quick work of him and Isaiah. The following morning, surrounded by six armed men, Cicero rode out of Davis Bend forever.

Second Time Around

To Coahoma County, January of 1874

Cicero was mortally weary as he boarded the Bartable II, hardly having slept the night before. He walked over to the cargo rail of the steamboat and leaned against it. The river at his back gave him a certain security after the danger-filled ride into Vicksburg. He hunkered down as so many around him were doing as they got underway.

The overcast morning draped Cicero's weary shoulders like the pearl gray cape he wore. By the time the boat paddled away from Vicksburg and headed into Milliken's Bend, swift current from the clear northern channel caught them. The steam boat shuddered as cinders flew and engines churned to break the river's grasp and move ahead.

Cicero pulled himself away from the railing and joined the passengers toward the rear, grateful for their body heat. The cold steel of Blacksmith's pocket pistol seemed to burn through his shirt. An ice-fanged wind still slashed at his hands and face.

A horn blast scrambled gulls into the air. When an unseen boat answered, quite a few abandoned their sheltered places behind a pile of cargo to run gawk at the second boat, and Cicero squeezed into the still air. Dropping to his rear, he removed his stove pipe hat and placed his portmanteau atop his legs for whatever warmth it might bring. A woman with four children who'd left to look at the passing boat were back crowding around.

"Are you alright, mister?"

Cicero nodded as the woman knelt alongside.

"I got these beans for my chil'ren, and you welcome to some if you feel up to it."

"Thank you, but no."

The children were munching on what looked like frozen hunks of cooked beans broken out of a sack.

"My name's Clothilde, mister. Goin' back into them Miss'ippi Bottoms to try'n find my pa. He used to live in Arkansas, and he always said to look for him in Helena if we got separated. So I'm comin' for him, now that we free. You got people up there too?"

"A sister and a very close friend."

"Um hunh! Lots of our people got families all busted up. I got my first son livin' up on a Mister Alcorn's plantation. I'm stoppin' there first to find him."

"Nigga Jim Alcorn!"

"Yessir, he the one. Used to own me 'till his wife had me sold to a man from Natchez. If you need direction when we get to Friar's Point, I used to live there."

Cicero napped intermittently, the black river falling away behind the boat. Perhaps because of the nearness of the woman with the children, he came out of a dream thinking that Rose was beside him. When he called out to her, she faded. He awakened that night to find himself wedged between Clothilde and her children.

Cicero did not fully awaken again until sometime before sunrise, but he'd missed a morning in between. The boat was easing along shore, and winches had begun whining to lower the gangway. Now, he struggled to his feet with Clothilde's help.

It was bitter cold, though the wind had died. Cicero huddled as long as he could in the shelter of the cargo until half of the others had disembarked. That was when, in the light of lanterns hung along shore, he saw the men. Identical hats and long coats flapped in the breeze.

"Them men looking for you, maybe?"

The cold grabbed Cicero as a group in front of him headed down toward the gangway. His smile broke off in a cough, and he lost his hat to the resurgent wind.

"Would you," Cicero asked, "unfold your blanket around my shoulders—here, take my cape, please. Tell anyone I'm your husband."

While Cicero was disguising himself, the men stepped onto the gangway and examined the passengers onboard. There was a commotion forward as someone lost control of a crate of chickens. It hit the deck and broke open. The birds fluttered over the side and into the water. The owner of the chickens jumped into the river and got one of his legs tangled in a line. A boatman pulled him out, but the man was so bedraggled even the two armed men began to laugh.

"Mister, what you involved with?"

"I was a politician. Some think we should all be ambushed."

"Just stay with me'n the children until it git more light."

Cicero exited with his arm around the woman, Clothilde, and they walked to a cargo area and sat on the dock where they bundled up as best they could, and they waited. There was no visible sunrise, just a darkness that turned more grey. Clothilde walked over to the boat merchants and began asking directions to where she was going. Then she sought transport for Cicero. A black man loading a freight wagon bound for the interior said he'd take a passenger for a half-dollar.

Cicero started out sitting on the wagon tail, but a hacking cough was convulsing him so regularly that he sought shelter among the wagon's freight from the rising wind. Nor did he remove Clothilde's blanket except to don his cloak underneath. He sat looking backward, marveling at the wildness of everything. Trees forty and fifty feet tall played court to giants over a hundred. Along the horizon west of the Mississippi, they created a funereal tapestry of bony spectral arms against the gray sky. An occasional evergreen intruded, sometimes a few together in clumps like dusty jade.

The wagon hit a rut and bounced off the edge of the log-covered road. The driver cursed, then struggled with his wheels trailing off the edge of the logs. When he jumped them back on top, the jolt doubled Cicero over.

"Is that there yours?"

Cicero turned to face forward.

"Is what mine?"

"That there pistol."

Cicero hadn't noticed his pistol fall onto the wagon bed. When he looked up, the driver held his own pistol.

"Ain't want to strand a man out here, so I best hold onto this little gun. Gotta search you, too."

Cicero submitted to a search in the cold air. The driver pulled off Cicero's blanket, his cloak. Inside Cicero's jacket he found a letter. The man opened it and read Abyssinia's name.

"You know Abyssinia Morgan?"

"She's my sister."

"Be damned, fella, if that ain't a woman I knows. You shiverin' somethin' fierce. Git wrapped back up'n lay down."

"Looks like a storm coming."

"Like dancin' devils, ain't it. I got tarpaulin. You just lay back."

As the wagon moved ahead again, Cicero couldn't stop shivering. He was sweating underneath his clothes, and he had no feeling in his cheeks.

Rose was in her rocking chair looking out through the open door at the snow coming down. A fire was roaring in the stone hearth to her back. An unusual silence had descended on the swamp, and it held until melting snow began to sound like a growling bear. Hours had passed in meditation. Rose walked outside and lifted her face to taste the blowing errant flakes.

Before Rose walked back inside, the wind banged her door shut, made her heart beat fast. The trees began rustling as if victims of the slave pens at Land's End were crying down to her. A swirl of snow and winter-burned leaves sprayed off the cabin roof into her face. She hurried inside and reached for her plum wine.

As evening approached she came awake. Wine preserved with whiskey had deadened her caution and the rest of the day. It had commenced snowing again, more heavily. Her throat felt scratchy, so she dipped hot water to steep rosehips. A mongrel chill had slunk inside while she was sleeping. It kept nipping at her until she crawled back under her bed covers.

Back in bed, she was soon drifting in between sleeping and waking. Her thinking and dreaming left her body, the cabin. She felt threatened until she began seeing her time at Davis Bend, not her welcome time with Cicero but the aggravation of Abyssinia. Only once had she seen the headstrong young woman since their winter together. Abby had been walking across the new Sunflower River bridge at Clark's Landing. Sitting in a boat on the river, Rose had said nothing.

Dawn coming in through the shutter found her awash in the frustration of incomplete clarity. On went pants and sweater, a dress over them. Her throat felt better, but she still carried a disagreeable sense of something to be discovered. She drew her rocking chair close up to the hearth, rebuilt the fire and watched it catch. As the sun burned away the overcast, an urge to paddle up to Clark's Landing and walk among people ripened.

She settled instead for going out to feed the chickens. The storm front had passed, and melting snow was steaming off tree limbs. She had to stretch to place corn inside the chicken cage because it was suspended high against varmints. Then she gathered the eggs and walked leisurely back toward the cabin. Off-trail, she had piled stones left over from building the fireplace. A nice warm stone heated in front of the fire would feel good that night. Unfortunately she could free up only one hand by shifting the eggs to the other. So she used her foot, tapping the stones repeatedly to knock snow loose. Then she kicked harder and the pile shifted. One stone rolled free. When she reached for it something stung her hand and she dropped her eggs.

A rattlesnake fell from her arm. It had holed up among the stones for winter and was sluggishly wriggling without direction. She kicked it away and walked inside.

Inside the venom-born enchantment thoughts could expand to fill hours. She barred the door, closed the shutter and put more wood on the hearth, then dabbed her wound with an oil-saturated lamp wick to help it heal. A little dizzy by then, she settled into her chair by the fire.

Drowsiness weighted her eyelids, and sound gave birth to itself inside her head. Warmth from the fire soon lured her into it, but as she gave herself over to the comfort, the dull ache in her hand interfered. The throbbing grew and spread until it mated with her beating heart and echoed in waves of disquiet.

This was the dream world, where trying to think made her mind separate from her body, where distance took no time to travel and past was present. At the same moment she was both in The Bottoms and at Land's End, and when the thinking, moving self came to rest, she felt the sea wash over her in the same instant that she and her Jasper were entering the waters of their pond.

Water was still touching her feet when she heard the wind die. In front of her was a sunken freight wagon, its victim shrouded and gasping. Overhead, a woman Rose recognized as Abyssinia was wringing her hands and pleading to be told what to do.

THE FOLLOWING MORNING, a crystal dawn cheered Rose up-river. When she reached the point where the trees had been cut back from shore, the wind sprang up, and she pulled a knitted cap from inside her bearskin to cover her head. Her thick hair—recently invaded by a few gray strands—resisted the mashing down.

Around a bend in the river, the Indian burial mound beyond which John Clark was marking off his town came into view. Rose pointed her boat toward the cross-river ferry dock.

"Mornin' Miz Rose!"

"How do, Nathan. I need directions."

"You give me whiskey on credit. I owe you."

Abyssinia's house had a front gable rising from a roof that sloped over a porch screened on front and side. The door opened before Rose reached it, and a red-eyed, pale woman whose skin looked as if the sun never touched it ran onto the porch.

"Rose! Momma Rose—I'm so glad to see you. Tell me what to do."

"You tell me what happened—is he shot?"

"No ma'am."

"That's a relief."

Rose hurried out of the parlor and into the adjacent bedroom where light from a lamp was flickering in Cicero's face. He was thrashing around, gasping, making puny efforts at coughing.

"He gonna live, Rose?"

"Not from you worryin'. Who that in your back room?"

"That's Mr. Gene Woods, a local businessman."

"Got anything to do with my Cicero?"

"Gene's wagon brought him."

"Ahhhh, he's your man."

"No ma'am, we just friends. I needed somebody to do for my brother."

"I'm here now. Go on about your business."

"Are you sure?"

"You lived with me. Ever know when I wasn't?"

As Abby joined Gene Woods in back, Rose kicked off her boots and pulled skins for her feet from the pouch inside her coat. Before putting them on, she sat in one of the bedroom chairs and stuck her toes close to the fire.

After warming herself, she changed the bed sheets. She dressed Cicero in a dry shirt from his bag. Then she mixed a potion of dewberry leaf tea and dribbled it into his mouth. He was anointed with coal oil before a bowl of pine sap in boiling water was placed on his chest, its steam captured by a sheet over two straight-backed chairs. As quickly as beads of sweat popped out, Rose would towel them off. All night, she tended him. Toward morning, she fell asleep.

Rose came awake after an upstairs door opened. Abyssinia's footsteps rang out on the back stairs as she descended from a loft where she had spent the night. Rose stirred herself and walked back to report. In the kitchen, Abyssinia was dressed in a starched bib apron tied over a gray dress.

"Morning, Abyssinia."

"Sure is," she said, turning with a sigh. "Cold, still. One day the Lord bring mornings like this without us having to work."

"You a church lady now?"

"Got to have somebody, Rose. Seem like I lost or run away from everybody else."

"Well, your brother will be with us a while."

"Praise the Lord."

Back in the front bedroom, Cicero opened his eyes. A light that was more a stream of honey colored his delirium. When Rose returned and blocked it, his eyes opened again, and she took his hands. When she touched his cheek, he asked, "Are we dead?" and she started crying.

Gene Woods drove Abyssinia to work. As soon as she departed, Rose pulled Cicero out of his soiled clothes and shirt and bathed him. She dressed him like a mummy in dry sheets pulled from Abby's other bed. In the back yard a fire was built for laundry, and into the pot went all the soiled sheets, Cicero's personal clothing. Then Rose brewed a tea of yellow mullein, hops and red pepper to settle her patient's stomach. Red clover and wild lettuce were added to make him sleep.

All day Rose kept the two-sided fireplace in the wall between the parlor and the front bedroom stoked up. Cicero slept, even as Rose forced more tea into him. After she had finished rinsing and hanging the laundry to dry, she lay by his side and slept.

Cicero awakened as Abyssinia stood in front of him with a steaming bowl. Then Rose moved into view. It was to her that he spoke.

"You can't imagine."

"Missed you, cherie. You can't imagine neither.

"What can't I imagine?"

"Oh, Cicero, I have waited so many evenings, so many days."

"Hello Abby. How've you been?"

"Better than you by looks of things."

"Is this your house?"

"I kept store and did all sorts of work. Are you really alright?"

"Don't worry about him," Rose said. "You go on to work."

"No, he needs to eat, and I want to help."

"Rose? I thought that was you in the light . . . When was that?"

"Yesterday morning. You've slept a full day since then."

Rose opened her hand to Abyssinia for the bowl.

"Bless you, Rose. I'm late for work."

Boiled cornmeal had never been a favorite of Cicero, but he ate. Abby had dribbled honey all over it. Mainly, he sat and stared at Rose, recalling moments of their brief life together. She cleared her throat, pushed back her hair.

"You don't talk as much as you used to."

His mouth was full.

"Go on eat."

When she offered the spoon, he turned away.

"So what," he said, "should I talk about first?"

"What are you doing here?"

"Don't you know?"

"Come for your sister, me—what?"

"I have never been closer to anyone than you. I have a life to live, don't I?"

"Shape you was in you needed a place to die."

"Just as I remember, tongue sharp as a blade. If you only knew what I've been through since—"

"I asked you why you come up here?"

"I came to find you. Rose I've never felt like one person with anyone else."

"Oh sure. Do you think I'm a simple fool?"

"Well, you asked me . . . And why are you angry?"

"You just spent ten years away from me. Got nerve to ask me why I'm angry."

"Oh, so it was my fault?"

"Whose would you say?"

"Excuse me!" It was Abyssinia. "I'm gone, Rose. Hope y'all have a nice chat."

Rose followed Abyssinia to the door before returning to the bedroom with more mush and a piece of bacon.

"Cherie, it wasn't right what I said. Tell me what you want, when you want."

"I'm not sure where to start." His hand held off the spoon. "I got elected like I wanted to."

"Really did, hanh?"

"Yeah. No idea what I was getting into."

"What was it like? You was up in what they call the capitol with all the white folks?"

"We had forty elected by the time I left—I mean we had forty of us elected in '71. There was talk of Federal laws being enforced for the first time against holdover Confederates. The new governor seemed about the best we could hope for. There were just enough of us to make me think building a new life after slavery was right around the corner . . . Overnight, it all changed."

"Um hunh, spect so."

Rose placed the bowl of mush on the bed table. With her fingers, she caressed the stubble on Cicero's face.

"Yes, that was the big surprise, what happened amongst ourselves. We never had the numbers to run things, but instead of concentrating on the poverty we all had suffered through as the main issue, we started going every way, one to build a farming business, another off to Washington and then back to run a new college. Some of us began bragging about how our success was an example to the next generation, and then there were a lot of us who weren't very successful about anything except in showing the white delegates we could think like them . . . Every one of us knew that nobody should have to grow up poor and misused, but we could never make that our program. The old masters were never challenged."

When Cicero awakened that afternoon, there was not a sound, not even a floorboard creaking.

"Rose?"

He felt her hand on his arm.

"You called?"

"Where were you?"

"Restin', thinkin'. I ain't never claimed to be perfect, so 'scuse me for getting ahead of myself this morning."

"You remember *Mr. Cicero's Book*? Helping those refugees made me feel less guilty for me'n my family staying behind while people I'd grown up with got sent everywhere. My pa . . . My pa was probably the greatest man I've ever met. Not the politicians, they turned out to be just ordinary."

"Keep on talkin'. Git it all out."

"We had so much hope after I was first elected."

"What about the people back at Davis Bend. Mr. Ben, your momma?"

"Momma died some years back."

"Let it go. Let it all out."

"She didn't get a chance . . . to enjoy much of my life or hers."

"Kin I lay alongside while you talk, cherie?"

Cicero was encumbered by the sheets he was wearing. Rose pulled him free of them then bounced out of bed and pulled Cicero's freshly laundered shirt from his bag.

"Here. Put it on and cover yourself."

"Speaking of momma makes me real sad . . . I have a son."

"You what?"

"I have a son . . . Momma Nancy never saw him. She died in the cookhouse where she'd worked."

"I know how you feel."

Rose leaned over and stroked his forehead.

"There was a young woman . . . Old George the Butler's daughter by the younger woman he later married. They called the girl Old George's daughter . . ."

"Why are you smiling?"

"George was way too old to be that girl's poppa."

"Sound like the old man had his reasons to claim the child."

"I suppose . . . One night—"

"Forget about you'n her. Tell me about your boy."

"Buck is his name. Four years old this April."

"Don't hang your head. I ain't been a bump on a log neither."

ABBY KEPT BEGGING Rose and Cicero to go to church with her. One Sunday, she bribed Rose with a new dress—in gratitude for her help, she said. It was a wonderful dress, and Rose wouldn't put it down, kept rubbing its lacy collar and panels covering the bodice like so many wagon traces across the shoulders from front to back.

"I ain't a churchgoer," Rose said.

"Well, it ain't only about shoutin' for the Lord. My brother needs to meet the right people."

"I'm not a businessman. I'm not sure how safe it would be for you either."

"You have such a good background. Let people see you all dressed up. I've got a little money saved that you could put into a business."

"That reminds me . . . This house cost more than you could make in ten years."

"So what, I always liked nice things."

"You couldn't have saved up to buy it."

"Land is cheap. Eugene got me a special deal . . . Besides that, I had a sponsor of sorts."

"A sponsor?"

"Leave it at that . . . Will you talk business, now?"

"No. Shall I explain again?"

"I am just trying to help you."

Abyssinia rushed out ahead of what might have been tears. Rose signaled Cicero to keep silent. A door slamming marked Abby's departure.

"Do you feel up to walkin', cherie? Such a fine day outside even the air look pretty."

"You look gorgeous yourself, Miz Rose."

"Oh, hush up. You shouldda told me that when you first come awake."

"Well . . . "

Rose turned away and sighed, began fingering the faded dress she was wearing.

"Okay, mister man, just for you, I go dress up. I know a safe direction for us to go promenade and still be away from the white folks."

The dress was a high-necked affair whose trim lay crisp and white against Rose's skin. Cicero dressed in his suit and pearl gray cape.

As they entered the sunlight, Cicero squinted and sucked in crisp air tinged with smoke. He started fastwalking, speeding up whenever Rose tried to come abreast, and then suddenly he stopped. Rose stumbled into him, and Cicero held her close.

"Don't," she said, gently pulling away. "We shouldn't go no closer in toward the river."

"Just relax. I'm the one they're after."

"Who after?"

"Did I say that?"

"Yes, you did!"

"My arch-enemy is John Clark's brother-in-law."

"You perfect fool! So what're you doing here at Abby's?"

"She was easy to find."

"I got to go home, soon. My boy was off makin' liquor. He don't know where I'm at."

"Does Jasper have a family yet?"

"Non, non . . . Worries me 'cause living in the swamp make you feel alone."

"You—alone? I thought your swamp was heaven on earth."

"Don't play with me. I have wants like your sister, but I rather live out there than under these white folks."

For the time it took Rose to fix Cicero's eyes with hers, to touch her lips against his, they said nothing. He took her hands and began kissing them gently, until a breeze brought the smell of frying bacon.

"Hungry again?" she asked.

He nodded and put his arm around her.

"I know that you have to leave for home. I'll go with you."

By noon they had made their way to the rear of John Clark's house on a hill along the Sunflower River just north of the settlement. Abby opened the kitchen door with her finger to her lips, then eased outside.

"Old darky ain't supposed to have comp'ny when she workin'."

"I'm leaving with Rose. Thank you for taking care of me."

"Wasn't me. It was Rose."

"You did your part, and I'm grateful." Cicero gestured toward the mammoth house behind Abby. "I'm leaving now because I want no dealing with all this."

"That's crazy. We got worthy folks just like white people."

"I don't want my being here to involved you."

"What do you know about livin' in the swamp?"

"I know enough," Rose said, "for him and me both."

Abby's lips quivered. She was about to speak when a voice from inside the house called her.

"'Sinnia! You cannot go to church if you work like the other lazy niggers around heah."

"No ma'am, comin' right in . . . I got to go," she said, wiping at a tear. "You goin' into that swamp will make a lot of people who could help you wonder why you don't want their company." Then Abyssinia took a deep breath and smiled. "I know. You're different. I'm happy you come find me."

Rose put a hand on Abby's shoulder, and the women hugged.

"Rose, take him back by the Alligator Lake, please."

"River be more direct, cherie."

Cicero said nothing, remembering a second letter from his sister that had spoken of 'the alligator lake,' and of a child. Abby turned to her brother.

"You a schoolteacher, Cicero. Certified and all from our college. I got a son whose daddy promised you could teach the boy when he got older. He's a white man, and now's the best time for you all to meet . . ." She paused, then went on even though it seemed she couldn't find the precise words she wanted. ". . . Going there dressed like this, you look better."

"As you wish . . . Rose?"

"Yes, cherie."

"We'll go by way of—Alligator Lake, is it?"

"'Sinnia!!" The white woman again.

Abby flew inside like a startled bird, but she stopped behind the screen door and waved.

"C'mon, Cicero." Rose said. "That white woman be raisin' more Cain if she see us."

Rose led Cicero across the Sunflower River out of town heading west. There was a narrow swath through a thin forest whose largest trees had been harvested. Ahead, the world Cicero knew fell away. Back toward the Sunflower, trees stretched off to the south without a break. Toward the Mississippi River, new fields draped the higher ground between stretches of bayou water. Smoke trails rose like clans, spirits of unseen farms below. And then the path turned more due south into the heart of the swamp.

Alligator Lake was narrow and curved like a scimitar. Rose led Cicero off the main road, west along the southern shore. The settlement was only a couple of houses among the original towering oaks. The store of Abyssinia's interest had been built five years earlier, Rose explained, by an Irishman who blew gruff and jolly as his moods swung and who adored women, black and white. They asked for Jim Dolan, but his clerk directed them to Dolan's house.

A half-hour later they passed a low-lying marshy area filled with woody anise gone yellow and brown in the cold. A dozen burial mounds loomed on the left creating an oddly pleasant rolling family of little hills in the surrounding flatness. They found the trail the clerk had described, and Dolan's house soon came into view.

A dark-haired, stocky boy with green eyes yanked open the door.

"Who you?"

"Is Mr. Dolan home?" Cicero asked.

"Who you?"

Rose eased to the front and smiled. "You're Mr. Dolan's boy, non?"

The child nodded once.

"Is your pa home, cherie?"

He darted away and returned leading his father. Eyes of father and son were the same emerald green.

"I'm Cicero Morgan, Mr. Dolan."

"Aye, aye! Expecting you one day, I've been, and judgin' from your clothes, you're a gentleman."

Dolan stepped outside, closed the front door behind himself, and offered his hand.

"My sister said you'd be expecting us."

"And right she was!" Dolan said. Then he lowered his voice. "If you don't mind, I'd prefer to keep this conversation brief on account of the lady inside who keeps me company has a tender sense o' these things, but I know why you're here, and it suits me. You've met the party in question. I intend to give him what I missed as a lad. Know what I mean, Mr. Morgan?"

Cicero nodded.

"The boy's too young now," Dolan said, "but in the fall, a year hence, come spend a week with us. Find me at the store, or here—wherever."

"I could give you references."

"And why would you be thinkin' that necessary?" Dolan leaned close. "A gentleman of quality, you are—Abyssinia's kind. Afternoon, Rose. How's business?"

Rose said nothing beyond a dismissive motion of her hand. Dolan saluted them and turned back inside. The boy's voice rang out.

"Who's that with the medicine woman, pa?"

"A Mr. Cicero, lad. 'Tis a gentleman he'll teach you to be."

The sun was almost below the tree tops as they walked away. The smoke spirits trailing above Alligator Lake had grown blacker and more numerous in anticipation of a cold night as Rose led them to the home of a woman who had befriended her. A pallet of quilts for Cicero was placed on the floor outside of what their hostess pointedly called Rose's room. They asked for some whiskey and a kettle of hot water for Cicero's medicinal needs. Rose brought it back to the room and sat at a doily-covered table to pour.

"Boy seems likely enough, Mr. Cicero."

He grunted as she handed him a toddy.

"Why so quiet, cherie?"

She sat next to him on the bed and began massaging his shoulders.

"Somethin' stuck in your craw?"

"No."

"White man called you, mister. Next thing, you tell him who you be an' all, but he don't care. He already know enough to suit him. Maybe he don't care 'cause you just another nigga . . ." Rose dug her thumbs into Cicero's shoulders. ". . . Him havin' a baby by Abby. Had to talk to him and you so mad at them people."

She stopped rubbing and draped her arms around his neck.

"You making a problem inside your head don't need to be. That man's feelin's don't count."

She walked over to the table and poured herself a toddy.

"You got brand-new feelings against 'em. They strong, like when I first made my escape. I would of made a war if it hadn't been for others in the family. They knew better. I needed time to simmer down and focus on living my own life."

Rose bent from the waist and kissed Cicero. She took his cup and returned to the table.

"Are we goin' to bed now?"

Cicero nodded, and opened his arms. When Rose walked into them, he pulled her close against his chest and rubbed his hands up and down her arms. She pushed him backward and scattered friendly little kisses all over his face. A noise from outside the room made them pause. Rose pulled away to struggle with her boots. Cicero stripped off his jacket, pants and outer shirt and lay shivering in the frigid room. Rose leaned over him.

"Cherie, if you want me now, I'm yours, but we gonna have better than a cold room and tired feet."

In a lassitude born of warm whiskey and fatigue, Cicero watched Rose as she wiggled out of her trousers. He grinned as she yanked her dress over her head and shivered quickly under the cover beside him. As soon as his cold hand touched her thigh, she yelped, and she returned the favor.

"Take your cold hand off me!"

"Cold man cain't complain, cherie."

He tried to kiss her only to feel a cold nose thrust into his neck.

"Yowww!

"Shhh . . . quiet."

"Then yield, woman."

Each struggled to hold the cold hands of the other at bay to the accompaniment of noisy bedspring.

"Cherie, the woman bedroom behind that wall."

When Cicero hesitated, Rose thrust her hips up and almost dislodged him. Moving against each other ignited stirrings of passion long remembered, so much and so intensely felt that for long minutes cold hands were forgotten. They watched each other's face reflect the ecstasy of touching as it possessed them.

To avoid the squeaking bed, he helped her to pull his pallet into the room. There on the floor, between the pallet and quilts pulled from the bed, they exhausted themselves in delights of sharing a single skin.

Of Wilderness Love

Inside the Swamp, March of '74

"Heaven is findin' the juice of life."
Rose, to her church-going friend

Jasper bristled into camp gun in hand. When Rose opened the door, and Jasper watched his mother wrap her arms around Cicero, he broke into a huge smile.

Together Cicero and Rose slept, ate, Cicero followed Rose around as she did cabin chores, she sat and listened to more of how his thinking had change. In those first days they became one person again. Neither gave any thought to differences that might still exist. It was enough to be children at play.

In some sense of granting his mother privacy, Jasper disappeared for over a month wandering through the swamp before returning to his mother's camp. When he did, building Jasper a cabin became the men's first chore. Jasper insisted they not cut timber close by. Instead, the trees were felled far to the west and floated in as close as spring flooding of the Hushpuckena River allowed.

The new cabin was to be erected a mile southwest of where Cicero and Rose lived. By the time Cicero went off for the cabin raising, Rose followed to cook for him and Jasper. When they did not return home, she remained to sleep on the ground. She it was who began to teach Cicero to hunt.

When the cabin work ended and Cicero and Rose returned home, chopping wood became Cicero's job, but there was only so much wood to chop. Soon, Cicero found himself with more time than he knew what to do with. He had no reading library, no correspondence with former associates. So he began to go off alone exploring.

Rose cautioned him to be careful, but it was not her way to force anyone, certainly not a grown man, to avoid danger. During one such trek away from the cabin, Jasper visited his mother and discovered that Cicero had disappeared into the swamp. Seeing anguish on his mother's face that she would not give word to, he swept a quantity of food into a sack and headed out tracking.

When he located Cicero, he waited hidden until Cicero attempted to ford a small stream. Jasper yanked on a creeper that continued across the water. When it began to move near Cicero's leg, Cicero panicked. He dropped his rifle into the water and ran.

"Where you goin'?"

"Who is that?"

"This Jasper. Look how you just lost your rifle. If you don't know about this swamp, you best wait until you do. Aside from the cutthroats, you got quicksand, water moccasins, bears. Stay at home unless you with me or momma."

The exchange soured the air, but they didn't have time to pick at one another. By the time they returned to camp, Bill Williams was sitting there.

Rose hadn't mentioned him, though Jasper had spoken of his whiskey partner. From the way Rose hugged Bill, Cicero quickly concluded there was some personal connection. Cicero held out his hand.

"You're Bill Williams."

"So you the one belong to her."

They all had a welcome laugh. Bill offered Cicero a drink and Rose some new tobacco. They sat and talked for several hours before Bill stood up and, without a word to the others, led Cicero away whispering he needed help gathering provisions for the whiskey season. Though Cicero had just returned home, it pleased him to go off alone without Jasper at his side.

"Corn cost 25 cents a bushel. It make two and a half gallons of whiskey. Sell it for maybe dollar and a half a gallon."

"And you trade last years whiskey for corn?"

"The cheap stuff, that's right. It come off the line first and last. Farmers glad to git it 'cause they ain't got no money."

For two whole weeks, Cicero lugged gunny sacks of sugar and bushels of corn back into their part of the swamp from across the Hushpuckena River. A constant backache reminded him of leaving Davis Bend, what he had previously assumed were nerves. To remedy Cicero's back, Bill fed him a potion of cornshucks boiled in something vile.

Their next job was mixing the mash.

"We mix the corn with water and sugar in barrels. Then we bury them inside a cage in the ground."

"A cage in the ground?"

"Critters like mash. We dig a hole, put down thick cane stakes, tie them together along the top with cane—that's the cage. We put the barrels inside."

"Sounds like a lot of work."

"Only when you startin' out. It last for years. Use it over and over. Got to make it strong. Varmints dig it up if we don't."

"You don't expect me to build one."

"No, the cage ready. After we bury the mash, we leave it alone. When we come back it be near ready to cook."

"I'm thirsty. What do you do for water?"

"Try this."

"Ach . . . It's good whiskey, but I'm thirsty."

"Take this piece of cane. Go down to the river and suck the water up from underneath the spores."

"What about your canteen?"

"That's whiskey, too. Got a little water in it. Want some?"

"What an awful taste!"

"Ground water around here got sulfur in it. Same as the smell of the blue mud. White folks got a name for it."

"Why is Rose's water different?"

"She catch it off her roof. She keep enough for a long time in the water barrels behind her cabin. 'Till it rain again."

"So you mix whiskey to kill the taste of ground water."

"You learnin'. Drink up."

"I'm drunk already."

"Then answer me a question."

"What?"

"You going to make Rose your squaw?"

"My life is hers, hers mine. I don't think I can make her into anything."

Bill stuck out his hand.

"My life hers, too, but she was waitin' for you."

CICERO STARTED MIXING ground water with whiskey, drinking a pint or more a day, and the alcohol began to tinge his time with mellowness. After returning from his travels with Bill Williams, he passed whole days marveling at the sound of his breathing, the feel of wind on his skin, the absence of so much weight in his mind.

As those crafts necessary to keep life going occupied Rose's time, Cicero was happy just watching and helping where he could. Rose worked a deer hide into a shirt of astonishing softness to go with the baggy trousers she had been sharing with him to keep his suits from being ruined.

He began to notice her mystical side—her visions, her herbs and secrets. Often Cicero awoke to find her gone, only to return later with some root or flower still wet with dew, when its potency was described as high. The first time he saw her use rattlesnake venom, he thought she was crazy. Until she explained about tolerance and offered to initiate him. When he declined, she shrugged and offered the whiskey jug.

Cicero cut a lot more wood than they needed, and he piled it for later use. Then he again turned his time to hunting, the solitude of which he rather enjoyed. Toward the end of summer, he took up swimming in earnest, either in the Sunflower or in the pond Rose used for bathing. The active life hardened his body, spread the balm of fatigue over him. He was happy.

One day Cicero hunkered down and allowed his alcohol-tinged mellowness to focus on an old log tracked all over with termite trails. Little tracks eaten into the wood just below the bark. The insects were gone, but their spoor lingered. That was when the idea for a chronicle of the lives of people Cicero had known took shape.

If the spoor of bugs lingered, so ought the life of a human being. Cicero was amazed how clear the notion was, and none of the books he had ever read told the story of black people beyond the respect that most of them had been slaves. None told of their struggles, happiness, real accomplishments. None told of men like him taking responsibility for making a new world. None celebrate how Rose had, in fact, created her own.

Cicero didn't get back to the cabin until just before dark. He opened his mouth to tell Rose what he'd been thinking, but she was arms-deep in a batch of plums for wine.

Morning found Rose just as busy again, Cicero in his quills and paper. After eating, helping clean up the cabin, Cicero sat against the sunny east wall going at his memories. First, from

the viewpoint of his mother, Rose, Jasper, Mr. Ben, Isaiah—
even some of the white folks who'd stirred in his life.

"Come sit awhile," he said. "I missed you yesterday."

"Let it wait, cherie! This fruit sit overnight in skins like this,
wine be bitter."

On such note, their summer turned to autumn. They all
were busier than ever preparing for winter, each in his or her
own way.

Cicero shot his first bear, a small one not more than a couple
hundred pounds. Jasper was almost as pleased as if he had
shot it. He showed Cicero how to cut it out of its skin. How not
to damage the pelt.

"Too little for a coat. Make a good vest. Good and warm
this winter. You kin put it on over anything. Tough, too. Them
burrs and thorns wont tear it."

"What about the parts you're cutting off?"

"Oh we use them too. Make leggin'. Wrap 'em around your
legs and arms to protect and warm you."

The bear finally dressed down to about thirty pounds of
ham. A couple of good-sized shoulders for roasting. Most of
the rest went into the rendering pot for lard. What was
skimmed out after the cooking was lightly salted for keeping.
It had the most delightful taste to Cicero. Nothing like the
crunch of pork cracklin, this meat had not been allowed to
cook hard. It was juicy and flavorful. His tasting turned into a
gluttony that forced him to lie down and sleep.

The weeks passed, and the intense preparation for winter
eased. Rose became free to talk when Cicero wanted to. She
even persuaded Jasper to cooperate. Cicero hunted so many
turkeys for quills that Rose complained she had eaten enough
turkey for a lifetime.

One morning, after a late night with candles and his quills,
Cicero awakened to a full-blown doubt whether writing words

on paper was worth the effort. He lived in no most perfect world, and he doubted if anyone in either of the worlds he did live in would ever read his book.

So he went hunting with Jasper and Bill. All day they walked, they drank, and they walked and drank some more. When they arrived home, Cicero was drunk.

Rose kindled a fire in the yard, and the men kept it going. Rose joined in the drinking, and they sat around the fire celebrating. Bill started singing and Rose joined in. Night cautions were ignored. Afterwards, Jasper hung around his mother's cabin listening while Bill and Cicero swapped tales.

"Tell me about bein' a political nigga," Bill said. "Rose say you know."

Rose passed Bill a pipe of tobacco. Cicero began a rambling tale beginning with how he was persuaded to run for the constitutional convention and how going off to build a new government had seemed a welcome change from keeping records for the navy. Then he began to explain the hidden detail: the men meeting in a party convention who make decisions the people never learn about; how the party picks issues and passes them to the newspapers so the people end up arguing about the party-selected issues as if from their own heads while questions of real change never get discussed. And he told then about meeting Charles Caldwell—Blacksmith—about his unshakable will to live and to protect those around him. As the night wore on Cicero began bragging about how Blacksmith and he had escaped lynching on the streets of Jackson.

". . . and without so much as a second thought, Charlie Caldwell drew out his pistol and—bamm—wounded the rash white boy through his head. I was there, you know. Only nigga I know of ever killed a white man and got off from the law."

"That there's the part makes me smile," Jasper said, poking Bill in the ribs. "Bamm! Solve a lotta problems goin' on now."

"Like what?" Cicero asked.

"Silly niggas goin' around callin' theyself grown, and they all scared to vote next year. Embarrass me to see a man gonna let some white man keep him from doin' anything he want to. Course, I ain't see no sense in votin' no way."

Late, after sleep claimed the others, Rose got up without lighting the lamp, pulled her rocking chair close to the bed.

"Cicero?"

"Um hunh."

"Most men feel a woman part of their life. She got to do for him, help him do whatever . . . Old Bill wanted that. But I don't want that. You just enough different that I wanted you here with me."

"I want to be here, Rose."

"Are you sure?"

"Well, yeah."

"But you ain't sure."

"I am certain about how I feel, Rose. I do wonder what to do with my time."

"You ain't through with politics yet."

"I have no plans."

"Non, non! All you got to do is make up your mind."

"Hell you mean?"

"If you got to leave me, go. If you stayin', stay."

Cicero moved out of bed in his underwear, shivered past Rose and stood by the fireplace.

"Maybe I'll go spend a few days with my sister."

"You do that."

"I owe Abby a visit. I'll work some things out."

"Decide what you want, please."

When Rose started around toward the bed, Cicero touched her arm.

"It wasn't about you and me tonight. It was me hearing Jasper talk about things outside. I just want to see what's going on."

CICERO PADDLED ALONE to visit Abyssinia. All he owned was
a formal suit and traveling cape, inadequate against both cold
and rough swamp trails. So he wore the new bearskin vest over
a pair of Rose's baggy trousers, and his feet were wrapped in
skins. Abby reported sick so they could spend time together.
Right away also, she bought Cicero new clothes—rough
shoes, denim trousers, another of twill and two cotton shirts.

It was the first opportunity for brother and sister to take
each other's measure as adults. They spent night after night
talking, about Davis Bend, the death of their mother, Abby's
trip into the swamp with Rose, Cicero's time in Jackson. Abby
persuaded him drive her to a soiree northeast of Clark's Landing on the edge of the place called Shufordsville. Joseph
Woods, a carpenter, brother of the man who'd driven Cicero
to Abby's house months before, was to be their host.

"Joseph is a well-off man," Abby said as her wagon neared
the house. "Good-looking family, friendly. His brother lets
me use this wagon for things like today, for shopping and
the like."

Amused by Abby's smile as she spoke of the man who'd res-
cued him, Cicero went ahead and parked the wagon. Joseph
Woods was opening the door.

"Come in, Miz Abyssinia—wife! Abyssinia's come. She got
her brother, too. Welcome to the both of you."

A thin nervous woman, presumably the wife, rushed up
and waited until Joe finished hugging Abby.

"Eugene's inside, Abyssinia," she said. "We was all hoping
you could come. Let me take you to him."

"That leave us to talk awhile, Mr. Morgan," Joe whispered
behind his hand. "Ain't gonna deny Miz Abby put me up to
this, but I'm gonna talk to you man to man."

Cicero smiled.

"What I got to say is—well, your sister helped me get started. She was housekeeper for the General Store. Mr. Stephen Levy owns it now. The man used to be his partner hired me to build that store."

"That would be Jim Dolan."

"Correct. When our people seen me workin' for a white man, well, the business just poured in."

"You built Abby's house too, didn't you?"

He nodded.

"Most important, we went 'round to all the Northerners, some others. Told 'em they owed it to my race to give one of us a chance. Wasn't no sense leavin' all the rebuilding after the war up to them white boys moved down from the North. I ain't met a white carpenter yet know what I know."

"I saw this downstate, Mr. Woods. No sooner had we got free, than a conspiracy rose up to keep us from working any-where except on the land."

"You know what you talkin' 'bout, Mr. Morgan."

"Oh, I don't know. A lot of successful people like you think I'm crazy."

"Naw, they don't, and I knows what you referrin' too . . . See us forward-lookin' colored mens got to bow'n scrape a little. We tryin' to coax the white man into actin' right. Now, course he don't want to, but times like now the onliest time we can come forward.

"It's all politics, you know. Well, what I really want to say is I heard your sister say you was a wild-eyed Radical don't want nothin' to do with white folks—naw, don't say nothin. I un-nerstan'. We was comin' outta slavery. I become a business-man, you went into politics. Ain't neither of us got what we set out to git. Now, when you arrived, my brother says you wasn't only near dead, he say you was ate up with hatred. Been marked as a Radical. Shot at. I wouldda felt the same as you about dealin' with the white folks if I'dda been in yo shoes. But now you had time to cool off. If you wants to open a school here—"

"A school?"

"Abby say you been a teacher, college trained and all. Me'n my brother Gene would be pleased to stand behind you."

"Joseph!"

It was his wife calling.

"C'mon, Mr. Morgan," Joe said. "We'll have other folks here soon, and my wife wants to meet you."

"What of the local sheriff?"

"You don't want to get too close to him."

"Why?"

"He a Northerner. Wasn't a slave like me'n you. Don't appreciate our ways."

"How so?"

"Look, I introduce the man to the woman he married, local gal named Missouri. He let some carpetbaggers mash his head outta shape and push him up against me. He fancy hisself a big race leader."

Rose sparkled upon Cicero's return. When he asked why, she wouldn't say. By mid-November, the light in her eyes went out.

"Thought I was carryin' a baby."

She gathered up a basket of clothes and headed toward the pond.

"How come you're so sure?" Cicero yelled after her.

"Got my monthly, that's why."

"How can that be?" He ran behind her. "I mean, you aren't sick, are you?"

"No, I'm not. No more than you."

He tagged along, waiting, unsure what to say until the pond came in sight.

"Is it," he said, "too cold for bathing?"

"Not for me, mister school teacher man."

Cicero stuck his hand in. The water was cold but not painfully so. The sun had warmed the shallows, and neither had been accustomed to heated baths. Crouching along the edge, Cicero waited for Rose to begin talking again, but she didn't.

"Do you want a child?" he asked.

"Yes, indeed. Don't take this the wrong way, but why you think a woman my age couldn't seem to get enough of you, cherie. Not that I don't enjoy every moment we lay together, but I was hoping . . . On the other hand, I got no need. Children are for family living, even if family is just two people like me and Songhai. I could of been momma to one, and I would of loved it like I didn't have time to love him." She nodded her head in the direction of Jasper's cabin. "Him and me was runnin' all the time. Survivin' was more important than huggin' and playin' games. I had more life than my boy when I was a child, because I had a momma didn't go nowhere."

Rose dropped away from Cicero to begin bathing, but continued talking.

"Problem, cherie, is you, me and the world."

"You are full of the world these days."

"Don't make fun. You ain't sure what life you want. I 'spect you be leavin' sometime, maybe your school teachin'. You that kind of man. For Jasper, surviving was enough because he was there. I had no choice but to keep us living."

"I don't understand."

She caressed his face.

"Gettin' cold," she said, moving out of the water and reaching for her untouched washing.

The bickering that had cropped up before Cicero's visit to

Abby ceased. He and Rose were cordial, romance flaring anew as each of them seemed moreso to let the other go. Coming back together was sweeter, more intense. Each seemed better to appreciate the other's need to go off in his or her own pursuit. Some shift had occurred. Space between them was once again blessed.

In such good feeling, Cicero persuaded Rose to go visit Abby for Christmas. Jasper and Bill decided to go pass the holiday with a group living deeper inside the swamp.

They arrived at Abby's around noon on Christmas Eve.

"Got a surprise for Rose," Abby said.

"Whatcha buy this time?"

"I cleaned your dress—the one I bought while my brother was sick. And look at these."

She pulled a pair of shoes from a bag.

"Ballroom slippers," Cicero said.

"And covered in a shiny white cloth. They'll look so good with my dress . . . Where are you pullin' me off to, Cicero?"

"I want to see you in those shoes. The dress is beautiful, but I want to see your legs in those shoes."

That night, as accessories to the new dress and slippers, Rose wove rust-red leaves of a wintering cypress around her hair, more at her waist. The house was decked out, too, thanks to Eugene Woods "He's just real nice, Cicero. He likes to do things for people," was Abby's response to her brother's teasing.

Gene cut fir boughs and tied them to Abby's doors. Just inside the screen porch he set up a table with cups and a jug of water. He placed whiskey jugs underneath the table for those who would insist on serious drinking. In the dining room, a large bowl of punch on a lace-covered table was Abby's centerpiece.

Gene Woods' brother, Joe, and his family were the first to arrive. Caroline Edwards—in her sixties but a bosom buddy of Abby's—rode in with the Woods family from Shufordsville. Abby hugged her lovingly. The woman pulled Cicero aside and demanded to know all about him. She was the one who had introduced Abyssinia to her church. Cicero also heard the woman comment that she had introduced Abyssinia to the father of her child.

Rose moved about, keeping to herself. She fortified the weak punch and soon was walking around watching the festivities with what one pesky old codger called a man-eating smile. Each time Abby introduced Rose, she described her as a woman from the outskirts of town. When Rose finally blurted out that she lived in the swamp, Abby walked away. Later, to Gene Woods' inquiry about what was going on, Abyssinia whispered, "She's a friend of my brother's from the old days."

Midway in the evening, somebody said that Captain Brown was tying up his horse. Gene Woods ran outside, and Cicero followed.

"Welcome, Mister Sheriff," Gene said. "Miz Abyssinia would be here herself, but she got her hands full."

"I understand," John Brown said. "And this must be the Honorable Cicero Morgan."

"I haven't been addressed like that in a while."

"Don't expect you have. They call me Captain Brown."

Cicero accepted his hand. Brown was a ruggedly-built and tallish man.

"Please call me, Cicero."

Gene Woods was looking on curiously.

"Do you mind if I have a few minutes of the sheriff's time, Gene?"

"Oh! Well, of course not. I'll go back inside."

Joe Woods opened the door for his brother. The sheriff and Cicero saluted both of them.

"What," Brown asked, "do you know of me and of the men yonder?"

"An important man is ever on view."

"Us together even more so."

"Did you move here on business?"

Brown shrugged.

"I mustered out of the army and came here to work for General—I mean governor—Ames when he was appointed governor. One of his men convinced me to support Ames when the locals of James Alcorn's persuasion bolted our party for their own. That's how I became sheriff—Ames appointed me. He knew he could trust me up here in Alcorn's county. When I ran for office in '73, I got as many Northern votes as black votes. Joe Woods and some of the rest voted for the Alcorn candidate."

"Why did you settle here?"

"For land. Ohio is a hard place."

"So why does Joe Woods mistrust you?"

"I'm an interloper, an outsider who doesn't show enough respect for him or for the good white people like Alcorn that he supports. They always called the white man 'captain.' 'Captain Brown' is their little joke—I carry myself like a white man . . . I've grown fond of my name."

"Nobody thinks everything through, John."

"You're a philosopher, too?"

"Oh no, but imagine my own disappointment when folks I'd grown up with turned their backs on me a year ago."

"Yes, it was a rough time. How our focus narrows. We always end up at odds amongst ourselves. I wonder if we'll ever be able to pass even that one message down, to keep another generation from committing the same error?"

"What keeps you pushing on? Beyond providing for yourself."

"I made a commitment to be the first sheriff to treat a black life same as a white one. I got a hunch we're a lot alike. Men like us feel guilty sitting back watching the world go by . . . You know, I don't usually speak this straight."

"And I never dance with folks don't know the steps."

They both smiled.

"I didn't come seeking this job," Brown said, "I just took it on."

"Even though you could get shot?"

"Oh, every little nigga hears somebody tell him what a great thing it is to work for the race. I did . . . So there I was, trying to buy up some land with a little money I'd saved, being called a fool by my family back in Ohio for coming into this hellhole. I figured I could do something for my people, do myself a little good as well."

"Bravo. You didn't confuse your success with progress."

"Have you seen my office in Friar's Point?"

"I was through there, but I don't remember it."

"Friar's Point is the seat of government, a Democratic stronghold, though we have some people of color in town. The great majority of our people still live on plantations or in Joe Woods' community near Shufordsville where those who could afford it moved after freedom. My own farm is between here and Friar's Point. Armed men refuse me access to the old plantations. I've been shot at six times."

The front door opened. Abyssinia leaned outside and beckoned. Rose was standing just inside. As she pulled Cicero away, he whispered, "I apologize for ignoring you. This has nothing to do with a school, either."

"It's a party, cherie. I done a little dancin' myself."

"Come visit after the holiday," Brown called out. "We outnumber white voters in this county almost two to one. As sheriff, I intend to make sure we can vote."

County of The Red Panther

Beginning of the Year, 1875

That winter in Coahoma County, a cold and biting wind stripped the cypress trees naked. Morning frost smothered the ground, and the sun warmed neither the land nor people. They wandered about bundled against the cold and each other. Rumors of bloodthirsty nigger soldiers chilled the blood of white children. Ghost Riders in prairie dusters were more than rumor to black children.

The name of the county derived from Choctaw words for red panther, though a red panther hadn't been seen inside of the county since before the war, at least not by those who lived within islands of cleared land. The county actually took its name from a beautiful young Choctaw woman named Red Panther by her father, a man of power reduced to a being trader after being conquered by those who now claimed to own the land.

Inside the swamp itself, always sheltered by its tree walls, life proceeded pretty much as usual. Bears and wild cats exacted caution. The unseen serpent glided soundlessly. Killing and dying happened in the nature of things. Trying to survive dictated a certain order, but human feeling was awry.

Bill Williams knocked on the door. He had returned the night before with Jasper from their holiday in the deep swamp.

"Hey Rose, I brought up more tobacco this trip."

"Been almost a month since Christmas, where was you?"

"I was walkin' in the swamp with the boy."

From leaning on his rifle barrel, Bill turned toward Cicero who got up from the rocking chair and offered it as a courtesy to Bill. Jasper pushed inside to warm himself at the fireplace as Bill lay his tobacco on the table. He paused to look at Cicero staring out the window, then turned to Rose.

"Why your man ain't kept you happy?"

"Happy ain't got nothin' to do with where you'n that footloose son o' mine been."

Rose was sitting on the floor, a quilt around her legs as she attached hide strips to a piece of deerskin. Ignoring the chair, Bill ambled over and sat beside her.

"Come on, Rose. What's wrong?"

"You tend to your business. I tend to mine."

Bill struggled to his feet.

"Guess, I'll walk Jasper to his house."

"Hello, momma."

"Hello, cherie. Tell me what all happen—I'm curious."

"What you wanna know?"

"Just talk! Why everybody got to pick at me?"

"You'n Mr. Cicero didn't have much fun, that it?"

"What it is, he spent all night drinking with a man called the sheriff. Ain't talked about nothing but politics. If it ain't that, it's teachin' school. My house just a little pond, and he a big fish."

Cicero whirled around from the window.

"Quit blaming me for what I haven't done!"

Jasper beckoned to Bill.

"We goin' to my house. If y'all have need, come git us."

Bright and early the following morning, Cicero packed his portmanteau for travel and left it against the wall. Neither he nor Rose said a word about it. That evening, when Rose put plates on the table for supper, Jasper stuck his head inside.

"Come on in, shut the door. Nothin' but show up and eat."

"Aw, momma."

"Just sit down. I'm putting it on the table."

Rose was glaring at Jasper when she moved toward a cookpot in the fireplace, and she bumped her leg on a corner of the bed.

"What's wrong, momma?"

"Just keep quiet!"

One hand on hip, the other on her forehead, Rose closed her eyes and took a long deep breath. Her rocking chair had been pulled up to the table beside Cicero's. Moving toward it she bumped her shin on the rocker.

"Ah, Rose, let me help."

"Goddamn, Cicero—siddown! You can help me by burnin' that skinny-assed suitcase."

Rose pulled away from Cicero. Then she twisted her chair away from the table and collapsed into it. Jasper went and fetched the pot. Inside was a stew of hominy and tomatoes.

"Ain't we got no meat?"

Cicero startled everyone by springing up to open the larder and search around for whiskey, which he then brought to the table.

"We have to talk," he said to Rose. "I'm grateful for everything, but I've got to . . . You don't have to cry."

To hide her tears, Rose walked over to the fireplace.

"I don't have to do nothin', and neither do you."

"Rose, please. I know the people living out there."

Rose picked up a poker, smashed a coal in the fire.

"When will you'n me be together for good?"

"We're together now, always will be."

"Oh, Cherie, don't tell me that. Last time I felt like this I didn't see you for ten years."

"I'm going thirty miles up to Friar's Point. I'll be there,

down at Abby's sometime—I'll come home every week or so."

"Ain't Mr. Woods helping you start a school?"

"I never said I was going to do that."

"You ain't said nothing. That's the problem. Now, you going to live with your sister, and I know she do anything to get you outta this swamp."

"I wish you'd believe me. I can't live out there, so I can't be a school teacher. It's just that there is a very rare political opportunity here. We can win."

"That again."

"Time is passing. This'll be my last chance to change a little bit of the world."

"I don't like it. I don't like it."

"Sometime, Rose, you feel too much for your own good."

"Y'all quit fightin'," Jasper said.

"I am not fighting," Rose said.

"Well, whatever . . . I'm goin' home."

"No you don't. I want you to go with him."

"But, it's like war out there."

"So go on home," Cicero said. "Don't meddle in my business."

"Non, non! You git yourself killed, and momma be more sad."

"Ain't seem like you been so concerned."

"Aw, momma, I just—I hate his writin' and stuff."

"Writing and stuff is my life."

"You be dead playin' with them white folks," Jasper said, "'cause they ain't playin'."

Cicero reached for the whiskey.

"That's why I have to help the people I met."

"Help!?" Rose said, whirling from the fireplace. "Help who?" She slung her poker away and it crashed through the tiny glass window. "*You* need help! They will kill you out there."

"Our people have to stand up for each other."

"And who is our people?"

"Isn't your skin black?!"

"What can you do now that you couldn't before?"

"Things are different up here."

"How different?"

"Yeah," Jasper said, "tell us how it is."

"More of us to vote. We have a sheriff. I'm going out there to help us take control and turn the government over to the people."

"Shit!"

"Jasper, I can't abandon my family and friends."

"I don't know about all you been through," Rose said, "but you been telling me about Mister Charles Caldwell. One thing he said is so true. Your heart too good for your health."

The door opened and slammed. Jasper was gone. Rose sprinted and yanked the door open again.

"Get back here!" She yelled over the noise of the wind. "I want you with Cicero—and you stay with him!"

"Then give him a rifle," Jasper's voice said. "I come for him tomorrow."

THE MONTHLY Loyal League meeting was always held in Friars Point. Instead of paddling the entire distance, Jasper and Cicero left their boat with Nathan the ferryman in Clark's Landing and hired two horses. It was evening when they reached Friars Point, and Sheriff Brown walked out of his office to greet them.

"So glad you came, Cicero."

"This is a young friend of mine. His name is Jasper, and I want him to taste how it feels organizing our government."

Jasper stood silent in his bearskin coat, two rifles cradled in his arms. His face was somber, more grayed than black with an ashiness from the raw wind outside.

"Pleased to meet you, Mr. Jasper. Looks like you know guns."

Jasper remained silent. Others inside the sheriff's office walked outside and began milling around the door.

"Don't leave yet," Brown said to them, ushering Cicero and Jasper inside. "Here's a man from downstate you all should meet."

"Greetings, Cicero," Joe Woods said. "You a little late."

"Just wanted to pay my respects."

"Why don't you," the sheriff said to Woods, "go over what we've been talking about."

"I don't," Cicero said, "want to hold anyone up, perhaps your steering committee could fill me in."

"We ain't got none," Woods said. "All decisions together. None o' that committee shit they had back in '73."

"It wasn't," Brown said, "our fault the Alcorn people bolted and tried to take over the steering committee."

"You outta order," Woods said, "I got the floor . . . You all know things ain't been so good since our Mr. Alcorn fell out with us Republicans and went over to his own party. Now he's making noises like he a good Republican again, even though it's their own white-Republican stuff."

"Don't back off," Cicero said. "Alcorn is not to be trusted."

The room quieted. Brown clapped Cicero on the back for support.

"I'm surprised at you, Cicero," Woods said. "White folks done what was to be expected, what with Captain Brown here not willing to let them kinda run things in they own areas, but—"

"Just a moment," Brown said. "Would you please introduce our guest from downstate. Not all know him as you and I do."

"Oh, yeah—we have here, the Honorable Cicero Morgan. Used to be a member of the state house from Warren County."

The applause was scattered. Brown stepped up beside Joe Woods.

"He is the Honorable Cicero Morgan, member of the House of Representatives from Warren County. He grew up with and was a part of the famous Montgomery family, and he was a delegate to the Constitutional Convention. He was associated with Charles Caldwell, T. W. Stringer and the other stalwarts in our defense. He—Cicero, that is—was instrumental in the defense of Mr. Caldwell against his murder charge. Cicero also, I think, told me he was an associate of Gambrel Allington White, scion of an old Massachusetts newspaper fortune some of us know from his abolitionist days. Now . . . that is who you have in front of you."

The two deputies applauded with gusto, along with a man Cicero had taken to be the only white man in the room.

"I have heard of you, Morgan," the fair-skinned bespectacled man said. "I am John Cochran, county treasurer."

"Alright, so he was important some time back," Joe Woods said. "He's also the brother of sister Abyssinia. Y'all know Miz Abyssinia."

Several of the men nodded. A friendly comment arose.

"Thought y'all 'preciate that. He ain't no wild-eyed crazy man."

"You oughtta be ashamed, Joe. Mr. Morgan helped form the Councils of Elders. Are you implying that men like him were crazy?"

Joe Woods opened his hands in capitulation.

"Thank you, Mr. Sheriff, for fillin' us in on all that *old* history. Sittin' beside Mr. Morgan is a young friend of his named Jasper. His family clearin' land out in the swamp down below here. Believe me, it's true! He Mr. Morgan's son by marriage."

"I don't clear no land," Jasper said. "Only way to keep away from white folks is livin' in the swamp."

"There you have it," Brown said. "Not everyone is a businessman."

"I think," Cicero said, "we would all be wise to keep business and politics separate. I understand the pressures upon you good people, Joseph. But what you can't do, others can."

"Well, last election, Alcorn made me look real bad, and he

wasn't happy neither. Like I told you when we met, I'm in charge, and I want that clear."

"I assure you," Cicero said, "that I shall be guided by what you all decide."

"Now, if you folks hold off leaving, I want to explain our local organization a little bit more. Despite what the sheriff just said, we ain't no Radicals. All we been doin' today, Cicero, is gettin' ready to send word around the county so our folks know who we going to nominate come convention time."

"Which is the most important thing we have to do," Sheriff Brown said. He laid his hand on Jasper's arm. "Would you be a messenger for us?"

"Sheiiit!"

"We need men who wouldn't let themselves be pushed around. The people must learn what we're doing. That's how building a government starts."

"Don't press the boy," Woods said to the sheriff. "He know his own mind."

"No problem at all," Cicero said. "My young associate was commenting on how small a task carrying messages is."

"Didn't sound that way to me." Woods said.

"The young man and I will do what we can to help you. I will never run for office again, but I do want to help. I want Jasper to become part of what touched me as a young man."

"Mr. Jasper is a fine marksman, I'm sure," Captain Brown said. "Perhaps, he can help me guard some of your families."

"At least that make sense," Woods said, "and he ain't got no job to lose."

"Momma said to stay with you," Jasper whispered to Cicero. "Cain't do that if I carry messages."

"Don't worry. Unless I miss my guess, there won't be trouble so early in the year."

"I do it for you, but don't tell momma."

After the meeting dispersed, Sheriff Brown brought Cicero up to date on the local scene. The Coahoma County Loyal League had no funds. They needed money to pay those unlike Jasper who could not both earn a living and carry on the political work. The League had postage expenses, needed to rent horses, wagons from time to time.

Of one mind, they began working that night, writing letters to Isaiah Montgomery and T. W. Stringer and to several former abolitionists including Gamble White in Boston begging contributions. Brown made a list of Northerners who'd settled in the state and introduced him to Governor Ames as well as a list of his supporters and family back in Ohio. Plan was, in the following days, one of his deputies would copy the same letter to all and Brown would sign it.

He would also send a telegram to the governor advising him of Cicero's arrival and reminding the governor that some guns promised for the sheriff's office had not yet arrived from the armory downstate.

They also made a list of a hard-core group whose position in the county did not hog-tie them, who would not bow under pressure. An invitation would go out to them to assemble as soon as possible before the next Loyal League meeting.

A HANDFUL OF THOSE considered resolute were brought together on short notice. Brown and Cicero took great pains to avoid any hint of a secret meeting coming to light, knowing that it would rip the League apart. Not all of the fifteen they had identified had yet been contacted. Cicero, Brown and Treasurer Cochran held the meeting in the sheriff's office. They were joined by Jasper and Bill Pease, a heavy-eyed man singularly proud of having been a Union soldier. It was Pease who had been in contact with plantation representatives from Greengrove, Hopson and Big Creek. He reported them to be rock solid and willing to support any action taken by the League.

Pease was also the man Brown had identified to Governor Ames the previous year to head up a local militia what with the white power structure in opposition to Brown's law enforcement. Brown's thinking at the time had been that the mere existence of a local militia would deter violence come the election. For some months, it hadn't been safe for Pease to go home so he had lived camped out north of Clark's Landing with a couple lieutenants laying plans for the militia and interviewing applicants.

It was Pease who detailed why Joseph Woods was so sensitive about secret meetings. The steering committee of the League in '73 had been taken over by Alcorn after getting Woods, in the name of racial balance, to leave the sheriff and county treasurer off the committee in favor of two white Alcorn supporters. A motion was then rammed through to change the local party name to The Republican Party of Mississippi. Despite a hastily convened full meeting of the League that overrode the Steering Committee, Alcorn had it reported in the *Weekly Delta* as a done deal and further evidence of his favorite son leadership.

On Jasper's first swing through the county carrying information about the League, his biggest task was to relax. A maroon to the core, he would ride until he saw someone in the distance, then ride down off trail and wait for them to pass. Until he got tired of wetting his feet in the wintry water usually found below the outlying trails. It took him two weeks to cover the pockets of farmland east of Clark's Landing carved out of the edge of the wilderness.

During that trip, he took a boat along Moore Bayou to reach a settlement growing up around a Mr. Jones' store. Jones was no longer around. Alcorn had foreclosed on his acreage to recover a legal fee incurred in Jones' murder trial some years before. That was where the Senator was now assembling a new plantation called The Eagle's Nest.

On the nearby farms, Jasper searched out his contacts. They then introduced him to the handful they could trust. Which forced Jasper to trust people he didn't know. Though none of them wanted their activities known, being cooped up in a house from which escape would be tricky made Jasper break out in perspiration.

It pleased Jasper to be looked up to on the circuit, and Cicero, Bill Pease and others were actually relying on him. Never before had men his senior dealt him anything but scorn. Though he'd not once been shot at, all of the fear he'd worked through left him convinced that no one else could have done what he was doing, and he felt proud.

Jasper returned along Moore Bayou and retrieved his horse. His final stop was back toward the Mississippi River near Yazoo Pass in the north of the county. He had been instructed to stop on a Mr. Armistead's plantation to introduce himself to the League contact.

Approaching Armistead, Jasper crossed a narrow-gauge railroad running toward the Mississippi River. Along the line sat a cluster of farm buildings and one large house. Stretching off in both directions from it were sharecropper cabins, their green wood all warped and oddly pitched during the hot summers since freedom.

By now, Jasper felt more assured. From memory as instructed, for he could not read, he headed for the third cabin down the tracks. A woman his mother's age was sitting on the porch surrounded by four children, an infant in her lap. The two younger children, girls perhaps seven or eight, were stirring an iron pot over a fire.

"Evenin', ma'am."

The two girls hopped up onto the porch closer to their mother, who quickly turned the infant over to one and pointed toward the door. The girls disappeared inside, but two teenage boys hesitated until the woman whacked the youngest with the stir-stick from the wash cauldron. Jasper pulled up in front of her.

"Fine day, ma'am."

"Evenin', mister, what's your business?"

"You be Miz Clothilde?"

"Why you askin'?" the woman edged toward her open door.

"My name's Jasper. Sheriff John Brown said you was with the League."

"Oh shucks! Then git down off that horse. I was bein' careful 'cause Mr. Armistead threaten to get rid of anybody cause him trouble, and I know he ain't gonna be happy he find out about me'n the League."

"Ma'am, we gonna have a slate of delegates like always, and maybe some other things I don't know yet. That's why I come to find out if the people give us your name was tellin' the truth 'bout you workin' with us . . . You got a man I should talk to?"

"Talk to me. My baby's daddy got run outta these parts . . . Y'all c'mon back outside," the woman said to the children listening in the doorway. "When that happen, I swore to do what I could to change things."

A train whistle broke the silence that followed. Still in the saddle, Jasper clutched his rifle.

"Don't be scared," the woman said. "That's the cotton train they float back and forth from Arkansas."

In the center of the settlement, two white men walked out toward the track. One held a gun, the other a red flag. Jasper quickly dismounted, led his horse behind Clothilde's cabin.

"This a train stop," the woman repeated. "Don't be scared."

"Why he carryin' a gun then?"

"Mister Armistead been havin' too many croppers hop that train to the Helena ferryboat before he know they gone and ain't paid his store. So that there's the overseer. He come out with his gun when the train go by so nobody can leave."

HARRISON REID was the *Weekly Delta*'s former owner. He was also a lawyer, and with great patience he was conferring with a client.

"General, what's done is done."

"Alcorn's handling of the paper—and the niggers—just ain't cuttin' the mustard."

"Yes, Alcorn has an odd streak. Do you think it's in his blood?"

"Don't make me say something you'll repeat, Harrison."

"Cherokee or nigger—take your pick."

"I ain't about to fight no duel. I'll whup him when he run for governor."

A wagon pulled up outside the hotel. Through the lobby doors, two men could be seen stepping down. Harrison Reid excused himself and walked to greet them at the door.

"Welcome, Senator" Reid said, "and you, Mr. Clark."

General James Chalmers did not move. He waited until Reid brought the new arrivals inside.

"When John Clark drives JL Alcorn to see me," Chalmers said, "something's up."

Oh, hush up, General," John Clark said. "I have come about this new Loyal League development."

"It disturbs John's dancing lessons," Alcorn said. "Pity to take a man away from his cultural pursuits."

"I am not ashamed to be a man of culture. I have no time for the rest of your political nonsense because I have no ambitions in that direction."

Alcorn turned to Chalmers, extended his hand.

"General Chalmers, good to see you fit and virile."

With a politeness that did not extend beyond formality, Chalmers shook Alcorn's hand.

"So now," John Clark said, "let us hear what the renowned general proposes to do about the colored?"

"You saw," Alcorn said, "our front page article, didn't you?"

"Niggers don't read," Chalmers said, "and I did not think your running that story very bright."

"I agree!" John Clark said, then to Alcorn. "Your picture of the radical Morgan only served to show the colored what he looks like."

"Dear brother-in-law, he is not a candidate. Besides it also shows any number of white men with rifles what he looks like."

"What?" Chalmers pulled a cigar from his pocket. "Something I don't know about?"

"Be patient," Alcorn said. "Harrison and I practiced law way before the war. We've talked more about this new Radical push than anything. First—and this is for you General Chalmers—me refusing to sell the newspaper has nothing to do with running against you. After loosing to Governor Ames, I began thinking that I may have used up my political capital. There are many who'd vote against me but support any other white man. Much of what I hoped to accomplish already has been. Our state is up and running again, and we are an election—maybe two—from turning the colored vote into an insignificant thing."

"All of you relax a moment," Reid said, snapping his fingers. "I have ordered refreshment in the salon. Would you follow me?"

The four men entered a dimly lit room furnished with a chaise lounge and two stuffed chairs.

"Always did have a healthy opinion of yourself," Chalmers muttered to Alcorn.

"Enough to see there was no use fighting against Reconstruction. I was elected by the colored. I let you folks jump all over me."

"Are you tellin' me," Chalmers said to Alcorn, "that you have no intention of runnin' against me?"

"I am here today," Alcorn said, "to propose a partnership."

"What's he talking about?" Chalmers asked.

"What is happening," John Clark said, "is a coming together of all political stripes. Jim and I—a few others—have begun to see the need to subsidize activities we had not thought necessary until now. My own home and land are secure. I moved here when all considered the Sunflower River godforsaken. My own father had died in New Orleans with me at his side, and I had no prospects beyond a gentleman's education and debts. To pay them, I came here to cut and raft out timber for one season only. I stayed for another, and then I realized I should be foolish to leave.

"I sell timber and land. The war didn't threaten me, but the prospect of vindictive coloreds taking over my county is most alarming. How would they treat us? Why, like we treated them."

"Sometime you sound," Chalmers said "like the high-born Englishman you prob'ly ain't. Speak up."

"I would not," Clark said, "wish to shout in the face of President Grant."

"Understood," Chalmers said. "I just don't see where you goin'."

"We want to teach the colored," Clark said, "that they will die should they approach a polling place this year. All was well until John Brown teamed up with this Morgan fellow. He's the brother of my housekeeper—heaven only knows how it came about, her so refined, him so . . . Being a charming boy was probably his ruination."

"We are willing," Alcorn said, "to make monies available to the statewide plan."

"The Miss'sippi Plan?"

"Yes."

"And you have no problem," Harrison Reid asked, "if mischief should befall this brother of your housekeeper?"

"She worked for the Davis family. I assume you recognize the name. None of this is her fault."

"Some of us," Reid looked toward Clark, "have been raising money right along."

"As U. S. Senator," Alcorn said, "I cannot associate myself with that, but I am willing to help pay your men from Texas to tarry a longer spell in this county."

"These are military men," Chalmers said, "who fight under—"

"No names," Reid said. "Their work has been done all along the river, in Vicksburg, Greenville—you may make inquiries."

"No need," Clark said. "We are aware of the riots. So wonderful, James, that one may turn a killing into a riot with the magic of a newspaper."

"Things got out of hand in Vicksburg," Reid said. "We took no part in the continued shooting. A mass assault on the colored in this county would serve no landowner's interest."

"Hear, hear!"

"Thank you, John." Reid cleared his throat. "The monies Senator Alcorn and Mr. Clark contribute will be forwarded."

"Seems," Chalmers said, "all to the good, but let's go back to the matter of the Senator running against me?"

"General, you are such a common person."

"John Clark, you a goddamn snob! So-called architect, you up and forgot how to be a military officer before a shot was fired. You want me to keep talkin'?"

"Gentlemen, gentleman."

As Reid raised his hands, Alcorn examined his empty glass and began speaking into it.

"Trust me when I predict that the national government will just go away. If we succeed this year in holding control of this county, there won't be another colored vote of any magnitude because they will be afraid to vote. That is a prospect of such historic value that I should yield myself perhaps never to run again."

"Why didn't you," Chalmers said, "come to me before? John Clark ain't no fighter, but you, James . . . Nerve enough to call his new plantation the Eagle's Nest. Man call hisself a eagle."

"Thank god for difference," John Clark said, "but members of the white race stand together in India or in Mississippi. I suppose you, General Chalmers, know nothing of the East India Trading Company."

"More refreshments, gentlemen?" Reid said.

"No," Chalmers said, "let's get a little more out on the table, so's I understand. I do not imply that any gentleman here would lie . . . What of General Forrest?"

The men looked from one to the other. Clark made a dismissive gesture, walked to pour himself another drink.

"I should tell you how chagrined we all were," Alcorn said, "when he killed that colored man. Think of the impression that made on the national government. General Forrest is still a liability in Washington."

"His Klan," Clark said, "is an association of ruffians. I do not favor them."

"Why not?" Chalmers asked. "Keep the niggers in place."

"Every time Nathan lights up a cross," Alcorn said, "I have one or two hard-working croppers who pack-up and disappear."

"Too many niggers anyways," Chalmers said.

"No," Alcorn said. "We need every able body for the land. Only the Radicals are expendable."

Editorial

Radicals and outside agitators have descended upon us. Sheriff John Brown is one. He was appointed by the Governor, who must be considered a Radical sympathizer. With the clandestine arrival of the very architect of the Radical cabal in the Constitutional Convention of '69, the nest of vipers grows. (See February 22 article:"Radicals Among Us".)

That you may know the local malcontents, we publish the names of those who have joined the Radical conspiracy under color of the local Loyal League:

_____

_____

_____

Clothilde, Armistead Farm.

_____

We salute the good proud American colored who labor long and hard.

Weekly Delta

WHEN JOSEPH WOODS convened the next Loyal League meeting, Jasper came to his feet.

"My name is Jasper, and we got to protect folks workin' with us. They cain't run off like me."

"We always keep our posse massed against big trouble," the sheriff said. "We can't patrol everywhere."

Bill Pease cleared his throat, pounded his rifle stock on the floor.

"The Governor appointed me head of the local militia. Now I got some advice. Sheriff, you send whatever posse you got around so it do some good."

"Troublemakers would avoid a regular schedule, and the League has voted for me not to make unannounced visits to the plantations."

"Don't raise that issue again," Woods said. "White folks told you they ain't gonna stand for us sendin' niggas with guns near where they live."

"Us businessmen," another said, "got to look white folks in the eye every day. We cain't all be heroes'n give up our livin'."

"Folks is being beat," Pease said, "they calling on Jesus, and y'all niggas still believe the white man love you."

"I have a suggestion!" Cicero said, moving in front of Jasper and Pease to address the group. "For you who want to do something—shhhhh! I know, Bill, I want folks to be safe as much as you, but just listen."

"Then what do we do?" Jasper asked.

"Some of you may think that my head is in the sky," Cicero said. "But power never gives itself away. The one lesson I learned going from being a slave to becoming a member of state government was the importance of pushing against the people who oppose you."

"Don't," Woods said, "start that Radical talk."

"No more radical than letting a man work his own land."

There was a murmuring.

"Downstate," Cicero said, "all the land was developed, no swamp nearby to give us an option. We were thinking of the government advancing folks money to buy plantation land, except for those might come up here and relocate in the swamp. What if enough white landowners get religion and let us rent the land? We won't have to buy it. And even if they don't, think of the swamp . . . The state government is pretending to be on our side—at least for a year or so while a Northerner is head of it. It would probably sell the land on full credit as it does to plantation folks. Railroads get it for free."

Cicero paused and looked around the room.

"Just consider, withdrawal of even a third of the experienced laborers and sharecroppers in Coahoma County will force white folks to compromise with us—at least that!"

"White folks talkin' 'bout bringin' Chinese out of San Francisco," Gene Woods said. "You'll put our folks outta work."

"One man in the county tried." The voice was that of John Cochran, county treasurer. "Chinese left the next year and opened a store."

"Thank you!" Cicero said. "They can't bring enough of anybody here quick. We'll cripple the yields of the big landowners because they could never replace every missing black family. And keep in mind, more than a half million acres is still state land. Adelbert Ames should let us buy a little of it. Those of you worried about losing jobs and sharecropping can look forward to owning your own land."

A murmuring arose in the small crowd.

"Give a listen, now," the sheriff said. "Mr. Morgan's idea is not new. You all know this. It's been discussed before, but never so timely. White folks are united. Something like this could split them up. Some might not want to play all-or-nothing with their plantations."

"A life beholden to no one!" Cochran added. "Every family will choose where to make home."

"And we whom they label Radical will do the pushing," Cicero said. "You business people can blame us, if you need to. Tell anyone it was us Radicals."

"What if they threaten to kill us?"

"They already doin' that," Pease said. "Anyone who gets in too tight a spot can come in here to the central county. My militia can give them more protection than they have on any plantation."

"Yes," Cicero said, "that's the other thing. Instead of tryin to patrol the whole county, which we can't do, if people feel too threatened, they can come to a central place to stay a few days until they make plans."

"Are we agreed, then?" Sheriff Brown said.

Joe Woods was talking to his brother. From volunteers congregated outside the sheriff's office came an enthusiastic cheer.

"We don't need a show of hands," John Brown said. "Let's just agree to agree. That way anybody in here who wants to say he didn't vote for what we do can say that."

As soon as the land withdrawal was announced, John Brown made Jasper his deputy. More often that not, Jasper was the one left in charge back in Friars Point while Brown went off on law enforcement or League business.

Joe Woods and others of prominence chose not to speak out, not even Magistrate Van Bibber or George Chatters, the Clerk of the Circuit Court, both of whom were Africanamerican. That burden fell on Jasper and Cicero and on some of those living on sharecrop acreage who concluded they had nothing to lose. Cicero became a celebrity. Every organizer wanted him to come speak.

Over time, a single metaphor emerged. When first he'd been elected, Cicero explained, land and jobs had seemed like rose blossoms you simply had to nurture. He hadn't reckoned with thorns on the established stalks, the gnarled old roots that resisted change. To have new growth, courage and hard work was all he asked, to cut the existing plantations off at the root if they did not begin to set more blossoms for the people.

Farmers Jasper had often disdained as timid agreed to confront their landlords. Moreso on some plantations, like Armistead where Clothilde's children had already run miles up and down the track to convince people, or to announce Cicero or Jasper coming to speak. Near Jonestown, Jasper jumped up in a meeting and slugged a burly laborer who tried to make him leave without speaking.

It took the spring rains to bring League's politics to a halt. After threatening for weeks, the dark sky opened up and poured. By the second day, the few country roads had become impassible by wagon, a struggle to walk. Jasper and Cicero picked up their boat on the Sunflower where the ferry tender was keeping it and headed back into the swamp.

SUMMER CAME AND went. Cicero and Jasper put in more months of tireless effort. If more sharecroppers were offered wages, they would win. Wage earners being offered a lease of land would be a much bigger win. Any offer of land in the swamp from the governor would be the biggest victory of all, and Governor Ames had telegraphed his support to Brown, though he refused to consider any plan concerning swamp land until he saw the details.

In high spirits after receiving the governor's telegram, Cicero decided to surprise Rose with a visit, but she had not been told he was coming home and was away. Coming back out of the swamp, Cicero paused at Clark's Landing.

"What you wearin' cain't fool me," Nathan the ferryman said.

"My good clothes are in the bag, Nathan. Got a very important meeting up in Friar's Point."

"I hears things sometime. White folks think a nigga got wood in the head. They gonna cut Captain Brown's money off. They holdin' a supervisors' meetin' while we talk."

"Up in Friar's Point?"

"Yep."

"Are you certain it's today? That's the meeting I was supposed to attend with Brown. I thought it was tomorrow."

"Well, I ain't sure it's today, but one thing I do know. There's been men around I ain't seen before. They got shiny boots and Stetson hats and they askin' about a fancy-dress negro."

"Long coats, army issue pistols in scabbards?"

"Yessir. You seen 'em?"

Cicero nodded.

"Then you know you a marked man."

Cicero left his boat with Nathan and headed toward Abyssinia's house to warn her to take a few days off work and move in with Eugene Woods, if possible.

Inland lay a rocky depression that was simply referred to as the Pit. Out of it was quarried some stone, but not enough to make a business of it. It lay between the Sunflower and Abyssinia's home. As Cicero approached, a whinnying horse made him crouch and move more stealthily. Then he saw the horses tied among the trees, white men lounging, the shiny boots and long coats. Cicero turned from the path that he was on and fled. He skirted The Pit on the west and on northward toward Shufordsville.

When he arrived, Gene Woods was away driving freight. Joseph was about to leave for Friars Point. Alcorn wanted all sides of the Loyal League present at the county supervisors' meeting. There was to be discussion of awarding a contract to build a new courthouse.

The Parable Of Demographics

September, Second Sunday

Inside the silence before dawn, five figures climbed out of the deep channel of the Sunflower River. Bill Williams cursed the crumbling riverbank, pulling himself from bush to bush just behind Jasper. It was autumn, and the water was low. Patches of the grass covering the top of the river ridge were dry and brittle. Jasper slid backward into Bill Williams.

"Ain't you know how to climb?"

Two men following them began chuckling. By now at the ridge top, Rose reached down to give Bill a hand up.

"Thank you for helping me round up the two gentlemen behind us."

"I do what I can even if I ain't yer husband."

"I know what I seen. My Cicero in big trouble."

"You real sure what gonna happen?" Jasper asked.

"Yes, and I aim to be up at Clark's Landin' by noon."

"Yes'm," Bill said. "We all know you got the sight."

When they reached the camp, Rose walked into a clearing lit by torchlight.

"Merlene! . . . This here is Rose!"

From bushes on either said of the house stepped figures shadowed in flickering light.

"Come on in then," a woman's voice said. "I ain't knowed who it was, but you know we ain't never let nobody git the drop on us . . . Hey there, Rose. You know Luther. Them other two is friends of ours."

"We need guns, Merlene. A spell come over me. Seen my Cicero come into peril."

"You sure?" Luther asked.

"He been helpin' people git ready to vote. Come home from gatherin' my winter roots, I walk inside my house and I got so dizzy I fell to my knees."

PILGRIM'S REST WAS *the* black church, and the second Sunday of the month was *the* Sunday. Some had had to leave home in the early dawn and drive for miles. The congregation included the Caroline Edwards, and her young friend Abyssinia Morgan.

"Abyssinia!" J. W. D. Van Bibber yelled, running down off the church steps to greet her. "Come heah'n let me greet you proper, young woman."

"Lordy, lordy," Caroline Edwards said. "Sure glad I retired from all you men. Else, I be truly jealous."

"My beloved, Caroline," Van Bibber said, "how you doing?"

Joseph Woods' carriage bearing his wife and daughters parted an admiring crowd. Gene Woods leapt down and Abyssinia opened her arms to him.

"Humph!" Caroline said. "Let's go on in, Abby. Preacher up there wavin' at folks."

Caroline Edwards led the parade up to the door and inside, all the way up to her prized bench second from the front.

Behind her walked the family of Joseph Woods, then Gene. Bringing up the rear was Abyssinia.

"How're you, Joe?"

"Not too good Miz Abyssinia. Damn county supervisors got my stomach in a knot."

As Abyssinia tiptoed in to sit beside Caroline Edwards, the minister cleared his throat and began.

"Good morning esteemed colleagues and guests . . . Judge Van Bibber . . . Clerk George Chatters . . . Greetings all and sundry, ladies and gentlemen, boys and girls . . . We are grateful for the bounty of these times for we have been a most burdened people. Most grateful indeed. And on this day, we thank you for the dedication of our Sister Abyssinia Morgan. . ."

There was a sustained outpouring of applause.

". . .and we are most grateful to Mr. John Clark, a most refined gentleman who is Sister Abyssinia's employer . . . But it is Sister Abyssinia whom we must to thank first for the largest offering this congregation have received since this building were built. Is it not a beautiful colored glass window?"

Caroline stood up.

"Praise the Lord! Rev'n Jackson ain't told y'all the half of it. Abyssinia had to teach the white man why he owed it to you."

"Amen!" said Reverend Jackson. "Tell it sister!"

"I'ma tell it alright. Abby know how I used to tell my old master what to do, how I used to just slide the thought into his head."

"She a true beautiful sister," Gene Woods said.

Abyssinia colored and nodded in his direction.

"I'ma praise Jesus special this mornin'," Caroline said. "The white folks is givin' to us this time. Such a beautiful picture—St. Peter at the Pearly Gates."

"Hallelujah!" Reverend Jackson said. "He waitin' for all of us beyond this vale o' tears."

"Reverend!"

"Yes, Judge Van Bibber."

"Far be it from me to claim that Joseph Woods need help tootin' his own horn—"

Laughter filled the church.

"—but Mr. Woods built that window frame—no, no! You don't have to clap . . . He the best craftsman around. And don't y'all forget the election next month. I won't say more 'cause I know the church got to keep from being involved."

"Praise the Lord!" Reverend Jackson said. "A word from Mr. Woods? I see you rising from your seat."

"No, reverend. Y'all excuse me."

Joe Woods eased himself out of his bench. As he exited, his wife could be heard saying ". . . right on down to Mr. Levy's store. He fix your stomach."

THE SUNFLOWER BAPTIST Church was more affluent than Pilgrim's Rest though the matter of affluence is culturally filtered and always confused with judgments concerning quality. Some Christians have equated it with godliness, but then, some might offer that Jesus Christ was a poor man. As a matter of history, owners of slaves built Sunflower Baptist before there were former slaves.

It was a wilderness church, steps caked with mud in spring, dirt in autumn. It sat across a teacup bend in the Sunflower River from Pilgrim's Rest.

"I do wonder," Eliza Clark whispered during a lull in the service, "why you waste our money on that lazy 'Sinnia."

"Ahem," John Clark said, "if you are tired of sitting quiet in church, I am eager this afternoon to attend a fiddle concert."

"I'm talking about the money you wasted on that stained glass window 'Sinnia talked you into."

"You have no appreciation for what I do. All I ask is that you leave me to my pursuits."

"What a fool you are."

To the right of the Clarks sat James Alcorn and his wife, Amelia. They were not members of the church, but it was founder's day, and Alcorn had allowed his sister Eliza to prevail. Amelia Alcorn overhead the Clarks' whispered conversation. As it got more heated, she pulled her husband's sleeve, nodded surreptitiously.

"*You* believe in god, Eliza," John Clark hissed. "I believe in Mi'ssippi bottom land."

"Brother-in-law," Alcorn said. "Might I offer a word."

"You," Eliza Clark said, "tend to your business."

"And that, my precious sister is why I counseled your husband to make the gift. It is sound business to support good colored people."

John Clark's wife was a charter member of the church and made it a considerable part of her life. By the time the service had ended, she was meeting and greeting one after another. Clark and his brother-in-law strolled away only to be buttonholed by General Chalmers.

"I am on my way down to your settlement, John."

"On the Lord's day?" Alcorn asked, repressing a smile. "Surely the business of sin can wait."

"Ain't about sin."

"Some of us know about your handsome friend down on John's farm."

"Don't take liberties 'cause we ain't that close . . . I'm going down to keep our po' folks out of mischief."

"And whose mischief would that be?" Clark asked.

"The Grangers and their foreign notions of brotherhood in land."

Clark and Alcorn watched Chalmers mount his horse and ride away. Clark pulled his brother-in-law's sleeve.

"Eliza just won't see what a master stroke of politics that small gift of colored glass was."

"It was a nice piece of business . . . When Cicero Morgan is dealt with I should find it helpful being known as his sister's benefactor, too. It would support me being just as aggrieved as any colored person over his death."

"Ahh . . . Then do just that."

"Do what?"

"Let my gift become *our* gift. We ride over to the colored church. Nothing political, just go shake a few hands and take a look at our gift."

CICERO HAD SPENT a sleepless night on the floor in the sheriff's office. All night and into the morning he had been humming the same two lines.

> *Mine eyes have seen the glory*
> *of the coming of the Lord . . .*

He was dyspeptic, feeling none of the righteous energy of the song. The afternoon before, the Board of Supervisors had met down the street in total confrontation—armed black deputies on one side, armed white vigilantes on the other. The white supervisors couldn't kick the black sheriff out of office because he had been elected. Instead, they cut off his money. No more for horses, or deputies or bullets.

"The county board," Cicero said, "will arm more vigilantes."

"Good idea you had to write out exactly what we need in armament for Governor Ames. He can't use that as an excuse to delay shipping us guns and ammunition any longer."

"Amazing that he would ask for a written proposal about the swamp land. So I figure . . . I better go warn Bill Pease he may have trouble coming."

"Sorry, you got the short straw, but if I leave this office today, I'd have to shoot my way back in."

Cicero set off. At the edge of town, one of its main roads continued up over a stretch of levee. Beyond it lay the headwaters of the Sunflower that seeped out of a tangle of sloughs and marshes off the big river. Cicero trudged across a small bridge over the main channel.

As the road climbed the ridge, Cicero paused and scrabbled up a handful of wild pecans. Nothing like the big meaty nuts that grew in Joe Woods' grove. A noisy squirrel complaining overhead made Cicero dream of squirrel roasting. Because he could not dismiss a bitter nut hull residue from his tongue, he walked down to the water to drink.

As soon as he dropped to his knees to dip, he began to feel uneasy. There was an explosion of pain. He pitched forward, helpless.

A coarse rope was around his neck when he came to his senses. Someone pulled him back uphill and onto the ridge road. Three horsemen and two on foot surrounded him. One horseman spurred down off the road on the slope away from the river, which began a jug-handled bend to the right a half mile ahead. The horseman seemed intent on cutting across the bend in the river through a stand of trees. The rider waved for the rest to follow, and the other horsemen did.

The two holding the rope around Cicero's neck doggedly kept to the ridge. The one pulling Cicero along was unshaven and baked brown by the sun. He wore a ragged gray jacket of Confederate infantry and was being ordered about by a cousin who seemed protective.

"Bring the nigger on, Clarence!" the cousin in charge yelled. "We got a couple miles 'fore we reach them niggers playin' soldier."

Grunts and squeals erupted from Clarence, and a sound like "hoongary." His cousin reached into a rucksack and pulled out shortening bread. Clarence dropped Cicero's rope and fell to his rear stuffing his mouth with the bread. Meanwhile, the distance between them and the men on horseback grew.

A mile further on, they let him rest. As he gasped for breath, he stared down at Shufordsville ahead across the river, open square to the north and frame buildings around what he recognized as the Sunflower Baptist Church as a rider returned.

"Top o' the mornin'," he said. "'Tis nigger business we have or I'd not be disturbing your rest."

The other two riders joined him. Clarence was staring blankly and open-mouthed. He shied away when the first horseman dismounted near him. The protective cousin came to his rescue.

"Whyn't you go back North, Irishman. Me'n Clarence stood up to you Yankees. Them what set us to singin' Johnny Reb is wearin' fancy store bought and sittin' pretty mares like yourself . . . My cousin ain't acted right since you nigger-lovin' Yankees turned him outta prison."

"Nay, I never fought for 'em. Buildin' levees right here for Mr. Alcorn, I was."

"Hold, gentlemen," another horseman said. "We have business with them niggers ahead if you're lookin' to collect a bounty."

He rode off, and the other horsemen followed. The dim cousin grabbed Cicero's rope and set off to keep up with the horses. Cicero took only a few steps before someone tripped him.

"Hold on, Clarence. Nigger got new boots."

They also took his pants and shirt. The Irish man rode back and, as if to bond with the able cousin, began beating Cicero with a coiled rope. Cicero started running ahead but a piece of rope struck him across the face. A shot rang out.

Cicero fell to his stomach and covered up. The cousins were rolling toward the river. Two of the horsemen had dropped to the ground. The third had his mount by the reins and was running downslope away from the river toward the trees. He was unlucky. Another rifle shot, and he crumpled.

Hundreds of yards away, two of Pease's horsemen were galloping toward Cicero as he scrambled toward the water and tripped, rolling head over heels to land near the cousins at water's edge. Clarence started bawling and running back uphill. His cousin tackled him. Cicero seized the opportunity to jump in the river and swim away. As he neared the opposite shore, he recognized Pease wading out into the water.

"Come on we gotcha, brother."

By the time Cicero had coughed up the water he had swallowed Pease was looking at his bruised face.

"Brother man, they almost lynched you."

The other militiaman was opening a blanket. Cicero's teeth were chattering too much to express gratitude as he snatched it around himself. Pease helped Cicero astride his horse, and they rode to join the rest of the group.

As soon as he dismounted, Cicero blurted out how the white-controlled county board had armed its own vigilantes. Peace laughed.

"John Brown don't realize we ain't got no better choice than stay right here on this ridge. It's better than low ground, and the river protect us on one side."

Tired and cold, Cicero collapsed onto someone's bedroll and closed his eyes until the men about him began to murmur. When Cicero opened his eyes, people were walking toward them, two wearing bearskin coats.

"Hello, Rose. What brings you up here?"

"You, cherie. Been telling you stay 'way from danger, but no. Well, here I be, and if I hadn't come on when my sense told me, you likely be dead."

WHENEVER THE members of Pilgrim's Rest gathered on Second Sunday, Stephen Levy opened up the nearby General Store. Down from New York in '63 before Grant captured

Vicksburg, he had been a cotton buyer chasing contraband during the Union embargo.

Levy unlocked the doors without enthusiasm, walked outside and stretched. When church let out he would see a good run of business. He walked back inside and behind the counter to pour himself a drink.

A group of people appeared headed in Levy's direction. Thinking them possible customers he rushed to lift a jar of picked eggs, two cheese rounds, some sausages and crackers onto the top of his counter. As he looked more carefully, he realized that the people he had glimpsed were white. They were from the white Sunflower Baptist Church and would not patronize him.

Levy unstoppered a new crock of whiskey, but before he could drink he heard the door open. Joseph Woods stood there, holding his stomach.

"Come share a drink with me."

"My wife said you sell stomach potions."

"Well, that I do, but sometimes what a man needs is what my old partner used to call 'a drop of the creature.'"

"No, thank you, Mr. Levy. I got a real upset inside."

"Suit yourself."

Levy walked to a small cabinet of patent medicines. He pulled a brown bottle out, shook it, blew the dust from it and held it out.

"That'll be fifty cent, please."

"Well give it here. White folks' medicine oughta cure what they cause."

Levy froze, then turned.

"Surely, sir, you are not referring to me."

"Oh no, Mr. Levy. My troubles ain't yours. Here late, my business been slacking off."

"Mine likewise."

"Po' assed white trash is tryin' to tell all the rich white folks to quit hirin' colored. I built this store for you'n Mr. Jim Dolan six or seven years ago. That gimme a good start, but I just make do. Mr. John Clark brought in them men from Illinois to rebuild his mansion. That set the pattern."

"But aren't you in line to build the new court house?"

"*That*, Mr. Levy, is what got my stomach in a knot. Democrats ain't worth shit where the colored man concerned. It all depend on Mr. Alcorn."

"I never did trust him."

"Oh I still trust him, Mr. Levy. His people say come see them next month after our convention."

"**A**RE YOU ALL right?" Jasper asked.

"Just a scratch or two."

"You haven't looked at your face," Rose said.

"I was careless. Nothing more to say—How're you, Bill?"

"Better than you. Come on home with your woman. Or don'tcha want her no more?"

Jasper and Cicero laughed along with the woman named Merlene.

"These here your people, Mr. Cicero?"

"This is my wife. Rose, this is Bill Pease."

Barely nodding to Pease, Rose busied herself draping her bear coat around Cicero, and he began shucking off his wet undergarments for pants and a shirt someone scraped up. No one had extra boots, so Jasper pulled out some skins, and Merlene, the woman from the swamp, produced a bag of rawhide strips.

"Here somethin' else, too."

"My pocket pistol. Thank you, Merlene. I sure didn't want to lose that."

Rose was stony-faced.

"Walking around without even a decent gun, tsk."

Cicero tried to stand and pull Rose up with him.

"Don't take me nowhere. Say what you got to right here. Where the guns you been talking about?"

"Just a few more weeks. We'll have our own officials nominated, and our militia will have guns."

A cheer went up among those listening in.

"No, cherie, y'all got hard times comin'." She turned to the men around them. "Where I live the swamp ain't been cut, and it feel real good to be safe away from the white folks."

There was mainly silence.

"Maroon was more than a color," Rose said, "back when I come along. During slavery time, it meant a free life. We were outlaw folk."

"Do tell," Bill Pease said.

"No maroon would let her hand be stuck to a hoe in some slave nightmare. To be maroon you have to go into the wild where white folks cain't get at you, where no underground railroad stops and north is only a direction."

"We 'preciates your offer, Sister Rose," Bill Pease said, "truly we do. But goin' off into a swamp . . . It ain't for most of my people."

"We ain't disposed," one said, "to give up bein' civilized."

"Shit on that!" Jasper said. "I'm as good as you, and I live better."

"The best thing," Cicero said, "is that you would have neighbors willing to help you learn the life, a free life. The boycott is just one way. Living in the swamp is my way."

"But it's too many trash people out there."

"Maybe is, maybe ain't," Jasper said. "Before I was grown I killed a man. Killed plenty of 'em. You wasn't a man 'till you did. So least I'm a man. Who you callin' trash?"

"Now, cherie," Rose said. "Don't talk like you dote on killin'."

"Y'all called me the Nightflame. Said I put a fear in all them planters' hearts." He turned toward the men listening around him, thumped his chest. "They had to hire a constable down where I lived just to be safe. Knowed the swamp better'n anybody—even Mack, the headman. Ain't that right, momma?"

Rose was smiling, Bill Pease, too, amused by Jasper's bragging. But the rest appeared no more disposed to consider the living in the swamp than before.

"Like I figured," Rose said to Cicero. "You better let me have that bear coat. I'll need it this winter. Y'all get him some blankets—Jasper!"

"Yes'm?"

"C'mon home with me. You can bring him back his other clothes tomorrow."

"Momma, I got work to do here."

"Hush up! . . . And when he come back, Cicero, he gonna stay with you—I said, hush up, Jasper! . . . He ain't gonna get killed for you, but he bound to stay long as you out here in this foolishness."

NOT MORE THAN two miles away in Clark's Landing, a troop of pubescent girls in what were billed as the latest in athletic bloomers were tumbling across the stage. They were farm girls of no particular grace, both lean and fat, sharing only an eagerness to show off what they already knew their fathers' and brothers' friends wanted to glimpse.

It was early afternoon. Tables had been spread with cloths, planks for benches driven in by wagon. A rough stage had been erected and trimmed with bunting. Nearby, on a newly denuded piece of land, stood the wooden footings of a new building. A banner overhead read, "Congratulations! Coahoma's New Grange Hall."

There were barrels of well water for the faint of heart. Kegs of liquor for those so disposed. It was a most festive occasion, as festive occasions for poor farmers go. These were not the same people who attended either the Sunflower Baptist Church or Pilgrim's Rest.

"I know it's s'posed to be a secret society," a man with a Grange ribbon on his hat said, "but Grangers is a family movement—picnics and such."

"I hear y'all against the church," a woman said.

"No ma'am, we ain't. Just ain't no church ourself. We for the little man, folks like yourself. Ain't no more jobs for us on most o' these plantations. Y'all folks is poor. Ain't got Democrats nor Republicans doin' nothin' for you."

"May I, sir?" a well-dressed man with graying hair curling back from his forehead said. "Some of you folks new enough, you may not know me."

"I know you, General," the original speaker said. "This here is General James Chalmers of our recent Confederate Forces."

"Pleased to make your acquaintance," the woman said, now shy and uncertain.

"I couldn't help overhearing," Chalmers said to the woman, "what this Grange man said."

"This ain't no debating society," the Grange functionary said.

"You spoke the name, Democrat, sir! I demand to make the record clear."

"Long as you know, ain't no politicians welcome here today."

"My dear lady," Chalmers said, "all of your political parties in this state have had to concern ourselves with the needs of commerce. But do not for one moment believe that we Democrats don't represent you people."

A small group gathered. A speaker mounted the stage, then walked to the edge of it to confer with another who pointed to the knot of people around Chalmers. The speaker cupped his mouth and spoke as loud as he could.

"I bid the good General welcome. He is a Democrat. Like all the rest, he take care of the railroads and the rich folks."

"I demand the right of reply!" Chalmers said.

"We ain't," the speaker said to the crowd busy consuming the chicken, sweet potatoes, corn relish and home-fried bread. "We ain't Democrats nor Republicans. What we is is red-blooded Grangers, Americans thru'n thru."

There was anemic applause. The food was still holding, appetites unsatisfied.

"Here in what is now to become Clarksville," the speaker continued, "we come together to dedicate our lodge. We got no concern in this war between the power-drunk colored and them who control everything else."

Gunshots rang out in the distance to the north toward the river. Everyone paused momentarily, glanced at their neighbors. When the shooting did not continue, the conversation and other noise, the eating and drinking commenced again. Up on the stage, the speaker continued.

"Now, they got white folks sayin' vote for Mr. Alcorn 'cause he our hope. Hell, he ain't our hope. He helpin' them what's already got the land. And he sendin' niggers to school. Don't none o' them need no nothin'."

Spirited applause greeted the remarks. Mothers began to quiet rampaging children.

"We ain't got nothin'. They promise us jobs when business is rollin' again, but who's to say. There ain't no more used to be. Them what's tellin' us there's gonna be jobs is the same folks sicked us into fightin' so's they could keep their slaves."

As the applause rose, General Chalmers climbed onto the stage and raised his hand.

"And I say that you got Democrats on your side!"

"And I say," the speaker continued, "we in the middle, 'tween the landowners and the niggers. We got to make our po folks voice heard. Alcorn and the niggers is Republican.

And then, there's the Democrats. Who they really for? Them who runs that party own land, too. They ain't poor. Now, folks like us need two things—niggers in they place, land on credit!"

The applause turned to cheering and shouting. Two banjo players ran up on stage and began playing the Confederate marching song. Folks held arms like a square dance, and promenaded all over the street. Chalmers tried to no avail to capture their attention. Finally, he smiled and accepted a drink of whiskey pressed upon him by the now friendly speaker. Black folks in the vicinity, who had been quietly watching what was happening from the fringes, just as quietly disappeared.

"There are plans afoot," Chalmers was heard to tell those who were listening, "to return the niggers to where they belong. Just don't try to overthrow our American way. This country is a place where a poor man can become a rich man. That is true opportunity. Ain't that really what you want?"

"May be," a man said, "but what's wrong with givin' us folk a little swamp land on credit like out west. It ain't all supposed to go to railroads'n them already own plantations."

Safety and Welfare
at Any Cost

Monday morning

A freight boat put in to Friar's Point. It carried cargo in a
hundred-foot forward space studded with timbers supporting
a tarpaulin roof. The pilot-house was aft built up over quarters
for captain and crew, below them the boiler room and massive
paddle wheel to the side. A suited white man with a blue military cape walked forward and yelled ashore.

"Would someone direct me to the sheriff?"

A black teenager approached along the shore and yelled
aboard.

"S'cuse me, mister, my name Booker T. I know the sheriff."

"Go tell him that I bring a dispatch from the governor."

"The governor?"

"Yes, young man. I must speak with John Brown."

"Right away, suh."

Booker T ran. He was an office mascot some thought to be
an orphan. When he reached the office he blurted out the
news, and John Brown and a couple of deputies ran out to

where the steamboat was tying up. As soon as the gangway thudded into place, Brown went aboard.

"You'd be from the governor?"

"Jim Moran, US attorney for northern Mississippi."

"I was," Brown said, "expecting the governor's representative from the armory downstate . . . What of the cargo?"

By the time Jasper returned with Cicero's clothes and they traveled with Pease to Friar's Point it was afternoon. Some semblance of a meal—a ham and bread, boiled eggs and a corn pudding—was being served in the sheriff's office. Two women who had provided food were easing their way out. Caught up in his stomach's happy expectation, Cicero walked straight toward the food, didn't notice the somber mood.

"Is it honorable for an Honorable to eat before greeting?"

"John Cochran!" Cicero mumbled. "What brings our county treasurer up off of his farm today?"

"Why, to have egg spit in his face by you."

"Seriously, now . . . Why?"

"I'd like to introduce James Moran," John Brown said. "He's from Floreyville, US Attorney, though I don't believe you've met."

"No," Cicero said extending a hand. "I think not."

"But I have corresponded with you," Moran said. "You and a Dr. Stringer, I believe—documents you mailed describing the violence before the '71 election."

"Sorry," Cicero said, "that I didn't connect you with the name. We did exchange several letters."

"Governor Ames," Moran said, "stands behind those who ran for office at his urging—men like you, Brown. Thus, his decision to supply the usual weapons for your defense. He regrets that local whites are trying to subvert the government."

"Regret," Brown said, "is not a very strong commitment."

"He cannot do the impossible."

"What the hell do you mean?" Brown said. "My ass is hanging out here, you talk impossible—what about the safety and welfare of the people who depend on me?"

"In the capital, the Governor can only *order* things done. If his orders are not carried out—by the legislators, or by those sworn to the executive itself—nothing can be done."

"You mean," Cochran said, "he refuses to dismiss whoever won't do what they're told?"

"Well, in a way."

"So explain," Cochran said, "about that."

"Be realistic, gentlemen," Moran said. "The governor is only human. The officers who control the armory will not carry out the governor's orders. No weapons from the armory in Jackson have moved for months. Until recently, the governor thought he could persuade them to do their duty."

"Kick the sombitches out!" Bill Pease said.

"Who would replace them? White Mississippians resist arming your race."

"Pick a black man," Cicero said, "like Bill Pease, here."

"Yes, yes but most certainly, no. He'd be assassinated, and even the more moderate on the governor's staff would rebel should we turn the armory over to . . . Well, you understand."

"The rebellion," Cicero said, "seems already to have begun."

"It is", Moran said, "a delicate time. The framework of government must be preserved, law and order."

"Law and order for who?" Cochran said.

"There is," Moran said, "no sentiment in Washington to come back in and take over running this state. The nation must pay its bills for the War, not hire more soldiers. Work and land for former slaves—the way the army talked about a new society—those are failed policies of the '60's. Governor Ames knows this. He and other Northerners making this state their home have had to adapt to the new consensus, become new-thinking Republicans."

"Aside from that," Cicero asked, "what did you come all this way to tell us?"

"That the governor is attempting to avoid both insurrection and a bloodbath."

"I showed up in town a few years ago with Brown," Cochran said, "just in time to run against Alcorn's Mississippi Republicans. Our esteemed Governor Adelbert Ames assured us that he would back us."

"Why doesn't Ames," Brown said, "at least declare martial law and request Federal troops? We cannot be worse off if he is refused."

"Alas," Moran said, "no white man would vote for anyone who asked for troops to be brought back in here. In reality, the governor would only anger the President who has made his position quite clear."

"So," Cicero said, "the good general wants to hang onto his job as governor. He presumes us too stupid to challenge him, and because we were slaves our dying doesn't count much."

"Of course not. I can only repeat that the governor remains loyal to *all* of us . . . What can I say. Mr. Morgan, you know politics."

"Ain't there no way," Jasper asked, "to get no guns?"

"I hope, young man, that Mr. Morgan will help sustain your people's basic faith in the law."

"We're facing insurrection!" Cicero said. "John Brown was duly elected. We have the votes to control the county board. Isn't that the American way?"

"Here in Coahoma," Moran said, "our governor wants you to know that he opposes all negotiation with you know who."

"Oh please!" John Brown said. "No guns, but you say, no deal with Alcorn?"

"Yes," Moran said. "No deal with Alcorn. The governor doesn't want him taking over anything, officially or otherwise.

"What a low down, scum sucking request!"

"Mr. Pease, I choose not to be offended."

"Well, I am," Cochran said.

"And with whom," Cicero asked, "do you suggest we are to compromise? If not with Senator Alcorn, we are left with General Chalmers and his Democrats, or maybe General Forrest and his Knights of the Ku Klux Klan? You choose."

"I am merely suggesting," Moran said, "that you not give up the fight. You may loose the election if your people don't turn out, but don't give up. Just go ahead and get out the vote. Don't let Alcorn become the great mediator."

"In other words," Cicero said, "Don't help Alcorn run for governor again."

"And teach the people," Pease said, "how to dodge bullets."

A whistle sounded, and with one mind all piled out of the little office. Taking his leave of John Brown, Moran walked back toward the steamboat landing.

"Would you gentlemen," Cochran said to the sheriff's deputies, "allow the rest of us to meet in private for a moment?"

Silently, the men carrying rifles began piling back inside the sheriff's office. The rest gathered apart in the middle of the street.

"Stay on, Brother Jasper," Bill Pease said. "I like at least one gun beside me."

"We have," Cicero said, "no choice left."

"None," Cochran said, "at all."

"I am *not* going to say how I felt about being left outta this 'secret' plan," Bill Pease said. "Me bein' jes a soldier in the army of the Lord, but I assume y'all are about to tell me now."

"For some weeks now," Cochran said, "there has been little government in this county. A couple days ago, when the Board of Supervisors cut John Brown's money off, they appropriated funds to arm a local force of vigilantes. Well hell, since it's my job to disburse all funds, I just refused to pay. Then I discovered money for roads being used to buy guns. So I have cut off *all* county disbursements until the Board comes to its senses or we work things out."

"Damn!" Pease said. "You alright, Cochran. Thought so but this prove it. But you ain't told the plan yet."

"My plan," Cochran said, pausing as the sheriff returned, "is to use county money to buy guns in Arkansas."

"We can't worry about proper authorization," the sheriff said. "There's not even enough time to call a meeting of the Loyal League."

"And I," Cochran said, "wouldn't want everyone in the League to hear of me using county money."

"If I can't arm my militia," the sheriff said, "and secure the polling places, there will be a massacre."

"So spill the whole plan," Bill Pease said. "Who buys 'em?"

"A certain white man of our acquaintance," Cochran said. "Most of you know Stephen Levy. He and a partner opened a general store selling to freedmen right after the War. Recently he has been trying to sell that store to me and Brown at a very low price. He wants something, maybe just an inside connection once we control county business."

"Well," Brown said, "Cicero and Jasper don't know all the background of our business circle. You see, Levy started out as an abolitionist before the war ended."

"Really?" Cicero said.

"Yes indeed. He even ran against Jim Alcorn for the Constitutional Convention in '67, but Alcorn painted him an outsider, even worse, an extremist. Levy's store sits in the black settlement near Shufordsville, but he could only get a few of his customers to vote for him. They supported Alcorn."

"Now," Cochran said. "Levy comes trying to do Brown and me a favor. Let's see if he really wants to be on our side."

"My sister, Abyssinia," Cicero said, "says he's always respected black customers."

"True," Cochran said, "and I learned a few months back that he's again taken up cotton buying. Yet I doubt if any of the white planters are eager to do business with a Jew."

"So," Brown said, "he wants in with us, and he has our same problem with the big white folks."

"Correct," Cochran said. "Who better than such a white man to go buy us guns? Even in Arkansas, no one would sell a hundred guns to a black man without too much hoopla."

And Light Is Said To Emerge From Dark

End of September, 1875

On the morning of the Loyal League meeting, a month before the Republican Party Convention, rumors about guns from Arkansas had election workers laughing and joking outside the sheriff's office. The rumor went, "Big white man in Jackson come through." Before Sheriff Brown could climb up on a barrel and convene the meeting, Joseph Woods ambushed him.

"Tell 'em," Wood said, "the truth about the governor, or I will."

"What do you mean?"

"You ain't got no damn guns is what I mean!"

"Mr. Woods wants me to tell you that white folks control the telegraph and the post office. The governor has no way to supply us guns from the armory at this time."

"What about from Arkansas?" a woman's voice asked.

"No, no . . . The only connection we have with the governor is through Floreyville down in Bolivar County."

"Are they," another asked, "gonna send in the army?"

"No," Brown said. "The people in Washington won't."

No one broke the momentary silence. The sheriff continued.

"Our League—our election effort—still requires that we go ahead and plan our convention, the candidates' parade, everything. Right now, though, I have to go meet with my deputies about security here in town today. I am turning the meeting back over to Mr. Woods."

As Brown walked off, Joe Woods took over. He whispered to an associate who pointed out several other League members. The business contingent was fully represented.

"We gotta drop this land protest," Woods said. "I been thinkin' that for some time, but then I thought maybe we would get some guns."

"Sheriff Brown oughtta be heah!"

"Cain't help that. Y'all heard him turn things over to me."

"Jes wait! Sheriff be back in a minute."

Woods looked toward his supporters, then shrugged as Bill Pease sent a man running to fetch the sheriff. They returned momentarily.

"What about," Woods yelled to the approaching sheriff, "the land withdrawal?"

Before anybody could respond, sporadic cheering began on the fringes of the crowd. From the north, a wagon was raising a dust cloud. As it closed, the crowd could make out a woman driving a wagon loaded with children. Cicero recognized Clothilde.

"Mr. Armistead," she yelled, "is offering straight wages plus food to anybody don't want to sharecrop!"

Another cheer went up as Clothilde stepped to the ground.

"I had to come tell you we fought a good fight. . ." Then her head dropped, her eyes seemed to gush forth. ". . . but they killed my baby! He ain't come home yestiddy, an' we found his shoe layin' in the road."

Cicero walked over and embraced the woman.

"Oh, Miz Clothilde, I am so sorry, so sorry."

As the two stood there embracing, the crowd nearby began to pass word of what was said. The festive noise swallowed itself.

"What," the sheriff asked, "will you and your children do?"

"We cain't stay out on that place no more." Clothilde began sobbing again. "Don't give up the fight. My boy give his life for it."

When the condolences and cries for revenge subsided, Joe Woods pulled away from a caucus of his business group and stepped forward.

"Madame, you have our deepest, deepest sympathies."

Mournfully, someone started singing.

"Ain't but a few white folks done like you report, Miz Clothilde," Woods said, "and after a lot of hard thinking we got to back off this land thing. My friends here want you to know we take care of our own. You and your children come on to the convention and let folks see a brave lady."

"I ain't no politician," Clothilde said.

"Just help us out and we help you," Woods said. He turned to the crowd. "Find this lady a place right here in town!"

The crowd applauded. Clothilde spoke before Joe Woods could.

"Me'n my chil'ren got to move from this place. Ain't no doubt about it. I say if you stick together, you can help yourself. Else, you better put this raggedy-assed place behind you."

Joe Woods put his arm around her shoulder.

"I move that we feed'n take care of Miz Clothilde and all her children until they can pull some plans together."

"I cain't let no more of mine git killed."

"No ma'am," someone said, "we understand."

"We are very sorry, ma'am," the sheriff said.

Woods turned away from Clothilde and opened his hands toward the rest of the group.

"This prove what I mean. We cain't go no further on this land pull-out thing."

"Shut up, you rat-lookin' nigga!"

Jasper moved toward Woods. Bill Pease stepped between them.

"Somebody," Jasper said, "oughtta make sure the boy ain't died for nothin'."

"Be still!" Cicero said, as Jasper again tried to get at Joe Woods.

"This discussion's closed!" Woods said. "We got election business, and that's all!"

"Damn if that's so!" Jasper said, finally elbowing Pease aside. "Bill Pease ain't got his guns yet, but y'all oughtta git the sheriff to go hunt for the young man. I know he dead, so ain't no sense in nobody thinking otherwise. But we do what we can. Respect what the boy done, and git you a gun from somewhere. Steal one!"

"Absolutely not!" Woods said.

"We can't decide all of that here," the sheriff said. "I'd suggest a committee look into what we should do."

"Damn that!" Joe Woods said. "We ain't talkin' about nothin' in secret. All we got is election business."

"Damn you, too!" Jasper screamed.

Sheriff Brown grabbed Jasper's arm to help Bill Pease restrain him.

"Just remember, Joe," the sheriff said, "a lot of folks who aren't here have nothing to lose. They'll have to pack up and move. After the election, if we stick together, our new supervisors could demand that the planters negotiate with us."

"Hell no!" Woods said. "Brown you ain't big enough to tell them landowners what to do."

"We'd control roads and levees. They'd have to listen."

"Look here, this land thing got to be over 'cause ain't nobody but us here had to face the pressure. Us businessmen the ones had to grin up in the white man's face . . . Maybe you ought to resign, sheriff."

"What you say, sheriff," another voice asked. "Are we gonna keep fightin' to rent land?"

Brown looked momentarily toward Cicero who was whispering to Jasper. After a pause, Brown jabbed his finger into Woods' chest.

"You've lived here longest—you decide."

"You out there!" Joe Woods said. "Look at Miz Clothilde here! We cain't be havin' folks like her git hurt . . . Yeah, I see y'all finally listenin'. What we got to do is take care o' these children . . . Now, all in favor of dropping the land thing, raise your hand."

MOUNTED WHITE MEN wearing Stetson hats and prairie dusters were seen visiting several plantations, and the county shut down. Black workers stayed at home with their families because no one felt safe.

John Brown sent his deputies to round up as many Loyal League board people as they could find for an emergency meeting at the home of John Cochran, the county treasurer.

"We still have an election coming up," Brown said, "but without guns to guard the polling places, there could be a lot of killing."

"We asked you here," Cochran said, "to let you know that it is our recommendation to go ahead and plan a slate of candidates for the convention."

"Ain't that what we was already doing?" Joe Woods asked.

"I think," Brown said, "that right now, the League should provide escort to any man woman or child who wants to move."

"Where," Woods asked, "are you gonna take 'em?"

"The only place would be with Bill Pease's men. That camp along the Sunflower is protected on one side, and some of the men have weapons. Once we get people there, they'd have some time to plan what next."

"Do you realize," Woods asked, "how much planters hate people runnin' off?"

"We already know that!" Cicero said. "If we do nothing, others like Clothilde will fall victim. You've dropped the boycott. Now we're protecting our workers."

"Go talk to your dear Mr. Alcorn," John Brown said to Woods. Let him know what we're doing. We don't want their vigilantes coming after women and children."

HELENA, ARKANSAS was not very different from Friar's Point except that it was bigger. On its outskirts sat Fort Penny and around the Fort a cluster of commercial activities related to troop movement and supply. Lately, this had become the debarkation point for settlers heading inland to form wagon trains into the Southwest.

From Cairo Illinois, from along the Ohio River a stream of immigrants poured. They would disembark off the Mississippi at Helena from which they would arrange passage west, usually buying a wagon and team, sometimes further boat passage along the Arkansas River from whose source they would continue overland.

Stephen Levy left the ferryboat and tip-toed over the muddy ground onto a planked walk. He wasted no time presenting himself at the Fort Penny Quartermaster. He was no expert on buying guns, but he had bought wholesale for the General Store, and his instinct for a quick bargain told him to test the market inside the Fort first.

"Good morning, sir. May I help you?" the civilian employee

said as Levy made his way up and down between rows of stacked weapons.

"These all seem to be powder and shot, a few cloth cartridge models."

"Correct, sir. These are not the latest of weapons."

"I want Winchesters—repeaters," Levy said.

"Can't help you there."

"I'm in the business of outfitting wagon trains, my good man."

"What's your name?"

"Stephen Levy, if you must know."

"Goddamn Jew! Go find a sheeneee to help you."

Within the hour, Stephen Levy arrived at a general merchandise store. He saw a few crates of the rifles he wanted.

"May I help you, sir?"

"How much for a crate of rifles?"

"Get 'em for you in two, three months."

"What's your problem?"

"Special requisition come in this morning from the Army."

"The Army?

"Goddamn Indians are breakin' outta the Territory and headin' toward the border. The army is payin' my retail price plus a premium."

"I have a party of settlers leaving in two days."

"Oh I'd sit here a few weeks until the fightin' clears up."

"I can't wait."

"How much is it worth to you?"

"Half-dollar over the cost of a rifle."

"Five!"

"One!"

"Two!"

"Done."

BACK ACROSS RIVER in Mississippi that night, a cross was burned on the riverbank within sight of Friar's Point. Brown put out sentries north and south of town.

Early in the morning, Booker T rushed in sleepy eyed and distraught from keeping watch.

"Y'all git up. Mr. Alcorn hisself comin'."

In the strange orange light of morning, stark of countenance rode Alcorn. At his side, rode none other than General James Chalmers. Ten men accompanied them. As they passed down the long street, window shades were pulled aside.

"Greetings, Brown," Alcorn said, dismounting.

"Good morning."

"May General Chalmers and I come inside?"

Sheriff Brown held out his arm indicating the way. He and Cicero followed Chalmers.

"My men will remain outside," Chalmers said. "The Senator and I come in peace."

"Close the door, sheriff," Alcorn said.

The deputy closed the door.

"State your business, Senator," Brown said. "It is not an occasion for pleasantries."

"No, no—why, bless my soul! Is that the Honorable Cicero Morgan?"

"Good morning Senator."

"Yes, it is indeed—or, I should say—it *would* be a fine morning but for what has recently come to my attention. No, don't get all agitated, Morgan. This isn't about you." Alcorn turned toward the sheriff. "I did not come to make an arrest."

"Arrest?" the sheriff said, "Whom, and on what charge?"

"Why you, sheriff, for theft. You know all about it. I just wanted to give you warning. I shall arrest you for stealin' close on ten thousand dollars of taxpayer money. I cannot prove how you came into possession of it, but I can prove that you passed it to an unnamed co-conspirator."

Cicero was about to open his mouth again, but Brown restrained him.

"What," Brown said, "is your evidence?"

"This is no court of law. I know what I know, and I intend to confront you publicly if you are still around on the date of our convention."

"When," Cicero asked, "did you re-join our Party?"

"I have never resigned, merely re-aligned myself."

"And I," General Chalmers said, "came here to show all white men united against Radicals like you Morgan and carpet-bagging thieves like Brown. I am so disappointed in you, boy."

"General," Brown said, "you may spare me that."

"Then, there's nothing more," Alcorn said. "We urge you to resign. With a charge pending, it would be the right thing."

"I see," Brown said, "and you—"

"With the General's concurrence," Alcorn said, "I and one of my sons would take over your duties on a temporary basis. Morgan knows that I am a civilized man."

When Alcorn and Chalmers departed, Jasper walked inside agitated.

"Let's go home, Cicero."

"We have guns on the way."

"I ain't seen 'em."

Cicero put his hand on Jasper's shoulder.

"Let's take a couple days off. We'll wait out Levy at Abyssinia's."

On foot, and keeping out of sight, it took the rest of the day to walk down to Pease's encampment. By then it was late afternoon. A wagon with parade bunting still in place from the recent League meeting was parked nearby. Those who had become marked for supporting the sharecrop holdout and fled their homes were camped in the vicinity.

Cicero and Jasper walked through shaking hands, commiserating. One group seemed of a mind to gather family and move away as soon as the convention was held. Most without family were eager to join the militia. Once alone, Cicero told Pease of Alcorn's visit and moved on.

He and Jasper reached Abby's house after dark. Cicero told Abby that if the convention didn't go the way he hoped he wouldn't be coming out of the swamp again soon. Caroline Edwards was visiting from Shufordsville.

"All this trouble," Caroline said. "Ain't no time for a woman to be living alone."

While supper was cooking, Cicero sat up front and luxuriated in the warmth of Abby's extraordinary fireplace. Jasper joined the women in the kitchen.

"Well knock me over with a feather," Abby said, "I didn't know if you'd come visit."

"Why?"

"Because I didn't."

"So why was that?"

"Hmmmmm." Caroline Edwards muttered, throwing an arch glance at each of them.

"Excuse me," Abby said to Jasper, "for raising my voice."

"It's alright, Miz Abyssinia."

"Don't call me that, I'm Abby."

"Ok."

"Is that all you got to say?"

"What more you want?"

"Well, well," Caroline said, "if you two ain't oil'n water."

Cicero walked in as Caroline leaned forward to give Jasper the eye.

"You is one of the prettiest black niggas I seen. Move your chair over heah, boy."

Jasper looked startled.

"Yeah, you!" Caroline said. "I'm older than your ma so do what I say. Come over heah'n hug me."

"I see that you are all having fun," Cicero said, turning back toward the front. "I'm gonna warm my feet some more."

"Go warm yours too, Caroline," Abby said. "Leave pretty boy and me alone."

An old brood hen giving way to the pullet, Caroline stood and showily shook down her voluminous skirts. She was laughing as she walked out behind Cicero. Jasper pointed to Abby.

"I been wanting to ask you something."

"What?"

"Why did you act like you did when I first met you?"

"How was that?"

"You know."

"No, I don't know."

"Yes you do. Girls like me."

"Boys was the same with me, so there."

"Why you didn't have nothing to do with me?"

"What kinda question is that?"

"Answer me."

"Some things I just don't want to talk about."

"You don't think I'm good looking?"

"I thing you're a fine boy."

"I said, good looking."

"You are a handsome boy."

"Ok, so how come you was like you was?"

"Jasper, are you a simple fool?"

"I ain't no kinda fool."

"Then tell me this, when I met you how much money did you have?"

"I had some."

"I had to look out for myself."

"Naw, you was in love in that Commander Grey."

"I wanted him to take care of me."

"Wasn't you in love with him?"

"I told you—oh, you don't understand."

"Then wasn't no reason for you not to be with me."

"I didn't want to live in no swamp." Abyssinia sighed. "If you'd been a regular person we could have spent a little time together."

"What's wrong with now?"

"How much money you got?"

Cicero's voice rode Caroline's knowing laughter in from the front room.

"Neither of you has one red cent of shame."

Such moments aside, the evening soon turned solemn. A preoccupied Cicero didn't talk much. Jasper talked on and on about the land withdrawal, and Caroline kept him at it. Even Abby showed curiosity.

"This freedom thing ain't easy," she said.

Jasper's eyes never left her. She allowed his hand on her arm, giggled and slapped it when he tried to hold her hand. Cicero sat there amazed. Old Caroline kept up the small talk, or what started out that way, until Abby again turned serious.

"I never helped you men in your fightin' with the white folks," she said, rubbing Jasper's hand. "I never figured you had no chance, no way. Maybe that ain't right. Sometime I get so mad at these white folks. Old lady I work for think she know more'n me about myself. One day, I'm gonna bust her in the nose and run join you, brother."

"Why don't you?" Jasper said.

"Oh no!" Caroline said. "You a example to the whole community. Got more culture than anybody I know."

Abby chuckled and stood up. She clasped her arms about herself.

"I know that seems extreme. I mean what kinda life can you live, off in some swamp without a good job and everyday people. So I keep trying out new ways to act when that woman I work for say somethin' about us colored. *Got* to keep 'em guessin' how you really feel. I act stupid, and that's they way she think of me. I hate that old woman . . . Oh Lordy, freedom is strange."

Insurrection

October

The day after Jasper and Cicero's night with Abyssinia, someone spread the word in Friars Point that Bill Pease's militia had been ordered to surround and take control of the town. Brown sent word to General Chalmers that the only reason the militia was scheduled into town at all was because of the convention. Every Loyal League convention began with a parade to show people who couldn't read who to vote for.

Chalmers dismissed the explanation. Black people voting, he said, turned the order of nature on its head. Holding a black convention in town was as bad as, his words, "negroes with guns."

That afternoon, even before the messenger returned to Brown's office, white people began moving out. Logistics of the withdrawal was a passive-aggressive and ominous fact, how well it had been organized, Chalmers and his vigilantes escorting white people out of town, and carrying more guns than the sheriff could ever muster.

John Brown hadn't survived by being a fool. All logic told Brown to defuse the situation, to buy enough time to see if

there were something somebody wanted, something nego-
tiable. He convinced John Cochran to send messengers to a
couple county board members to offer release of some county
funds if the board would agree to fund the sheriff's office
through the next three months, which would have covered
the convention and election to follow. Only one white board
member lived in town. He had nothing to offer. That night,
Brown rode to Chalmer's house. The sheriff's militia would
not march into town.

The square outside the Friar's Point courthouse was filled to
overflow early. Wagons unloaded from Jonestown, Greengrove, Sherard, Yazoo Pass, and about fifteen other plantations. Picking candidates was a celebration. It wasn't every day
that former slaves had a reason to leave their backbreaking
work behind, and what they didn't learn at the convention
about who the candidates were they never would.

The town square was roped off. Africanamerican townspeople stacked barrels of water along the edge. Fires had been
lit that morning, and four sides of beef were cooking. All provided by the business wing of the League attempting to
smooth over hard feelings that had lingered since they killed
the land withdrawal. It was a festive day, and not a single white
face was to be seen.

Toward ten o'clock, a rider carrying an American flag
trotted into the square.

"Parade this evening—parade!" he yelled. "Children welcome . . . Know who John Brown is?"

"Sheriff!" the crowd roared back.

"John Cochran—you know *him?*"

"Treasurer!"

"Board o' Supervisors?"

A confused rumbling turned into laughter.

"Hush!" the mounted man said. "Ain't no way you could

know. You got to join the parade and find out. Learn who we gonna pick!" He continued on toward the end of town, repeating himself for those who'd just arrived.

    Eugene Woods showed up and demanded to speak to the sheriff alone. He kept insisting until Brown allowed himself to be pulled aside. Nearby, Cicero was trying to calm the nerves of Clothilde who had agreed to give a speech telling of the success of the land withdrawal on her plantation. Then there was the tiny courthouse in which the convention was scheduled to be held. Not even a hundred people could squeeze inside. No amount of tact and diplomacy soothed hurt feelings when those who'd arrived early were asked to allow official delegates to replace them and take their seats.

    By noon, somehow, they convened, and the sheriff become chairman by acclamation. He wasted no time calling for the Nominating Committee's report.

    That was when the meeting erupted around the Woods brothers. They stood up with several others and yelled to get the sheriff's attention. He seemed taken aback until the rear doors opened, and a small group of white faces appeared, yelling,

    "Point of order! Point of order!"

    They plowed into the crowd and shoved roughly toward the front. Bill Pease was sergeant at arms.

    "Go back, goddammit!"

    "You don't talk to the Senator like that," a man with the group said.

    "Senator or not, stay where you at!"

    "Let them in, Bill," the sheriff said. "Give 'em seats."

    "Seats my ass!" someone yelled. "Let 'em stand up."

    Jasper and Cicero were near the rear door when the uproar began, and they now pushed toward the front. Jasper stopped midway up, but Cicero moved on, leaving Jasper grabbing at his coattail. One of Alcorn's men kept yelling something toward the folks who were refusing to give up their seats. When the white man couldn't get seated, he charged the rostrum.

"We come here to speak, sheriff. You gonna let us?"

"Ladies and gentlemen," the sheriff said. "I beg your indulgence, but certain folks want to make a speech, do you want to hear them?"

The response was a resounding, no, along with booing and stamping of feet. Brown raised his hand.

"Now that you've let them know our mind, I say we have nothing to lose . . . Senator Alcorn, you have the floor."

Bill Pease was muttering under his breath as Alcorn walked to the front flanked by two armed men whom Bill made no move to disarm. Sheriff Brown stepped down off the little raised speaker's platform, and Alcorn replaced him.

He began by calling the sheriff a thief, and he demanded that Brown be replaced as chairman of the convention, all to resounding boos—except for a timid and almost symbolic show of hands by a small group of black delegates. Alcorn stood there for a moment silent, staring back and forth from his small knot of support into the otherwise hostile audience. When Brown stepped up beside him, Alcorn grew red in the face.

"You are doomed!" Alcorn said under his breath to Brown. "I am your only savior."

When the booing continued as lusty as ever, Alcorn shouted into the crowd.

"No black empire will be built on our graves!"

The people grew more angry. Even Brown couldn't get them quiet. Alcorn stepped down and tried to rejoin his retinue. From outside, people who were not delegates tried to press in to join the booing. The other white men inside moved toward the podium presumable to link up with Alcorn, but Bill Pease blocked their way.

"Y'all wait in the back. You cain't come up and take over."

A tussling match ensued, right in front of Cicero. He turned to see Jasper pushing through the aisle. A white man standing guard near Alcorn pulled a revolver, and Bill Pease struck him over the head. When another man grabbed Bill, Jasper lifted his rifle and fired, though not before someone knocked his arm toward the ceiling.

As the shot echoed, the room erupted in screaming. Guns were drawn all around. Cicero started pulling on Jasper and clearing a way toward the rear.

"Arrest that blackguard, sheriff!"

The voice was Alcorn's, but up front, the crowd had the white folks locked in as Cicero and Jasper pushed their way toward the back.

"Cicero!"

It was Brown yelling, but Cicero kept going. At the podium, Brown fired a pistol to capture the room's attention. By that time hundreds outside were trying to push in, even through the windows. Fist fights broke out on the perimeter near the back doors and in front where Alcorn's group was mixed together with the delegates. Near the doors, Jasper was knocked aside when two fighting men crashed inside. Cicero grabbed Jasper's arm and pulled him on out into the space others were giving those fighting. Somehow, Bill Pease reached them.

"Brown says you brothers got to go away until the convention over. Come to his office in the morning. Ain't gonna arrest the young brother. Y'all git gone. Take them two horses over there." Before he let go of Cicero's hand he pulled him close and whispered. "Guns bein' unloaded tonight."

Through the milling crowd to the horses, Jasper and Cicero ran. Once mounted, they galloped away. Jasper led the way toward a piece of wilderness that lay between Friar's Point and Moore Bayou further inland.

"How does it feel?" Cicero asked. "Wait'll your momma hears what a Radical you've become."

They reached a good-sized cane break a half-hour later and hacked out a clearing far enough inside not to be visible from the ridge path. Jasper refused to move anywhere else through open country, and whiskey water helped them nap.

Along about midnight, Cicero awakened and suggested they get a jump on the following day and go back to Friar's Point.

"Not yet. Wait, maybe another day."

"Jasper, I have waited all my life for this opportunity. Finally, our people will have a government not owned by rich white men. We may be able to start something that will catch fire in other places. Do you understand what would happen if just a few poor white people joined us? It's about taking the government away from those who use it to promote their businesses."

"I hate you for bringing me into this . . . I feel bad about Miz Clothilde. Damn all this election shit."

"But with the guns—"

"If they got the guns, they don't need you tonight. Could be somebody lookin' to arrest me. Wait another day."

NOT TEN MILES AWAY toward the Mississippi and north of Friar's Point, a wagon with two men eased along. Joe Woods turned to his brother.

"I hope that fella we left word with got to Alcorn. Else it look like we planned all this."

"But Joe, if Alcorn don't know—and Mr. Levy bring the guns—it'll all work out for the good."

"How so? You think that fool sheriff smart enough to take on all these white men, all the generals and judges and everybody."

"We got judges, too. What about Van Bibber?"

"He got elected 'cause he was black like you'n me. What that mean? He ain't nobody."

"Ain't that why all folks git elected, 'cause they like the people vote for em?"

"Just shut up, Gene . . . I swear, you got too much nature. Need you a woman keep you in trim."

Gene Woods quit talking. The freight wagon turned off the main trail into an approach to the River that had not been used since before the war when the abandoned town of Delta upstream was a trading stop.

Fifteen minutes later, Gene slowed his team and pulled into a smooth expanse of sand and grass between two trees occupying the high ground on a sand ridge. It was clear and bright, not unusual for the time of year. Movement on the river caught Gene's eye almost immediately, and he stepped from the wagon.

"Three flashes of light just like old Levy told me."

He walked down closer to the water. Drifting straight toward him, outlined in the crisp moonlight, was an old flatbottom boat looking like a ramshackle raft because it was riding so low in the water.

"You see the raft?"

"No, I don't."

"Look!"

Closer and closer came the boat. A man on deck was poling mightily toward shore. When the boat struck the shallows, the man leapt into the water and yelled.

"What he yellin' for," Joe Woods said. "Sound like he tryin' to git caught."

While yelling toward shore, Stephen Levy was floundering in the water, grappling with a rope to keep the raft from floating off. By the time Gene Woods decided to go help, the boat slid away from shore and headed back out into the river. It was all the two men could do to catch up to it, hold it fast and then slowly drag it back into shore. As Gene dropped to his knees to rest holding onto the rope over his shoulder, Levy lit a lantern and swung it overhead.

"Mr. Levy, what you doin' that for?"

Sound of a branch breaking nearby made Gene's heart leap. He became aware of men moving and talking behind dunes and trees just off the river. He came to his feet and ran toward his wagon.

"Stay wheah you are!" A voice out of the night commanded.

From all along the riverfront, out of low places between hillocks of sand, from the edge of the woods, men emerged. Panicked, Gene dashed to his wagon.

"Git outta here, Joe, drive!

"I cain't. Look in front of us!"

"Oh, sweet Jesus!"

Around them a group of twenty men on horses were closing, their skins frighteningly white in the moonlight.

"Gentlemen, how wonderful our business will conclude so promptly."

"That you, sir?"

"Yes, Joseph, it is I."

"I wasn't part o' this, you know that."

"I did get your message, but I am not sure what to make of it."

"I was reporting them guns soon as I could, sir."

"But your brother was part of this gun thing from the start."

"Oh no sir, Mr. Alcorn," Gene Woods said. "I went told my brother here just as soon as I could."

"Let us not quibble—Ah! the good Mr. Levy. Have you brought us our guns?"

"I have, Senator," Levy said, "just as you suggested."

"Merely putting the colored's diversion of funds to some good. Our own vigilantes—as they call them—need those guns."

"May I," Levy asked, "return to my store. I've been away for four days."

"Why of course, Mr. Levy, and now that you have begun to atone for your damnable past, come see me when this blows over. We won't forget that you brought us word of this conspiracy. Innocent blood might have flowed, but for you. Mazeltov."

"Would you gentlemen," Stephen Levy said to the Woods brothers, "drive me back home?"

"Give him a horse," Alcorn said. "We need that wagon."

"What's that, sir?" Joe Woods asked.

"You boys pull down your tailgate. My men will load the guns and we'll go surprise Brown before he can figure out some other way of arming."

Stephen Levy waited as the guns were loaded. Joe Woods joined him, and both stood as if in the exercise of some special privilege as Gene Woods helped load the freight wagon.

"Why you do this?"

"Do what, Mr. Woods?"

"Ain't you supposed to be a Radical?"

"When John Cochran brought me the money, and pressed me to go buy guns, I didn't trust him. For all I knew, he was working for Alcorn's people. I asked him about you, and he said that none of you business people knew what he was asking. I wasn't supposed to even mention it to you."

"You didn't answer my question."

"But I am . . . Think back to '67." Levy hesitated, looked around to make sure he was not being overheard. "I ran against Alcorn there. None of your people would take me seriously. Said Alcorn was a good white man. Now, I'm suppose to trust Cochran who tells me none of you business folk are in on using county money to buy guns? I'm supposed to stick my neck out?"

"Why not just turn him down?"

"You people don't stick together. Why blame me?"

"You a Judas."

Levy stepped back a pace, cleared his throat.

"Jewish, colored—same logic. We're all businessmen. I want to buy cotton. You want to build a courthouse."

THAT SAME MORNING, Cicero rode into half-deserted Friars Point. Refuse was blowing through the public square. As he rode closer to the sheriff's office he noticed that the window was broken. Three nervous guards were keeping Cicero in sight.

"Hold it, fella!"

"Let him go," Booker T said. "He all right . . . I take your horse, Mr. Cicero."

None of the gas lamps were lit inside the darkened office. Stretched out on the floor without a mattress, the sheriff was still asleep. His boots were propped against one another, the toes pointed in opposite directions. The smell of sweat and liquor and something else was overpowering. On a desk lay a dead rooster, a miniature noose around its neck, its feathers scorched.

Cicero stooped to rouse the sheriff.

"Wake up, John . . . Come on, now, wake up."

Brown stirred, moaned and licked his dry lips. His eyes were rheumy and red, his hair matted.

"What time is it, Cicero?"

"What's going on? The guns?"

"Levy went over to the other side. That's how Alcorn found out about the money he accused me of stealing."

"Who told you this?"

"The Woods brothers. The vigilantes have taken our guns."

"Well damn me to hell and back!"

"I've been promised a lynching. Most of my deputies have headed toward Floreyville to catch a riverboat. General Chalmers arrived before the Woods boys had left; he's even offered me a boat ride to Arkansas if I surrender and make it easy."

"Do you trust him?"

"No sir. I have written the governor one final official letter. One of my ex-deputies will post it in Floreyville."

"How could we have been so wrong about Levy?"

The sheriff rolled to his knees and reached a mail packet from his desk.

"This came for you. Seems it was mailed last year, but it took a while for it to find you. It just came in off a boat."

Cicero ripped open a letter whose writing he recognized and silently began reading:

December 15, 1874

My dear, dear friend,

I hope this letter finds you well and in possession of all your health as I and my loved ones are. My wife sends her heartfelt prayers for your continued well being.

Cicero paused and touched Brown's shoulder. "It's from a man I served with in the legislature." He continued reading, now out loud:

Not all is well. You and I have known for some time of the violence against our people. But I daresay not even I—certainly not you—would have imagined the evil doings come upon us lately.

In Vicksburg, eighty teachers, ministers and Loyal League organizers were shot or beaten to death this December. The authorities argue over the number because some died outside the city and are said to be unrelated.

During a parade intended to show our candidates to the people, troublemakers fired into the crowd. The local authorities did nothing to stop the carnage until it was too late. From the first unknown hot-heads, it spread citywide by nightfall. A group of white women were encouraged to take target-practice while sipping lemonade. The black deputies who stood and fought were killed.

There is a traveling band of cutthroats called Modocs, trained in Texas but named for what are said to be the most fierce of our Indian brothers in the mountains of California. They travel well paid and provisioned by boat, train and horseback.

The newspapers have reported practically nothing about events in Vicksburg. Only after our handful of Federal troops were mustered out to quell the violence (but did nothing except bivouac in the public square) did accounts closer to the true extent of the carnage begin to appear out of state. Amazingly—if we are to believe all the evildoers are Democrats—it is the Republicans and their newspapers exercising the greatest restraint, for they have printed none of the evil in these events. You would think so many killings had never happened.

My dear friend, the whole state is involved in a conspiracy. As if death were not an infinitely greater evil, the Jackson newspapers are now explaining that the "excesses of a few" (the murderers) must be understood as a natural reaction to political corruption and the general vagrancy of our people.

Dear, dear friend, I cannot warn you earnestly enough to take care and utmost precaution for your well-being. I fear for myself, but I see how things are, and if I am to die, I shall die.

I must lay down my pen. Trusting we may always share affection, I remain,

Very truly yours and always a poor and ornery
Blacksmith

As Cicero stood shaking his head, John Brown pulled on his boots and walked over to the window.

"My wife is carrying our first child, and my farm will surely be burned. I'm driving her into Tunica County where we can hide. I'll try to contact the governor again before I leave the state. Trouble is, once I leave Friars Point, white folks will take over . . . I'm tempted to ask you something beyond any man's duty to the cause."

"What is it?"

"Sheriff!"

It was young Booker T along with two people from the town.

"This here," Booker T said, "is Clyde Childress and his wife, Marge."

The man was peering back outside even as Booker T was speaking.

"Pleased to meet you," the man said, then to his wife. "I'm sho scared. We oughtta took off with Mabel and Charlie."

"No, no," his wife said, "this ain't only home to white folks."

"A few of us," the man said, "still got guns."

"We ain't here," his wife said, "to join no militia, but ain't hardly nobody out on the street now. If you all need to go somewhere, now be the time to leave."

"What," Cicero asked Brown, "do you want us to do?"

"I want you and Jasper to barricade yourselves in this office with whoever will volunteer. That way, the office would remain officially open on the chance that the governor might act."

Jasper had joined them. Brown smiled at him and continued.

"Jasper knows how to move, run if and when he must. I'm deputizing him along with you and any of these others who'll stay."

"What's the point?" Cicero asked.

"To keep this office open for as long as we can. That would keep white people from just walking in and taking over, and maybe, just maybe in a day or two some of the local Northerners if not their fucking governor might come to your aid."

"Non!" Jasper said. "Ain't never let fools shoot at me."

"You could put out sentries," Brown said. "That's the main thing I've been using my deputies for. You'll know ahead of time if trouble threatens, and you keep your horses saddled. With the white folks gone, you won't be ambushed inside town. Meanwhile, I'll be sending as many telegrams to those who used to claim to be our allies as I can muster. Surely some of the old abolitionists will take note and shine a light on what's happening here."

"Stay wit us, Mr. Jasper." Booker T. had a rifle in his hand. "We put some lead in they ass."

Within the hour, the sheriff of Coahoma County stepped into a wagon driven by his wife. Before they had passed from sight, Young Booker T took one end of town, Jasper the other, and they waited—the five of them including one deputy and a volunteer from town.

BY SUNDOWN, the tension had drained them all. Cicero sent out the deputy and the volunteer to keep watch. Jasper and Booker T curled up to sleep.

Long after midnight Cicero took to the street and walked until it began turning light. Just north of town was a place no black person had dared enter since white people of the town evacuated in that direction. Cicero saw shadows moving in the distance, and he turned to see the deputy coming to warm him. They continued back to the office.

"Take my horse and ride," Cicero said to Booker T. "Tell Bill Pease that if he has men with guns and horses, to send them now. Make sure he knows that Levy brought us no guns."

Booker T ran outside and rode off. Jasper hurried to call in the volunteer keeping watch south of town. A stand-off was possible because the vigilantes wouldn't burn the office without fear of the fire spreading to the whole town.

Within the hour, two groups of riders gathered, one in clear view up on the levee along the Mississippi where it curved across the view north. The second group closed from the east. There was a single shot in the distance.

BOOKER T THOUGHT he was hit, but it was his horse that faltered and dropped. There was a sudden great jolt as he tumbled head over heels. The horse snorted and lay dead. Booker T scrambled to his feet and started running.

He ran for what seemed an impossible time, until his chest pained and he was sucking at wind. His lungs felt like they would burst, but he ran on. Soon he was beyond breathlessness, and each step produced only a measured ache. The smell of coffee swirling up out of the river gorge told him that he was approaching Shufordsville.

Then he tripped and took half a minute to catch his breath before struggling up. This time, when he opened his eyes, he could see the smoke from Bill Pease's campfires rising across river, and he let himself roll head over heels down to the water. Then he was in it, floating and swimming, being pulled out on the other side.

"Tell . . . Mr. Pease. . ."

"Here I am young'un."

"You know . . . me."

"Take your time."

"White folks . . . plum crazy. Mr. Cicero say . . . you come quick. Just the men with guns."

"Exactly what happened?"

"Yessuh . . . The vigilantes got him pinned inside by now. They gonna hold out 'till you git there."

"Where is Sheriff Brown?"

"Oh, he warn't there, suh. He run away up to Tunica County yestiddy . . . Left Mr. Cicero and Jasper in charge."

"Goddamnit! What of our guns?"

"There ain't none. Mr. Levy went and told the white folks what he was doin', and that's why they was claimin' the sheriff stole that money."

"So how come you know so much?"

"I were listenin'."

Winking to a nearby man, Bill said, "You wouldn't be workin for the white folks would you?"

"Oh no, suh."

"Come on boys," Pease said, "we gotta ride quick."

"What we gonna do?"

"Men with horses and guns, head out with the boy here. Ride straight on in if you can. Else, turn aside to that big oak grove this side of town."

"We ain't got but ten horses, and some mule wagons."

"Just the horses with the boy. You men know what real soldiering is about. This ain't no drill."

Rumors of what was happening had the encampment awake and streaming in toward where Pease was standing with Booker T. Pease raised his hands and spoke.

"You folks just calm down. You ain't no army, so go back'n relax."

Despite Pease's words a few teenagers began to chant John Brown, John Brown.

"You young un's shut up!"

Unfortunately, by some alchemy of hormones and rebellion, a group of boys headed toward Friar's Point. Their taunting triggered a surge of men, women and children to follow in their wake.

"Get ahead of them boys and stop 'em!" Pease ordered his horsemen.

"Do we ride in like you said?"

"Goddamn right! Just git ahead of them young fools first and turn 'em back."

A RIDER UNDER A white flag came down to the sheriff's office. At the same time, Modocs in shiny boots were leading horses off a steamboat. The first casualty was a dog who came snarling toward them. They mounted up and rode slowly toward the sheriff's office.

"Don't waste your bullets," Jasper said. "Aim and shoot."

Their first volley dropped three men, and the rest neatly split into two groups and withdrew to the ends of town out of clear shot. Meanwhile, down from their perch on the levy the local vigilantes charged, firing wildly. Riders thundered along the street past the sheriff's office in both directions. The defenders could only fire when vigilantes passed in front. Clyde Childress from the town burst in.

"Folks up'n down is shootin', too," he said. "Just wanted y'all to know. I'm gone."

"We can't stay here much longer," Jasper said.

"We oughtta," the deputy said, "git outta here while the white folks is worried 'bout gittin' shot."

"Where to?" Cicero said.

"South of town is a big oak grove. I heard the sheriff and Mr. Pease talk about defending inside o' there."

They gathered as much ammunition as they could carry and stuck their heads out. Straight ahead was the River. A distant volley rang out before the local shooting began to quiet.

"What's happening?" Cicero asked.

"That way-off shootin'," Jasper said, "is Bill Pease's folks, I expect. We ought to run for it now."

Down the street south, they ran, then between two buildings into a partially cleared field behind town. When they started to run again, a shout went up, and a small group of Modocs south of town rode after them. The roughly plowed field slowed the attackers enough to allow Cicero and Jasper to hurry back in between the last buildings on the edge of town where they hunkered down under fire. In the distance, there was another volley.

At that moment, the main force of vigilantes from the other end of town charged. They galloped on the street in front and a few rode in the field behind town. Townspeople hidden away inside homes began firing again, and the street cleared out. Bill Pease's horsemen came into view on the ridge road in the distance.

"Gather fire!" the deputy said. "Shoot into the field!"

When Cicero's group started shooting again, the closest white men—Modocs in the field behind town—gave ground back toward the main bunch.

"Take this wagon!" a voice yelled.

A man who had run between the sheltering buildings pointed to a hitched wagon on the street. Everyone turned around and ran for it. Jasper leapt aboard first and strapped it into motion, kept strapping for all he was worth as the last clambered aboard.

For the time it took a hawk overhead to circle, nothing much happened. The vigilantes had gathered and seemed to be watching the closing black men on horseback. By the time the wagon reached the stand of trees, Pease's horsemen galloped in behind them. Pease's lieutenant turned to the rest.

"No way we gonna re-take that office. We got ten men here, a wagon and a few horses—two been shot."

"Let's join up with Bill," Jasper said.

"Don't think we could make it."

"What then?" Cicero asked.

"Bill's whole group is marchin' this way, women and children with 'em. Civilians would be in the line of fire even if we did go join 'em. We cannot ride toward them."

From a distance, came singing. A sudden quiet came over the town. By now, the vigilantes had worked their way back through the center of town and were massing south of it. Along the ridge road, the distant singing became a chant.

The vigilantes were forming up into four groups. Alcorn sat at the head of one, James Chalmers another. What little wind there was died, and the sound of the marchers became more distinct. "John Brown, John Brown."

Chalmers moved in front of the four groups and raised his arm in signal. When he dropped it, the white men galloped toward the ridge road. Those inside the oak grove opened fire, but the tight order of the vigilantes divided and flanked the woods at a distance. Pease's lieutenant turned to the men around him.

"If we do any more shooting, our civilians be in the way." The man held out his hand to Cicero. "Was my pleasure to know you."

The men separated. Jasper and Cicero ran toward the rough along the river south of town. They climbed a sand dune to look back toward the ridge along the Sunflower. Far-off gunfire erupted. Distant figures were running in every direction. White men on horse back sat the high ground firing as if on whim. One mass of figures seemed doggedly moving on toward Friar's Point through a gap in the ranks of vigilantes.

"Ain't nothin'," Jasper said, "you can do with your puny little gun. Like the man say, it's time to go home."

For hours they moved along the river, then cautiously east to the Sunflower at Clark's Landing, which was deserted. Jasper cut a boat out of a line moored to shore, and he and Cicero shoved off.

"Paddle, Mr. Cicero! Anybody can pop off either one of us. We got to git on down below that burial mound south of town before we safe."

Their arms were heavy as driftwood by the time they had covered the several miles south and turned into the hidden piece of river bank behind a mammoth fire-cratered cypress tree where they usually left the water. Cicero waited for Jasper to secure the boat, and they started walking.

"Cicero."

"Yeah?"

Jasper ran around and stood in front of Cicero.

"Stay with momma an' me."

"I'm too tired to talk, Jasper."

"All I'm sayin' is momma want you to stay, but she don't like to ask for nothin'. I don't care if you ain't a swamp man."

"You don't?"

"You don't have to be like me, and it don't have to be all the time, neither—just mainly. I understand about the outside, now."

Jasper turned and set off toward home. Cicero understood he had been accepted. That and being safe inside the swamp for the first time in over a month filled him with an indescribable pleasure as he entered the clearing around his cabin. Through the window he saw Rose in her chair watching the fire dance. Her head was cocked listening.

"Come on in, cherie."

She was standing up when he entered. Her expression made him notice that his woolen cape was matted with burrs, dress trousers he'd worn to the convention caked with mud. He pulled off his cape and stepped back outside to whack at some of the mud.

"A little chilly, this morning ain't it?"

Cicero nodded. Something in the fireplace exploded, causing both of them to jump. When Cicero stepped back inside,

Rose yawned and stretched. Her dress pulled against the back of her hips, outlining the classic curve out and away from a waist that had thickened a little over the years.

"Hope you like this dress." She moved to the table and pulled away a cloth revealing bread and cooked sweet potatoes. "Go on, sit down. Rest of the food be ready soon."

Cicero trudged over and flopped down on the bed while Rose went out to rummage up on the cooling shelf before reappearing with half a ham.

"You get tired of venison and gamy critters. I traded for this and my dress."

"You don't have to go to so much trouble."

"Judgin' by your looks, cherie, you ain't won no election. In my little world, I want you to smile."

As Rose turned to prepare the meal, Cicero walked over and caught her up in his arms from behind.

"Thank you, for wanting me home."

"You callin' it home?"

"Yes."

Rose leaned back against him, patted his arms about her. Then she twisted around to face him.

"You're full of love. I could always see that."

"Then why are you crying?"

"These tears from that wind outside 'cause I known it longer than you, and better. It don't run off—not for long. Always by me to say hello and goodnight." Her voice softened. "Know how to touch me, too. An' it don't pay no peckawood or nigga more attention than me."

They kissed, separated tenderly, and Cicero sat on the bed.

"What's next, Rose? I don't know who I am, can't look myself in the eye."

"I been a drifter, Cicero." She sat on his lap. "Keep that in mind. Drifters don't look past today."

"No more politics, I know that."

"Non?"

"My son, another generation will have to carry on. What you give me, I don't have to strain for."

"My, oh my."

She kissed him.

"And I love you . . . This is my home. Family, friends will have to join us here."

"Now, you a maroon."

"I want us to have a life. What better world could I imagine if it didn't begin with you."

"Oh Cicero! That's the whole point. You'n me together."

That night lying in bed Cicero heard the wind rise, and he wrapped his arms about himself. As he did so he closed his eyes and gave in to a kaleidoscope of feelings, thoughts.

Blacksmith had warned him about the world. Were heroic impulses no more than stuff of childhood? And whom could his people depend upon? Not all black people, not all white, and yet to ignore color was foolhardy in a world where it still carried significance, acted as a badge of slavery or of distaste or in justification of cruel and selfish impulse. What—as old Bill Williams kept saying to Jasper—would be the lesson for Cicero to teach his child? What had he learned to help Little Buck avoid errors of innocence? Had he learned anything one ought teach a child?

He thought back to Bill Williams' tales of the white people coming upon his Choctaw relatives in the Great Swamp. Now Cicero found himself wondering whom had the Choctaw displaced from the land, and who, in turn, would displace the Alcorn tribe from Coahoma County. Land was the gift of the One God to all creatures, laws to the contrary a justification of conquest.

No one owned it, not in the long view. Each new group imposed new ways and laws, and the law always served those in power. Kindred spirits dedicated to principle did not rule. Nor had anyone found a way to insure that those wielding power would look backward or forward far enough beyond their own ambitions to understand that theirs was a temporary custody limited by the needs of others.

Cicero got out of bed and pulled his rocking chair up to the window. The moon was full and low, as if it owned the sky. He sat there sipping from a whiskey jug until a teary film made the moon shimmer. His feelings were resonating with the pulsing of his blood. So he reached for the good ones and felt a delicious satisfaction in recalling Stringer saying that young people feeding on principle was the only source of a power big enough to change old ways. After the heady good feelings, a kind of late-night loneliness took over, and Cicero went back to bed.

When he finally drowsed, thoughts continued running in and out of his brain. Dancing, he was, in an empty room, and crying, such a frightful flow of tears they burst like a flood through the walls, sweeping him into a desert, a place of sadness, some haunted place of moaning shadowy forms rising up and falling back into the muck only to reconstruct themselves.

Here were friends, family, people of so many descriptions he didn't even know, all of them bogged down in the muck of survival and fighting with each other. Closest was a woman in a hideously soiled and wrinkled Dutch collar and smock—one of Blacksmith's owners, he sensed—her gray face smudged with soot and perspiration. She took shelter in Cicero's arms, and there began a chanting, "Ghost dancer, ghost dancer."

Dancing across the sky, they all were, images breaking-off and flowing into one another, to places Cicero did not recognize. He could see the whole continent—fields of dusty brown and yellow, colors herringboned together in tight tiny rows. Elsewhere ridges starkly white beside black water places—and him straining to calm her in his arms and then the next and the next who joined them out of the muck. He now wanted to dance with all of them, as brother with a brother or sister, his joy being to banish their sadness, to end the conflict of those newly risen from the muck. He sensed a sweetness in the air.

A shadow came out of the west, menacing, a giant eagle screaming, Tuscayon! Here wind walks with the panther, the snake flies with the eagle and sky fills the hole in the ground. And Cicero shivered. Way to the south, a feathered snake rose up showing fangs, and Cicero hastily withdrew north, only to startle some chameleon-like apparition that blinded him as it turned into a white bird frantically trying to hide the north pole under a blizzard of tiny crystal copies of itself. Cicero knew that it was only a dream, the parts having no clear meaning.

And then, he sensed weeping underfoot, below him and his dancing companions. In their progress, they were trampling on others in place before them. A new multitude was marching toward them out of the sea, humans on top of humans. A people linking arms rose out of the muck like an ancient branched tree against the face of the moon, pulling up old roots from a far place and putting down new as its branches found space to dance in the wind. But new multitudes began to link up with those already on top and they shrouded the dancing tree. Its young branches snapped and fell and fed a river of souls flowing nowhere, women showing heels to men who boomed out anguish as their movement became indistinguishable from what had gone before so many times. Cicero stopped dancing. Voices wailed and screamed of Armageddon.

When Cicero awakened, his heart was pounding. He was drenched with sweat and empty. Rose was whispering,

"Whatever it is don't have to be. Dreamtime is like that."

They would tell people later that it was a fairy tale moving into each other's life, how their hunger turned loving, and even their tears were filled with joy. So many occasions for laughter, they celebrated evening and morning. Doing for the other was never work, play could transform any chore, and shimmer on rain seemed to rush skyward wishing them well, just as long as they remembered they were living inside each other, marooned.

Acknowledgements

Thanks to my Aunt Rose for her story one New Year's Eve of a war over a road in New Africa, Mississippi.

To my deceased friend and classmate, Professor Barbara Christian, and to all of the other serious readers of the manuscripts, especially the woman I live with, Jennifer Ways, thank you. Thank you: Dick America, Pershing Anderson, Clyde Childress, Faith Childs, Lige Daley, Mildred Daugherty, Dick Daugherty, Doris Davis, Alice Dear, Hedi Desuyo, John Harris, La Joyce Henderson Debro, Vern Henderson, Leif Helverson, Lois Jones, Larry Kennon, Joyce Langford, Reginald Lockett, Jabari Mahiri, Melody McDowell, Joyce McNair, Ted Pontiflet, Clayton Riley, Barbara Rodriguez, Morris Scroggins, Tracy Scroggins, Olivier Sylvain, Lee Wallace, and Doris Ward. A very special appreciation to Lucretia Jones.

A thank you to Sandra Starks Smith for her thesis on former slaves building an all-black town; gratitude to all of the people, many passed on, who shared about the old days in a nearby community called New Africa; thank you Harry Abernathy for buried headlines.

The West Oakland Writer Workshop was, for a few years, the best. To Jean Langmuir Blinn of the Oakland, California, Public Library, your manuscript reading and comparison reading suggestions were a gift of great value; to Coahoma, Bolivar and Washington county Mississippi librarians for helping locate Works Progress oral history and old newspaper files; special thanks to the Army Corp of Engineers warehouse employees in Vicksburg who gave me run of the place. It would have been nice had Mississippi Department of Archives people been more helpful, but unlike a guard in the Clarksdale Levee District office, no fat archivist wearing a gun jammed me up against a wall.

To parents, Willie and Lillian, and, for his caution, as writing took over my life, brother Bill. Genes, aside, I owe a heavy debt: to Smitty and the logic of raw onion; to O'Leary and Lambert who authorized thinking beyond the rules; to Bill Miller who warned of rough road.

Thank you Saunders Redding, John Hope Franklin and Haitian writer Jacques Stephen Alexis for showing and confirming.

I bow to my design crew, Chris Hall and Dickie Magidoff—also Andy Parks of RCB Publishing—for helping my publisher seize the moment.